# COMING APART

## The Disillusioning Art of Shell Formation

### Volume I

"Faith is like a bird that feels dawn breaking
and sings while it is still dark."

—RABINDRANATH TAGORE

A NOVEL BY
NICOLE GARBER

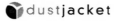

Dust Jacket Press
PO Box 721243
Oklahoma City, OK 73172

www.DustJacket.com
Info@DustJacket.com

The characters and events in this book are fictional, and any resemblance to actual persons or events is coincidental.

Cover art: Abby Stiglets aby3.com
Graphic Design: Lyn Rayn

This book is dedicated to Jimmy, my living,
breathing Alex Loving.

# ACKNOWLEDGEMENTS

*A* special thank you to my Father, for absolutely everything.

And thank you to everyone who has helped me along the way:

My husband Jimmy, for believing in me, encouraging me along the way, and for giving me something to write about.

Adam Toler, for sharing in my excitement and for believing in my book enough to send it to print.

To family and friends who read and edited and read some more. It has been an amazing experience.

Mom, for the two little books that you gave me from which I derived so much inspiration. Thank you for your selflessness.

Dad, for your prayers and for being the perfect definition of love. You are a living example of 1 Corinthians 13:4.

Karen, for reading my book three times before it was even published. XOXO.

To the super talented Abby Stiglets, for a cover that is so much more amazing than I could have ever imagined it to be.

Kara Choate, what can I say? You are like a sister to me. Plus, you are a master with the camera. Thank you for all of the encouragement, for your strong friendship, and for making me look ten years younger.

Susie, for being the friend that God has placed in my life.

Pastor Craig, for speaking directly to me.

Jean and Isaiah, for stopping by.

And last but not least I want to thank Brooks and Madison. You have beautiful and giving hearts. Your compassion is contagious and you inspire me each and every day.

# CHAPTER ONE

"To open your heart to someone means exposing the scars of the past." The first time I heard these words was when I was eight years old, sitting at the table in my Nana's pink and white flowered, 1940's style kitchen, explaining to her why I wasn't in the least bit concerned with making any friends. It was in my grandparents' house that I felt the most comfortable and once a year, in July, when my parents and I came to stay with my Nana and Papa, I could spill my heart and not regret it. The words just seemed to flow from my lips and the childhood pains from my heart. I could tell Nana everything, almost everything, within the walls of her pink and white kitchen. I could ask her anything I wanted and she would almost always give me the answer that I didn't want to hear. On those July afternoons, I would often climb into my Papa's baby blue El Camino that was loaded up with fishing gear and sandwiches, and we would make our way to the small lake on the outskirts of town. I would lie on a blanket under a tree, nibble on a sandwich, and watch Papa fish. But on that particular afternoon something else had caught my attention. "Look, Papa!" I shouted. "Look at those fish with their heads sticking out of the water!" In the murky water, close to the middle of the pond, there were five or six little bumps that would bob to the surface and then sink back down. "Those aren't fish, Sunshine, they're turtles," Papa told me. While Papa continued to fish, I watched the turtles as they moved through the water, heads out of their shells. I watched as one turtle climbed on a rock near the water's edge, neck stretched long in the sun. Before that moment, if someone had asked me to draw a picture of a turtle, I would have drawn a beautiful and strong shell decorated with little brown and green squares, but the turtle's head would have been tucked inside where it was safe. As I lay on my belly with my chin resting in my hands, I noticed the turtle on the rock had been joined by another; their necks stretched out and their noses touching. I realized at that moment that a turtle did indeed live outside of its shell, when it felt safe, and as the pond was a place of safety for the turtles, so was my grandparents' house for me. It was the one place that was familiar and the only place that never changed. Every July, I was welcomed by the same framed photos positioned on the painted white mantle over the brick fireplace, the same green velveteen, Victorian-style sofa, the same kitchen, the same front porch, the same old wooden floors and shaggy rugs, and the same smells. But my favorite was that I always slept in the same bed. It was mine.

I think that under normal circumstances I would have been a rather normal girl. I can still vaguely remember a time, long ago, when I had dreams of being popular, the prettiest girl in school. In my dreams, I always had plenty of friends and the perfect smile. I had a bedroom that was decorated in pink and it was the only bedroom that I could remember. I had a normal life and normal parents. In my dreams, tragedy didn't exist and I still had a sister named Laney. But, when morning came and illuminated the white walls of my bedroom,

I was reminded that consistency was a wish that I was never granted and an ever-changing address was the only life I knew.

My parents were physicians . . . sort of . . . they were shrinks. They preferred the term psychiatrist but at school, if anyone bothered to ask, I would just tell people they were doctors. They could legally dispense medicine and help people with their mental maladies, plus, they had MD behind their name and they never let anyone forget it. My parents had never been the typical doctors that worked in a hospital or a clinic. That would have actually been kind of nice. My parents worked for an organization called A-Omega and their assignments were always overseas. On occasion, Mom and Dad would reminisce about living in the states, but I don't remember much about it. For as long as I can remember, our home had been up and down the coast of Europe; we never stayed in one place longer than a year or two. Working for A-Omega meant dedicating their lives to helping the less fortunate and frequent relocation went right along with it. It always happened quickly; they would receive a letter in the mail and the next morning, with all of our possessions stuffed haphazardly inside nine pieces of worn out luggage, our family was en route to another country. I was comforted only by my mother's unwavering voice and my father's anxious smile. It happened time and time again. Eight countries in eleven years; I was bound to hold some sort of record. I detested moving and everything that went along with it: new surroundings, new climates, new cultures, and new schools. I was bullied. I was belittled. I was the new kid by definition and it was torture.

Not long after the visit to my grandparents' house, I began to consider the turtles that I had seen at the pond with my papa. I envied them in that they had a shell to protect them from pain. I wanted a shell to protect me from pain. I wanted a shell to protect my heart. I imagined it made of steel and rivets with locks and chains. It would let nothing in or out. It was on that day that I began to construct my shell. At first, the shell around my heart consisted of only a

9

single layer, but with each move, my heart grew harder. The layers of my shell became thicker and less permeable. Soon, the pain was gone. I was numb, comfortable, and I was detached from the rest of the world. After nine long years, life inside my shell had become manageable. But when we moved to Oklahoma, everything I had worked so hard to build began to crumble.

My life began to change upon arrival. Oklahoma was different than the Europe I had left behind. My parents purchased a house in the country, which was in fact better than the small, furnished apartments that I was accustomed to. Gone were the days of white walls and worn out luggage. For the first time, we had things of our own and my parents painted our walls a pleasing hue. This was our home and it symbolized the consistency that I had so badly wanted as a child. Both my mother and father still worked for A-Omega, but only on special assignments. They had decided to settle down and find new jobs: my mother now worked in the psych ward at the local hospital and my father at a small clinic in Tulsa that specialized in rehabilitating children and teenagers who had been victims of abuse. It seemed as though we were here to stay. My parents had traded in their erratic careers for something a little more stable and predictable; however, I couldn't help but wonder why they had waited until my senior year in high school to do so.

I stood looking at myself in the full-length mirror, staring at the only thing that seemed forever unchanging, the one thing in my life I wish would change. I looked thin, waif-like, with not a sign of any curves. My mom said I would appreciate my youthful beauty later in life; I wasn't so sure. My charcoal hair curled loosely around my shoulders but still framed my pretty, childlike face.

My eyes were a warm, see-through blue, like the foam off the ocean; I guess I had my mom to thank for that. Otherwise, I looked nothing like either one of my parents. With my rich, olive complexion, high cheekbones, and prominent nose, strangers would often jokingly ask where I came from.

"Rae!" my mom called from downstairs. "You don't want to be late on your first day of school."

I grumbled as I threw on my black, jersey knit skirt, floral embroidered tee, and All Stars. The understated ensemble I put together last night seemed the perfect fit for a wallflower. I gave a sullen nod to the full-length mirror and trudged down the stairs.

"Good morning, Sunshine," my mother mumbled from behind the kitchen counter, her right hand moving quickly to cover her mouth full of cereal.

"Good morning," I responded darkly.

"Did you sleep well?"

"I guess so."

My mother was naturally beautiful with soft, brown hair cut in a short, pixie style fashion. Her skin was perfect, porcelain white, like a china doll, and her eyes a dazzling, translucent pale blue. This morning she was wearing a sleeveless shirt, revealing a long, raised, pink scar that ran down her arm. Europe was perfect for my mother. The frequently cool weather allowed her to choose clothes that concealed it. The scar had taken some time to heal, but the accident left behind emotional scarring that she was still recovering from. I don't think she minded the slight disfigurement, but the attention it drew brought back painful memories. I don't remember it. I was told that I was the size of a pea when it happened. I do mean a pea, barely even a person in my mother's womb. We never talked about it. She liked it better that way.

I stared at my eggs, picking at them as if they were something strange and foreign. My granola looked just as unfamiliar, so I opted to at least drink the juice on the table for the sake of my mother's sanity.

"Are you anxious, Sunshine?" she probed. I could tell she was as nervous for me as I was for myself. She hated that they had to uproot me on an almost routine basis.

"Not at all," I lied, and quietly grumbled at her consistent usage of the word "Sunshine," her most favorite term of endearment.

"Do you have everything you need? Paper, pens, lunch, your keys, class sched . . ."

"Mom!" My near shout startled us both. I took a deep breath and bit my lower lip. She raised her eyebrows slightly, but wasn't surprised by my murky demeanor. My parents were accustomed to it, and although I did love them, they were allowed only glimmers of my affection.

"Sorry," I said without meaning it. I poured the rest of my juice in a plastic cup and stormed out of the house with my bag.

"Don't forget to talk to people; they'll mistake your shyness for rudeness," she sang after me.

Her cheerfulness provoked me; however, I couldn't stay angry for long. My anger was immediately followed by a wave of guilt. I felt guilty that I couldn't seem to be nice despite her every attempt to soothe me. Perhaps I wanted her to share in my bitterness. Perhaps I wanted her to feel as dark as I did at this very moment. Misery loves company, I suppose.

The sun was blinding as I stepped out of the house. It beat down on the field of tall native grass that grew in front of our house, each yellowish-orange blade glistening in the sun, hissing and thrashing aimlessly in the wind. The feel of dirt in the air, which left a residue of grit on my tongue. The quiet chirp of crickets and the constant drone of cicadas in the tall pecan trees surrounding our house. The wind whistling through the cracks of the dilapidated, metal barn behind me, pieces of loose metal slapping against its old, wooden skeleton. The smell of asphalt melting on the driveway at 8:30 AM in the midst of an August heat wave. All of these things were overwhelming and new, the dog days of summer. This was Oklahoma. I had never seen such barren land, wasted and desolate.

I opened the door to my old Honda Accord and began down the gravel road, stirring up sediment in the process and creating a dusty fog. I slowed as I neared the highway, glancing in my rear view mirror at the tiny bits of earth swirling behind me, forming into a small, funnel-shaped cloud. I rolled down my window as I pulled onto the pavement and let in the hot morning air.

I could see the high school from a distance. A three story, white, concrete building that spanned an entire city block. Bartlesville High, home of the Bruins, with an average graduating class of 400, give or take a few, much larger than any of my classes had ever been. As I pulled into the school, the lot was getting full. My old car stuck out like a sore thumb amongst all of the bright, shiny, new, and mostly expensive ones. I sat in my car, frozen, hands tight around the steering wheel, contemplating whether or not I should turn around. I hated the first day of school. More precisely, I hated the first day at a new school, and I knew that it had everything to do with Anna Sinclair.

It was my first day at The American School in London, ASL for short. My parents thought it was important that I have an education following the "American" curriculum because, even though my life was not consistent, my education should be. My day began as I dug through my three pieces of luggage trying to find something to wear. The only closet we had in our tiny apartment was the one by the front door and it was so small that we would barely squeeze three winter coats inside. My parents had been bickering all morning. They usually did this the first few days after a move.

"We don't have that much," my dad snapped. "I don't see why we can't just keep our belongings in the luggage."

"Why can't we just go and buy a small dresser? That's not too much to ask, is it?"

"Because, Sue, we can't take it with us when we leave. It's not worth it. We have no idea how long we'll be here."

"Well, this is no way to live. This is no way to raise our daughter, living out of luggage."

"I think you have forgotten that we have no choice in the matter."

My mother was silent for a moment. She seemed to have cooled off a bit. "It still doesn't make me feel any better. She needs some clothes, Will, and somewhere to put them. We have to make her life as normal as we can."

"Fine, go buy a dresser," my father said as though he had given up. My mother didn't ask for much, but when she did she was persistent.

"Fine, I plan to," Mother said as she left the room.

"Fine, pay cash and tell them I will pick it up myself. You know the drill. Don't leave behind any breadcrumbs."

I thought of Hansel and Gretel as I continued to sift through my clothing, finally, choosing a black and white, plaid jumper with white knee-highs to match. I remembered the crumbs that Hansel and Gretel left behind as I laced up my worn-out sneakers. And then . . . I remembered just what happened to them and I felt scared of what my parents were talking about and I wondered what in the world breadcrumbs had to do with a dresser.

My mom put my hair in pigtails and then dropped me off at school, late, and I walked into a sea of swarming students. I looked down at my outfit; it was babyish compared to the more stylish clothes that the other girls were wearing.

14

Anna Sinclair was her name and I will never forget it because it was Anna Sinclair who started it all. It was Anna Sinclair who made my third grade year a living hell. Anna was perfect, tall, and blond, with light brown eyes and a little ski slope nose. While most third graders are busy losing and re-growing enormous and very crooked teeth, Anna Sinclair had perfect teeth and the perfect smile to match. Anna was who every third grade girl wanted to be. She sat in the back with girls huddled around her and boys trying to pretend that they didn't notice her, while I cowered in front of the blackboard waiting to be humiliated after I introduced myself as the "new student."

"Baby. B-A-B-Y. Baby," Anna chanted softly in the back of the room and the entire class broke into laughter.

"Quiet, class," Mrs. Madison shouted, tapping her pencil on the desk. I wanted to grab Mrs. Madison's pencil out of her long, spindly fingers and use the eraser to wipe the nasty smile off Anna Sinclair's face. Instead, the tears in my eyes erased her smile, her face, and the rest of the class became a blurry, watery mess in front of me. I held my eyes open because I knew that if I closed them, the wetness would squeeze out and roll down my cheeks and the whole class would see me crying. The outfit, the pigtails, the tears. Maybe Anna was right; I was a baby.

Anna smacked on some pink gum that she wasn't supposed to be chewing, with each smack showing off her perfect set of third grade teeth. I trained my eyes on my feet as I recited to the class my name and where I was from. I told them I liked birds and that I loved to color. I tried to focus on the sound of Mrs. Madison's rapping pencil instead of the giggling that was coming from the back of the room.

"That's good, Rae," said Mrs. Madison. "You can take your seat."

"Thanks," I murmured, my eyes still focused on my worn-out sneakers. I wasn't sure why I was thanking her for a most humiliating experience, but I was. My gaze shifted from my sneakers to my desk, which sat directly in front

15

of Anna Sinclair's. As I drew closer, Anna simultaneously mouthed the word "baby" from her perfect glossy lips and chomped on her huge clump of hot pink gum.

When I got home that afternoon my mother and I stood in the doorway of our little London apartment and together we cried. She held me tight where I felt safe and then she walked me down to O'Grady's salon to pay someone to cut the bright pink clump of bubblegum out of my long, wavy, black curls.

Slowly, I opened my door, being careful not to ding the silver Range Rover that was parked next to me. I took note of the personalized license plate that read F-O-R-C-E before heading towards the front doors of the school. Groups of kids formed around me without actually taking notice and we all dragged to the school in unison.

## CHAPTER TWO

*I* was standing in front of my locker when I met Claire Kirpowski. I had been standing there for some time. I felt safe there. I felt like I was inside a bubble or something, a bubble that made me invisible. Strange, I know, but my locker was assigned to me and that tiny, metal compartment was the only thing I could call my own. The music room was about ten feet away from where I was standing and I could hear the sound of a high-pitched flute wafting out of the half-open doorway. Sometimes I thought about playing an instrument, but if I did, it wouldn't be the flute. A flute reminded me of love and little nymphs flittering around in bright green grass. I was not a flittery kind of person. I would play something a little more melancholy. Maybe the tenor sax, but I would play something like *Solitude* by Duke Ellington and absolutely no Kenny G. I would play something slow and a little sad. The shrill flute solo was now accompanied by the more pleasing sound of a piano. I continued to listen while observing the students as they walked by. I noticed how they seemed no different than the kids at the other schools I had attended. There's always the class clown, the jock, the stuck-up, overly manicured girl . . . or guy, the nerd, the gossip, the musician, and the misfit. I realized that this school, despite its enormity, was no different and I wondered where I would fit in. My mother told me that staring wasn't polite, but I was still staring, chewing on my fingernails, halfway hypnotized and halfway terrified by the student body, when I heard a very sharp and monotone voice beside me.

"Hello," she said. I turned to face the girl whose locker was next to mine.

"I'm Claire." She looked quickly away, focusing back on the combination lock that hung from her locker. She had a mechanical voice that reminded me of a robot. It was without a hint of emotion. Empty. And yet, her introduction seemed to break the ice that made the school so cold and uninviting.

Claire was quirky. She was a small girl, shorter and stockier than myself, with an athletic build. Her hair was straight and black, an obvious dye job, and her bangs were bluntly cut across her forehead. She reminded me of Carly, the friend I left behind in Amsterdam, my one and only friend, and the only person on this planet that understood me. I missed Carly.

Claire had an entourage of three girls behind her, two of which were chatting impatiently, one of which was silently looking me up and down. She paid them no attention and focused instead on me.

"I'm Rae," I said with hesitation. "I'm new." I silently groaned at my stupidity. I couldn't believe that I had introduced myself in such a fashion. All of the chattering stopped and four sets of eyes were now staring at me.

"So is Chloe," Claire offered, sensing my discomfort. Claire's offering, however, made me feel worse, not better.

I immediately began to wonder what it was about Chloe that was so magnetic. She was new, but still, two girls were standing beside her, one on her left and one on her right. They were doting over her in such a way that made me think they had known each other for years. I had never been this lucky. Friendship had never come easily to me. I took one look at Chloe before I attributed the attention she was getting to the way she looked, if for no other reason than because it made me feel better. She was pretty in an exotic sort of way. Her long, straight, black hair fell to her waist. She was tall and thin and wore designer clothes; the kind you might find in New York or Paris, not the kind that you could pick off the rack at the mall or even at an expensive, local boutique. She looked a model. She had blue eyes like mine, but they were icy and cold. They were the same unfriendly eyes that were inspecting me just moments ago. She had a sour look on her face, and I decided that it was definitely her clothes, not her charisma, that gained her instant popularity.

"Oh, and this is Jen and Megan," Claire said, pointing to the other two.

Jen was about my height with reddish blond hair that hung to her shoulders. She was small but not skinny. Her hair was perfectly tussled. I'm sure she had spent an hour to get it to look like she hadn't spent any time on it at all. She had on fitted jeans that accentuated her hourglass figure and a tight, white tee with a trendy scarf around her neck. She dressed the way my mother wished I would. I'm sure Jen was a nice enough girl, but I could tell instantly that she was the type who loved to gossip. I could easily see her being part of the in crowd, the one that I didn't belong to.

Megan was shorter than I was, probably only five-foot even. She had spirally, blond ringlets that I knew she didn't need to mess with; they did whatever she told them to. She dressed anything but plain. She had on a black, vintage rock tee and a tight, denim mini with footless, fishnet tights and peep toe heels.

"Hello," I whispered. I gave them a half-hearted wave.

"What lunch period do you have?" Claire asked as she looked back inside her locker. Her voice was now a muffled drone.

"Last . . . I have last period," I fumbled with my words. I couldn't believe that she was actually speaking to me. I hardened my expression to hide my surprise.

"So do we." Claire peeked hopefully from behind her locker and then motioned to Jen, Megan, and Chloe. "You can come with us, if you want," she offered, now focusing her attention back on me. Chloe rolled her eyes, and with a snarled lip, shoved her elbow without discretion into Claire's ribs.

"No . . . but thanks." I eyed the peanut butter and honey sandwich that was resting on the top shelf of my locker. "I brought a book to read. I'm sort of in the middle of it." It wasn't a lie. I had brought a good book and that definitely outweighed trying to start a superficial friendship. Honestly, I was shocked that I had been invited to lunch at all. I guess I should be thankful. Nine years ago I would have been delighted by such an invitation, but today, it felt more like an obligation, an uncomfortable one at that. I had become accustomed to keeping myself company. I had become a creature of habit.

My eyes drifted back to my locker. It was an untidy mess already, the result of tossing in all of my first day necessities after the new student orientation the night before. Books were thrown haphazardly in both a horizontal and vertical direction. Pads of paper were jammed into all the cracks. Pens and all of the other loose items were thrown on the little shelf at the top. The mirror that I attached to the inside, just below the three little vents, was the only thing that seemed to be in alignment. I glanced at my face in the mirror and thought that it looked much like the state of my locker, a hopeless mess. I continued to dig through the books, pulling out the one that I needed before heading to class.

The morning moved at the pace of a snail. My stomach started to growl and I pressed it hard with both arms across my abdomen, wishing that I had been more interested in my breakfast. Each class seemed to drag as a class typically does on the first day of school; teachers were trying to jam in all of the introductions, class outlines, and expectations for the year into a forty-five minute period. On a positive note, no one made fun of my name or tried to trip me. My books were still on my desk instead of the floor and there were no spit wads tangled into my curls. Best of all, I didn't have to go to the front of the class to introduce myself. I was completely ignored by students and faculty alike. I was invisible; a ghost amongst the student body and it was heavenly. Math was first, followed by AP biology, government, French, history, and English Lit was just before lunch. But it was in art, room 209, where my shell, the one I had worked so hard to build, began to crumble. I didn't actually know that this barrier of mine was cracking at the time. I had symptoms of course, but I had no sure fire way to tell that my heart would soon be fully exposed. I can imagine that it's comparable to having a life-threatening disease and not knowing it. You're aware that you don't feel right, but you don't know why. The unveiling process wasn't complete until sometime late in October, the unveiling of my heart that is. It wasn't until then that the shell that I had worked so hard to create had completely disintegrated. It wasn't until then that I felt the liberating effects. What I now know is that from the moment I walked into room 209, I didn't have a fighting chance.

The room was not unlike other art classrooms. It was clean and neat with easels lining one side of the wall and pottery wheels taking up a majority of the other. It smelled of paint and turpentine, a smell that, oddly enough, I loved. There were no desks in the room. Instead, there were six large, raised tables that held four chairs each.

Mr. Bradley was the teacher. His desk sat on an elevated platform in the center of the room and he peered crossly down at the students from behind his wooden abode. He was a stern, middle-aged man with thinning, dark brown hair and a small mustache that curled at the ends. His face was thin and angular with a lacy, red pigmentation that brushed across his cheeks.

I continued to scan the room, and then, without control, my eyes involuntarily positioned themselves on the table catty corner and three rows up. I couldn't blink. I couldn't turn away. My eyes were frozen, fixed, focused. My heart began this strange, new, and irregular beat. Not like a heart attack. It felt good. My chest was heavy as I stared at the most beautiful person I had ever seen. He turned his body in my direction and our eyes locked. I could not look away. He had rugged features on a square face and his ruddy complexion was a sharp contrast to my olive one. His pale, icy pink lips had a

21

small freckle on the lower, left side that stood out to me, even from a distance. I must have stared at him for the entire forty-five minute class period. I could have stared all day. My heart was pounding hard. I had no idea what was going on with my body. I had never been boy crazy, but this boy had my mind swimming in every direction. I felt stronger than I ever had, yet weak at the same time. I felt agitated and calm, excited and nervous, skittish, yet relaxed. My mind was garbled, but clearer than it had been in my seventeen years of existence. I wanted to pounce on him and at the same time run away. I felt every emotion at once, each one pulling me in a different direction. Thankfully, art was the last class of the day.

As I walked from the school to my car, I felt much different than I had on the way in this morning. Nothing had changed. I was still surrounded by a crowd of unfamiliar faces. A very small fish in an enormous and ever deepening sea. But, instead of feeling the drag in my feet, I felt light and weightless.

# CHAPTER THREE

*M*y mother was chopping onions when I walked into the kitchen for breakfast. The clock on the oven said 6:45. She was ready for work, dressed in her favorite pale yellow, cupcake print scrubs. I still hadn't figured out why a shrink would need to wear scrubs. Seemed like an excuse to wear pajamas to work if you asked me. My dad was standing in the corner of the kitchen watching her over the top of his wire rimmed glasses, sipping his coffee and looking slightly concerned. Dad usually did most of the cooking . . . when he was home. My mom only cooked when she was upset and, by the looks of it, the onion she was working on was receiving the entirety of her wrath.

"Why are you chopping onions at 6:45 in the morning?"

"I'm putting a roast in the crock pot. We've got to eat, right?" she sniffled and, without setting the knife down, wiped her right arm across both eyes. "I was going to make it tomorrow night for Nana and Papa, but Papa has changed his mind about coming," she huffed.

I walked closer to her, peering over her shoulder. Mom was making onion puree without realizing it.

"I thought you were supposed to leave the onions chunky for a roast. You're pulverizing the poor thing." My mother ignored me and continued to chop, a determined look on her face.

"So, why aren't they coming?" I asked, peeling the wrapper off of a granola bar and taking a bite. Dad was giving me his version of a "don't even go there" look. His face was scrunched up, his lips were pursed tightly together, and he was shaking his head behind my mother's back.

"Nana's had a rough week. Papa said she wouldn't even know us if they came." Mom moved the back of her hand over her left eye in one quick sweep. "These onions are killing me," she said with a sniffle. Now Dad gave me an "I told you so" look and picked up the morning paper, pretending that he was engrossed in an article.

"Here, move over," I told her. I set my granola bar on the counter and, without protest, my mother loosened her grip on the knife and I began to chop the onion into bite-sized pieces. It was obvious that my mother was upset, and not without reason. Nana had been as sharp as a tack until about a year ago. Papa started noticing little things around that time, like finding Nana's favorite jewelry wrapped up in foil inside a coffee can in the freezer. There was also the time, a year ago last October, when she wound up in the emergency room because she had forgotten to take her heart medication for a solid week. She had sworn up and down that she had taken it and did everything short of throwing a temper tantrum in the ER to convince him of it, too. When Papa got home, he found all of her pills still in the day of the week medicine dispenser, which was hidden near a large potted plant on the back patio. The last time I saw her, she was beginning to get the days of the week confused, but she hadn't forgotten my name.

"So, how was your first day at school?" Mom sniffled again. "I can't believe I forgot to ask. What kind of mother am I?"

"It was okay."

My dad lowered his paper. "Make any new friends?" he asked hopefully.

"I met a girl. Her locker's next to mine."

"You like your teachers?" he probed.

"They're okay. Looks like it's going to be a repeat of last year, at least in English Lit and biology."

"I told you all of those years in private schools would pay off."

"If you say so." I used the knife to scrape the onion into the crock pot. My mother was watching me from a barstool on the other side of the counter.

"The carrots are in the fridge," she offered.

"You know it's not too early to start applying to the local universities. Your mother and I prefer OU, you know that, but after all, it is your choice."

"Yeah . . . right," I muttered under my breath as I dumped the bag of pre-washed baby carrots into the pot and turned the switch to high.

There wasn't a time that I could remember my dad not being an OU football fan. Even when they were lousy and we were thousands of miles away, he was still loyal. Both he and my mother had gone through med school at the OU Health Sciences Center in Oklahoma City. That was where they met . . . in shrink school. They thought for sure that I would be following in their footsteps. In fact, that could be the only reason we moved to Oklahoma in the first place. They could have chosen to settle down anywhere. But no, they chose Oklahoma. Smack dab in the middle of the prairie.

School was no different today than it was yesterday. I was completely ignored and I couldn't have been more pleased. I made a fruitless attempt to concentrate on my calculus. Mr. Martinez wasted no time in assigning home-work, but instead of trying to finish some of it in class, I doodled lots of hearts and swirly-ques on my folder with my purple gel pen. AP biology went by quickly. The teacher sent us in alternating groups to the gym to sign up for extracurricular activities. The gym was full of tables set up in rows lining the outer edges of the room, each table manned by a volunteer to answer questions. It smelled sweaty and stale. I was certain that I would find nothing at all in this cold and unremarkable room, but I pretended to have some interest, finally, stopping at the cross-country table. I loved to run. It wasn't that I was particularly fast or competitive for that matter, but it was something I could do regardless of where I lived and it didn't involve teamwork.

After lunch, I bypassed my locker and headed straight to art. I made it to class, room 209, with ten minutes to spare. The art room was empty, not even the teacher was there. I noticed the room was arranged differently. The tables had been moved and different stations were set up around the perimeter of the room. The easels that lined one side of the wall yesterday had been spread out. The pottery wheels were still on the other side, but today there was a large lump of clay on the center of each one.

"Hello."

I wasn't aware that I had any sort of expectations for what his voice might sound like . . . until he spoke, and I realized that it was nothing like I had imagined it to be. It was smooth . . . unsettling . . . intoxicating.

Startled, I whipped around to find him staring at me, the beautiful boy. His eyes fixed on me felt hot; they were burning through my body. I took a deep breath, returning his gaze, and I realized that no amount of focus or concentration could keep my heart from doing somersaults inside of the small, steel, encasement that it occupied. It was thudding against its familiar hard shell, begging to be set free. He was more beautiful up close than he was from a distance. His eyes were amazing, like nothing I had ever seen, and yet, they looked familiar. They were an indescribable shade of hazel. The dark pupil in the center of each eye extended out in about eight spoke-like fingers that reminded me of a pinwheel. The tip of each spoke perfectly touched the edge of the yellow ring that outlined his eyes. He had a small scar at the outer corner of his right eye that was very subtle, like it had been from an accident years ago.

He pulled out the chair next to mine and sat down, a nervous smile on his face, an unexplainable kind of excitement radiated from every inch of his body. I knew it wasn't his appearance that brought about this oddly intimate sensation. It was the way he made me feel. I was certain I had never seen him before; such striking features would surely never be forgotten. I continued to stare at his flawlessness. I was gawking. It was something I couldn't control. The classroom was empty; all of the open stations and he boldly chose the easel next to mine.

"Hello," he said again, without breaking eye contact for a second. "I'm Alex."

"I . . . I'm Rae," I stuttered. I wanted to say more, but I couldn't come up with anything, nothing at all. My mind was blank, like a plain, white sheet of paper. I turned to face my canvas.

"Rae," he repeated my name, rolling it off his tongue as if he had said it ten thousand times before.

My tongue, on the other hand, felt like it was tied in an extremely large knot and my throat felt like I had something stuck in it.

"So . . . how do you like Bartlesville High?" His voice was smooth . . . hypnotizing.

I cleared my throat several times to ensure I wouldn't sound like a croaking frog.

"Okay, I guess."

"I saw you at the new student orientation a couple of nights ago."

My eyes were still glued to the blank canvas that rested on the easel in front of me. My heart was pulsing through my chest. I did not remember seeing him. I would have remembered. My mind was twisting and turning, cranking round and round.

"I didn't see you," I spat, still searching for answers and the tone of my voice unintentionally testing him. Again, I wondered what it was about him that seemed so familiar.

"I sat in the back. I was late," he offered. He paused, waiting for me to say something . . . anything. I was silent. "I just moved here last week," he hesitated. A bit of seriousness returning to his voice.

"From where?" My voice cracked.

"Up north," he said with ambiguity, a smile forming at the corners of his mouth, just before he pressed his lips into a smooth, straight, and serious line. "And you?"

"We moved here at the beginning of the summer. From Amsterdam . . . this time," I scoffed. The words felt jagged as they passed over the huge lump in my throat. I hoped he hadn't noticed the effect he was having on me. I wanted to know everything about him: what his interests were, his favorite foods, what his family was like, what kind of toothpaste he used. I bit down hard on my lip to prevent the abundance of words from dropping out of my mouth.

"You're Dutch?" A wrinkle formed between his brows and once again, the corners of his mouth began to curl upward into a knowing smile.

"No. I'm from Kansas City . . . Missouri . . . originally," I said abruptly. I began to twist my hair around my finger nervously.

"You don't talk much, do you?"

I responded with silence. He began making this clicking noise with his tongue on the roof of his mouth. I ignored him and began to look around the room. During my trancelike state, the classroom had filled with students and the teacher sat behind his desk staring at me like I was a disruption.

My head jerked quickly back to my canvas. Bradley rambled on about the course of action for the day. Half of the class would be getting started with oils on canvas and the other half would be starting on the wheels. He explained that a few students had never worked with oils and today we would be spending most of our time learning technique. Tomorrow, there would be a live model and we would begin our masterpiece.

I spent most of the class wishing I could start painting. All of the mixing and playing left me yawning, but I could feel Alex's intense stare and it warmed me. The bell rang, prematurely I thought. The class went by fast, much too fast. Strangely, I was hoping it would drag on for days. I could get used to sitting in the warmth of his presence.

"So, what classes are you taking?"

I felt the sting as I unclenched my teeth from my lower lip, and I wondered if there might be a permanent indentation. I cleared my throat again as I got up from my chair and slung my bag over my shoulder.

"Just the basics. Biology with Mitchell, English Lit with Brooks, history with Canton, calc with Martinez, government . . . ."

"Basics, huh," he interrupted with a bit of humor in his voice. "Aren't those all AP teachers?"

I shrugged sheepishly.

"So, tell me about Amsterdam." His honey voice was coaxing me to speak.

"It was coldish," I responded, trying hard not to elaborate.

"Just . . . coldish?" he asked, probing for more information.

"It was pretty too."

"Coldish and pretty." He repeated my choppy summary in one irresistible breath.

I reached my locker with him dangling behind me like some beautiful and misplaced charm. He stood there for a moment, staring at me. I felt uncomfortable.

"I guess I'll see you tomorrow, then?" His voice sounded hopeful.

"I'll be here," I responded. My heart sank as I watched him walk away. I wanted uncomfortable back. Uncomfortable was so much better than empty. Empty and sad and lonely and anxious was what I felt when this beautiful stranger was gone.

# CHAPTER FOUR

*T*here's a saying about a watched pot: it supposedly never boils. In my case, it's the watched clock that never ticks. My new obsession with the clock that hung on the wall in every classroom would surely be the downfall of my overall excellent GPA. I would watch every movement of the second hand as it counted down in small steady increments, each movement bringing me that much closer to my favorite period of the day. It was in art that I might get the chance to sit next to him, that I might hear his voice from across the room, that I might be lucky enough to smell the scent that my brain had already labeled as his, that I might brush my fingers across his on accident in the supply room, or that I might feel the warmth that I was used to feeling every time our eyes met. I loved and hated when he looked at me. I loved it because it gave me the tingles and made my heart beat faster. I hated it because my face would turn red, causing me to look quickly away. I hated it because it reminded me that I was insecure and scared, too afraid to go after those things in life that I desired.

My life had fallen into a routine, a very predictable and unnerving routine. Each day began with the blowing Oklahoma heat that felt like a hair dryer fanning across my entire body. Lunch was always the same. I ate by myself, usually at the park by the high school. I bypassed my locker whenever possible, an attempt to avoid the mindless gossip of Chloe and Jen. I learned that my first impression of the girls was dead on, but I was surprised to find that Claire was growing on me. There was a degree of warmth that lie behind Claire's impassivity. Sometimes we would talk . . . when Chloe wasn't around . . . and every once in a while, I was able to overlook the mechanical nature of her voice.

My parents seemed content with their new lives. We were now closer to Nana and Papa and, because Nana wasn't well enough to travel, Mom was preoccupied with the planning of a trip to see them soon. Dad was just as busy with work as he was before the move, so for him, nothing much had changed.

When I stepped outside that Thursday morning, it was dark and dreary, unseasonably cool for early September with the lack of any breeze whatsoever. I was accustomed to the wind making instruments of nature: a rustling, whisper-like sound as it blew the grass in a circular motion, a deeper and more frightening tune as it blew the heavy branches of the hundred-year-old pecans, a shaking and rattling noise as it forced its way across the guttering that clung to the edge of our roof, and a high pitched whistling as it blew through the cracks of my father's barn. This morning the music was gone, not even the birds were singing, and I wondered if there was some sort of secret that I hadn't been let in on. It felt like the calm before the storm, but I took no time to appreciate the stillness.

The first half of the day was unremarkable. Lunch came quickly. I was expecting to see the girls huddled around Claire's locker, but they were standing across the hall waiting on Jen. Their voices carried through the hall that was noisy with students. Leaning against my locker door, I watched them and listened as Jen talked about the Masquerade Ball that was coming up next month. She was going through a list of possible costumes that included a 1960's pinup girl, a vampire, a gothic princess, and sexy pirate wench amongst other things. I could see her smile inflate each and every time she got approval from Megan and Chloe. I wanted to gag. Every once in a while Chloe would look in my direction. She would give me a menacing look and then say something very hush-hush to Megan and Jen. Claire seemed to be listening as well, but unlike me, she wasn't staring. Instead, Claire focused on her locker. She didn't seem herself. I thought I was the only one that found Jen boring and superficial, but apparently, today, Claire shared in my opinion. Something about Claire was different. Her previous warmth was replaced with something cold and untouchable. I watched her from the corner of my eye. She was distracted and aloof. I hated to admit it, but it was nice to have someone to talk to, even if it were only a few simple words. I continued to observe Claire from behind my half-open locker door. Other than the hint of sadness that lingered in Claire's eyes, her mannerisms were much like her voice, robotic and cold. She reached up and slammed her locker door. I expected her to walk over and join Chloe and the other girls, but instead, she walked down the hall by herself and I was left standing all alone. Once again, I was reminded that I didn't fit in. I scowled and poked my face back inside my locker. I tried to focus on something else, like tonight's information meeting for cross-country. I had to admit that I was a teensy bit excited, not to meet the coach or the other cross-country girls, but to mark the practices on my calendar, just as I did at all of my other schools. This made my life feel monotonous and predictable, but at the same time, I found it comforting to know that I finally had some sort of schedule. Every time we moved, the pieces of my life became scattered and unorganized. Cross-country was one of the familiar pieces of my life and I loved these familiar pieces, because I knew exactly where they fit in.

Art was completely worthless. I tried to concentrate on the model in the middle of the room, but I couldn't bring myself to lift the brush a single time. The bell rang and I realized that my canvas looked the same as it did when I set it on the easel at the beginning of class. I could hardly blame myself. I was completely uninspired by the subject matter and decided that a bottle of gesso might come in handy tomorrow. I would use the gesso to make my canvas white again. It would let me start from scratch. I loved gesso. I loved its thick whiteness and how it was so forgiving. I loved brushing it on heavily over my marred canvas. It made the canvas look new and clean, without a single blemish. I wish they made gesso for the soul, because if they did, I would slather it on thick. I would create a new me. I, too, would be new and clean, without a single blemish.

I had a good three hours before my cross-country meeting. Just enough time to go home, finish my homework, and shovel down some food before heading back to the school. My mom was working the night shift in the psych ward at the local hospital. She had decided to cut back to part time when we moved to Oklahoma. My dad preferred the clinic setting. Between his hefty workload and the hour he drove to and from work, he was rarely home for dinner. He promised that it would slow down once he got into the swing of things, but we had been here several months and I had yet to see a change. I finished my homework and was left sitting at the desk in the kitchen with nothing to do. I got up and looked out the window. The slight breeze that was present at lunch had picked up a bit; the sky was grey with ominous clouds that hung so low to the ground that it looked as if they were touching tops of the trees. My mind shifted to Claire and I wondered how she could be so friendly one moment and distant the next. I thought about the sadness that I saw in her eyes. I thought about Chloe. I wondered how someone beautiful could be ugly. This was one of those times when I felt like giving up on people altogether and also one of those times that reminded me of why I built the shell around my heart to begin with. My shell protected me. It made me indifferent and uncaring and that made my life so much easier.

I made a sandwich, grabbed a Diet Coke from the fridge, slung my bag over my shoulder, and hopped in my car. I ate while I drove. I had to admit that the clouds were a little scary, not like those warm summer days when you look up at the clouds and see funny faces in them. When I was little, I would do this. I had seen a cloud that looked like an elephant standing on a ball, a cloud that resembled a horse jumping over a fence, a robot, a shoe, one of the seven dwarfs, a princess, and even a sailboat with a monster about to eat it. But tonight, the clouds did not form any funny little faces. They came together, forming a wall, as if they were getting ready for battle. I focused instead on the road ahead of me, noticing how little drops of rain were splattering on my windshield, slowly at first, but steadily picking up speed.

I rushed into the school out of the pouring rain, soaking wet and running late. I walked silently into room 115, my history class, and took a seat in the back. The coach was also my history teacher, Ms. Canton . . . surprise, surprise. All of my cross-country coaches had taught history. I wondered if it were a prerequisite. I listened and copied practice times into my agenda and scowled when she informed the team that we would be practicing during the wee hours of the morning until the weather cooled down. I looked out the window and noticed that the rain was now pounding. Large drops coming together and then rolling down the glass in one continuous sheet. My eyes then drifted over to the blackboard, taking notice of the homework assignment that was written neatly at the top of the board in yellow chalk. The homework assignment that I had neglected to see on my way out of class and the one that would require my history book, which was on the third floor somewhere at the bottom of my locker. I now realized that I would be reading history tonight instead of watching my favorite show and that made me a bit crabby, but not as crabby as I would be without Tevo.

I had never actually considered what a school might be like when it was empty. It would sort of be like wondering how the ocean would feel without water or what it would be like if my mom was without my dad. It had just never occurred to me that the school might feel very different without students . . . until it was. Certain things just fit together with such perfection that I had never stopped to wonder what one would be like without the other. For instance, I was accustomed to the perfect combination of piano and flute flowing out of the music room and intermixing with the sound of laugher, chatter, footsteps, and the rustling of papers. This was the sound that a school made. But tonight, as I climbed the stairs into the darkness of the third floor, the halls were totally silent. The odors were different, too. Tonight, the hallways smelled more like cleaning supplies than cafeteria food infused with perfume and hairspray. Nothing remained the same. Even the lighting was different. Darkness poured out of the paned glass classroom doors and cast shadows onto the milky colored, linoleum tiled floor. The sun that usually streamed in through the windows was gone and the overhead fluorescents that I had never actually noticed flickered and buzzed. Contrary to what I might have previously believed, the school was a rather cheery place to be . . . in the daytime.

My locker was halfway down the hall, between the stairwell and the exit sign that glowed red in the darkness. It was a bright orange locker that was made dreary with chipping paint and a heavy, black combo lock. As I was twirling the combination around, listening to the clicking noise the lock made as it spun, I noticed another sound; it was a more pronounced clicking coming from the opposite direction.

Squinting my eyes to see the numbers on the lock, I turned clockwise to twenty-four, counterclockwise to seventeen, and then clockwise again to twenty-nine. Presto, my locker opened like magic and I pulled my history book from the bottom. It wasn't until I turned and began walking in the direction of the stairs, my history book tucked tightly under my arm, that I noticed two things: one—the clicking noise that I had heard in the distance had come to a stop, and two—at the end of the hall near the stairwell was a shadow that I hadn't noticed on my way up. Without thinking about it, I stopped in my tracks and stared into the darkness, studying the black silhouette that fell away from the dark wall and spilled into the hallway. The shadow had taken the shape of a tall, thin body with legs together and one hand on its hip. Creepy, I thought. I took a deep breath and began to walk closer to the stairwell when I could have sworn that I saw the shadow in the distance shift; the arm that was, just seconds ago, on its hip was now at its side. But had it moved? I doubted it, but still there was an uneasiness inside of me that was making my heart beat faster by the second and, until I sucked in a large amount of air, I hadn't realized that I had been holding my breath. I thought about the other set of stairs at the back of the building and quickly turned back toward my locker. I was just about to round the corner out of sight, when the pronounced clicking noise returned. It wasn't until I had picked up the pace, the rubber on the bottoms of my black All Stars squeaking loudly across the floor, that I heard another sound. This time it was a sound that I could pinpoint, the sound of another set of feet pounding hard and fast through the hallway. There was someone else here with me tonight, and the footsteps were coming in my direction. It didn't matter to me what their intentions were. It could have been the janitor for all I knew, but there was no way I was going to stick around to find out. Torn between instinct and curiosity, I craned my neck over my shoulder and continued to run.

All at once, the clicking came to a halt. It was silent, completely silent except for the rain beating down on the roof. I couldn't even hear my own footsteps. But I was still moving. I couldn't feel my feet beneath me. I was weightless. My stomach dropped. I felt a crushing pain right before everything went black.

I can only assume that it was the similarity of circumstances that caused me to flash back to that fall day in Prague. As I lay in darkness, my body unmoving and broken, I felt no pain; instead, I felt trapped and angry. I was twelve years old and my mother was getting ready to drop me off me at school. The morning was cold and damp. It had just begun to rain and already the odors were rising from the city streets as though Mother Nature had just given the drains on the side of the road a quick stir.

"You and Dad are so overprotective. I'm not a baby," I told her. I wanted to walk to school, by myself, just like everyone else did. She wanted to accompany me on the metro and escort me to the front steps of the school, waiting in the semicircle drive until I disappeared behind the secured double doors. It was embarrassing. I wanted to spread my wings. She wanted to keep me under her thumb. I wanted to fit in. She wanted me trapped inside the tiny bubble she and my father had created. Inside this bubble, I could see the world but I could not touch. I had never attempted to break through . . . not until that cold, wet day in October. By the time the bell rang for dismissal, I had a fairly good but risky plan for escape, and it completely depended on a boy that I barely knew. Jan Jorgenson was his name and he was the tallest and roundest boy in my class. He outweighed me by at least fifty pounds.

That he towered above me was normally intimidating, but today, if I stayed close to his side, I would be able to walk, unnoticed, past my mother, who always waited for me on the bench right outside the doors. The walk to our tiny apartment was a little over a mile and it would take me less than thirty minutes. I didn't see the harm in that. The heavy mist had burned off in the afternoon sun, leaving a beautiful fall day with only a few clouds in the sky. Sticking to my plan, I stayed close to Jan Jorgenson's side and, as I breezed, unnoticed, past my mother, I felt so many things at once: brave, nervous, independent, free, and scared. The city looked different as I walked the streets alone. For the first time in my life, everything seemed real. I had stepped outside the bubble and finally felt the stimulation and excitement of the world around me: the narrow, cobblestone streets, a man and a woman embracing on the corner, a boy riding a scooter with a girl snuggled tightly behind, two men fighting behind a delivery truck that was loaded with bread, and shoppers carrying bags from fancy stores. The buildings were fascinating: tall and narrow with distinguishing colors. Most of them were five or six stories high. Some of the buildings had balconies and others had windows with flower boxes hanging below. It was as I stood on a bridge that arched over the Vivata River, admiring the painters who transferred their perspective of the city onto the canvas, that something inside of me changed. As I watched the artists at work, I noticed that, even though they were looking at the same river, each painting was very different. I wondered if everyone saw the world this differently. At this moment, the world looked very different to me, too, different than it did inside the bubble where my parents kept me. The drizzle from this morning had returned and I noticed that the artists were packing up their supplies in a hurry, easels under their arms and heavy, black cases filled with supplies swinging by their sides. I heard the bell of a church toll somewhere in the distance. At that moment, I realized that it was much later than I thought and that I was lost. Several hours had slipped by without my noticing and now I found myself in an unfamiliar place. The Vivata River was several miles past our apartment and I knew that I had gone too far. Instantly, my knees felt weak, my heart accelerated, and the confidence that swelled inside me this afternoon had dwindled to nothing. Darkness had come more quickly now that the heavy mist from this morning had returned. The only light came from the glow of infrequent lampposts. I passed back over the Vivata and headed toward the shops that I had admired earlier this afternoon, the shops that were now closed. The drizzle had changed quickly into a heavy rain. The streets had become deserted, only a few scattered city dwellers hustling about. I tucked my books tightly under my arm and slipped off onto one of the many narrow, cobblestone streets, nervously watching my tiny body cast an enormous shadow onto the side of the building. The night was quiet with the exception of the church bell tolling, loud and reliable, somewhere high above me. The noise of the city was drowned out by the steady drumming of water on the cobblestone streets. Walking quickly, I passed shop after shop, each one closed for the night, *zavreno*, until suddenly, I came to a stop in front of the huge plate glass window of a business, and read the name that was scrolled across the glass.

## PIERCE AND ASSOCIATES
### International Relocation and Job Placement Services

The bold red lettering stood out, bright, against the image of a lion in the background. I peered into the window and found the building to be practically vacant, with the exception of a rickety desk and an outdated typewriter that was sitting on top. I found it odd that such an elaborate storefront would house nothing more than a desk and an old typewriter, but what initially captured my attention was the name of the business: it was written in English. I shrugged, stepped back, and took notice of my shape reflected in the plate glass window, noticing how my once enormous shadow on the wall of the building had shrunk to a more realistic size in the glass storefront. I studied myself: my wet hair that hung heavy past my shoulders, the outline of my pleated skirt that fell just above my knees. My legs looked ultra thin from where I was standing, two twigs sticking out of a pair of boots. Just as my eyes were shifting down to examine my wet and tattered books, I caught a glimpse of a second, less distinct reflection in the window. A figure amongst the shadowy backdrop, detected only by its sudden movement. Without thinking, I whipped around to face the shadowy figure; instead, I found a deserted street. But I didn't feel alone. I could sense the presence of someone else there with me. I curled my fingers tight around my books and edged away from the storefront. At first, I walked slowly away, but when I heard the sound of heavy padding close behind, I picked up the pace to a slow jog, my spindly legs shaking beneath me. I could hear the sound of the church bell tolling. I could hear the sound of the church bell tolling half past the hour. I didn't dare turn around to face the figure that was behind me. Instead, I kept my eyes focused on the road ahead. And that's when I saw it: a large bend in the road. I quickened my pace so that I was now sprinting. Out of breath, I raced around the corner and tucked myself into the dark shadow of an empty alleyway. Nervously rolling one of the pink crystal beads on my bracelet between my thumb and index finger, I waited. It was the bracelet that my parents had bought for me on our first day in Prague, but right now I was hoping that it would bring me a bit of luck.

The time ticked by and I was cold and nervous and scared. I wrapped my coat, tight, around my body and had just begun to edge myself out of the shadow, when I heard heavy footsteps coming in my direction. I slid back into the darkness and froze. I was completely still when the figure approached. The stranger was no longer an indefinable shadow. The pale glow of a distant lamppost partially illuminated his body, revealing the long, charcoal grey overcoat and fancy, wing tipped, leather shoes of a man who was holding a medium-sized case in his hand. The man stopped for a moment, less than five feet from where I was standing. If the rain had not been pounding, I was sure that he would hear me breathing, my teeth chattering. I pulled my coat tighter around my body and I watched the stranger walk into the darkness and away from the shadow in which I was standing.

"Rae . . ." The words were fuzzy and distant as if someone were speaking to me from the end of a long tunnel. As the voice became more distinct, the memory that I had been reliving while lying unconscious on the floor of the high school began to fade, returning itself to the portion of my brain where it belonged. I opened my eyes to a mere squint, but the light was blinding and forced them to shut immediately. I felt a throbbing throughout my entire body. I could feel my pulse heavy and hard in my head. With each beat, my head felt as though it was about to explode.

"Rae . . ." The voice came again.

I opened my eyes, squinting and holding them like that for a moment, adjusting them to the light, and then they fell shut. I had no control, my lids felt heavy and then blackness took over once again.

My next memory was waking up in a dimly lit room, a more comfortable space where I was able to open my eyes and look around. I was lying on a narrow bed inside of a room that was enclosed by a curtain. My mom was sitting in a chair beside me while my dad paced back and forth at my feet.

"Mom . . . Dad." My voice was weak; it surprised me. My father came rushing to my side when I spoke.

"Where am I?" I asked through clenched teeth.

"The ER." My dad was now hovering over me, blocking the little bit of light that was still shining in my face. My mom was still seated, staring blankly at the wall.

"What? Why?" I struggled to pull from my memory anything that would cause me to wind up in the Emergency Room. My head felt heavy. My mind was garbled and fuzzy.

"How do you feel?"

"I don't know . . . sore. My head hurts...bad," I said as I lifted my left hand to touch the back of my head. My arm was stiff and felt swollen.

"What happened?" I could feel tears forming behind my lids, but I held them back. I hurt, but I was also angry that I couldn't remember.

"You fell down the stairs at school." My parents looked at me as if they were hoping I would supply them with an answer, any answer that would make them feel better about their daughter falling down eighteen stairs in a dark and empty high school.

"How did you know?"

"Someone called 911."

"Who?" I asked.

My dad shrugged his shoulders. "I got a call from the hospital saying that you were here. Mom was seeing a patient on the fourth floor and she came right down. I got here just as they were taking you back."

"I was there for a cross-country meeting. I remember that."

"Don't push it, just rest. It'll come back," my father said with encouragement in his voice that did not match the concern in his eyes.

"Can I leave now? I want to go home."

"They want to do a CAT scan. After that we can leave."

"Why? Am I hurt?"

"No," my father paused. "You hit your head pretty hard, just precautions, I suppose." My father paused again, longer this time. "Strangely enough, there's not a bruise on your body. Pretty remarkable for falling down a flight of stairs."

"That's hard to believe," I said, grimacing in pain. "Every inch of me hurts."

"I guess you're just one tough cookie," he said in the most reassuring voice that he could pull together.

My mother was still sitting in the chair beside my bed, her legs were now tucked tightly to her chest and she was rocking back and forth like a child in pain. My father looked down toward the floor with his lips bunched together as if he were in deep thought. He was shaking his head in rhythm with my mothers swaying body. I could now hear my mother crying. Soft sobbing. Uncontrollable tears. It wasn't often that my mother cried, but when she did, it frightened me.

The next morning, I wasn't sure what to expect. But when I woke, I found that everything had returned to normal. It was as if nothing had actually happened. The tears and anxiety from last night were gone. In their place was strength and distance.

I wasn't expected to go to school the next day, which was Friday. I felt fine. I had taken a couple of ibuprofen and it stopped the pain from last night; however, it didn't stop the school from calling to check on me. Maybe they were concerned that there might be some sort of lawsuit. I liked to think that they were just being compassionate.

The rain continued hard and heavy throughout the weekend. I took advantage of the fact that I wasn't expected to do any homework for the time being and I picked up my dad's copy of *Angels and Demons*. I sat on my bed in my pajamas, keeping my nose in the book until it was finished. It was a perfect weekend.

# CHAPTER FIVE

*I* arrived at school early, anticipating that I might get in and out of my locker before the students filled the halls. I was sure that by now everyone had heard about my accident on Thursday night. I was thankful that I wasn't here on Friday when the news was still hot. On Thursday, I had been the invisible new kid, but I was sure that today everyone would know my name. I hated that from here on out my name would be irreversibly linked to my most recent fumble. The rain was still pounding outside and my hair was soaking, leaving my curls heavy and pulling my black locks midway down my back. I felt like a wet rat. I was sure that I looked like one as well. I was quickly learning that the humidity in Oklahoma had absolute control over my hair, turning my once soft curls into a very full and frizzy heap.

"You don't believe in umbrellas?" came a smooth and familiar voice from behind my shoulder.

My heart skipped a few beats. I now understood the meaning of butterflies in the stomach. I would have killed for a change of clothes and a hairdryer right about now. Yes, I was sure that I looked like a wet rat and I grabbed my hair and began to wrench out some of the extra water.

I turned slowly to face him. I was trying hard to come up with something smart to say in return, but his appearance took me by surprise. He was as dry as a bone. He was wearing a long sleeved, white, button up with the sleeves rolled, some worn jeans, and a pair of blue and black vans. Not a drop of rain on his perfectly pressed shirt. He was beautiful . . . painfully so. I couldn't breath. He was now standing just inches away from me, his eyes focused on mine. A million thoughts were swimming through my mind in no particular order, a whirlpool of questions.

Why did he have to smell so good?

Did he have this effect on all of the girls?

Why couldn't I move?

Why couldn't I open my mouth?

Why couldn't I think about anything other than pinwheel eyes and the skin that lie beneath his perfectly pressed shirt?

Why couldn't I be one of those beautiful girls that made men weak in the knees?

Why was I so ordinary?

Why was he standing at my locker at this very moment?

Without uttering a single word, I flipped around so that I was once again staring at the inside of my locker. I sucked in a chest full of air and then began to rummage through my books, pretending to be looking for something

I couldn't find, when I did it. With one small fumble, the entire contents of my locker came streaming out onto the milky colored tile floor. At that moment, the only thought running through my mind was how I wished he wasn't here to witness my natural clumsiness and how I wished I could just crawl into my locker and make this whole mess go away. My face was red, my eyes were closed, and my body was tense as I turned slowly around to pick up the mess I had made.

"I've got it," he whispered. It was at that moment when I realized why Alex was standing at my locker. He felt sorry for me. Who wouldn't? He had heard about my accident on Thursday night, and he was standing at my locker out of pity for the poor girl who fell down the stairs. I wanted to tell him to stick around and see what else I had to offer. I was sure that I could top it if he gave me just a couple of days.

I slowly unclenched my eyes and was now staring at Alex, the heaping pile of books stacked neatly in his arms.

Claire's inquisitive eyes were watching our every move, but still she seemed distant.

Alex was gently biting on his lower lip while the other side of his mouth was turned up into a wry sort of smile. I wondered if he could sense my discomfort and found it amusing.

"Do you have plans for lunch today?" He stood in front of me, still holding my books in the crook of his arm. He was irresistible.

"I . . . I don't have any plans at all. Nothing." My mouth was running more than it should. I'm sure a simple yes or no would have sufficed. The words were being pushed from my mouth. I had no control.

"Good, I'll meet you here." He glanced at my still cluttered locker with a look of disbelief, as if he were planning on placing the books neatly back in but wasn't quite sure how to go about it. He handed me my stack of books and began walking backwards, away from my locker, but with his eyes still focused on me.

"Where are we going?" I raised my voice above the sound of the students. I couldn't believe that I had agreed to go somewhere with a boy I barely knew. I had absolutely no backbone . . . or maybe . . . I had absolutely no choice.

"You'll have to wait and see." He gave a slight wave, turned around, and then merged into the crowd of students filling the busy hallway. I was instantly reminded of how much I hated surprises.

I continued to watch, soaking up every last bit of him, when I saw Chloe coming in his direction. The same sneer across her ruby lips. They both seemed to stop in their tracks for a moment. His shoulders stiffened and then they continued on in opposite directions. Did he know her? This idea immediately made me jealous and instinctively protective.

Claire looked at me again with expressionless eyes before shutting her locker and turning away. Her coolness reminded me that nothing had changed. Yes, I had been invited to lunch with a boy, but this school was no different than the others. I was no different than I was before. I was not popular. I was not pretty. But most importantly, I still didn't have any friends.

I placed the books back in my locker, not taking the time to stack them neatly, when one of the books caught my eye. It was my history textbook. All at once the events of Thursday night flashed before me. I could now remember every last detail: the dim red glow at the end of the hallway, the shadow in front of the stairs, the clicking sound, the rain drumming on the rooftop, the echo of my footsteps through the hall, and the powerful pounding of another set of feet. I remember feeling scared and running away with my history book tucked tightly under my arm. I was certain that I had taken my history book out of my locker and couldn't imagine how it had found its way back in. My mind was cranking round and round, trying to put together a puzzle for which I wasn't given all of the pieces. If I could have only seen through the darkness, if I could have seen what was happening behind me. I headed down the hall, unintentionally letting out an audible sigh, ambivalent to the whispering and the multitude of eyes that were following me.

I don't recall the topics of my morning classes. My body was physically present in every classroom, but my mind was somewhere far away. When the bell finally rang for lunch, the butterflies that had been cooped up all morning were set loose and my stomach felt as if it were moving in many directions at once.

When I reached my locker, Alex was already there. I opened it quickly, throwing the book in and slamming it before anything could fall out.

"You keep a tidy locker, don't you?" he said with sarcasm. I had never been a particularly neat person, but I couldn't believe he was commenting on it.

"So, where are we going?" I asked, hoping to direct his attention off my messy locker and back to the topic at hand.

"I told you, you'll have to wait and see. Come on."

I trailed behind him, making a beeline for the parking lot into the sea of shiny, new, and beautiful cars. I could see my car in the distance.

"This is me," he said.

Before I could disagree, he had the passenger side door of an old Jeep Wagoneer opened and ushered me in. It caught me off guard. I realized that no one had ever opened a car door for me. I wasn't sure I liked it. It went against everything that I held dear. It threatened my independence and came dangerously close to jeopardizing the shell I had created around myself. He slid into the driver's seat, turned the key in the ignition, and with a rather large roar, brought the old beast to life.

It felt like we had been driving for miles. The old wagon took all of the bumps surprisingly well. I wondered if his parents had taught him how to drive. Even though I was eighteen, I had only been driving for a couple of months. Shortly after we moved to Oklahoma, my mom taught me to drive my dad's old truck in the field by our house. She made me practice for weeks before we went to get my license. My mom was terrified with the idea of me behind the wheel and she saw to it that I had more practice than I probably needed.

He slowed, pulling into Jo Allen Lo Park. It was pretty here. He drove through the park and drove over a dilapidated bridge before killing the engine. I opened my door quickly, not giving him the chance, and walked to the front of the car to admire the surrounding beauty. I was surprised. I didn't know Oklahoma had this potential. The rain had stopped, but the ground was damp. The cover of trees was shielding the grass from the now harsh sunlight. It was magical. Little bits of light trickled down through the umbrella of leaves and reflected off the drops of rain, each droplet creating the tiniest rainbow of light. I inched my way to the back of the Wagoneer, positioning myself just a few feet from the now open tailgate. He was seated comfortably inside with his legs hanging over the back bumper. I leaned up against the side of his car, struggling to come up with the most coordinated way to hoist myself into the back of his Jeep.

"I got you peanut butter and honey," he informed me as he pulled a foil wrapped sandwich from the small bag that sat inside his car. "Is that okay?" he asked knowingly.

"Yeah," I muttered, shrugging my shoulders. I had no intention of letting him know that was my favorite.

Cautiously, I put one knee on the bumper and then twisted my body so that I was sitting on the back end of the Wagoneer, a good arm's length away from Alex, and a perfect landing I might add. My body wriggled in the quiet discomfort that surrounded us. I had never been much of a talker, but I could feel his silence prompting my mouth to run like a faucet that I couldn't shut off. Someone had once told me that silence was golden, but there was something about his presence at this particular moment that provoked me to chatter without direction.

"What did you get?" I asked, unwrapping my peanut butter from the shiny, silver foil.

"Turkey and Swiss," he shrugged.

"Did your mom make these sandwiches?" I regretted my choice of words as soon as they dropped out of my mouth.

"My mother passed away seventeen years ago."

"I'm *so* sorry." I could feel my cheeks warm and was certain they were the color of the tomato on his sandwich. I was searching for something intelligent to say and was thinking; thinking about how, when I did open my mouth, I always seemed to stick my foot in it.

"She died in a car accident in Alexandria when I was two."

"Alexandria, Virginia?"

"No. Alexandria, Minnesota. It's a small town in the middle of the state." His expression was blank, which further provoked me. Without control, my mouth dropped open once again and words came gushing out. I wasn't even sure where I was headed with this conversation, but I was certain that in exactly two seconds, I would regret sharing such personal information with a perfect stranger.

"You know, I lost a sister," I spat. I was again reminded of the "silence is golden" rule, but it didn't stop me. I had no idea what had gotten into me. I never spoke of my sister, especially not with a stranger. But for some reason, he didn't really feel all that strange. He felt familiar. "I never really knew her," I continued. "She died before I was born. My parents don't talk about her much."

"I'm sorry." His voice was full of sympathy, but lacking the bit of surprise that I had expected. I picked up my peanut butter and honey and nibbled it a bit.

"I'm sure that has to be hard for them, losing a child." I could hear a bit of anguish in his voice.

"Where did you get your car? I like it. A rare find I'm sure," I said, changing the subject. "My dad had a car similar to this once upon a time, before we moved to Europe. It wasn't a Wagoneer. It was a Scrambler, I think. Yeah, it was Jeep Scrambler." I continued on in a methodical sort of way about the pictures of my dad's old Jeep, describing to him how it was a Jeep in the front and a pickup in the back, an off road version of an El Camino.

"This was my dad's car," he told me. "I don't know if you would say that he saved it for me, but it was still around when I was ready to drive. I just worked on it a bit and now it runs like new." He took another bite of his turkey and cheese.

"You're one of those handy kind of guys, huh?" I asked. I could hardly imagine the same boy who was so clean and dry during this morning's tsunami being covered in the grease and grime of an old Jeep.

"You can pretty much do anything if you put your mind to it." He didn't sound prideful at all, just honest. Besides, he wasn't saying anything that I didn't already know. I had pegged him for perfect the second I laid my eyes on him.

"I disagree; there are just certain things that I will never be able to do, no matter how hard I try."

"Like what?"

"Like singing."

He wrinkled his nose, his mouth twitched ever so slightly, and then he turned to face me, looking me directly in the eyes. I bent my head down so that I was now staring at my knobby kneecaps, which were sticking out of the holes in my jeans. I hated my kneecaps. Actually, I hated kneecaps in general. They were really the least flattering part of the human body, and here I was with my kneecaps sticking out of my jeans for everyone to see.

"What else?"

I sucked some air between my teeth, which made a mousy sort of sound. "Well, I can't bake cakes." I said, still staring at my knees and the little blond hairs that sat on top of them. The same blond hairs that I neglected to shave off in the shower this morning out of pure laziness. I discretely moved my hands over the tops of my knees and focused my eyes on Alex.

"Well, that's really not so bad."

I shrugged silently.

"Did you like your sandwich?" He eyed the empty piece of foil with a knowing smile on his face.

"Um, Yes," was all that I could find to say. Right now, if I only had one wish, I would wish that my drippy faucet of a mouth would turn back on. Even dribble was better than saying nothing at all. I bashfully crumpled up the foil and threw it in the brown paper sack that it had originated from.

"You have just a little bit of peanut butter on your mouth," he whispered, leaning over and gently wiping the mess off of my lower lip, leaving me breathless and embarrassed. We sat silently for an infinite second, neither of us speaking a word. I began to relax a bit as I realized that he was probably just as uncomfortable as I was. He was tapping his finger against the inside of the window, a nervous habit I was sure.

"So, do you come here a lot? I mean, how did you find this place?" It looked to be the older section of the park, completely neglected for years.

"It's one of my favorite places, so far, in this town, anyway. It's quiet. It reminds me of home." I wondered if he had moved from Minnesota, the place where his mother had passed.

"Do you miss home?" I asked.

"Not really."

"Do you think you'll ever go back?"

"Someday, I'm sure. It's hard to say when. Doesn't everyone usually find their way back to where they started from?"

"Not me," I said ruefully. "I've moved around so much that I barely even remember where I was born." Even though it was an exaggeration, I did feel that way part of the time.

"Well, you've gotten to see a lot of things that most people only dream of seeing . . . I'm sure."

"I guess you're right." I paused momentarily before changing the subject. "So, what do you like to do?" I asked. "When you're not at school."

"I write some. I love art."

"Like books?"

"No, not books."

I waited for him to elaborate, but he didn't.

"Who's your favorite artist?" I asked.

"Picasso."

"Really?" I guess I must have had some sort of wrinkle between my eyebrows because he had this slightly offended look on his face.

"You don't like Picasso, huh?"

"No, I do. Really, I do. It's just I'm more of a Renoir kind of girl, I guess. I like paintings with lots of details, something a little more complex. You know, like a painting of a group of people. I can spend hours looking at one painting . . . imagining what they're talking about . . . the people in the painting I mean."

"Picasso's complex. I think he is, anyway. His paintings are simple and complex all at the same time. They all have distinct lines and boundaries. I wish the world were more this way . . . you know more black and white. There's so much gray in this world. Everything is not always what it seems."

"I guess so."

"We'd better go, I don't think we should be late to Bradley's class, that guy kind of scares me." He brushed a chocolate wave of hair from his eyes and then removed himself from the back of the Jeep.

We walked through the door just as the bell was sounding, and we caught a "just in the nick of time" look from Bradley. We made our way to the easels, but our near tardiness had consequences. The only two easels left were at opposite ends of the room. It was probably better that way. I would have never been able to focus with him sitting next to me; however, I did long to see what his hands could paint. I put a thin layer of gesso over the canvas, covering two weeks of work, and I waited for it to dry. The white looked beautiful and fresh and by the end of class, I had started to sketch out something abstract with a charcoal pencil. It wasn't until the bell rang that I realized I had drawn a very rough outline of Alex's face. I hoped I was the only one who noticed. I quickly took my canvas to the supply room and pushed it to the back before anyone had the chance to see it. I walked out into the hall and waited for him to join me.

## CHAPTER SIX

$T$oday was September the thirteenth and it was my birthday. It was an occasion that my parents never took lightly and one that I tried to avoid at all costs. If it were up to me, I would stay in bed and pretend that this day didn't exist, but every year September thirteenth would roll around, and I would be reminded of every reason why I detested this mark on the calendar.

The festivities began as soon as I woke up. We would start with breakfast and then follow with the unwrapping of gifts, one of which was always a birthday collage that my mother had spent the year working on. The collage was something that I looked forward to getting. The large, square piece of poster board was filled with a year's worth of family photos and other bits of nostalgia; plus, it was small enough to fit in my luggage. I now had seventeen of them, and I was about to receive my eighteenth.

Birthdays were supposed to be fun, or at least that's what I had been told, but it was the purpose of this day that filled me with guilt. I felt guilty that I was alive and that my sister had not been given so much as a chance. I couldn't help but wonder if my parents thought about Laney on this day every year. I did. I loathed this day and I would trade all of its attention in a heartbeat for the sister I was never allowed to meet.

I crawled slowly out of bed, dressed without showering, and plastered a fake smile onto my face as I headed down the stairs. I paused at the bottom, closed my eyes tightly and silently reminded myself that I could do this. I was strong. Strong enough to hide the sadness in my eyes and strong enough to convince my mother that I was delighted she had given birth to me eighteen years ago. It didn't seem quite fair that I wasn't allowed to wallow in my pity. I knew such actions would cast my mother into a deep pit of darkness. I had made this mistake once before, ten years ago on the eve of my eighth birthday. My idea of paging through an old scrapbook seemed good at the time . . . until she caught me. I remember the piece of white paper that she ripped from my fingers, the program for Laney's funeral that had been stuffed between pages of photos. It was a beautiful, bright white program with Laney's name, birthday, and date of death embossed in silver on the front. I never got the chance to open it, but I didn't need to. Everything I needed to know lay before me. I hadn't realized until that moment that Laney and I had something in common. The date that brought me into this world was the same date she departed. It was the first time I felt such sickness, such remorse, and such guilt. My parents told me that my sister died before I was born. This was true . . . sort of. What they didn't tell me was that she died on the exact same day. I couldn't help but think that there was more to the story, that there was something else they didn't want me to know.

After all of these years, my parents had no idea that I knew the truth, and I had no intention of telling them. Laney's death brought darkness upon them and even though I longed to know how and why she died, I couldn't bring myself to ask. I didn't dare ask them if it was my fault. That my life began the day that hers ended could in no way be a coincidence. I couldn't bear to see them in that state of emotional grief, so I never spoke of it again.

The conversation was flowing as we ate breakfast, but our expressions were forced and tense, as if someone had come into our house while we were sleeping and painted smiles on all of our faces; frozen, unmoving, fake smiles that made me feel cold and uncomfortable. I rushed through my breakfast and opened my gifts: a new pink iPod, a slinky silk designer top and, of course, the long-awaited birthday collage. I thought it was impossible for me to feel any darker than I already did, but when I scanned over the pictures of the past year of my life, I began to miss the things I used to despise. Now, I clung to these memories as if they were all I had ever known. My eyes fell on a picture of Carly and me on my seventeenth birthday. I missed Carly. She was thousands of miles away, and I was undeniably miserable. I set the collage atop the rest of my presents, thanked my parents in the most cheery voice that I could muster, and as I closed the front door behind me, I felt relief spread through my body. No more pretending to be happy. For the next seven hours, I gave myself permission to be self-loathing, and in a very unusual sort of way that excited me.

I was relieved to find that school was going on just as it usually did, which was one advantage of attending a large high school. The accident on the stairs had been brushed under the carpet by the latest bit of gossip and I walked through the halls unnoticed. More importantly, no one wished me a happy birthday. I stood at my locker, my safety zone, and began twirling the combo round and round.

"Do you have any plans after school?" A smooth voice came from behind me and in a one single second, the dark clouds of my day lifted and a bit of light was forced through the cracks of my shell. I shook off the twinge of happiness that I was feeling, shut the door to my locker, and turned to face him. I noticed that for the first time since we had met, he looked unsure of himself. He had a questionable expression on his face. There was a hint of apprehension hiding somewhere deep behind his unique green eyes.

"Um . . . let me think." I wasn't actually considering my alternative, which was going home and spending the rest of my birthday with the parentals, but none-the-less, I pondered and twisted my mouth so that I might lead him to believe I could possibly have something more important to do.

"No," I said with finality. "Why?" My mouth was deliberately spread into a thin, flat line, a poker face of sorts, expressionless and indefinable.

"I want to take you somewhere. It's a surprise, but I think that you'll like it."

"One hint." I asked without pleading.

"I'm going to Tulsa . . . if you want to come with."

"*Tulsa*? That's at least a forty-five minute drive, if not an hour. What's in Tulsa?" I was becoming more and more intrigued. A good hour there and the hour back into town, plus the time spent doing whatever it was that he planned to do. It would be a full three or four hours. I would most certainly be missing dinner with Mom and Dad, and if luck was on my side, I could potentially avoid any interaction with them at all. How cruel and inconsiderate of me. I tried to mask my smile.

"You said one hint, and I gave you one. No more questions. So, are you in?"

"Alright," I agreed, and then watched as he walked briskly away. Very mysterious. He had me. Hook, line, and sinker. I was in.

The rest of the day passed quietly, very unremarkable . . . I couldn't have asked for more. The first twenty minutes of the car ride were no different, quiet, but uncomfortably so. I bit my lip so that my mouth wouldn't try to compensate for the lack of conversation. I focused instead on his hands, which were clenched tightly around the steering wheel. His knuckles were white from gripping with such force. I turned to look out of the window. We were no more than a mile outside of town and already the small city feel had been replaced with open pastures, cows grazing, and an occasional horse bucking and running aimlessly through the field as if someone had just given its tail a hard tug.

"I was thinking we could play a game." His words surged over me, breaking the silence and I felt somewhere in between relief and dread.

"What kind of game," I groaned. Games were not a part of my normal September 13th routine. In fact, I frowned upon any sort of games that took place on this day.

"I call it the 'OR' game."

"Like a boat ore?" I asked.

"No, like this 'OR' that. I will ask you a question and give you two choices and then you have to pick one answer 'OR' the other. You can start if you like." I paused for a moment and then jerked my head quickly back toward the passenger window. "Fine . . . Chocolate or vanilla?" I scowled.

"Vanilla." He responded quickly and smoothly, and I flipped around to look at him in disbelief.

"Really, how can you not like chocolate?" I was stunned. "Chocolate milk, chocolate cake, chocolate ice cream, peanut butter and chocolate sandwiches . . . " I glanced back down to his hands, which had now loosened up a bit around the steering wheel, his knuckles returning to their normal color. I moved my eyes slowly back up to the profile of his face and held them there discretely.

"Who eats chocolate on a sandwich?" He turned now to face me, his eyes far from the road and his nose scrunched up, forcing a heavy wrinkle between his eyebrows.

"Europeans do. It's called Nutella. It was the best thing I learned while living overseas. You can put Nutella on anything. Toast, apples, waffles, pancakes, chips, bananas . . . ." I dramatically whirled my head back in the direction of the passenger window, flipping my hair in the process, and trying my hardest to pretend that I wasn't the least bit interested in this game of his. I knew it was the perfect excuse to find out anything and everything that I wanted to know about him.

"Okay, my turn. Organic Food or not."

"Does it matter?"

"Yes," he answered with potency.

"Okay then, I think I'd rather not have bugs on my food, so not."

"Let me rephrase. Organic food or food laced with chemicals and injected with hormones and dyes."

"Well, when you put it that way, organic, I guess . . . my turn."

"80's or Indie?" I asked.

"I love Indie."

"I agree."

"Hmmm . . . age gracefully or plastic surgery?" he questioned.

"That's a no-brainer. Plastic surgery." I answered with confidence. I could feel my mood begin to lighten against my will. My eyes drifted back toward him.

"We'll get back to that later," he groaned. "You're up, prima donna."

"Fine." I rolled my eyes. "If you were a dinosaur would you be a herbivore or a carnivore?"

"What kind of question is that?" He laughed and I twisted my mouth trying hard not to laugh right along with him.

"Just a question, so answer."

"A carnivore, I guess. I can't live without my red meat."

"Ewwh!"

"You asked, I told. My turn. Do you like your coffee black or with cream and sugar?"

"I like a nonfat, three Splenda latte," I told him.

"I don't like coffee. I didn't realize you were so picky. And here I thought you were so easy to please with your peanut butter and honey . . . or peanut butter and chocolate sandwiches."

"Oh, I have one. Crest or Colgate?"

"Close-up." He smiled, showing off his teeth the best he could.

"You're kidding. Isn't that the cinnamon toothpaste with the commercial of two people kissing?" Suddenly, the commercial made perfect sense, toothpaste laced with a pheromone. Yummy. I'd put that on the grocery list.

"Well," he urged.

"Aquafresh. Right now I'm using Aquafresh because that's what my mom bought. Sometimes it's Crest and sometimes it's Colgate. I think it depends on which one comes with the free toothbrush."

Now we both were laughing for no particular reason, or maybe because we were talking about toothpaste. I was laughing because it was a little bit funny but mostly because I was happy. It was my birthday, and I was actually happy. My whole body was shaking with laughter that had been building up for years and now that I had unleashed it I was unable to control it. The last time I had laughed this hard was when I was little and my papa would push his false teeth out of his mouth with his tongue and clap his dentures together. Now this thought sent another uncontrollable wave of emotion through me. It was a perfect mixture of elation, wonder, and amusement with only a touch of fear, fear that my guard was being let down and I was unable to do anything about it. I bit my lip, holding back the laughter, and caught a glimpse of several tall structures poking up into the horizon, interrupting the flat and golden fields of wheat. Prominent structures of steel and glass, I supposed, but still shadows from the distance. I felt longing to be there amongst civilization, amongst culture, amongst the hustle and bustle of the big city that I was so accustomed to. It was a Mecca in the middle of the prairie and it was beautiful.

"I'm up," he said through hiccups of laughter. "Dog or cat?"

"Dog, of course." I thought of my dog Cocoa, who was taking just a little bit longer with her journey back to the states than expected.

"Cat."

"Why?" I asked, my voice revealing an unreasonable amount of disgust.

"They're easy."

"They're evil."

"Nooooo. Besides, evil is a choice not a predestination, don't you think?"

"I try not to give it too much thought. My grandparents used to have this cat named Truman who was a self-nursing meerkat," I told him.

"Like Harry Truman?" He looked confused.

"No. They named her after *The Truman Show* with Jim Carrey."

"I don't follow."

"They never let her outside."

"Her?" He had a perplexed look on his face.

"Yes, her."

"Poor Truman, no wonder she was so odd, she didn't stand a chance from day one with a name like that. Now, if they would have named her Fluffy . . . but back to the self-nursing, meerkat thing."

"I don't know, I think she was weaned from her mother too early. She would lay on the sofa and nurse herself."

"Did she actually get any milk?"

"Nana and Papa said no. They said she did it for comfort."

"And the meerkat thing?"

"She sat on her haunches. You know, with her front feet in the air. She wouldn't walk around, or anything like that. She would just sit there and look at you. It was a little creepy if you ask me."

"Now see, you're missing the bigger picture. Truman was a truly gifted kitty."

"If you say so."

"Pencil and paper or Word when writing a paper for English Lit?" he asked.

"Pencil and paper, for two reasons. First, I like to have everything in front of me. I like to be able to touch it, move it around, cross it out, and doodle on the edges of the paper. Then, when it's finished, I type it out."

"Isn't that like doing it twice? That's just a waste of time." The look on his face let me know that he in no way understood how my mind worked.

"Maybe, but you didn't let me finish. Second, I don't mix well with technology. If somehow my paper gets deleted, I still have the original. What about you?"

"Word on a Mac, for sure." He looked excited just talking about it. "I'm up again."

"You've already gone twice in a row," I protested, but then realizing I hadn't a question ready to ask him, I quickly gave in. There were so many things I wanted to know, yet all of these curiosities seemed to escape me under pressure of the game and the questions I did come up with were, for the most part, trivial and essentially useless in uncovering the mysteriousness that surrounded him.

"Tattoo or piercing?"

"Tattoo."

"Really?" He looked surprised. "Neither."

"You can't say neither, you have to pick one," I reminded him of the rules and he ignored me.

"So, where would you put it, this tattoo of yours?"

"I would have a sleeve of flowers and swirly-ques down my right arm with lots of greens and reds and hints of bright white. It would probably be a lily, I love lilies."

"Seems like you've given this a lot of thought."

"A little."

"Haven't you ever heard of starting out small?" he questioned.

"Haven't you ever heard of the bigger the better?"

"You have nice skin. Why would you want to cover it up?" he asked.

"Thank you . . . I think. It's wearable art. It would make me unique . . . like no one else."

"You're already unique." He blushed. "Believe me when I tell you that you are like no one else." Now I blushed, and he looked down.

"Well, you are . . . . unique," he murmured as his cheeks turned a ruddy color against his will. It was as if the feeling of awkwardness was as contagious as a yawn.

"Republican or Democrat?" I changed the subject.

"Undecided," he answered with confidence.

"Hmmm. Me, too. I guess I just don't like being defined by a group of people. It's better to pick the best of both."

I now realized that we were somewhere in the heart of Tulsa. There were older, stately looking homes surrounding us on either side of the narrow, winding streets. A small outdoor shopping area was on my left with high end stores and expensive cars nestled outside of them. There were green parks with children playing. Mothers and fathers taking advantage of the beautiful weather as they pushed carriage style strollers along the trails by the greenbelt.

"We're here," he said as he squeezed the Wagoneer into a tight, parallel spot on a busy, narrow, street in front of one of the huge estates.

"Are you going to tell me where we are or are you going to keep me guessing?"

He smiled. "It's a museum."

"A museum?"

"A museum . . . you know, lots of art . . . it's like a miniature Louvre."

I nodded without saying a word and slammed the car door behind me.

The estate was grander than it had appeared from the street. Of course, the tall stucco wall did a good job of blocking out the specifics of the monstrous, twentieth century, Mediterranean style mansion. Creamy, soft, copper stucco expanded across the grounds, surrounding the building like a fortress. In contrast, a rather modest stone walkway led up to the multi-arched entrance. Red terracotta tiles blanketed the roofline and four large chimneys protruded, their soft, butter cream hue standing out perfectly against the bright, blue sky. Several large, white clouds hung low, precisely over the center of the museum to create a masterpiece of collaborated efforts. It reminded me of a Van Gogh, with the soft yellows, bright blues, and swirly whites. Tall, bright green cypresses resided on either side of the arches. Inside, the pristine, white marble floors stretched across the foyer and up to the edge of an imperial staircase. It was out of a storybook, it was a palace, it was enchanting, and time vanished. The day of the year escaped me, and I felt as though I should never leave.

"Have you been here before?" My voice cracked and an uncomfortable echo filled the lobby. I cleared my throat.

"Only once. It's not a huge museum, but there's more here than we can look at tonight." His eyes scanned the room. He appeared to be having trouble deciding which way he wanted to take me first.

"Let's go this way. There's a painting I want you to see. I think you'll like it." He led me up a set of wooden stairs with a large, multicolored, floral carpet running from the bottom all the way to the top. I ran my fingers up the wood and wrought iron banister and listened to the nearly inaudible noise that our feet made as they padded against the plush strip of flowery fibers. I loved the quietness of museums, much like I loved the atmosphere of a library, the art much different but the respect still the same.

"We're getting close." I could hear the excitement in his voice. He stopped in front of an opening that led into a separate room. Six paintings held within its walls. I walked into the room, spellbound by the painting that hung on the back wall. I knew the painter. I continued closer, still amazed that it was here in front of me.

"I didn't know they would have a Renoir."

"I thought you would like it," he said knowingly.

"I do. I love it." I stood in front of the painting, admiring each brushstroke that the artist made. I felt the warmness of his body from behind me and tingles spread their way down my arms and legs. My heart fluttered and I sucked in a chest full of air. My lungs felt so full they could explode.

"17 'OR' 18?" He whispered. His breath was warm down the back of my neck, which made it difficult for me to focus on the question at hand. At first, I didn't realize what he was asking. I stood frozen, my gaze focused on the Renoir in front of me but no longer appreciating its beauty. "So, which is it? Is it better being 18?" And all at once, the brief period of happiness escaped me and I felt the darkness of the day return once again. Even if it was only momentary, he had taken that darkness away. No one had done that before.

"How did you know it was my birthday?" I responded coolly.

"The birthday board at school." He placed his hands gently on my shoulder and turned me so that I was now facing him. He was smiling. I wasn't.

"Where's that at?" My tone was on the hateful side; it was something I couldn't control. I thought that the enormity of the school would somehow prevent the staff from recognizing anyone's birthday, or I had hoped. A birthday board was better than the full-fledged birthday recognitions that took place at my other schools.

"Right by the office." His voice had an unfaltering smoothness that was completely unaffected by my change in mood.

"I haven't seen it," I tested him.

"You know, you really shouldn't be so cantankerous on your birthday. It doesn't suit you," he said as he reached into his pocket. At that moment I knew exactly what he was about to do and I cringed. My body tensed as I saw the small box that he held out in front of me.

"I hope you don't mind. It's nothing much, really."

"Well, I do . . . I mind." I swallowed hard and focused on the box, not daring to look him in the eyes. I could hardly believe I was being so rude, especially to him.

"Are you going to open it?" he asked. I looked up at him. He was biting on the corner of his lower lip making the freckle disappear. He looked nervous, which made me feel bad.

"Yes. I'll open it." I sighed and reached for the gift, holding it for a moment before peeling off the paper. It was a small blue box with a lid. I lifted it gingerly and peered inside.

"Do you like it?"

I was speechless. I couldn't say a word. The resemblance was remarkable. I pulled the small oval locket out of the box. I ran my fingers over the intricate, raised, floral detail as it brought back a certain pain.

"Is something wrong?"

"Nothing's wrong . . . it's just, I used to have something exactly like this."

"I told you it wasn't much."

A strange mixture of emotions crept through my body. I pushed the button on the side of the locket and closed my eyes. I knew that what I was looking for wouldn't be inside. I knew this couldn't be the same locket, but as I held my eyes closed, I imagined that it was, and I imagined that he knew, and I imagined that I had already shared with him the story of how I had lost a locket just like this once upon a time.

"It's empty. You know, so that you could put the picture inside that you want."

I opened my eyes. My heart felt like it had stopped beating in my chest. My heart felt heavy. "Are you going to put it on?" he asked hopefully as he eyed the box.

"Tomorrow, I will . . . . I hope you understand, it's just I can't today."

"I do . . . . more than you know . . . I understand." And in some strangely impossible way I thought he must.

"Did you know we have absolutely nothing in common?" He laughed as we walked back to his car.

"Yeah," I said. "You say potato I say patata."

"Rae, there's something I think you need to . . . . There's something I want to . . . " He was still fumbling with his words when my phone began to ring.

"Hey, Mom . . . yeah . . . Okay! . . . Bye." I was ecstatic. Cocoa would be flying into Tulsa tomorrow at 4:30 after months of being in quarantine.

"Good news?" he asked

"My dogs flying in tomorrow . . . so what were you saying?"

"I forget. Hop in," he said as he pulled open the door for me.

And just like that, my day became more twisted than I could have ever imagined. It was easier being morose on this particular day, but now, I sat willingly next to a boy who had the ability to make me happy like no one else could, holding a gift that had more meaning than he could possibly know. His presence was changing everything and I was left feeling confused and frustrated.

## CHAPTER SEVEN

*I* woke up this morning to the annoying chirping of my alarm clock. It had pulled me from a rather dark dream and so for that, I was thankful. The dream had been so unbelievably real just seconds ago but now it was fading, the details fuzzy with bits and pieces missing. I remembered scattered trees and tall, yellow-orange grass. I was running . . . on a path. I remembered a pair of dark eyes and feeling scared of what might lie behind them. Lastly, I remembered a bright light and feeling safe. All of the specifics hidden away somewhere in my subconscious. So strange how the mind works.

I slammed my hand down on the snooze button and the dead bird stopped chirping. Note to self . . . get a different alarm clock, maybe one where the bird actually sounds alive and halfway excited about waking me up in the morning.

I had always been a vivid dreamer. My imagination ran wild during the day; I'm not sure why I thought it might be any different at night. Most people think that dreams are related to our inner most feelings. This theory didn't hold water in my case. I was the exception. My dreams were always taking me to far off places, places I have never been with people I had never met. Most recently, or I should say, since the move to Oklahoma, my dreams have all been about the same. I am lost on a long, narrow path and I can see nothing for miles and miles. The sky is dark and lonely, but I am never alone. Someone is always there with me. I have never seen their face; their identity is never revealed. But I'm scared. I think I'm scared of them.

I wrapped up in my plush, hoodie robe that my mom liked to refer to as my uniform. I argued with her that it wasn't a uniform. A uniform is something that you MUST wear everyday, and so my robe could never be a uniform. I loved my robe and always looked forward to slipping it on just before bed, first thing in the morning, sometimes after school over the top of my clothes if the weather was cold, most of the time when I went out to get the mail, or at night when I lay on the deck to look at the stars.

Today was going to be an exciting day. Cocoa was coming. Cocoa was my black Golden Doodle that had been in quarantine ever since we moved from Amsterdam. She was two years old and my parents had given her to me on my sixteenth birthday. Since I never had too many friends at school, they thought she might make me a good companion. And they were right, so you can imagine that this time of separation from my beloved pet and friend was just short of torture for me. Cocoa had been the best and the most unlikely gift I had ever received. I had never been given anything that couldn't fit inside my three suitcases and suddenly my parents had given me a dog. It bothered me that I might have to leave her behind if my parents decided to skip town again. Before Cocoa, we had never had anything to tie us down. My parents told me that if it became a problem, having a dog, then Nana and Papa could always take care of Cocoa, but they assured me that it would be okay. They assured me that we would be settling down soon, and when we did, Cocoa would come with us.

I scurried down the stairs in an unusually chipper mood, only to find my parents bickering over my father's hairy back. She was inspecting it closely, pointing out spots that needed some work.

"All I'm saying is that you should take care of that."

"What am I supposed to do about it?" he chuckled.

"Go get it waxed or something. I think that would fall under the category of what they now call manscaping."

"Oh, they're naming it now!"

"Why don't I just call Rose, she does my eyebrows and my lip. I'm sure she could handle your back."

"Ewwh!" I shrieked. "Can't you go do that somewhere else?"

"Hey, I can't help that I'm a hairy wildebeest."

I stuck my finger down my throat and made a gagging sound before dragging over to the kitchen counter and pouring some granola, not taking the time to slice my usual strawberries over the top. My parents could sense a change in my mood. They glanced at one another. My father gave my mom a reassuring nod. I was indeed capable of emotions. I had spoken without prompting. There was still a glimmer of the sweet eight-year-old girl somewhere inside my teenage body. Unspoken words told me how badly they wanted her back. But they didn't know . . . that I knew their secret, the secret that I kept tucked away inside myself to spare their pain, the secret that I kept hidden to avoid the heartbreaking confirmation. I was the reason my sister died.

I poured a cup of coffee, dumped in three Splendas and some flavored creamer, and balanced my breakfast in my hands as I headed for the stairs.

Cocoa would be coming in on a plane, and we would have to pick her up from the airport around four thirty or so. My dad suggested that he pick me up from school so that we could make it there on time. Cocoa was a bit of a princess around our household, so God forbid if Cocoa had to wait an extra couple of minutes in the airport. It's not like she hadn't already been waiting for months now. I agreed because I could hardly wait and because I made him promise that he wouldn't do anything to embarrass me on school grounds. I didn't mean to sound harsh, and I know many kids are embarrassed of their parents, but given my parent's track record, I most certainly had reason to be.

This morning, I had cross-country practice. In the late summer and fall, we were scheduled to practice in the wee hours of the morning to avoid the Oklahoma sun. In the winter and spring, we would shift our schedule to fit the changing weather. I looked outside and it was still dark. I slipped on my running tights and my long-sleeved Under Armor tee and swept my wavy curls into a high ponytail. After I finished dressing, I walked into the bathroom and picked up the small, blue box off the counter. I opened it carefully and pulled out the tiny, silver locket, but this time I didn't open it, and I wouldn't open it again, not even to slide in a picture. It would remain empty. I unhooked the latch, fastened the silver chain around my neck, slid it beneath my shirt, and started down the stairs.

By the time my Dad dropped me at the path, light was beginning to peek its way from the edge of the trees. It was never fun getting up at the crack of dawn, but seeing the beautiful hues emerge from the sky was reward enough. I liked to tell myself that I was the only one getting to see this beautiful array of colors and that if there was a God, he was definitely showing off for me. Then, the other runners would arrive and I would realize that He was showing off for them as well, but it didn't make me feel any less special.

Apparently, Chloe had decided to sign up for cross-country at the last minute. Just two days ago when Ms. Canton passed out the final roster, Chloe's name was nowhere on it; but here she was, sitting on a bench beside the path, adjusting the laces on a pair of brand new, pink and silver Saucony. I wish that I could say that it was nice to see a familiar face. Instead, her presence was a dark, heavy cloud hanging low over the running path which was my sanctuary. Chloe didn't look so intimidating without her fancy clothes and her friends. She had her hair pulled up into a ponytail and was wearing black running tights with a long-sleeved tee. Her outfit looked like something I would wear. I had never noticed it until this moment but, without all of the expensive clothes and makeup, she looked a bit like me. I adjusted my laces until my feet felt perfect inside my shoes and had just began to scroll through the playlists on my iPod when I looked up and saw a sign that read "Robinwood Park Entrance." I had seen this sign before but only on paper. Shortly after we moved into our house, the realtor brought over a welcome basket and inside, amongst a selection of other pamphlets, was a map entitled "Pathfinder Parkway—A Walk in the Woods." Below the title was a diagram of a large, circle shaped monster with many appendages. The body of the monster was exactly eight miles around, an easy and harmless trek, but each arm slithered away from the body and threaded its way into unknown territory, each appendage promising the partaker a different type of terrain. Per Ms. Canton's orders, the team was to stay on the main body of the path. The arms were off limits because, according to the coach, it was not wise for girls to go trekking off into the middle of the woods, not even in numbers. My thoughts exactly.

I couldn't help but notice that no one spoke as we ran, a result of still being half asleep at 6 AM, but that was fine with me. I would much rather listen to my iPod than yip yap. I started off strong and stayed that way, at the front of the pack. Every ounce of energy that I had at this early hour was invested in the run: body, mind, and spirit. It wasn't until I had been sprinting for nearly five minutes and the muscles in my legs began to burn that I realized the reason I was trying so hard. I wanted to outrun Chloe. Inside the walls of the school, Chloe could defeat me with her menacing looks and whispers, but running was mine, and I was not about to let her beat me at that, too. For the first thirty minutes, I felt something like pride as I held strong at the front of the pack but, when I ran past mile marker four and peeked over my shoulder to check on Chloe's positioning, her absence flooded my body with frustration. Was I angry because Chloe was not there to see me win? Possibly. I continued on, the anger only pushing me harder, until I realized that, even though I might finish first, Chloe was clearly the winner. Instead of enjoying the run as I usually did, I was obsessing over Chloe's absence. It was no longer just her presence but now her absence was getting the better of me, too. She was taking the enjoyment of the run away from me and so, without another thought, I pushed Chloe out of my mind, turned up the volume on my iPod, and began to focus on the run instead of the win.

The morning run was energizing; however, the warm shower in the girls' locker room lulled me back into a near slumber. I was now standing at my locker, staring at it as if I were in some sort of trance, a trance that comes from waking up at 4:45 AM and throwing myself almost immediately into an eight mile run. I blinked a couple of times in order to break the hold my eyes had on the bright, orangish-red locker, and began to fumble with my combination.

"Your hair's wet again." If honey had a voice it would sound like his, smooth and warm and just sweet enough without being syrupy. It had a quality about it that stuck with you and a taste, which, I could only imagine, left you craving more.

I reached up and touched my still damp hair. Now that the air had cooled off a bit, I wasn't having such an issue with the frizz. As I pulled my soft curls up into a ponytail, I felt his warm breath down the back of my neck. It sent goose bumps down my legs. I turned around so that we were standing face-to-face, my heart thudding so loudly in my chest that I was certain he could hear it, my mouth open slightly, taking in tiny gulps of the air that seemed so thick around us.

"I had cross-country this morning. I just got out of the shower." I managed to let a few words escape my mouth as I stared at him staring at me. "I mean . . . that's why my hair's wet."

"So . . . is that what you do for fun? You run?" He looked perplexed.

"Yeah, is that lame?"

"Lame isn't the word I would choose," he said as he began twirling one of my curls around his finger. I could feel Claire's presence as she lingered at her locker, desperate to catch any bit of our conversation. I paid her no attention. I focused on Alex and the black tee that clung to his lean but muscular chest, his charcoal colored jacket, his ravished and holey jeans, the same blue and black vans, the spicy and sweet smell that seemed to exude his perfection, the tiny freckle on his lower lip, his hazel eyes, his chocolate hair, and his warm, peachy skin tone.

"What word would you choose then?" I asked, practically hypnotized by the twirling motion of his finger through my hair.

"Self-inflicted torture is the first thing that comes to my mind," he answered, and I rolled my eyes, unable to think of anything smart to say in return.

The morning was creeping. My mind was preoccupied with Cocoa's arrival. I could hardly wait. Lunch was by the bridge. Alex brought the food and I had been anticipating my peanut butter and honey sandwich all morning. Much to my dismay, he pulled something out that looked more like fresh roast beef than processed peanuts and handed it to me.

"I didn't have time to make anything, so I just picked something up on the way to school."

"What is it?" Roast Beef?" I asked, picking apart the bread to have a look inside.

"Just eat it." He could sense that I was apprehensive. I took a bite so that I wouldn't appear rude.

"It's good," I said, shrugging my shoulders.

"Don't tell me you've never had roast beef before."

"Never . . . I usually don't eat anything that has the word 'beef' in the name . . . or 'loaf.' I never eat anything that has the word 'loaf' in it."

"Well, it doesn't hurt to change it up a little bit, now does it?" He laughed.

"Sometimes it doesn't hurt, but there's nothing wrong with sticking with what you like, either. If you know you like it before you eat it, then your pretty much guaranteed to not be disappointed," I said, trying my hardest to be difficult.

"Rae, disappointment only exists so that we can appreciate. How can you appreciate if you have nothing bad to compare it to?"

I knew he was right, but I was stubborn, and I held my face in a tight pinch to disguise the fact that I thought he was insightful amongst other things.

"So, when do I get to see the painting you're working on in Bradley's class?" he asked, changing the subject to something even more uncomfortable; uncomfortable because the masterpiece that I had created in art was a larger than life painting of his head.

"Oh, I don't know, how about never," I responded coolly, still brooding over the fact that he seemed to be right about everything. Brooding over the fact that he was perfect. The same perfect that I seemed to be helplessly and irrevocably drawn to.

"I do know where you hide that canvas of yours." He nudged me and then watched as the pinched expression on my face unwillingly turned into a smile.

His presence had a way of making me forget about everything, even Cocoa. For this, I was grateful; it made the day pass more quickly. I made little progress on my painting in art. I was overly paranoid that Alex was trying to look over my shoulder. I was afraid what he might think if he saw it. I shoved it to the back of the supply closet when the bell rang and made my way to the front of the school. As promised, my dad was waiting for me in the semi-circle loop by the door. He stayed inside his car, only sticking his hand out of the cracked window to catch my attention.

"Hey there, sweet pea."

"Hey there, wooly booger," I greeted him in a singsong voice.

"You aren't ever going to let that go, are you?" He chuckled. His eyes were warm and safe. I wanted him to reach out and hug me. I wanted him to hold me and tell me it wasn't my fault. I wanted him to make the pain go away. But he didn't.

"You know I can't help it, it's a hereditary thing," he continued. "My dad had hair on his back as did his father before him. It's a legacy of sorts. Now, my grandfather, he was really furry. On a positive note, it seems to decrease with each generation, so there might actually be hope for my great-great grandson."

"Okay, okay, enough. But speaking of furry, are we going to be on time to pick up Cocoa?"

"On time with a few minutes to spare," he confirmed.

My dad prided himself on being punctual. He could never understand why I couldn't seem to get myself together in a timely fashion. He often joked that I would be late to my own wedding. I told him that I would have to find someone interested in marrying me before he could bring that up again.

Just as my dad said, we arrived at the airport with a few minutes to spare. We headed straight over to the security desk where Cocoa would be delivered after her flight arrived.

"Do you think she'll remember us?"

"Who, Cocoa? Of course, she will."

"I'm going to go grab a magazine and something to drink. Do you want anything?" I asked.

"No, thank you."

I wasn't in the mood to read. I was too anxious, too excited, yet I needed something to distract me, but it had to be mindless. I decided on a tabloid and a Diet Coke.

"Did you really just spend three dollars on that trash?" my father asked.

"It's not trash, and it cost three dollars and ninety-nine cents. Besides, I need to know what's going on in the world."

He picked up a New York Times that someone had neatly discarded under his seat and shoved it my direction.

"Read this, then. This is what's going on in the world."

"That stuff is just too depressing," I said as I glanced at the front-page article titled *Eastern European Sex Trafficking Out of Control.* "I can't understand why anyone would want to read it."

"Well, it's a sad world that's for sure. When I was a boy growing up on the farm, we just didn't have to worry about the things we do now. Things might not have been easier, but they were certainly simpler and without a doubt more . . . oh, look, Rae, here she comes!"

I glanced over in the direction he was staring and saw a man with a large crate on one of those rolling luggage racks, the kind that my father most always refused when we were scrambling through the train stations with our hands way too full of bags. My father didn't believe in paying someone to wheel his luggage around when he was perfectly capable of doing it himself. My mother thought otherwise, and it was often a source of conflict while traveling.

"Dad!" I gasped. "Did you bring the leash?"

"Got it right here," he said as he pulled it out of his coat pocket. Dad really did love Cocoa secretly, but he would only dote on her when he thought no one was looking. I'm not sure if that's a man thing or just something peculiar with my dad. He made all of these tough rules on the day they gave me Cocoa, like no dogs on the furniture and especially the bed, and the dog gets dog food only, no table scraps. He acted like giving my dog attention stripped him of his masculinity; however, on more than one occasion, my mom and I found him asleep on the bed with Cocoa curled up on the pillow beside him. It was also my dad who would sneak tiny bits of steak and other human delicacies under the table to appease Cocoa's whimpering.

Cocoa was getting closer now, and I could see that she was showing her teeth at the airport security while letting out a small but very effective growl.

"That's my girl," Dad muttered under his breath.

"Oh, don't worry, she's all bark and no bite," I offered to the guard who seemed relieved to have Cocoa taken off his hands.

"Yeah, she's a *reeeeal* lover," my dad said sarcastically.

"She's been howling and carrying on ever since I loaded her up on the cart." The guy seemed very out of sorts. He had sweat dripping down his face and rings under his arms. He looked like he had bitten off more than he could chew with Cocoa.

"Well, she really doesn't like many people." I tried to apologize for my dog's rudeness, which made me sound even more ridiculous and at the same time infuriated the guard.

"I have a number for a good doggie training school if you decide you want to make her behave."

Now I was the one who was showing my teeth at the guard and I could have sworn that Cocoa had a very pleased look on her face when I did it.

Mom was just as excited to see the pooch as we were. Cocoa danced around her in the kitchen letting out little squirts of pee that I cleaned up with 409 and a paper towel. My dad let out a few words of praise before he stood up straight and stiff to reclaim his masculinity. My mother said something along the lines of, "Oh Will, lighten up." And then I said something like, "Yeah, lighten up you wooly booger," and then Cocoa pounced on him with her front paws, nearly knocking him to the ground. At that moment, I thought it must be hard on Dad to be in a house with three women. Cocoa was so excited to see us. You could hardly blame her. Being in quarantine was comparable to doggie hell, I'm sure.

We stood together in the kitchen, not really talking, but laughing and playing with Cocoa. It felt strange. It felt good. I felt alive.

Cocoa slept with me, sprawled out at the bottom of my bed. She made intermittent trips up to my face, licking it, making sure that I was still there. Everything was falling into place for me in a way that it never had before. I had my mom and dad and Cocoa in our new home, but I had much more than that. I think I was getting pretty close to having a boyfriend, something I had never had before, and I was enjoying all of the new things that went along with that: the butterflies, the red cheeks, the tingling, the rapid heart rate, the shallow breathing, and the warmness that ran from the tips of my fingers to the ends of my toes.

The days passed and fall was starting to chill the air. Lunchtime by the bridge was the highlight of my day. I was continuing to learn more and more about Alex, and despite the strong and familiar connection we had, I felt as though he were leaving something very important out. I felt there was something that he couldn't bring himself to tell me, and the boy that I was falling in love with was just as mysterious to me as the day we first met. He was still unpredictable in a predictable sort of way. He still loved to surprise me, he still loved to have the scales tipped in his favor, he still held secrets that I couldn't begin to uncover, and he was still perfect; I had yet to find a single flaw. But he seemed just as smitten with me as I was with him, so I overlooked all of this irritating perfection, learning to live with it the best I could. I had even learned to let him open my car door for me on occasion, but only if no one was looking. He had walked into my life and he was getting dangerously close to cracking the tough shell that I had built around myself. I wasn't sure how I felt about that. It was the only form of protection I had against the outside world. He hadn't cracked it yet. Maybe he had taken off one tiny layer, but it was still intact. I was toying with the idea of letting him take off just one more layer. I knew I was playing with fire, but I was beginning to like how his brightness was filling the inside of my otherwise dark cocoon. He was changing me, of this I was sure, and I was also pretty sure that I liked it.

# CHAPTER EIGHT

*T*he sun was blinding, shining in through the kitchen window and hitting the little prism that my mother had hanging over the sink. I had given her the prism for Mother's Day when I was just ten years old and this spectacular, circular shaped crystal took up residence over the kitchen sink in every apartment where we had lived. I was fascinated by how the light of each new climate could make it behave differently, but I had never seen it shoot out such an array of colors before, shooting out rainbows in every direction.

It was October, but the air was still surprisingly warm. Actually, it was pretty close to perfect and in a way, I sort of liked it here. I was beginning to feel more at home in Oklahoma, more at home than I had anywhere else. I was getting used to the weather, my new home, my new school, and most of all, I was getting used to all of the things Alex liked. I loved knowing that his favorite sandwich was turkey and Swiss on wheat and that when he looked at me, he tilted his head a little and his face filled with a smile that he couldn't control. I loved that I seemed to be the only one who could make him smile that way. I felt safe when I was with him, a kind of safe that I had never felt before, a kind of safe that was more powerful than my nana's kitchen. I felt like I could tell him almost anything and, because of this, I was well aware that he knew more about me than I did about him, and it bothered me, but not enough to keep him from knowing even more. I never really knew what love would feel like and it was unexpected how quickly I had fallen.

I pulled the turkey and Swiss out of the fridge and the bread from the pantry. Cocoa was dancing around my feet, begging for food and attention. I looked out the window and began to assemble the sandwiches, my mind somewhere far away, a place that it seemed to go quite frequently these days. I wondered what we would do at lunch when the weather got too cold to eat outside, when a blanket of snow covered the ground surrounding the bridge. I was surprised to hear that it snowed in hot and windy Oklahoma. In a state with such temperature highs, I found it hard to believe that the weather could change so drastically. Yes, I was beginning to love living in the land of hot and cold.

"You have a big appetite today, Rae," my dad said as he snuck up behind me, startling me right out of my dream-like state. I gasped. Air rushed into my lungs, filling my body with oxygen and bringing me back to reality.

"What?" I responded, oblivious to the mountain of food that I had unconsciously placed in the bag on the counter.

"I've never seen one little girl eat that much food. You have enough there to feed a small army."

I looked over to the bag. Maybe I had over done it.

"No, I'm not feeding an army," I informed him with as much sass as I could muster.

"A friend, maybe?" he prodded

"Maybe," I answered vaguely. My eyebrows lifted, putting a heavy crease in my forehead, and my mouth twisted into the typical know-it-all pout that any dad could expect from his teenager daughter.

"Could this friend be a boy?" he asked with slight amusement in his voice. He seemed to know the effect his question would have on me but it didn't stop him from asking.

"DAD!" I shouted and then followed it with a large groan to let him know I was irritated. I could tell my parents everything, but I in no way felt comfortable telling them about Alex, perhaps because I had never said these feelings out loud. It felt awkward trying to discuss it with anyone, especially my father.

"Alright, alright." He seemed to have gotten the hint from the tone in my voice. "I was just wondering if I could meet this fellow." He pushed the envelope even further.

"DAD!" I winced as I pulled the bag off the counter and headed out the door, my arms loaded up like I was moving out of the house rather than going to school.

"Have a good day, honey," he called after me. I could feel his smile, warm on me, as I continued to walk to the car.

"See you tonight," I sang.

I got to school early and patiently waited for Alex to grace me with his presence. Punctuality was never one of my God given gifts, but punctual was something that I was quickly becoming as it meant adding additional minutes to my Alex time every morning. Claire had come and gone and still no sign of him. I cleaned out the scraps of paper from my locker, organized all of my books, and stacked my folders neatly on the little shelf. Still, I was standing alone. The five-minute warning bell sounded and I headed for class, walking slowly, hoping that he would rush through the hall at the last moment, saving me from forty-five minutes of worry and anticipation over why he was absent. My imagination could come up with 101 reasons for his tardiness, none of them good. My snail like creep was beginning to draw a bit of attention, so I picked up the pace and stepped over the threshold into my own personal torture chamber, math. It was the chamber that would hold me hostage for nearly an hour and cram my head with insane scenarios for his tardiness. And that's just what it did. I spent the entire class period filling my head with explanations for his absence instead of solving equations. Maybe he was sick, or maybe he was just late, or maybe he was mad at me and bypassed my locker altogether, or maybe he thought we were getting too close too fast and he was backing off a bit. As each class ended and lunch grew closer, all hope that I had for seeing him dwindled at an exponential rate. I went by his locker . . . he wasn't there. I sent him a text . . . no response.

Lunch at the park by myself was looking inevitable, and at first it sounded gloomy and dull, but the idea was growing on me. I had paid enough attention at the park to know that it was indeed beautiful, but I had to admit that most of my attention was on Alex. His beautiful face, his flawless features, his perfectly smooth and hypnotizing voice. I would look around a bit more and enjoy the things that I couldn't focus on when he was there.

The bell rang for lunch and my near sprint made me the first one out of the building. The silver Rover was parked beside me, each day pulling up so close I had only inches to squeeze through my door. I unlocked my car the old fashioned way, with a key, and then squeezed my narrow frame through the small opening and into the driver seat. With my right hand, I reached up and adjusted the rearview mirror, which was askew and pointing toward the floor; with my left hand, I slid my seat forward until my toes were touching the pedals. Strange, I thought. It appeared as though someone else had been driving my car, someone much larger than myself. Without considering it any further, I turned the key in the ignition. Instead of the soft purring of the engine, I heard the repetitive choking of a car that wouldn't start. I turned the key once again, giving it a second try. The engine turned over while letting out an awful groan. This was followed by the front of my Honda heaving and bouncing up and down in distress.

"Come on," I muttered to myself, followed by a begging plea for my car to behave. Through all of the choking and spatting, I heard a tiny chirp come from the car next to mine.

"This cannot be happening," I said, still talking to myself.

I was too embarrassed to look up. My car was performing for everyone right in the middle of the parking lot and the driver of the Range Rover had a front row seat. I turned the ignition to off, pulled the key out, and then shut my eyes. It had been a long time since I had prayed, but I held my eyes shut and tried to remember how.

"Please, let my car start. Please, just let me get to lunch and back. Please, make everyone stop staring."

I lifted my head, exhaled, and then, testing my faith in God, plugged the key back into the ignition, shut my eyes tightly, and turned again. With the soft and gentle purr, my car came to life.

"Thank you. Thank you. Thank you. Thank you!"

I threw it in reverse and backed out of the lot before I could attract any more attention. I felt relieved that I didn't catch a glimpse of the mystery driver and that the mystery driver didn't catch a glimpse of me.

As I pulled over the rundown bridge onto the soft, green grass, a feeling of doubt stole over me. It was beautiful here. Crisp and cool, but still bright and sunny under the colorful canopy of leaves. The beams of dancing sunlight were showing through the red and yellow foliage of fall, making me feel as though I had just entered a magical place. It was perfect and seemed far from the rest of the world. I should have felt comforted; instead, I felt disturbed. I felt vulnerable. I didn't feel safe, not like I did when I was with Alex. I opened my door, enamored by the beauty of this spot, and quickly forgot about Alex ignoring my text, about my embarrassing mishap in the parking lot, and about how I was hopelessly imperfect and permanently flawed. I spread out a blanket on the grass and lay down flat on my back, letting the cool fall air blow over me. I closed my eyes and listened. The squirrels were scurrying, rustling the newly fallen leaves beneath their feet. The birds seemed to welcome me with their usual cheerful songs. The wind was whispering in a low and lulling tune as it blew the bright leaves that wearily held onto their branches. The stream under the bridge made a slow constant gurgle that I had never noticed and I felt myself slipping, relaxing, until there was no longer any light shining through the lids of my eyes. It was dark now, with the exception of tiny, silver sparkles that danced beneath my still closed lids. My head rested on the ground beneath me, and I allowed myself to slip further into a place that seemed a million miles away.

Before I could even open my eyes, I knew that something was wrong. The air felt cooler and it was quiet, completely silent. The absence of any noise seemed unnatural. The birds had stopped chirping, the squirrels had found another place to scurry, and the sound of the gurgling brook was gone. Eyes still closed, I reached out my hand and expecting to feel the soft cotton of the blue blanket that I was lying on, was startled when I felt something crunchy and dry between my fingers instead. What I saw when my eyes popped open only confirmed my suspicions. I was not at the park by the bridge. The bright, beautiful, and dazzling beams of light were gone. Instead, there was a soft glow of light on the forest floor as the sun pushed its way through the thick, red and yellow foliage. I rubbed my eyes, attempting to wipe away the hazy film that covered them. With my eyes finally adjusted, I looked around at my surroundings and almost immediately, I knew where I was. In the distance, about twenty yards ahead, I could see mile marker four, and I knew I was on the running path that wound its way through town. I had passed this portion of the path dozens of times, but today the path looked different: more heavily wooded and the leaves on the trees were brilliant colors of red and yellow, so bright they were almost glowing. I sluggishly picked myself up off the ground. My body felt heavy and beaten. I glanced down at my jeans. A large hole revealed several scrapes on my knee and my long sleeved cotton tee was torn at the elbow. I felt as though I had been given some sort of sleep-inducing drug, something that would knock me out and forbid me to have any recollection of the time in between, a drug that would leave me clueless in the middle of the path with torn clothes and a bloody knee.

I sighed, turned in a half circle, and found myself standing directly in front of one of the trails that fed into the path. So many times I had passed it by without the slightest amount of consideration, but today it seemed to be calling my name. I drew closer, noticing how the arm of the path differed from the body in which it extended, tapering into a narrow lane of hard-packed dirt that was rough and uneven. With more courage than I had ever felt before, I stepped onto the path, but before making my way through the dense cover of trees, I paused to take notice of the unusual feature that marked the start of the trail. A large tree that looked as though its trunk had been twisted into something that resembled a piece of licorice was rooted at the left side of the opening. The tree was doubled over so that its top was almost touching the ground. I had never seen anything like it before. It had an almost fairytale like quality about it. The path was dark but beautiful. Trickles of light shone through the canopy above leaving large, shiny, diamond-like patterns on the dirt floor below. I felt like I was in a very beautiful dream . . . until it turned into a nightmare. The deeper into the forest I walked, the darker and more quiet it became. I turned around and tried to walk back in the direction from which I had come, but I could not. An invisible force seemed to be pushing me deeper and deeper into the woods. Silence was now filling the air with a thickness that made it increasingly difficult for me to breath.

Shaking: a physical manifestation of fear.

I was well aware of fear's stages, both biochemical and emotional. My parents were shrinks. The biochemical part was easy. Anyone who experienced fear experienced these reactions: shaking, sweating, increased heart rate. The emotional part was more complicated; it was the stage of fear that told you who you were and what you were made of. Would you fight or would you take flight? It wasn't until I felt my legs trembling beneath me that I finally accepted what I already knew all along, I was terrified. Now what would I do? What was I made of? Unfortunately, I was not given a choice. I had tried to flee but was unable. Something wanted me to continue on, but what? What was this force that pushed me further and further into the woods? As the leaves thickened above, the tiny bits of light that had previously shone down on the path like jewels disappeared and I was left in total darkness. It felt like I had been walking for miles and just as I was beginning to think that the scenery would never change, I saw a light at the end of the tunnel of trees. Very gradually, the forest began to thin and large blades of native grass began to emerge.

It was a distant whisper and the crunching of leaves that first broke the surrounding silence. And it was at that moment I knew I wasn't alone. What should have been a comforting thought sent spiky waves of panic through my body. I could hear the footsteps behind me; they were distant but moving closer by the second. Without thinking, I ran in what felt like slow motion toward the light that emerged from behind the last row of trees. I was now standing on a narrow, asphalt path in the middle of a grassy field. Desperately, I searched for a place to hide, and without any other option, I took refuge in the tall, yellow, native grass that covered the ground in a splotchy, haphazard manner. I knelt down, concealing myself as I peeked through the wide blades of yellow. I could see nothing. The crunching of footsteps continued to get louder as another pair of feet joined in, each step alternating, creating a constant pounding. And then, it stopped. The silence seemed to last an eternity before being broken by a hushed voice. It was the strong voice of a man, but his accent was strange, thick, heavy, and definitely out of place for Oklahoma. He paused, leaving an eerie stillness, and once again it was broken, but this time by the voice of a woman. Her voice made the hairs on my arms stand on end; goose bumps were rising up out of nowhere. I couldn't make out what she was saying, I didn't need to, I knew everything I needed to know. They were looking for me. Once again, there was silence, followed by the sound of crunching. They had ventured off the path and into the grass where I was hiding. One set of crunching getting louder, the other set fading as if they were splitting up. A search party of sorts, and the target . . . was me. The part that left me baffled was why. I couldn't imagine that I had done anything to deserve such attention. I curled up into a ball on the grassy floor, desperately wishing I would wake from this dream. Wake up, wake up, I chanted under my breath as I waited for my assailant to find me. I prayed that the large blades of grass would conceal me just enough to save my life. Crunch, crunch, crunch . . . and then, it stopped. The shallow sound of breathing was so close now that I could have mistaken it as my own. Every sound and every smell was familiar. My dreams had taken me to this spot before. I had so quickly forgotten, but now the splotchy details came rushing back. The eyes . . . that's what I remembered the most, the deep dark eyes that stared into mine. The eyes that told everything, the eyes that told me I didn't stand a chance. Ever so carefully, I lifted my head, making sure not to disturb the grass below. I was now staring up at fragmented pieces of the sky, giant clouds blocking the sun, the world around me dark and cold. I rolled my head to the side, expanding my field of vision. I was now focusing on a black and red symbol. The breathing continued, heavy and in unison with mine. My eyes were still trying to make sense of the small and intricate shape. I shut them again, tightly, wishing I was home, safe . . . wishing that all of this made sense, wishing I had trusted my instincts. I shouldn't have come to the park by myself. My heart was racing. I was panicking. Just as I was about to inch myself away, the sleeve of my shirt was violently tugged upward and a terrifying, blood-curdling scream escaped my lips. I could see the symbol with ease; it was a lion with his thick mane blowing and his mouth open, ready to devour his prey. I focused beyond the black symbol, now staring at the peachy color that surrounded it. It was at that moment when I realized I was staring at a tattoo on a man's arm. I was now in the hands of my captor. My eyes moved slowly upward to get a look at the face of the person who held me, wondering if the face held the same deep, dark, and brooding eyes that I had dreamt of just days ago.

# CHAPTER NINE

$R$ae!" A voice shouted. A voice that nearly deafened me it was so loud.

My eyes popped open, and I was lying on the soft, blue, woven blanket in the middle of Jo Allen Lo Park. Alex was hovering over me, one hand on the ground, one hand on my shoulder.

I looked frantically from left to right, gasping for air. My breathing was irregular and heavy. I realized that I must have been having one of my elaborate dreams and felt instant relief. My vitals were beginning to fall back within the realm of normal as he scooped me up and pulled me close to his body.

"Were you dreaming?" he whispered, now brushing his fingers softy through my hair. It took a moment for me to realize that this was actually happening. He was touching me, holding me, and it was so much better than I had ever imagined.

"I guess I fell asleep," I whispered back, my head lying softly on his shoulder. I noticed that the sky was still bright, just as it was when I arrived. Everything seemed just as it was before, just as it always had been: peaceful, calm, beautiful, heavenly, and perfect.

"Why were you out here by yourself?" he demanded.

I was immediately reminded of the reason I had come to Jo Allen Lo Park alone. I was also quickly reminded that the hour I had for lunch had most likely expired, but at the moment, I hardly cared.

"What time is it?" I asked, my head still lying softly on his shoulder.

"It's almost 4:30," he murmured.

I paused briefly to exhale. "I missed art," I informed him. My voice was flat, almost trancelike. My breathing was deep but quiet as I focused on the softness of his tee shirt beneath my cheek, the warm tickle of his lips brushing across my hair, the slight quiver in each breath that he took, and the security of his embrace that left me melting in his arms.

"Will your parents be mad?" His voice was just above a whisper.

"Yes," I responded without a hint of concern.

We stood silently, our bodies semi-entwined and relaxed. My mind was wandering somewhere far away when I heard the sound of crunching leaves coming from the forest behind me.

Alex's shoulders stiffened and then his entire body froze, solid as ice. I eased my head away from his chest and looked into his eyes, which were focused on something in the distance. His pale complexion appeared even more ashen. He looked so pure, so innocent, so perfect . . . so scared.

"Is everything alright?"

"Everything's fine." His voice sounded hollow and empty and determined. His color remained pale, with the exception of the smoky red tint that now crossed his cheeks. As he continued to look past me, I sensed that anger had replaced the fear I saw just moments ago. Now I was the one who was scared.

"Are you sure?" I turned so that I might catch a glimpse of what he was staring at so intently. Nothing in the forest looked out of place. The semi-barren trees were still blowing gently in the wind, the grass was still green, the sky was still blue. Nothing was out of the ordinary.

"Come on, let's go," he said, sweeping my bag up off the ground and starting in the direction of my car.

I slid into the seat of my Honda without shutting the door and started the engine. All at once, the problems of my day came rushing back. My car sputtered and spat. Black smoke was coming from the hood. I shut it down and tried again, without a bit of luck. Smoke began to pour out, thicker this time.

"Turn it off," Alex demanded, coughing and fanning the smoke from his face. He reached down beside my foot and pulled the lever to pop the hood. He then walked around to the front of the car and I heard another pop. In an instant, the hood was raised and a huge, black cloud bellowed from within. He walked to the passenger side and opened the door.

"I think I'll just wait a minute for it to cool down. I won't be able to see a thing until the smoke clears." He coughed again as he slid into the cloth-covered seat. "So, what was your dream about?"

I stared out the window into the blackish-grey smoke in front of me. "Just another silly nightmare."

"This happens often?"

"Well, I've had the dream before. I'm on a path in the middle of nowhere. Someone is usually following me. The first time it was a man. Today, it was both a man and a woman. No big deal, really."

"The way you screamed made it sound like a big deal." He looked at me with concerned eyes.

"I screamed . . . out loud?" I was flooded with embarrassment.

"On a positive note, you have a good set of lungs."

"Good to know."

"What did they look like?" he asked, while biting his lip in a persistent manner.

" I don't know. Their faces were blurred . . . fuzzy."

"Mm." He sounded disappointed, so I closed my eyes and tried to pull from my memory anything of interest, anything that was worthy of awe.

"Well, the man in my dream today, he had an accent . . . and a tattoo. It was on his arm."

"What was the tattoo of?" he asked, now thumping his fingers against the side of the door in a nervous manner.

"It was a black and red lion. That's it. I told you it was a silly dream."

The car was quiet now. He stared out the front window, deep in thought, and I could tell he was trying his best to cover up his mixture of emotions.

"Your dreams have so much detail."

"I guess they're just a product of a vivid imagination." I paused for a split second as I studied my fingers, which were loosely formed around the wheel. "Do you ever dream?"

"I used to."

"So, is it something you can just turn off and on?"

"No, nothing like that." He paused. "I'm going to get out and look at your car."

The smoke was clearing. He disappeared behind the matted, blue hood and after what seemed like seconds, he walked back toward my side of the car.

"Um, Rae, have you ever changed your oil?" he asked, trying his hardest not to laugh.

"Yes," I huffed. "I had it changed just last week."

"It's as dry as a bone," he said as he walked back to the front of my car. He ran an old rag across the dip stick making sure it was clean before plugging it back in to get a second reading.

"Come on. Hop in my car, and we'll go grab some oil." He opened the passenger side of his car, and I slid into his perfectly preserved leather seat.

"Can't we just tow it? It would be faster," I suggested as I wiped the beads of sweat from my forehead.

"You don't know a lot about cars, do you?" He continued on without letting me answer. "You really shouldn't have driven it if you were having problems with it. You can ruin the engine if you drive it without oil."

"It was fine this morning. I just started having problems with it before lunch."

He had a perplexed look on his face.

"You probably think I'm helpless, don't you?" I said, rolling my lip into a pout.

"I kind of like that you need my help."

The pout was short-lived and once again, I was doe-eyed. I was useless around him. I had absolutely no control over myself whatsoever.

Thanks to Alex's heavy foot, we made it back to my car in fifteen minutes flat. He poured the oil in, shut the hood, put the key in the ignition, and turned. A perfect purr came from the once smoking car.

"Look, let me follow you home. Just to make sure you get back, okay."

I nodded in agreement, shut my door, and then pulled out of Jo Allen Lo Park en route to my little house on the prairie.

We made it to my house with no further problems. He seemed to have fixed my car. I parked on the asphalt portion of my driveway that looped in front of the brick stairs leading to my front door. Alex pulled in behind me. By the looks of it, no one was home. I took the bag of uneaten lunch goodies from the trunk and headed toward the Wagoneer. He was still seated inside with his window rolled halfway down.

"You can come in, if you want."

"You sure?" he asked skeptically.

"I think that's the least I could do. You fixed my car, right?"

"I really didn't do anything special," he said, shrugging his shoulders with modesty. "I like your house."

"Thanks. It didn't look this way when we bought it."

"Fixer upper?"

"That's putting it mildly," I scoffed. "We spent most of the summer fixing it up."

He stepped inside and paused, waiting for the guided tour I assumed.

"Where are your parents?"

"At work. They're shrinks . . . I mean doctors. They work a lot, but not as much as they used to."

We stood in the large entry in front of the L-shaped staircase leading to the second floor. He seemed captivated by the photography that hung neatly on the walls, appearing to appreciate it as if he had been there himself.

"Your parents are very neat," he stated. I could detect a slight bit of astonishment in his voice.

"And you're surprised by this because I am not."

"Well, let's just say that you have other things going for you." He laughed and I had to agree. Organization had never been one of my strengths.

"Pictures of Europe?" His question sounded more like a statement to me.

"Yeah, my dad took them. He's somewhat of an amateur photographer, I guess."

"They're nice. It is pretty there."

We walked through the dining room and into the kitchen. I set the gigantic lunch bag down on the island.

"Do you want something to eat?" I asked as I pulled the peanut butter and honey out of the bag.

"Sure, I'll have what you're having. Peanut butter again I'm guessing." His eyes glistened in amusement.

"I have turkey and Swiss, if you want."

"No, I think I'll try the peanut butter and honey, since you like it so much."

I searched inside the bag and pulled out another sandwich identical to mine.

"Diet Coke, Dr. Pepper, tea or water?" I asked with my face crammed inside the refrigerator.

"Diet Coke is fine. So is that all you eat? Peanut butter?"

"Pretty much." I handed him a sandwich just as Cocoa came running into the kitchen, sliding halfway across the floor, tail wagging in every direction, circling Alex, and licking him on the hands and face.

"Hey Cocoa," he said, patting her head with the palm of his hand. She licked him again, whimpering with the same delight she had when we brought her home from the airport. My body froze for a moment. I was sure that I hadn't mentioned Cocoa's name.

"You'd better watch out for your peanut butter sandwich; that's her favorite," I warned.

"A dog that likes peanut butter, huh. Sounds like she might be just a tad bit spoiled."

"Maybe, but she hates pancakes, just in case you ever try to give her one . . . she won't eat it."

"I'll keep that in mind."

"You know, Cocoa seems to like you. She doesn't really like anyone except for me . . . and my parents, I guess."

"I'll take that as a compliment."

"Come on, I want to show you my room." I picked up my sandwich and motioned him out of the kitchen. We reached the top of the stairs, my room was right ahead.

"So, this is it?" he asked nervously.

I knew that once we reached the top of the stairs the order that he had witnessed below would change into the chaos only a teenage girl could create. I wished now that I had picked up a little before I left for school. I had no idea what I might find lying on the floor to embarrass myself.

"It's a little messy." I pushed the door open, and his eyes became wide like saucers.

"A *little* messy," he repeated. His tone was emphasizing rather than questioning my warning.

I scanned the room, looking for anything that might send me running for the nearest hole to hide in. Cocoa was chasing her tail in circles and then she put her front paws on Alex's chest and licked him on the face.

"Cocoa, that's not nice. Get down, girl."

"She's fine."

"Do you have a dog or something? She's going crazy. I think she smells something on you."

"Yeah, my peanut butter sandwich."

"Hmm." I shrugged my shoulders.

Cocoa ran across the room and pounced on my bed. She rolled over and put all four legs in the air, begging for Alex's attention. Alex rubbed her belly and then made his way around my room, touching everything as he walked past it. He continued pacing slowly, studying every detail, as if my whimsical wallpaper would confirm everything he thought he knew about me. Besides the mess that I had created, my room was pristine. My parents installed brand new, mocha colored carpet and hung a vintage, floral print paper on my walls. I had a bed and a desk of my very own, but it was my new bookshelf stuffed with novels that I was most found of. Of course, I loved having a space that was my own and a room that was decorated to my taste, but I hadn't allowed myself to get attached to anything other than the books. I could wake up on any given morning and be en route to another country by afternoon. But the books, they were small enough to stuff into one of my three pieces of luggage and for this reason, they became my newest treasure. Alex seemed most interested in the small, yellow, wooden bird that hung from the chain on my ceiling fan. He spun it between his fingers, inspecting it closely.

"Be careful with it. That's my *most* prized possession."

He studied me, still twirling the small, yellow bird between his fingers. His eyes looked sad as he removed his fingers from the tiny yellow creature, but then, without hesitation, his attention was drawn to my huge collection of pictures. Across all of the walls were hundreds of photos attached to neatly installed bulletin boards. They were mostly pictures of me and my parents and lots of pictures of far away places with castles and vineyards, beautiful beaches and mountains. I wondered what he was thinking as he scanned the rows of photos, carefully studying each one. I wondered what his room looked like, if it were neat and perfect just like his car. Did he, too, have pictures lining his walls, and if so, what would these pictures tell me?

"You know, there's a lake just behind the house . . . much more interesting than my bedroom, I'm sure."

"I kind of like your room," he teased, but then he shrugged his shoulders and reluctantly followed me down the stairs.

He stopped the car beside the lake, and I quickly grabbed the door handle to open it before he could make it around to my side to open it for me. I knew that a man opening a door for a woman was considered chivalrous and most girls would love to be treated with such attention, but I, on the other hand, was not like other girls, and despite my hopeless romanticism, it made me feel helpless and weak. He grabbed a blanket out of the back of his car and spread it across the ground. He sat down next to me, still clutching his half-full Diet Coke in one hand.

"Do you like it here? I mean, do you like living in the country?"

"I don't know, I guess I'm not really used to it. It's sort of lonely . . . and windy. There are snakes. I hate snakes. And all sorts of nasty flying bugs. They must be indigenous to the area, because I've lived in a lot of places and I've never seen bugs like these."

"Sounds like you love it here." He smirked, raising one eyebrow while his lips formed into a twisted smile.

"You know, the bald eagle rescue is right there on top of the hill; you can see it if you squint," I said, attempting to swing my finger around to the top of the tallest hill; instead, my whole hand landed directly in the middle of his can of Diet Coke.

"I am *so* sorry. You're soaking."

"It's alright. Really, it's not a big deal. I think I have another shirt in the car."

"Yes, it is. It's probably ruined. I'm just a bit of a clut . . . " I stopped mid-sentence and watched as he quickly removed his shirt and walked over to the Wagoneer. He put the wet shirt in a bag and tied a knot at the top. His back was toward me, and I watched as he pulled on a plain, white tee shirt. I felt ashamed that I was staring, but it didn't stop me.

"The eagle's my favorite bird," he continued as if nothing had happened. "We should go up there some time if they'll let us in. I think my dad knew the man that ran the rescue. But that was a long time ago."

I cleared my throat. "I thought you said you just moved here before school started." My eyes now met his. I was trying my hardest not to blush.

"Just moved back," he corrected me. "Have you ever been up there?"

I didn't respond. My eyes were now fixed on his white tee shirt, but I was thinking about his chest . . . it was something I couldn't control.

"Have you?" he repeated.

"Have I what?" I swallowed hard.

"Been up there . . . to the eagle rescue." Once again my eyes met his for a split second just before they drifted down to my feet.

"No."

I picked a few pieces of dead grass from the ground and started to braid them in an attempt to distract myself. I was slightly flushed, but more upset with myself for being so embarrassed. It wasn't like I hadn't seen a man's chest before. I had seen my dad's plenty of times and, of course, at the movies. But this just wasn't the same. I felt my stomach twisting into knots. Even though I wasn't quite sure how I felt about religion, I had grown up around a few religious people. Wasn't I supposed to be good? I shouldn't be having these thoughts. My nana had taught me about the fruits of the spirit: goodness, kindness, joy, gentleness, patience, love, peace, faithfulness, and self-control. If I were a good person then all of these qualities should come easy to me, but they didn't. I was certain that all of my fruits were rotting on the vine, but it was my self-control that I was having the most trouble with at the moment. I wanted to kiss him. I wasn't sure what had gotten into me. I had never even considered something like this before. I was not going to make the first move, that much I was sure of. I would tempt him I decided. I flipped my hair slightly and put my lips into a semi-pout. He didn't notice. Instead, he picked up a rock from beside the blanket and skipped it with perfection to the other side of the lake. I inched my way closer, making a barely visible difference in the gap between us, and still he didn't respond. I twisted my mouth in frustration and focused on the lake. I focused on the rolling hills in front of us, speckled with hues of light reds and yellows, announcing that Fall was here despite the unusually warm weather. And lastly, I focused on the tall pecan trees high above us, their branches waving gently. A more perfect setting didn't exist. I stretched out my hand until I could feel his wrist with the tips of my fingers, and I wiggled them so that he might reach for my hand. He shifted his gaze up to the sky just before he looked at me. Concern filled his face, or perhaps it was anxiousness. I couldn't tell. He appeared to be making some sort of life changing decision, and then, all at once, he moved closer to me, our bodies almost touching. I could feel his warmth radiating onto my cool skin. He turned so that he was facing me, looking into my eyes, biting gently on his lower lip, not saying a word. His eyes shifted down to my hand and he traced the tops of my fingers with his. And then, very slowly, he leaned toward me until our lips were just centimeters apart. The warm sweet breath that I so often inhaled from a distance was everything I had imagined it to be close up. We seemed to be locked in the moment, neither of us advancing. It was as if we were playing a game of chess, waiting anxiously for the other to make their move, the move that would determine the outcome of the game. I made my move, advancing just a fraction closer, but still not making contact. The final move was his, and it was a move that most certainly wouldn't put the game to an end; however, in the game of chess outside sources most certainly do not influence the outcome. But we were not playing chess, and as he pressed his lips softly to mine, I could hear the rumbling of my dad's old work truck coming in our direction. He leaned back. I could see his heart beating through his chest. I hadn't moved. My lips were still slightly parted, trying to make sense of what had just happened.

"I guess I had better get going." His eyes followed my dad's old brown pickup.

He pushed himself up off the ground, then pulled me up with an effortless tug. He opened my door, folded up the blanket, and placed it in the back of his car.

"Next time, I think you should invite me to your place."

"We'll see," he said as he parked the Wagoneer in front of my house. "How about I pick you up in the morning. You shouldn't be driving your car anyway." His eyes still focused on mine.

"Okay." I shrugged. "See you in the morning, then." I turned to shut the door.

I sat on the brick stairs in the front of the house and watched him drive slowly away. I shut my eyes tightly and took in every sound and every smell. I wanted to remember this moment forever. I had just been kissed for the first time, and it was at this moment that I knew, without a doubt, I was in love.

## CHAPTER TEN

*I* frantically pulled everything out of my closet. I was beginning to share my mother's distaste for my wardrobe as I sifted through piles of jeans and tee shirts, finding nothing appropriate to wear to dinner with a boy I was trying to impress. I pulled out a long, black, tiered sundress from the back of my closet and cut off the tags. I found my favorite short-sleeved, white cardigan and pulled it on over the top of the dress. I stared at myself in the full-length-mirror. I felt uncomfortable. I took off the dress and sweater and threw it on the floor atop the mountain of other clothes that I had rejected. I reached up to my top shelf, pulled down a pair of dark denims, slipped them on, and then began to hunt for a top that would dress them up a bit.

In the past couple of months, my mother had become obsessed with buying me fancy clothes while she was out shopping. She would sneak them into my closet to avoid hearing my protests. She probably felt guilty that, during our previous lives, I never had much of a wardrobe, or a closet for that matter. Digging through all of the plush, silky tops was overwhelming and a bit frustrating but my persistence paid off; finally, I came out with an earthy colored, sheer one that had a little bit of lace detail incorporated into the low cut neck line. After I slipped it on, I decided it was okay; I still felt like myself. I clipped the tags off and picked a pair of wedge heels that had never been worn. I let my curls fall loosely over my shoulders and began to work on my makeup a bit. When I looked into the mirror, I barely recognized myself. I looked more mysterious and dark tonight rather than innocent and angelic and that pleased me. I was listening to the Kings of Leon, and I could barely hear the doorbell over *Talihina Sky*. Quickly, I squirted on some perfume and headed downstairs. I didn't trust my parents alone with Alex.

I peaked over the balcony into the living room and, sure enough, I could see my father giving Alex the third degree. I needed to save him from my parents or he may never come back. The clunk of my heels on the stairs made the conversation below come to a screeching halt. I could almost hear my parents' thoughts.

Is she really wearing *HEELS* out with *A BOY*?

I knew they were wondering what had gotten into me. Yes, I was becoming a woman and this was the first time that I had ever felt like one. Although this relieved my mother, it had the opposite effect on my dad.

I reached the bottom of the stairs and stood in the arch that lead from the foyer into the living room, feeling uncomfortable as three pairs of eyes focused on me, each pair revealing a different set of emotions.

"I love the top," my mother said with quiet excitement. "You just look so pretty." The tears were starting to ooze from her eyes, and I realized that her previous aspirations for me had just been restored. She exhibited the enthusiasm I would expect on my wedding day, not my first date. It was a defining moment, and I was halfway glad I was able to do that for her. She saw hope in my make-up smeared face and it brought a sort of happiness that I had never seen before.

"Thanks, Mom," I said under my breath. "You're embarrassing me."

"So, Rae, are we going to get a proper introduction?" My father chided.

"I'm sorry guys. Alex," I said as I motioned to my parents, "meet Will and Sue. Mom and Dad, this is Alex Loving."

The color immediately vanished from my mother's face. She stood still and rigid, with an expression on her face that I had never seen before. Not quite the reaction I was expecting. At that same moment, my father unconsciously jerked his head so that he was now looking at my mother. Her eyes were still fixated on Alex and her lips positioned as if she were about to say something but couldn't find the words. Alex stood motionless, like a statue.

"Dad? Mom?" My voice was full of apprehension.

For me, this moment was huge, and I hated that she couldn't share in my happiness. I was stuck somewhere between despondence and shock. I wanted to cry. Instead, I pushed back the tears and straightened myself into a defensive pose.

"You know you need to be back here by eleven o'clock and no later," my father snapped. He appeared shaken.

"My curfew is twelve o'clock," I argued

"Eleven o'clock, no later." He repeated with a stern but worried look on his face.

"Fine." I held my breath as I scooted out the door with Alex close behind. Finally, I heard the heavenly sound of the door shutting, and it was just he and I alone in the cool, night air. I let him open the car door for me. His hands fumbled in a way that seemed out of character.

"I'm sorry about my parents," I muttered.

"I like them," he said.

"Really? They can be a little overwhelming at times . . . and weird."

"I really like them, Rae."

I sighed as he shut my door. He moved around to the driver's side and climbed behind the wheel. He drove quickly, the gravel crackling under the tires. Once again, I had no idea where he was taking me. The car was silent. I reached over and powered on the radio, mariachi music filled the car and we both began to laugh.

"So . . . this is what you listen to, huh?"

He gave me a sharp look. A smile turned the corners of his mouth, his hands loosened around the wheel and we pulled onto the highway heading towards town.

"Your parents are just a *little* bit protective, aren't they?"

"That's putting it mildly."

"Do they act like that every time a boy comes to pick you up, or was it just me?" He looked at me with a knowing smile plastered across his face.

"I've never really been on a date before." I sounded pathetic, and I wished I could stuff the words back into my mouth, but instead my mouth continued to run. "So do all of your girlfriends' parents behave so rudely when they meet you for the first time?"

"Just yours." My heart sank a little. "Of course, this is the first time I've ever met a girl's parents . . . and I think it went well, considering." I tucked my bottom lip behind my top teeth in an attempt to disguise the smile that was emerging.

He slowed, taking a sharp left into a nice, older looking neighborhood. He flashed his pass at the guard and the gate lifted open. We climbed the hill, making a series of zigzag turns through the tree-lined streets. When we reached the top, he pulled into a long cul-de-sac dotted with half a dozen homes. Most of them looked to be built in the late 60's to early 70's, but they had a hint of modern curb appeal, as if they had been completely gutted and redone into a contempary masterpiece.

He drove to the end of the loop. The porch light gave off a soft glow, revealing a somewhat rundown split-level home. It was the only house in the cul-de-sac that hadn't been updated. It looked a bit neglected. The white, wooden exterior had bits of chipping paint, guttering was hanging loosely from the roofline in more than a couple of spots, and the walkway leading to the door was overgrown with ivy. He put his arm around my shoulder and walked me slowly to the door, pulling it open without even testing the lock.

"This is where I live," he said, very matter-of-fact.

"Is your father home?" I questioned, looking at the unlocked door.

"No."

"Do you have a habit of leaving your doors unlocked?"

"Yes."

"Oh." I raised my eyebrows in surprise.

"You worry too much."

The house was immaculate, so different from the exterior. The décor had a timeless feel. It looked staged, untouched, and a bit lonely. There were old but refurbished wood floors throughout. Every detail of the home was perfect. From the front door, I could see all the way to the far end of the living room. The house was very open, making it appear larger than it actually was. The walls were filled with photography, but it was a cluster of family photos on the far wall that drew me in for a closer look. There were several large photos of his mother and father; they appeared to be in their mid-twenties. They were a handsome couple, but my eyes gravitated toward a picture of his parents holding a baby who looked to be about a year old. The lack of any new pictures in the house suggested that perhaps his father had not moved on since the death of his wife. I thought that was sad and sort of sweet. She was his true love.

"Look how cute." Against my will I made a cooing noise as I approached the portrait. "Is that you?" I asked, adjusting my voice so that it now sounded more indifferent.

"Yes," he answered. He made the 's' hiss through his teeth as if he were irritated. I continued studying the picture of baby Alex, not taking his hint.

"Look, you have the same eyes that you did back then. They say that a baby's eyes can change after the first year, but your eyes are exactly the same . . . except the little scar by your right eye isn't there." I turned to look at him. He was studying me silently and it seemed as though he were trying to discern what I was thinking.

111

"What? Why are you staring at me like that?"

"No reason," he responded quickly.

"So . . . how *did* you get that scar on your eye?" I asked as I traced my finger along the right side of his face.

"It was a long time ago . . . I don't recall," he said with a blank expression.

"Didn't your dad tell you?"

"Do you want to see the rest of the house, or not?" he asked, completely disregarding my previous statement.

I nodded without saying a word. We were both quiet as we walked through the large foyer and into the living room. A huge wrought iron and glass coffee table sat in the center of the room with several magazines lying on top. Surrounding the table was an oversized, camel colored, leather chair and a pristine, white overstuffed sofa. A couple of large area rugs covered the dark chocolate hardwoods and a fire was burning in the stone hearth at the back of the room giving a warm glow to the otherwise lonely features of the house. One side of the living room had an enormous built-in shelf that was stuffed with books, most of which looked old and a little worn.

"Your dad's a big reader," I stated as I walked over to the collection and ran my fingers across the spines. I couldn't help but think how his father's library put my small collection of books to shame.

"He used to be."

"Not any more?"

"Nope."

"Have you read any of these?"

"No, I guess I don't have the same taste in books as my father did." I glanced over the titles that were at eye level: books on culture and society, the Cuban missile crisis, a plethora of books on World War II and Nazi Germany, books on Fascism, books on religion, several Bibles, a couple in NIV, one in King James, along with several Bible Commentaries. There was a wide variety of books on different American Indian tribes and a worn copy of War and Peace nestled smack in the middle of the bunch.

"Not exactly my taste either." I continued to gaze over all of the titles, my eyes jumping from shelf to shelf, scanning the huge collection.

"They all look so old."

"I think some of them were my grandfather's."

"Is he still living?"

"No." He took my hand and began to guide me toward the kitchen. I scanned the room one final time, my eyes falling on one of the magazines stacked on the glass top coffee table. It was *Time* Magazine, and on the cover was a picture of a man I didn't recognize. Quickly, I glanced at the date in the lower, left hand corner, and although the small print was fuzzy, I was certain that it read August 1989. The magazine was older than I was, a relic, a collector's item perhaps.

"Come on, I need to get dinner in the oven." I followed him into the long galley style kitchen. The jet-black, granite countertops were a perfect contrast to the stark white cabinets. The kitchen was spotless.

"You cook?" I smirked.

"If you consider warming up cooking, then yeah, I cook." He pulled two dishes out of the fridge and slid them into the oven. "I hope Chinese is okay."

"Perfect, I'm starving."

"This is going to take a while. Want to finish looking around?" he asked as he wrapped his arms around my waist and brushed his lips across the back of my hair.

I felt his hands loosen and he led me down the dimly lit hallway. He opened the door to what I guessed must be his room and flicked on the light. It was just as I had imagined. Everything inside his room was very neat and orderly, unlike mine. He had a platform bed sitting in the middle of his room and a long, sleek table under the window that held a simple iPod docking station and a laptop. I thought the furniture looked a bit modern compared to the rest of the furniture in the house. Unlike my picture-lined walls, he had only a few framed photos sitting on his dresser. I approached the pictures and then hesitated before I ran my fingers along the frame that held an older photo of a woman who appeared to be in her twenties. It looked like the picture of his mother that I saw in the foyer.

"Your mom?" I choked.

He approached me gently, taking the frame from my hands. "Yeah."

"She was so pretty." I stood admiring her small face and her long, perfectly straight, blond hair. "You have a lot of her features." I paused, trying to think of the right thing to say.

"I think I have her eyes."

I turned toward him, cupping his face in my hands.

"I'm sorry," I consoled him, knowing that our eyes now shared the same sadness.

"It's not your fault."

"I know, but I just wish I could do something to make your pain go away."

"You are what makes my pain go away. You make me happy." He tilted his head slightly, studying my face.

"You make me happy, too," I whispered.

He set the picture down on the dresser and started to lead me back into the hallway. I shook my head in opposition and made my way around his room instead, studying everything with interest.

"You didn't think I was going to let you off the hook that easy, did you?" I teased.

"A man can always try. Besides, I guess I have it coming to me after giving you a hard time about your messy room."

"What's this?" I questioned. I held up a worn, black leather notebook that was fastened shut with a piece of twine. It had been resting on the table beside his computer.

I began to twist the twine between my fingers. I was testing him. Teasing him.

"Please . . . don't." He was pleading. He moved quickly toward me, maneuvering the book from my fingers with ease. His humor had escaped him.

"I'm sorry. I didn't mean anything." Now my voice was pleading, and he was flustered. His cheeks were brushed with color and his breathing was an uneven rhythm that he was trying to control. "What is it?" I asked, my voice just above a whisper.

"My writing," he whispered back, his arm still folded tightly around the book.

"Can I read it?" I was pleading with him once again.

"It's just for me." His voice was soft, his breathing still uneven and rapid. He nervously bit his lower lip and brushed a wispy chocolate strand from his eyes. For a moment, his hazel pinwheels looked different. For the first time, I could see emotion behind the color. Desperation. Passion. Anticipation. Fear. But what did he fear?

"Well, you could read to me," I offered.

He inhaled deeply, relaxing a bit, and then began to untwist the twine, opening the book, but holding it close to his body. He flipped through the pages with precision, resting his finger on a page that was near the beginning of the book. A smile was now forcing the corners of his mouth upward. His eyes glistened. His lips began to tremble.

"*Please*," I begged.

"You're not going to actually make me do this, are you?" Once again, he bit his lower lip, playfully this time.

"I guess you don't know me very well then." I swallowed hard. My heart was beating in my throat.

"Better than you think." He smirked. I exhaled. I waited. "I'll read one page and that's it. No more begging. You promise?"

"Pinky Promise." I held my little finger up so that he could see.

He positioned the black leather book in his hands, and I could see the quiver return to his lips. My hand fell on my silver locket, and I nervously began to run it up and down its silvery chain in an almost trance-like motion.

His lips barely parted and his eyes focused on me, reciting the words without looking at the page. His voice was soft and raw with a hint of pain, but at the same time sticky and smooth like honey.

*My window is a little hazy*
*But I wipe it clean*
*So I can see*
*A piece of you*
*That's all I need*
*Sometimes I think I'm going crazy*
*When you come near*
*And look through me*
*It makes me sick*
*That you can't see*

*So I press my finger to the window and watch the world*
*below me twist and spin*
*I can only hope that one day very soon*
*You will finally see me for who I am*

*Will my heart ever quit this aching?*
*I close my eyes*
*You're in my dreams*
*You're next to me*
*Or so it seems*

*I am so desperate that I'm shaking*
*I break the glass*
*From you to me*
*The wall is gone*
*And now I'm free*


*So I reach my hand outside the window and feel the*
*world below me twist and spin*
*I know for certain that one day very soon*
*You will finally see me for who I am*


"It's poetry. I love it. So, is there anything you're not good at?" What I really wanted to ask was whom he had written it for. I wanted to know why he felt so misunderstood.

"I'm sure there are a few things."

"One more . . . for me," I begged.

"You promised."

"I guess I did, didn't I," I grumbled just as the timer on the oven chimed.

"Looks like dinner's ready." He returned the worn, black leather book to its place beside the computer.

"I thought you said you preferred Word on a Mac. You know a black leather journal is more my style."

"I only said that I preferred a Mac. I didn't say that I have always had one."

He led me back down the hallway to a pair of French doors that stood open to a large deck. Despite the darkness, I could see the outline of the trees. The night revealed the tall pines that surrounded the back of his house and gave the illusion of being in the middle of a forest.

"I'll be right back." He left me standing on the deck, staring into the dark, night sky, but within seconds it seemed, he returned with two plates loaded with rice and chicken and noodles and broccoli.

"Your house is amazing. I love older homes . . . I think all homes tell a story, but the older the home the richer the story."

I wondered what story lie within these walls. I bet it was a good one. I wished that I could have met his mother. I wished that he wasn't so alone.

We ate in silence, not an uncomfortable silence, but a silence that comes from being at ease around one another. And it was easy being with him. I didn't have to say a single word. He seemed to understand me, and although we had only known each other a short time, I felt he knew me better than anyone else.

We stared up at the stars. They were the same stars I had seen every other night, but they seemed more complete with him next to me. There was nowhere else I would rather be. I snuggled closer to him. I wished he would kiss me again . . . but he didn't kiss me. Instead, he reached out carefully, like he was unsure of himself, and pulled me closer to him. My heart was leaping out of my chest and my face was flushed. He studied me, looking deep into my eyes. His fingers felt warm on my cold skin.

"I've thought about this moment for so long. It's so much better being here, being with you, so much better than I could have ever imagined. You have no idea how . . . you have no idea . . ." His voice trailed, leaving silence and unanswered questions.

"I think I *can* imagine," I responded with all the certainty that I knew.

"No," he paused. His lips stayed parted as if he had something more to say but couldn't find the right words. "I never imagined that I could feel this way. You make me weak," he whispered. A frown formed on my face, the darkness unable to conceal it. He stroked my hair and then very softly kissed the top of my head.

"You make me strong," I said in opposition.

"I love you, Rae."

"I love you, too."

He looked down and we were both silent.

"Come on, I've got to get you home before your dad comes after me himself."

I sighed, but I knew he was right.

"Fine," I agreed begrudgingly. He got up first and then pulled me up with a single, gentle tug.

All of the lights were out when I got home. I snuck quietly up the stairs, hoping not to wake my parents, and fell back onto my bed. If ever there were a perfect leading man in a romance novel, it would be Alex. He was quiet and mysterious. He was kind and patient. He was handsome, and he was always saving me from myself. I, on the other hand, was not cut out to be the leading lady. I didn't have an exotic beauty, I was far from graceful, I was impatient, and in no way was I ladylike. I couldn't imagine what it was that he saw in me, but he loved me and he told me so, and right now, that was the only thing that mattered.

# CHAPTER ELEVEN

*I*t was almost the weekend. Time was flying much more quickly than it ever had before. The school was buzzing with anticipation. Chatter filled the hallways and the main topic of conversation was who was dressing up as what for the Masquerade Ball tomorrow night, Halloween night. Many schools had a homecoming dance that usually fell around the same time. I didn't see why we couldn't have just stuck with the norm. The student council thought this would be a change for the better, something new, more fun, more exciting. And for much of the school it was. So much for my luck.

Halloween was my least favorite holiday. Actually, that was an understatement. I hated Halloween. I couldn't stand dressing up. I hadn't even enjoyed it as a child. Alex tried to persuade me to go to the Masquerade Ball. I tried to convince him that dinner at his house was a far better option. We settled for a scary movie marathon instead. I didn't see what was wrong with repeating last Friday night over and over again. I couldn't think of anything better than lying under the stars with the boy I loved. I endured class after class filled with talk of wigs and fangs and masks and horns before it was finally time for lunch at the bridge.

The weather was starting to cool down ever so slightly, and I dreaded the snow that would come and turn our paradise into a cold and icy mess. He started to spread out a blanket in the usual, ritualistic manner, but there was nothing about today that felt normal. I relished every motion he made, as if I were noticing each movement for the first and last time. I reached into my bag, discretely pulled out my camera, and managed to take a few shots before he noticed.

"Hey, no pictures." He turned his head bashfully, so that I couldn't snap one of his beautiful, hazel eyes.

"Why not?" I put the camera strap around my wrist and approached him, playfully trying to turn him around until I could get a good shot. He was laughing, but not budging, trying to fight off my surprising strength while I gave it one last attempt, sending us both toppling to the ground with me now hovering over him.

"Perfect," I said, positioning my camera directly over his face.

"How can someone look as good as you and not like his picture taken?" I asked. "If I were that beautiful, I would have my picture taken all day long. In fact, people would pay me to take my picture." I snapped the picture just before he flipped me over. Now he was the one who was hovering over me.

"You're the most beautiful thing I've ever seen. You're like a dream that I don't ever want to wake up from," he said, slowly easing the camera from my limp hands, my entire body mesmerized by his presence and hypnotized by his voice.

With one quick snap, he took my picture then set the camera down beside him. "You're absolutely perfect and you don't even know it. And to me, that makes you all the more beautiful."

I watched him roll over to his side and prop himself up on one elbow, his free hand brushing slowly through my curls; a gentle, twirling, rhythmic motion that relaxed me and made me forget about everything else. The rest of the world and all of its pains had disappeared and it was just the two of us, alone in this magical spot. I'm not sure how long I lay with my eyes closed, listening to him breathe, to his heart beating hard beneath my cheek, but like waking from a dream, I opened my eyes and he was gone.

Art class was a foggy memory, and I found myself on a bench in the girls' locker room lacing up my shoes, preparing for the eight mile stretch that lie ahead of me. At the first sign of cool weather, the coach opted to change the practice to afternoons. Even though it was still fairly warm, the mornings started off cold. I guess Mother Nature was giving us a taste of what was to come.

My body was weak, limp, and felt completely unconditioned for a long distance run. I could still feel the twirling of his fingers through my hair. I could hear his heart beating as if his pulse had merged with mine. Every beat of my heart made me long for his touch. We followed the path that hugged the wall of trees, staying close to the outer edge of the woods. The girls continued to chatter, so I pushed on my iPod and filled my mind with thoughts of Alex. He loved me. He thought I was beautiful. How could I be so lucky to have him? I decided that I was beginning to like Oklahoma. I'm not sure if I would have even given it much of a chance if it hadn't been for Alex. I could be happy living in Antarctica if he was by my side. There were things that I missed, a certain friend to be exact. Even though I had become an expert at keeping people out, I had managed to pick up a friend along the way. I would be lying to myself if I said I didn't miss her. While lost in thought, I had become oblivious to everything around me. I was still running, but struggling to keep up. It was the sign in the distance that brought me back to reality: mile marker four. All at once, I realized that I was well behind the others and perhaps it was this new position that allowed me to see something that I had been missing all along. For weeks now, each practice had been the same. Fifteen runners would start but only fourteen finished. Up until this point, I had forced myself to concentrate on the run rather than on Chloe's whereabouts. But now that I was no longer in the lead, I was able to see something that allowed me to answer the question that, despite my best efforts, had been eating away at me all along: where had Chloe gone? When I saw Chloe slip off down one of the arms leading into a dense cover of trees, I stopped dead in my tracks. A million thoughts were blazing through my mind, but mostly, I was thinking about revenge. I thought about how, on the first day of school, Claire had befriended me and with one snarling look, Chloe had pushed her away. Was it because of Chloe that Claire and I no longer spoke? It didn't take a genius to notice that, like me, Claire was now alone. Did Claire hate me because her single act of kindness had cost her three of her closest friends? Had she been shunned because of me? If it hadn't been for Chloe, would Claire and I be friends? It occurred to me that, if I wanted to, I could get Chloe in trouble. I could tell Ms. Canton about what Chloe was doing. Ms. Canton had made it perfectly clear that no one was to venture off the path. But I had never been a rat and couldn't deny that I was curious. I had always been scared to run the path alone. But why wasn't she? I could follow her, I thought. I stood idle for a moment longer. I was torn between desire and fear: the desire to follow her onto the winding path and the fear of what I might find if I did. Something about this situation didn't feel quite right. Everything about this moment seemed familiar, but I could not place it. I felt as though I had been standing in this exact spot before, contemplating whether or not to take the path that veered off into the woods just before mile marker four. It was the twisted tree at the start of the trail that refreshed my memory. Twisted like a piece of licorice and doubled over so that the tip of the tree was touching the ground. Fantasy was becoming reality. I had seen this tree in my dream and yet, here it stood, no less mystical, right before me. In my dream, I had taken the path and the thought of what lie waiting for me on the other side was enough to send me running in the opposite direction. In an instant, fear won over desire, and I found myself sprinting, not stopping until I reached the others, finishing out the eight mile stretch and ending back in the parking lot where we began. My body was still shaking when I finished the run. Not my legs so much, but I was shaking from the inside out. Everything inside of me was trembling. In my entire life, I had never experienced anything so surreal. I took a couple of deep breaths in and out and tried to calm myself. I knew that Alex would be waiting for me in the parking lot, and I didn't want for him to see me shaken. The girls were lingering by their cars, finalizing their plans for the big Halloween bash tomorrow night. They were standing close but their voices sounded very far away. Chloe was nowhere in sight, and I had no idea what that meant, but her well-being was the least of my concerns. I scanned the parking lot, as usual, looking for Alex. He was leaning against the driver's side door, patiently waiting for me. It was when I saw his face that I felt calmness fill the spot in my body where, just moments ago, fear and anxiety had resided. My heart rate began to slow down, my body stopped trembling, and all thoughts of the dream and of Chloe magically slipped from my mind.

"How was the run?" he asked.

"Long," I replied, knowing full well that he could, in no way, comprehend what it felt like to run eight miles. He had never run a mile in his life. He didn't understand my obsession with running for sport. Running was something you did on an as-needed basis.

"Whose car is that?" he asked as we pulled onto my gravel drive. We both studied the white rental that was parked in the loop at the front of my house.

"Company, I guess. I didn't know my parents were expecting anyone."

"Lucky you."

"Do you want to come in?" I tugged playfully at his sleeve. "I promise you can leave if my mother freaks out again. Besides, if I have company, then I won't have to entertain theirs. You'd be doing me a huge favor, really."

"Sure, why not." He climbed out of the car and opened my door while I was busy gathering all of my junk off the floorboard of his car.

My parents were sitting in the living room. I could see the back of the red headed visitor they were entertaining. My parents were both seated, facing the door as we walked in. My mother stared at us with a blank and far away look on her face. My dad gave Alex a warm smile and motioned us into the living room.

"Rae!!!!!" A familiar voice bellowed as the visitor whipped around to greet me.

I had been longing for a friend all day, and now she was here. Crazy Carly; at least that's what my parents called her. My day couldn't get any better. I was happy; a kind of happy that I knew little about, a bouncy kind of happy that was so uncharacteristic of myself. It was bubbling up inside me. It was a kind of happy that I couldn't control. But somewhere in the back of my mind, I was reminded of Sir Isaac Newton's oh-so-famous words, "What goes up, must come down." I knew this kind of happiness couldn't last forever. Although I felt with every beat of my heart that the end was very near, I pushed the darkness away . . . but I couldn't push it out completely.

I met Carly in Amsterdam, and we were best friends from the time I was sixteen. Carly was a definite exception in my book of rules on friendship. It wasn't a traditional friendship, and I think that's why I allowed it. We were more like sisters. We shared secrets like sisters, we laughed like sisters, and we even fought like sisters. I didn't consider her just a friend; Carly was like family. But it was what drew us together that made our connection so strong.

Carly was different from anyone else I had met. She was very in tune to things, and that's part of what made our friendship so strong. We were the best of friends, and yes, there were secrets that she had entrusted to me, but there was one secret in particular that I couldn't bare to repeat. It was a secret that would cause a stir, a whole mixture of emotions to follow. It was a secret that would bring out skeletons, in a figurative sense, of course, and so Carly and I decided together that it would be best if we kept it just between ourselves.

It was around this time of year, two years ago. I was sixteen, and it was my first day at the American school in Amsterdam. The usual was going on around me. Girls were sizing me up, trying to decide if I was the right material for their group of friends. I watched as they bristled up like cats who had just seen something intimidating. Their smiles reminded me of a dog showing its teeth at someone who was trying to take away its bone. I wasn't sure if they were looking at the same person that I saw in the mirror every morning. I couldn't understand why an ordinary girl like myself was causing such a stir. Although I still noticed the whispering and the narrow, unfriendly eyes, these cruel and barbaric forms of initiation seemed to have little to no effect on me since the construction of my shell.

I remember when I first saw Carly. I was searching for my locker, and she was standing alone in the hallway, leaning up against a wall, reading a copy of *To Kill a Mockingbird.* She was wearing a pair of brightly colored printed leggings with a floral tunic that hurt my eyes. Her hair was a heap of fiery, red curls that hung midway down her back. Her face was pale and her cheeks were brushed with freckles. Among all of the oddities that Carly possessed, it was hardly the way she looked that caught my attention; rather, it was the way she looked *at* me. It was a look that, at first, I misinterpreted as disgust. Her face turned an even paler shade of white, while at the same time holding a hint of green. It was as if she were going to get sick at any moment. The look on her face made me turn immediately in the opposite direction.

It wasn't until lunch that very same day that I realized just why Carly had looked so ashen. She apologized then explained it to me in the simplest way that she could. I remember her words exactly. She set her lunch bag down beside me and said, "I can see her."

"Who? You can see who?" I asked.

"Your sister."

Now it was my face that was a sickly shade of green.

She explained to me how the living let off a warmth that she could feel and a glow that could be seen with the naked eye, or at least her naked eye. I can remember feeling sick to my stomach. Even though I had no reason to believe that what she was saying was true, every inch of my body was telling me that it was. I had always felt close to Laney, although I could never explain why. In a way, even though it freaked me out, I wanted Carly to be right.

As I listened to Carly recount the story of what she had seen, my stomach turned inside out. Carly described the girl that was standing beside me and the details of the little girls' outfit: her puff sleeved heart top, little blue jeans, the rubbery pink shoes, the heart shaped sunglasses, the curly blond piggy tails, the pale blue eyes, and the small red birth mark on the lobe of her left ear.

I went home that night and pulled a scrapbook off the shelf in my parents' closet when they were preoccupied in front of the TV. It was a scrapbook that I had seen on occasion. I would usually sneak away to my room and flip through it before sliding it back into place when no one was looking. It held pictures of Laney, and the presence of the book brought about a depression in our home that was thick and unsettling. Looking at these pictures brought about feelings that I would rather not stir up, and so I sat in secrecy. The entire album was filled with pictures of Laney: her birth, her first bath, her first time eating real foods, her first birthday, Laney at the park, Laney at the zoo, Laney's second birthday, and then, finally, a picture that made the hairs on the back of my neck stand on end. It was a picture of Laney and my parents standing in front of a large statue of a Viking. She was wearing the puff sleeved, heart top and blue jeans, the rubbery pink shoes, the little heart rimmed sunglasses with her hair in the same curly blond piggy tails, just as Carly had described. Below the picture were the words "Big Ole" in my dad's characteristically sloppy handwriting. After that, a bond was created with Carly that I could never have with any other person. A firestorm of questions followed, but there was one that I needed an answer to right away. Why was Laney beside me? Carly said that she didn't know, but she thought that Laney had been there to protect me. To protect me from what, I will never know. Laney would appear now and again, and even if Carly couldn't see her, she could always feel the coolness of her presence that counteracted my warmth.

Carly and her supernatural encounters became more than just a mere interest. Her stories both fascinated and frightened me. Of course, my parents didn't believe in ghosts. They knew that Carly claimed she could see them; the part they didn't know was that she had seen Laney. They thought of her stories as nothing more than child's play, and thus, she earned the name Crazy Carly. They loved her all the same. I think they thought of her as a daughter, and although she would never replace their Laney, my mom loved having two teenage girls running around our small apartment. Sometimes, I would catch my mother sitting quietly with her eyes closed tightly as she listened, a sort of peacefulness surrounding her that I had never seen before. I imagined that she was listening to the sounds that two sets of feet made as they ran through our tiny home, the hushed whispers of teenage secrets that lingered in the air, and the occasional bickering that any mother could expect and that she many times wishfully considered sibling rivalry. She would close her eyes to listen and pretend and that would be enough, but not enough to bring Laney back.

I looked around the room and realized that besides Nana and Papa, I had everyone that meant anything to me right here in this room. I couldn't have been happier. By the looks of the body language between Carly and Alex, I was beginning to feel that I was the only one who was delighted. Alex stood with his arms crossed in front of his chest and his head pointed in the direction of the door. He didn't appear to be upset, nor did he seem to be feeling left out now that my old friend had come to town and taken away some of the attention I was paying him. He appeared rather antsy and uncomfortable. I had never seen him this way. I had never seen him look so nervous around another person before. As for Carly, she was anything but nervous. She stared at him, her eyes intense, like she was trying to solve a riddle; a riddle that she wouldn't . . . couldn't leave alone. I guess I could relate. The first day in art class, the day I first saw Alex, I stared at him long and hard. I studied him. I tried to place him. I tried to determine why he looked so familiar to me. But Carly didn't seem as though she was trying to place him. I was sure that she didn't think he looked familiar, but rather unfamiliar.

"Carly, this is Alex." I broke the silence, hoping that it would also break Carly's stare. I loved Carly, but she was being just plain rude. "He's my one and only friend here in Oklahoma," I continued, giving Alex a quick hug to let Carly know that he was important to me.

Alex held his eyes low and gave her a small, stiffened hand gesture that only slightly resembled a wave, his eyes never resting on Carly's.

"Rae, I think I'll let you and your friend, Carly, catch up. I'll see you tomorrow," he said.

"Please, stay." I was being selfish and I knew it. I also knew that he felt uncomfortable, but this was one of my happiest moments and I didn't want it to end.

"No, I should go." He looked at me, his eyes pleading and I couldn't stand to argue with him. He wrapped his arms around me tightly and gave me a quick kiss on the cheek. I couldn't see his body shaking, but I could feel it. Was he shaking mad, shaking with fear, shaking with nervousness? He wasn't fighting. I knew that. He was fleeing, and I needed to know why.

"I love you, Rae," he whispered in my ear so that only I could hear.

"I love you, too," I whispered back.

He turned to walk out the door and I followed behind him, trying to make one last, silent attempt to keep him here. I could see in his eyes that it was useless.

"I guess I'll see you tomorrow," I said in a hushed voice.

He nodded again before shutting the door and walking to his car.

"Well, that was interesting," my dad grumbled as he rolled his eyes at Carly.

"What?" She sounded offended that my dad would even insinuate Alex's leaving so abruptly had anything to do with her.

"Carly, the bulldog," my dad chuckled and looked over at my mother who was standing as stiff as a board with the same indefinable expression from last Friday night consuming her every feature. She looked terrified. She was somewhere far away, not with us in this room. Her eyes looked glossy, and I wondered if she knew that she was ruining this moment for me. I couldn't understand this retched behavior during the happiest time of my life. I knew that she wanted happiness for me; she had told me so on more than one occasion.

"So, is he your boyfriend?" Carly's question seemed to bring my mother out of her stupor, her eyes focusing now on me, waiting for me to answer.

"Carly!" I nearly shouted; however, I couldn't force myself to be mad. I was still feeling the aftershocks of happiness rippling through my body.

"Will, I think that's our cue to leave." My mother hastily grabbed my father's arm and tried to pry him from his leather recliner. He didn't budge. He had a serious look on his face.

"I was just waiting hear Rae's answer." He focused his eyes on me.

"Carly . . . we can just go up to my room." I stared back at my father, wide eyed and irritated.

"That won't be necessary. Will, you're going to leave the girls alone. At least until dinner." Her voice was somewhere in between a plea and a demand. She jerked his arm again, this time with a little less patience, and he begrudgingly moved from his chair into the kitchen.

Carly watched them disappear into the other room before turning to look at me. I flittered back to the sofa, still quaking with happiness. I sat down and patted the cushion next to me.

"You seem a little tightly wound today," I smirked.

"*Is* he your boyfriend?" She cut right to the chase.

"Maybe. You don't seem to approve." My tone was a bit cool now. I did want her approval, but I doubted that her disapproval would change anything either. "So, what do you think of him, really."

"He's not bad . . . okay, he's gorgeous . . . but . . ."

"But what?"

"But . . . " She hesitated, taking a deep breath.

"Spill it, Carly." My patience was running thin.

"Rae, you remember Bernard Bodin?"

"Yessss," I hissed, fearing the direction that our conversation was heading. Bernard Bodin was the new boy at school. We called him Ben for short. He transferred to our school a year and a half after I did. He was gangly with short, dark hair, a pointy nose, and thick, wire rimmed glasses. Carly couldn't stand Ben. When she looked at him, she saw just Ben, no colors lining his thin frame and no noticeable temperate radiating from his body, just Bernard Bodin . . . and the thick, wire rimmed glasses that concealed his hollow and empty eyes. I think it bothered Carly that she couldn't read him.

"Alex is like Ben," she said quickly, just before looking away.

"Alex is like Ben. Whatever." I rolled my eyes. It appeared that no one appreciated my newfound happiness. Was my presence more bearable when I was gloomy and depressed?

"Well, he was blank. No color. There was no heat from his body, or coolness for that matter. There was nothing."

"You really are crazy." I hopped up off the sofa and headed to the kitchen.

"That's not very nice. I come all this way to see you and you won't even take me seriously."

"That's because I don't believe you. So, how long are you here for anyway?" I changed the subject, partly because it was nonsense, and partly because I thought that Carly might burst a vein in her head if she tried any harder to convince me of Alex's peculiarities.

"Here . . . just today. But that's what I've come to tell you, Rae. We're moving back." The determined crevasse in her forehead disappeared and little lines around her eyes formed as she squinted with the large smile that filled her freckled face.

I stopped short. "You're moving to Bartlesville?" I felt the excitement start to bubble up from my chest until it neared my throat, causing me to swallow hard before I could begin to speak again.

"No, not Bartlesville . . . but close . . . or closer. We're moving to Houston," she exclaimed, still sounding excited.

"That's still like eight hours away, Carly." I felt the bubble of excitement burst just as quickly as it had formed.

"Well, eight hours is better than being separated by an ocean." She looked disappointed that I wasn't as thrilled as she was.

"I guess you're right."

"We could go to the same college. We could even room together." Excitement filled her voice once again. I guess she had more time to think this thing through. The truth of the matter was that I didn't know what I would be doing after my senior year. What my parents wanted for me and what I wanted for myself were two totally different things. I had never said it out loud, but I was kind of waiting to see what Alex's plan was before I set anything in stone.

"Yeah," I agreed. She didn't seem to notice my ambivalence; she was preoccupied with the plans for our future.

"Did I hear you say you're moving back?" My dad whipped around the corner from where he had obviously been eavesdropping, and my mom followed closely behind him. They ushered her into the kitchen and set a huge plate of spaghetti and cheese bread in front of her and gave her the attention that she had been looking for from me. The entire dinner was spent planning our college careers. I was a little surprised that they didn't stop to ask me what I thought about going to the University of Oklahoma and majoring in pre-med. My life was being planned out before my very eyes, but it wasn't me that was doing the planning. It was as if I wasn't even here. I had immediately become colorless in their eyes, nonexistent.

How can you fall asleep after the perfect day? I had my parents, my makeshift sister, Cocoa, and Alex, the most important person in my life. My mind was 99.9% in a happy place, but there was still the .1% that felt dark and distracted, sending sickening pains to my stomach. I realized that it was because Carly had never been wrong. I recalled my own inability to read Alex. I recalled how he seemed familiar, yet there was so much that was still a mystery. Everyday, I learned something new about him, each day filled with more surprises than the last. For the first time, I was letting my heart, instead of my mind, control my emotions. There was something mysterious about him that was refreshing, intoxicating, and addictive. I was clay in his hands. I drowned all rules, intuitions, and precautions deep inside me until they were practically non-existent. But tonight, as I tried hard to keep these feelings of doubt submerged, Carly's words made them come bobbing to the surface. Her intuitiveness could be trusted, and it made me sick to think what her intuitions were telling her about Alex.

## CHAPTER TWELVE

*O*nce again, the blaring of my alarm interrupted my pleasant dreams. I lay in my bed, relishing the warmness and comfort of my dream; but just as abruptly as my alarm sounded, I was reminded that today was my second least favorite day of the year. Halloween. It wasn't that I minded all of the little kids running around in their costumes, begging for candy that would rot out their teeth; I just didn't like dressing up.

My earliest memory of Halloween was when I was five. I was so excited. I wanted to be Wonder Woman. She was so beautiful, the essence of a woman. I loved her long, black, wavy hair, and I remember looking at mine thinking that it had the potential to be Wonder Womanish. I had even spotted a Wonder Woman costume at Kmart and almost nothing could kill my dream of becoming this powerful superhero for just one night. Almost nothing that is, until my mother came home with a Mickey Mouse costume that smelled of a plastic beach ball. The one holiday that you get to become something else entirely. I might have even been able to live with Minnie, but Mickey! No five-year-old girl dreams of becoming a boy rat for Halloween. I remember the picture of myself sitting on the trunk of my nana's ancient blue car; my shoulders slumped as if I had given up entirely. I think that was also the day I gave up on Halloween.

Up until the sixth grade, my schools had always held a contest for the best Halloween costume. It didn't seem to matter where I lived, I couldn't escape Halloween. Kids would parade around the gym in the elaborate costumes their mothers had sewn or costumes they had purchased while back in the states for summer break. My mother had never touched a needle and thread, and she would usually be scrambling around the house on Halloween morning looking for something to change my appearance just enough to qualify as a costume. One Halloween, she cut off a pair of my jeans just below the knee and put my hair in pigtails. I donned a tattered, flannel shirt and hiking boots. She then spotted my cheeks with eyeliner and called me a hobo. My least favorite was when she wrote to my nana, asking her to send a costume in the mail. She was really proud of herself that year. Several days before Halloween, the box from Nana arrived at our apartment, and I wanted to know what was inside. She told me that it would be a surprise and that I would be delighted. I knew that it had to be a costume and even though I had become quite cynical of this particular day of the year, I hoped for something amazing. A costume that would bring back all of my excitement for the holiday. I can still remember her saying.

"Now close your eyes and don't peek."

I held them tight until she instructed me to open them. When I did finally open my eyes, I was staring at the most horrible clown costume I had ever seen; it even came with a big, fat, red, clown nose. I didn't get my way in the end, so I put the bright orange, floral clown suit on along with the red, curly wig and crimson nose and let her smear white paint all over my face. Needless to say, I never did claim one of the prizes for the best costume.

The doorbell was ringing downstairs. A long, continuous ring like the button had gotten stuck. I peeked out the window. It was Alex; he was early. I looked at the clock; no, I was running late. I was a little apprehensive about how I would discuss the happenings between him and Carly the night before. Maybe I wouldn't discuss it at all. It would be easier if I could just submerge those feelings once again. I halfway sprinted down the stairs, opened the door, and then fled to the kitchen to grab a granola bar, leaving him standing in the doorway. He was back to the old Alex: confident, happy, smiling, and most importantly, not shaking. I decided I liked him better this way and bringing up what happened last night would definitely be the wrong choice.

"Do you mind if I eat this in your car?" I asked, envisioning the pile of crumbs I would leave behind in the passenger seat. "I don't want us to be late to school."

"I don't care," he responded as though it truly didn't bother him.

I poured a cup of coffee and put a lid on it, my version of a kiddy cup, and headed out the door with my bag.

"Are you still set on staying home tonight?"

I wasn't sure why he was asking. It was something we had already discussed. We had agreed on watching scary movies at my house. Not that I was overly excited about that either, but it beat dressing up.

"I'm not going to the Masquerade Ball, if that's what you're asking."

"I had something else in mind." His enthusiasm captured my attention. He frequently had that effect on me.

"As long as it doesn't have anything to do with dressing up, I'm in." My mood lifted slightly and all of my apprehension from last night faded. "So, where are we going?"

"It's a little surprise," he grinned.

"You know I don't like surprises, especially on Halloween." He looked at me confused, as if he couldn't figure out how surprises and Halloween fit together at all. "Just a bad childhood experience involving a clown suit. Enough said."

He focused back on the road, a knowing smile spreading across his face.

Anticipation did nothing to help the time pass quickly. I couldn't wait until the bell rang. Listening to all of the chatter about who was dressing up as what was becoming increasingly obnoxious. I had to admit that I was also a bit excited to discover what Alex had planned. By the time I got home, my curiosity was killing me. I had thought about it all day and couldn't come up with anything good enough to match the enthusiasm in his voice.

I sat at the table with my parents, playing with my leftover spaghetti from last night. They didn't seem to notice. They were preoccupied with Halloween plans of their own. My mom seemed just as antsy as I was; she got up from the table without touching her food and began scurrying around the house, trying to put the finishing touches on her and Dad's costume.

"I can't believe you're making me dress up for Halloween," she howled at my father as she stormed off to get ready for the party.

I continued to play with my dinner, spinning the noodles around my fork and then letting them drop back to the plate like a slinky.

"Playing with your food again? You're supposed to eat it . . . with your mouth."

I rolled my eyes and grumbled temperamentally.

"What are you two going as?" The anxiousness that I was feeling was quickly replaced with amusement. I was now holding back laughter as I envisioned my mother dressed as a clown.

"Were going as Shreck and Fiona," my dad replied. I giggled, and he appreciated that I found it funny.

"Your idea?" I asked.

"Your mother's."

"Really? I can hardly believe that."

"I kind of liked the idea of being a werewolf for Halloween. I wouldn't even need a costume," he chuckled as he pointed in the direction of his hairy back.

"Ewhhh!" I shrieked. I was saved from any further discussion on the topic as my mom, Fiona, stood in front of us.

"Arrrh," my dad growled, showing his front teeth, bending his fingers like claws, and chasing my mom around the room.

"Arrrh," he continued.

"Oh stop it, Will." My mom was giggling. It was sickening and beautiful at the same time.

"Arrrh . . . I am the werewolf and you are the damsel in distress," he said as he pulled her to him. My dad was obviously overwhelmed with her beauty, just as I was, and he gave my mother a very passionate kiss that was totally inappropriate for young eyes.

"Okay, okay." I made my best gagging noise. I wasn't sure if I was more disgusted by the idea of a werewolf taking advantage of my mother, or if it was the fact that my dad was kissing my mom.

"Teenagers," my father said.

"Teenagers," my mother repeated, and then they slipped away to get my father dressed for the party.

It was dark when Alex arrived. I grabbed a jacket from the coat tree and threw it on after feeling the chill in the air. There was something about the cold air that brought stillness. The air seemed crisper, thicker, and heavier. I felt like if I yelled, my voice would bounce off the invisible particles making an everlasting echo. He made it to the passenger door before I did.

"Madame." He motioned his hand in the direction of the open car door as he ushered me into his chariot.

We drove down the long, dark, gravel road in silence. He took a left onto the highway, heading into town, in a hurry as usual. He continued on through the center of town, passing all of the shops and restaurants. The lights of the city were now behind us. He slowed down as he took a left turn onto a dark gravel road. As he flicked on his brights, I could see that the road began to twist upward. Finally, he came to a stop in front of a metal gate with a sign that read "Private Property".

"We'll have to get out and walk from here." His voice was filled with strength and confidence, which was more than I could say for myself.

"I don't really think were supposed to be here." I opened the door and climbed out, hesitation in my every move. "I mean, it did say private property, right?" Without a word, he slipped his arm around my waist and together, we walked up the winding gravel road.

"We're almost there."

"Almost where?" I asked as I stared into the blackness. Squinting my eyes, I could now see the words "hot" and "cold" spelled out across two cylinder-shaped structures that stood in front of us, the letters glowing under the stars.

"I'm taking you to one of my favorite places." He stopped in front of a ladder that was attached to one on the darkened structures.

"Are you ready?" he asked. "I'm going to let you climb first. I'll be right behind you to keep you from slipping."

"I don't think so. I don't climb up things," I told him. "Me and heights don't mix. Never have."

"Don't worry about it; you're safe with me," he encouraged.

"What about my shoes? Should I take them off? I can't climb up the ladder in these," I said, referring to the wedge heels I had chosen for our date. I was wishing that I had chosen my All Stars instead. They had served me well for years.

"Take them off if you want. You can just leave them by the ladder."

"Fine." I could see that I wasn't getting out of this. I unfastened the buckle, pulled off my heels, and threw them to the ground before climbing the first rung of the ladder. I was glad it was dark; I couldn't see what was below me. I used my sense of touch instead of my eyes to get me to the top.

"Careful," he cautioned as I neared the top of the ladder.

With the light of the stars shining down on us, I could see the top of what I had been climbing toward. It was an old water tower. I ducked my head under the railing that encircled the structure and waited nervously for him to join me. I held onto the railing for dear life. At this point, I was thinking that I should have opted for the horror movie and popcorn. He effortlessly ducked through the opening and met me behind the rail.

"See, that wasn't so bad," he teased. He wrapped his arm tightly around my waist, and I could feel the trembling start to diminish as I slipped into my safety zone. His face was gentle and reassuring. I felt my independence and my pride fleeing from me for the first time in my life, and I didn't care. I wanted him to be in control. I wanted him to take care of me now. I wasn't sure what was happening. I wasn't scared to lose control, to give in to him. I wasn't afraid to lose the shell that I had worked so hard to build around my heart, the one that had kept my heart from breaking each time I was uprooted as a child, and the shell that softened the pain of losing a sister that I was never allowed to meet. Losing my shell made me feel vulnerable and naked, and without it, even a very small wound could be fatal. I knew this and still, I was allowing the shell to crumble, I was allowing him in. I trusted him with every piece of my heart that I had to give.

"Let's go over this way."

We followed the circular railing to a long, wide, plank that connected the two structures together. Hot and cold water towers, and we were standing on a bridge somewhere in between. We lay down on the plank in between the two towers. The sky was clear and full of stars. I couldn't help but wonder what lie beyond them, beyond our galaxy. I had once read somewhere that astronomers estimate there to be around one hundred thousand million stars in our galaxy alone, and outside of our galaxy, there are millions upon millions of other galaxies. That I rarely think about others isn't something that I like to admit, but when I lay under the stars, I realize that there's something more, something bigger than me, something bigger than this world.

"So, what do you think is up there, just the stars, or do you think there's actually a Heaven?" I asked.

"I think there's a Heaven . . . but what makes you think it's up there?"

"I don't know. That's what I've always been told. Heaven's up there and Hell is a burning pit below us," I replied smartly.

"Everything is so black and white with you. I'll bet you also think there are little angels and demons floating around in the air."

"What makes you think there isn't?" I asked. I was getting the impression that he thought my mind was simple, and I was becoming slightly annoyed.

"It's not that I deny that there's good and evil. It's just that I don't think of it in the same way that you do." He started laughing, a quiet and restrained sort of laugh. In fact, he appeared to be trying his hardest to hold his laughter back. "Have you ever seen those old cartoons where the character is being tempted into doing something bad and there's a little angel sitting on one shoulder and a devil on the other. I think that must be how you see good and evil . . . little cartoon characters."

"That's not very nice." My heart sank.

"I'm not trying to be mean. I think it's beautiful, really. You're so innocent. If you had actually seen evil then you would know that evil isn't the black or white, it's all the grey in-between. It's sneaky and masked; it's deceptive and tricky. It's everywhere, Rae . . . it's darkness. Evil isn't a cartoon character dressed up in a devil's suit. It's the darkness that finds its way inside any one of us if we let it." He paused, looking up into the sky with a blank expression on his face, but I knew that he was thinking about something. I was just about to ask him what was on his mind when he spoke again. "So, do you believe that there's a Heaven?"

"Undecided. If there's a Heaven then there is a god? I would like to believe that my sister is in Heaven. But on the other hand, I have trouble believing in a god that would let Laney die. It doesn't seem fair. So I just wonder if there is a god, then where is he?"

"Someone once told me that life isn't fair . . . and they were right. But I don't think life was ever meant to be fair or perfect. It's not the tragedy, it's how we deal with it. It's whether we come out stronger because of it. It's not about blocking out the pain or hiding from it, it's about letting the pain shape you into someone better than you were before."

"How would you know?" I spat.

"I know what loss is, too," he answered.

"I'm sorry. It's just that's not how it works for me."

"How does it work then?"

"If you can't feel . . . then you can't hurt. I learned that a long time ago. If you push people away then they never get close enough to hurt you. It's easier to just have a shell around your heart."

"Maybe . . . but don't you think that the shell in itself is a bit disillusioning. It may do a good job of keeping the bad out, but it hardly ever lets the good in."

I didn't have anything to say in return. I didn't even want to look at him. I could feel rage building up inside of me and I wasn't sure why. Maybe it was because he was telling me that everything I had done to protect myself had been a giant waste of time. He was telling me that I was wrong. But what really made me angry was that, even though I didn't want to, I could actually see his point.

"Are you mad at me? Don't be mad at me."

"I'm not," I lied. "I guess we can just agree to disagree."

"I guess so," he sighed.

"So, while we're on the subject of Heaven . . . Do you believe in ghosts?" I asked as I swallowed the hard lump that was in my throat. He turned his attention away from the stars and focused his eyes on me. Even with only the glow from the sky, I could tell that the color had drained quickly from his cheeks and his face was now an illuminating white like the moon.

"That depends on how you define the word ghost," he continued without actually answering my question.

"You know, the dead coming back to the earth to visit the living." I gave a perfect dictionary definition of the word.

"Then, I guess I would say that I believe it could happen . . . who knows."

"Well, there have been plenty of accounts of people who have seen ghosts . . . I have a friend who sees ghosts." I swallowed harder this time and once again I knew I had taken it too far.

"Oh, Rae, you and your angels and demons and devils and ghosts." He paused for a moment before continuing. "I guess I would just say that I don't believe that those spirits necessarily fall within your definition of the word." I was silent. I couldn't think of anything smart to say.

"Do you really believe that she sees ghosts?" he asked. The amusement had left his voice and it was now full of concern.

"Yeah, I do," I said with all the confidence I could muster.

"Well, you should tell her to be careful. As I told you before, not everything is what it seems," he warned

"Careful of what?" Now I was scared. He ignored my question and changed the topic; for this I was grateful.

"Have you ever seen a shooting star?" he asked.

"No, not ever," I admitted. Staring at the stars was one of my favorite nightly pass times. I would often look up at the blanket of stars, because it made me feel safe and secure. It didn't matter what part of the world I was in, when I looked up, I always saw the same sky with the same moon, the same constellations with all of their eternal brilliance. It was the only thing in my life that stayed the same and the only thing that brought consistency to my ever-changing world. I felt small under the huge umbrella of stars, but I had never seen one fall. I had never made a wish.

"Look up there." He pointed with his finger directly above us, tracing an arc shape with his finger in the dark, night sky. And then, as if the star had received its cue, it fell from the sky like a puppet whose strings were being pulled, following precisely and without hesitation the map that he had made for it. I stared at the sky, sure that my eyes were playing tricks on me.

"Did you make a wish?" he asked, his question confirming what I had seen.

"How did you do that?" My voice was shaking.

"I guess I have a few tricks up my sleeve," he laughed, with no intention of answering my question. "Make a wish, Rae," he urged.

"I wish. . . . "

He stopped me.

"Not out loud. It won't come true if you say it out loud."

And so I made a wish, a wish that I would keep locked within my heart for an eternity. A wish that I would tell no one until it came true. And if it didn't, the wish would fall from the broken heart that held it like the star that fell from the heavens.

# CHAPTER THIRTEEN

$N$either one of us spoke as we approached my house. His mood was strange, a bit sullen for a perfect night under the stars. I was sure he had something on his mind, and it appeared that he had no intention of telling me what it was. The car was silent, and he pulled onto my gravel drive unusually slow. He put the car in park and turned to look at me. His expression looked torn, as if he were trying to decide between two options, each one equally damaging.

"Is . . . everything all right?" I hadn't planned on getting out of the car until he told me what was bothering him, but when he didn't answer, I reached for the latch to open my door. He pulled me gently back to him. He leaned closer and kissed me softly. His lips pulled away slightly, lingering on mine before he pressed them back again. It was quiet inside the car; the sound of every breath we took was amplified. I could hear the sound of the leather below us as we inched closer to one another. My body was beating together with his, our hearts beating at the same tempo, blood flooding through our veins, sending warmth and redness to our cheeks.

The darkness was interrupted as my parents turned on the front porch light. In an instant, he was someplace far away. He was staring out of the front window and his fingers were gently tapping the steering wheel. There were so many things that I wanted to say, so many things that I wanted to ask him, but couldn't. I turned to face him, the light from the front porch illuminating his face, and his dewy eyes sparkling like jewels. I desperately tried to take in enough air to fill my lungs, enough air to mutter out the words, "I love you," but he beat me to it.

"I love you, Rae."

"I love you, too," I said. "I'll call you tomorrow."

I grabbed the latch and opened the door, not sliding one foot out before I heard his honey like voice.

"Rae," he spoke with urgency.

"Yes."

"Goodbye, Rae," he whispered, his voice still quivering.

"Goodnight," I corrected him.

I climbed out and shut the door silently to avoid attracting my parents' attention. My cheeks were still blazing red, and I desperately wanted to avoid seeing them in the condition I was in.

The coast was clear, but I took off my shoes so I wouldn't make any noise going up the stairs. I lay in bed thinking about him, about how I had found the one. He loved me despite my oddities. Nothing seemed to scare him away. He was the one, the one I would spend the rest of my life with. I wanted to start the rest of my life right now. Nothing could keep us apart.

The bright sun streamed in through my window, shining directly onto my face and waking me before I was ready. My blinds were open, allowing the light to pour in, and I grumbled to myself for not shutting them before I went to bed. I glanced at my clock without moving. It read 10:00. I rubbed my narrowed eyes. I slid out of bed and shivered. It was finally beginning to feel like winter, and I threw on my robe before starting down the stairs. The house was quiet, and I breathed a sigh of relief. I sauntered into the kitchen, pulled a box of cookie crisp from the pantry, and poured some into a bowl. The kitchen was filled with the smell of coffee, but the pot was empty; they hadn't even saved me a single cup. I felt grouchy. I ate slowly as my eyes focused on the window above the sink. Little crystals had formed on the glass overnight. I opened my mouth wide and breathed out heavily, watching as the cold air made my breath visible. My parents had forgotten to turn on the heater. I shivered again and then made my way over to the coffee pot, tinkering with it a moment before deciding that it looked too complicated. I marched back upstairs, showered, blew my hair dry, and dressed before dialing his number. It rang twice before going to voicemail; I flipped it shut without leaving a message. Then I stared at my phone for a moment, toying with the idea of trying again; instead, I set the phone at the far corner of my bookshelf so that I wouldn't be tempted, flopped down onto my bed, and closed my eyes.

Something had been tormenting me since the day my mother met Alex. It was something about the look on her face that I couldn't force from my memory. Every time I shut my eyes, her fright filled the darkness behind my closed lids. I couldn't explain the fear that I saw on her face; it was an irrational, undeniable, undeserving fear. It was when I saw this look for the second time, the afternoon Carly had come to visit, that I realized I had seen this expression before, long before I met Alex. It wasn't until this moment that I realized the circumstances under which I had seen it. It was the same look that I saw on the eve of my eighth birthday, when my mother caught me with Laney's scrapbook, when my mother ripped Laney's bright, white funeral program from my fingers. It was the reason I vowed to never speak to my mother about Laney. And then, like a bolt of lightening it struck me. I realized the look I saw in my mother's eyes was not fear; it was pain. A deep and haunting pain that she couldn't bring herself to face. And still, I was unable to connect the dots. I lay for a moment longer on my bed, my mind filing through different scenarios to explain Alex's peculiar behavior the night before. I was becoming slightly annoyed that he could be affectionate one moment and so distant the next. I was pulling myself up off my bed when I heard the garage door open and my parents noisily enter the house.

When I walked into the kitchen, I found the two of them in an unusually chipper mood. It did little to pull me out of the funk that I was in.

"We brought you a latte," my dad said with a smile.

"Thanks," I replied, trying hard to disguise my look of satisfaction.

"Did you see our prize from last night?" my mother asked proudly.

"No . . . should I have?" Cynicism rang in my voice.

My mother cleared her throat, walked over to the fridge, pulled off the king-size, handmade ribbon and laid it in front of me.

"What's this thing for?"

"We won the prize last night for the best couples costume."

"Great . . . it's about time someone in our house had a good costume." My voice was full of sarcasm.

"Rae!" my mother said, surprised.

"Did someone wake up on the wrong side of the bed?" My dad chuckled. "A late night will do that. If you like, we could discuss the fact that you missed your curfew last night," he said, his voice more serious than before.

"I was home at 11:30, Dad. Technically that's thirty minutes before curfew," I responded smartly. My dad's eyes widened. He looked taken aback by my sour disposition.

"Perhaps you would like to go up to your room until you can talk nicely to your mother and me."

I shrugged my shoulders, grabbed my latte, and turned in the direction of the staircase without saying another word. Silence had replaced the previous chatter. It was so quiet that I could hear their thoughts, and I was burning inside because I knew they were right. I was being a grouch and yet, I couldn't bring myself to say I was sorry.

"Oh!" My father's voice rang. "I forgot to ask if you know a girl named . . ." I turned to face him just as he was glancing down at the morning paper that was resting on the counter, scanning an article with his finger. "Ah, here it is. Claire Kirpowski . . . do you know her?" His eyes were now focused back on mine, waiting for me to answer. I wondered if it were some sort of trick question.

"Yeah, her locker is next to mine. I don't actually know her," I responded coolly. I desperately wanted to rush over and rip the article from my father's fingers, but I didn't. I stood still . . . motionless . . . waiting. He didn't say a word. He looked back down at the article. The suspense was killing me.

"Why?" My feet were still planted in the middle of the kitchen floor.

"She was in an accident last night at the school dance." His eyes had replaced his finger in scanning the article.

"What happened?" I kept my voice flat and even to mask my concern. They both studied me for any sign of emotion. I held steady, my feet unmoving, my arms folded across my chest, my eyes hollow and indifferent. Finally, he spoke.

"The article makes it sound as though something fell from the gymnasium ceiling. According to the article, whatever it was, fell right on top of her."

"Like streamers and balloons?" I scoffed.

"No . . . like it was some sort of sound equipment, a speaker or something."

"Is she okay?" I could hear the beginnings of emotion in my voice. I bit my lip.

His finger returned to the page, scanning to the bottom of the article.

"She was released from ER with a concussion. That's all it says . . . I guess it could have been worse." He walked over and held out the paper. I grabbed it and turned once more in the direction of my room.

I flopped back onto my bed and thought about the Masquerade Ball and Claire. Even though she was still ignoring me, I was truly sorry that she had been hurt. I thought about the first day of school and how she seemed to befriend me. Her demeanor had changed so quickly from hot to cold. I then began to make a mental list of all things hot and cold.

1. Claire

2. The erratic weather in Oklahoma

3. The water towers

4. Alex . . . Alex . . . Alex . . . so hot one moment and so cold the next. What was it that he was hiding? What was it that he couldn't bring himself to tell me?

I waited until almost one o'clock before I dialed his number again and still he didn't pick up. I grabbed a book off the shelf, one that I had already read, and began to submerge myself in the lives of others. The weekend passed without a word from Alex. I had only dialed his number on two occasions to keep from looking desperate, and then, to no avail, I waited for him to call.

It was on Monday morning that I awoke unusually early from a dream. It was a disturbing dream, not a nightmare, but wrenching none-the-less. Not a single detail escaped my memory. I dreamt of Alex; he was standing on the bridge at the park. When I awoke, I could still sense the silence from my dream, the same silence that surrounded me as I watched Alex cautiously step onto the bridge. When I awoke, I felt the darkness that had engulfed me, and I remembered how my eyes narrowed in pain as I stared into the light that divided the structure in two. With each second that passed, Alex was drawn closer and closer to the light, further from the darkness . . . further from me.

His features transformed as he neared the light. He became a beautiful, pearlescent figure, a lustery silhouette, and then he was gone.

When I awoke, I could still feel the pain as though the pain was real. I was still shaking and I felt the coolness of stale tears on my cheeks. I wiped them away and sat up. The dream left me hurting and aching, my heart was still throbbing. I glanced over at the clock; it was 6:00 AM. Thirty more minutes until the dead bird would sound, a thought that would normally cause me to doze back off, but this morning, the idea of falling back into my dream was frightening. It still seemed so real. I sluggishly showered, dressed without thought, and headed downstairs to eat breakfast.

"You're ready early," my dad said as he looked at his watch. I shrugged my shoulders without saying a word.

"You feeling okay?" He seemed only slightly concerned as he poured me a bowl of cereal.

"I can get my own cereal, Dad, I'm not two," I spat, my tone of voice on the hateful side.

I reached in the fridge and pulled out the milk, pouring it clumsily over my bowl and spilling more on the counter than I poured over my breakfast.

"Are you sure you're not two?" he chuckled.

"I'm glad I amuse you," I said dryly.

"You fell asleep last night before dinner. You coming down with something?" he asked as he felt my forehead with the back of his hand.

"No fever," he reported, "Don't even think about asking to stay home."

I rolled my eyes and began to shovel down my cereal like I hadn't seen food in a week. Finishing, I poured myself another bowl, watching my dad's eyes look at me with the approval. He loved to see me eat. It reassured him that genetics was the reason for my ultra-thin frame.

I continued to sit idly, listening to the *tick tick tick* of the tiny cuckoo clock that hung on the wall in the kitchen. Each tick of the clock brought back memories of my family's time in Germany. The clock was a souvenir that my father had chosen; we were allowed one souvenir per country. I had lived in eight countries, so I had a collection of eight priceless trinkets. The only rule was that they had to be small. Our first day in a new country was always the same. We would find a tiny, furnished apartment tucked away in an unsuspecting part of town and then we would select our tiny souvenir. It became a ritual, and I found it comforting to know that this was the one thing in life that I could count on. In Italy, I had chosen a small, silver, jewel-studded cross. In Paris, I picked out a poster from the Musee de l'Orangerie that boasted Monet's garden. In Amsterdam, I selected a small, yellow, wooden bird that had hung in the window of the little shop near our apartment. When I saw the bird, I knew I had to have it. I couldn't deny my reasons for choosing the bird. The bird reminded me of me; it was a tiny creature in constant flight.

*Tick. Tick. Tick.* He was late. I called his cell but there was still no answer, so I begrudgingly drove myself to school.

Each class drug on and on; I could barely focus on my two favorite subjects. Art and English usually captivated me. I hadn't realized what an effect Alex's presence had on me until I had experienced his absence. Was I really this desperate for him that my life was meaningless and drab without him? My painting in Bradley's class was coming along. I loved to add depth to the canvas by painting in layers and using many different mediums. Today, I was adding yet another layer of light creamy hews with a palette knife to accentuate his angelic face. I highlighted his eyes heavily with a charcoal pencil to reveal the pain that I had seen in my dream last night and the pain that my heart felt when he was gone. Despite my previous embarrassment, there was no hiding the subject matter of this abstract piece, and when the bell rang, I didn't even bother to push it to the back of the supply closet. I wanted everyone to know the feelings I had for Alex. One day without him and I felt like I was losing him for an eternity.

I was loitering in the closet with the supplies, admiring the face I had painted, when I heard feathery footsteps behind me. I jerked quickly around, astonished to see Bradley making his way toward me. Logic told me that he could walk because he had to get to and from school some how, but up until this point I had never seen him leave his chair. He habitually shouted instruction from behind his desk. I watched as his emaciated body moved slowly and painfully in my direction. I had always sensed that he had a soft heart behind his gruff exterior, and as I saw him limping toward me, I wondered if his sternness stemmed from the pain he felt in his joints as he moved.

"Your work is good, Rae. It shows feeling." I had never received such a compliment from him, and I could feel my gloomy day almost begin to brighten as he boosted my ego.

"Thank you," I replied staring at my feet. I knew he was harmless, but still I had no desire to look him in the eyes.

"Will you still be able to finish it without the subject present?"

My body stiffened and my chest tightened. I couldn't breath. I placed my canvas up against the wall and moved past him without saying a word.

Once in the hall, I pulled my phone out of my bag and dialed Alex's number; this time, it did not go to his voice mail. A woman's voice on the other end informed me that his number had been disconnected. I flipped it shut and tried again. Once again, the same woman's voice indicated that I had reached a number that was no longer in service.

My concern was waining and I could feel anger replacing my compassion. I planned on letting him know his rudeness had not gone unnoticed.

I rounded the corner to my locker, my mind was swirling with thoughts, when an idea came to me. I stopped short, turned around, and marched to the office with a spark of hope in my hollow eyes. My mind was swirling with different stories that I could tell the office secretary in order to get information on Alex's whereabouts. I opened the door to the office. It was large and very organized with several ladies sitting behind the front desk. Chairs lined the walls forming an L-shape around the front part of the room. I noticed there was a line, so I took a seat in one of the uncomfortable, wooden backed chairs. Conversations of students were fading in and out until my eyes landed on a tall girl in the corner who was talking with the secretary. She was dressed in jeans and a long, puffy style coat. Suddenly, I began to tune in, my ears straining to hear their conversation. The girl was discussing the transfer of her records. She was moving, that much I could gather without making it too obvious that I was eavesdropping. I held my bag in my lap and pressed it against my chest. I was unaware of how hard I was squeezing it until I felt a dull throbbing against the upper part of my rib cage and realized that my biology book was jabbing me. I unclenched my fists from around my bag and tried to calm myself. Only now, at the final second, did I begin to fabricate a story that would get me the information that I needed. I couldn't believe that I had resorted to lying. Is this what love had done to me?

"Can I help you?" the office secretary asked as she looked at me and then looked back down at her paperwork.

I pushed myself up off the chair and headed to the counter, just as the brunette in front of me was finishing up. As she whipped around, my eyes widened. She was looking directly at me, her eyes blue like mine, but icy and cold. Her eyes pierced me, and I shuddered as a wave of coolness rushed over my body, chilling me to the bone. She flipped her hair and walked gracefully from the office. It was Chloe. I glanced around at the now empty room and felt a sense of relief that no one would be witness to my embarrassingly awful ability to tell lies.

"Can I help you?" The secretary was beginning to sound impatient. I gathered my thoughts, cleared my throat, and headed to the counter.

"Um, I was just here to pick up homework for Alex Loving. I think his teachers were supposed to send it here." My voice quivered, making it sound more and more unconvincing by the second.

The secretary, whose tag read Connie, was thin, so thin she was sickly looking. She had short, brown hair that was permed, and I wondered who would have agreed to perform such a hideous act on her hair. If you could somehow compare the career of a hairdresser to that of a doctor, giving a perm would definitely fall under the umbrella of malpractice. She looked up from her stack of papers with a confused expression on her face.

"I believe Alex Loving has moved. All of his paperwork was transferred several days ago." She twisted her body around and was now confirming with another staffer that Alex Loving had indeed permanently checked out. There was a lot of chattering back and forth before she turned to face me.

"Yes, I'm sorry for any misunderstanding, but he is no longer enrolled here," she told me, the look of confusion still consuming her face.

"Can you tell me where he went?"

"I'm sorry. I wish I could help you."

I could have been very proud of myself at that moment for telling a lie convincing enough to get the information that I needed, but the only emotion I felt at this moment was pain and it rose from my heart, filling my face with some awful sort of expression.

"That's okay, um . . . thanks."

I ran out the door, racing to my car before the tears could spill from my eyes. I fumbled with my keys but finally opened the door to my car just as the floodgate was let down, releasing years worth of tears, tears that had been pent up against their will. I thought that the shell had made me stronger, better, indestructible; instead, it had made me weak. I had neglected my feelings for too long. I had forgotten how good it felt to cry. For years, I had not let my body have what it craved most . . . healing. And then I realized that I was no longer crying only for Alex; I was crying for the loss of a sister that I never knew and had never allowed myself to mourn. I was crying because of the differences that separated me from others; the differences that isolated me and made me lonely. I was crying because deep down, I knew what Alex's departure actually meant. It meant that I was alone again, this time without a shell to protect me. So quickly I remembered the salty taste of a tear from my childhood and how sweet it felt to let them fall, how each tear had a temporary, but magical way of erasing the pain. I was fully exposed, a turtle without a shell. And even though the earth was still a truly miserable place to live, I was going to have to face it.

I walked through the door to my house. My mother could immediately sense my hollow mood, and I was sure she was getting tired of me flip-flopping through my emotions. Up until this point, she had lucked out, she had never experienced the rollercoaster ride of emotions of which a teenage girl is capable. Before Alex, I had been so even-keeled, dark and distant perhaps, but even-keeled. But, of course, she had my shell to thank for that. Now that the shell was gone, well . . . there was no telling what emotions I was capable of. I was beginning to surprise myself.

# CHAPTER FOURTEEN

*I* can remember how life felt before Alex. It felt decent enough at the time. Dull and colorless maybe, but decent. Even though I had always felt like there was something more to life that I was missing, I didn't know any different. The pit that I felt in my stomach each morning had become just another part of who I was. Life without him was far worse. Alex made me feel true happiness and peace for the first time. Not knowing if I would ever see him again made the pit in my stomach come back with a vengeance. School was torture; the days seemed to drag on. Alex had left me alone with my heart and my eyes wide open. Everything that I felt was magnified and my world without him was blindingly painful.

Everything in my life had become a duty. My parents became little more than an obstacle that I tried to avoid as I darted to and from my room. Months had gone by. Fall was turning into winter, and the trees had shed their leaves. They looked cold and dead without their beautiful foliage. All my free time was spent in the park by our bridge, rain or shine. The hope that he would magically appear filled my subconscious. Art class was something I longed for; my masterpiece had become the last shred of evidence that he existed. Most days very little work was done. I would stare at the eyes in the center of the canvas, wondering if I had imagined them. My mood was sullen. I was completely unaffected by the look of concern in my parents' eyes. I was happiest now in my sadness. It consumed me.

I remember the day well. It was December twenty-first, the first day of winter. It was on that day that I could undeniably feel my mother's pity for me. I had yet to tell my parents that Alex had moved, that he had left me behind. I guess I was afraid of my mother's reaction. I felt as though she would be pleased by such news and the thought of that made the pain even stronger. When I got home from school, my mother was sitting in the kitchen, waiting on me. I could tell by the look on her face that she wanted to talk, and I could tell by the look in her eyes that I could in no way escape this situation.

"Do you want to sit down and have a cup of coffee, Sunshine?" My mom's idea of coffee was powder out of a small tin labeled with an Italian name that you added hot water to.

"Sure, as long as you don't try to psychoanalyze me," I responded coolly.

"I promise that I won't. While we're sitting at this table, I am a mother, not a shrink."

"Okay, then." I reluctantly agreed. I was hoping that if I sat down with her for a minute or two and told her what she needed to hear that she would allow me to escape up to the lair which was my bedroom.

"You doing okay?" She seemed frightened to dig any deeper. I knew what she really wanted to ask.

"I'm fine," I said, trying to sound as convincing as I possibly could. My eyes followed her to the stove where she poured some hot water into a mug and gently stirred in the powdered mixture.

"You haven't been yourself lately," she continued as she walked back over to the kitchen table. "Your father and I are starting to worry about you."

"Alex moved," I said bluntly and then took a sip of my Café Vienna. There, I had said it, and I was surprised how easily it had come out. I was surprised by how good it felt to let those two little words roll off my tongue.

"I'm so sorry." Her voice sounded hollow. "I hadn't seen him around . . . I wondered what had happened."

"I'm sure I'll survive."

"Maybe it was for the best." Her voice was flat and cold.

"How can you say something like that? Could you not see how happy I was when he was around?" I was speechless. I was fuming. "Look, it was more than obvious that you didn't like Alex. I saw the way you looked at him. You've always told me that you want nothing more than for me to be happy. He was what made me happy."

"It wasn't that I didn't like Alex," she paused, audibly exhaling before she reached for her mug and took another sip of her Café Vienna. "He seemed perfect for you. He seemed to really care for you."

"Then what . . . what was it about him that made you so uncomfortable?"

"His name," she spat. "His name reminded me of something that happened a long time ago. When I heard his name, it brought me to a painful place. It really had nothing to do with him at all. It was my problem, my pain . . . it was my fault and I'm sorry." She looked more relaxed now that she had spoken. It was like a weight had just been lifted from her shoulders. "You know, everyone has skeletons in their closet. Some people try to get rid of them and others just shut the door and pretend as though they don't exist. I can't bring myself to get rid of the skeletons that live in mine. I feel pain knowing that behind that door, they still exist, but I'm afraid that even greater pain will come if I let them leave." She cleared her throat. "Enough about me. Are you doing okay? I mean, now that he's gone. Do you want to talk about it?"

"Sometimes I feel like he was never actually here, like he wasn't real. It all seems like a dream. I just want to close my eyes so that I can be in that place again."

"I do know what you mean. After your sister died, things changed. We left A-Omega and we did what we could on our own. I did my best to take care of you, but there were just some mornings that I couldn't pull myself out of bed. Your dad did everything. But when I slept, when I dreamt, all of my pain disappeared. It was a full seven years before your father and I decided to return to A-Omega."

It had been a long time since my mother had spoken of Laney. She had a painful expression on her face, but her eyes were soft and warm, and I could tell that she was in a good place.

"I wish I could have known her."

"You reminded me a lot of her as a toddler. Even though the two of you looked like night and day; her with blond pigtails and you with raven, black curls."

"Does it ever get better, after you lose someone you love?"

"No. But you have to decide if you want to let that emotion control your life, and you have to decide if you want for that pain to consume you. I couldn't handle the pain on my own; I had to hand all of that pain over to something more powerful than myself."

"Like what?"

"God." Her answer seemed so simple, and yet, so obscure. I wouldn't believe that one three-letter word could answer all of my questions and solve all of my problems. It just wasn't possible. It was such a cliché answer. God was an answer that people gave when they didn't know the right answer. God was the answer that people gave after they had already given up.

"That's it? Did it work?" I forced a smile to hide my skepticism. Besides, tears were forming in her eyes, and I didn't want to make matters worse.

"It's a continual process. I ask him to take the pain from me every morning. There are some mornings I don't feel that I can get out of bed. It's a choice that I have to make. I think God is more than willing to help those who ask, but regardless, He's there to catch us if when we fall."

"If God is so good, then why would he have let you experience so much pain? It makes me think that we're alone, that maybe there is no God." I glanced over to my mother who was trying her hardest to not look crushed. I expected to see more tears, but her eyes had gone from moist to completely dry in an instant.

"It's the dark times that help us grow toward the light. It's hard to see a candle burning on a sunny day, but on the blackest night, the candle becomes your only hope. You can either sit in darkness or you can find your way out. I chose to find my way out." She finished her sentence just as my stomach was beginning to growl. I pressed it hard with my arms folded tightly across my abdomen.

"Are you hungry?" she asked, glancing down to my stomach.

"I didn't eat lunch." I looked at her with a knowing expression, preparing myself for her motherly words of wisdom.

"You can't afford to miss a meal, Rae. You're skinny enough as it is."

"Well . . . what's for dinner tonight? I can cook," I offered.

"That would be perfect."

"What sounds good?" I had already gotten up and started rummaging through the fridge.

"I laid out some hamburger." She pointed to the sink where the meat was thawing. "I wasn't really sure what I was going to do with it."

"Do we have everything for lasagna?" I was already pulling ingredients from the refrigerator, relieved that we had finally changed the topic of conversation.

"I think so."

I fumbled through the cabinets looking for the right sized mixing bowl. I felt awkward around my own mother. Was it because I was sharing things with her, because I was opening up? I felt exposed and vulnerable. Had my shell really made me that hard, that insensitive? My mom started mixing the eggs in with the ricotta and Parmesan. I began chopping up the onion. My eyes were beginning to water and my nose burned.

"Mom, I can do this." I sniffled and wiped my eyes with my sleeve.

"I want to help," she smiled, trying to hide the small amount of pride she felt for getting me out of my room for more that five minutes. "So, do you think maybe we should head up to your room and tidy it up a little after dinner?" I stopped chopping and looked at her in a way that let her know she had taken it too far.

"I'm sorry, one step at a time," she said. She hesitated. The mixing stopped, the talking stopped, and she stared at the counter with purpose.

"Rae, I know what hurt is, and I'm not talking about your sister. I know what it feels like to have a broken heart. I've been there and it seems like a hole too deep to crawl out of some days, but you will find your way out." When she looked up at me, she seemed a bit wiser, more like a friend than a mother. I had never stopped to consider her anything other than my mom or my father's wife. I had neglected to look at her as a person, with real feelings and real hurts. It had never occurred to me that she might have actually had a life before she had me or before she met my dad. I didn't know what to say. I felt incredibly selfish.

"Oh." My eyes focused on the counter. I was ashamed of my own self-absorption.

"Well, it was a long time ago."

When I finished assembling the lasagna, I covered the casserole dish with a piece of foil and slid it into the oven. My mother was staring out of the kitchen window as though she were in a trance. Sometimes, I wondered if she were imagining a different world on the other side of the glass, a world with Laney instead of me. I grabbed the plates out of the cabinet and began to set the table.

"So, where's Dad?" I asked as I set his place.

"He'll be home any minute. He had a meeting that was running late." She pulled the silverware from the drawer beside the oven and began placing it on table.

"Well, dinner's in the oven. I might take you up on that offer to tidy up my room. Do you think we'll even be able to open the door with all of the clothes on the floor?"

"We'll see." A small smile flashed across her face and she nodded her head in amusement.

When we opened the door, it was like I was seeing it for the first time. It was disgusting. I couldn't believe that I had allowed myself to live this way. I couldn't believe that I hadn't noticed it until now. I'm surprised she had let it go on this long.

"Rae, I do not know what I'm going to do with you." She ran her hand through her short, brown hair. "When was the last time you did a load of laundry?" she asked, her voice somewhere between irritation and disgust. She had already begun sorting through the dirty clothes, putting them in piles of lights, brights, and darks.

"Um, maybe a couple of weeks," I lied.

"I didn't know you had that many pairs of underwear to get you through." She looked horrified.

"Don't worry, I'm not that hopeless. Wal-Mart is just a couple of miles away and they do sell underwear."

"Okay." The disturbed look was only partially removed from her face.

"I'll do better . . . I promise." And in a way, I thought that I actually might.

I could hear the beeping of the timer; the forty-five minutes we had spent in my room looked futile. It was still a huge mess.

"Well, this is a work in progress." My mother looked at me hopefully. Hopeful for what, I wasn't sure. Hopeful that I might straighten up or hopeful that I might allow her more of this mother-daughter time that she had been so deprived of.

"You know, Rae, you can talk to me about anything. There's nothing you're going through that I haven't experienced for the worse." Her eyes glistened, becoming wet with tears. "I love you more than anything . . . you know that, right?"

"I know."

It felt amazing to finally be able to say I knew without a doubt that my mother loved me unconditionally. I think that somewhere in the back of my mind I suspected that my mother resented me, that maybe I was the cause of Laney's death and that she blamed me. I still couldn't bear to ask her how it was that Laney died, but I could tell by the way she spoke to me that she loved me. She didn't blame me, and for now, that was all I needed to know.

That night, I lay on my bed watching the ceiling fan spin my yellow bird in vicious circles. She was in constant flight, spinning without direction and out of control. I wished that somehow I could set her free. I wished that I could give her rest.

## CHAPTER FIFTEEN

*T*here's no denying that my life began to change on that hot day last August, the day I met Alex. So much had happened since my first day at school: I had fallen in love for the first time, I had learned to live, I had experienced true happiness, and last but not least, I had allowed my shell to crumble. It was as if all of these events had happened in slow motion. If I had woken up on that cold day in March knowing what I know now, I would have held on for dear life, because on that day, my life was getting ready to change at a much faster and more dangerous pace than before.

It all began with a dream. A dream I hadn't had since that warm fall day when Alex found me asleep on the blanket by the bridge. Much like the others, it was a dream where I found myself on a path that stretched out long and flat for miles with tall grass surrounding me on either side. In my dream, the air was thick and quiet, making it difficult to breath. As usual, a stranger joined me on the path; his features were still blurred and distorted. With every step I took, he seemed to take five, thus approaching me at lightening speed. I stood frozen as I stared into his dark and determined eyes, unable to move. I felt my neck beginning to tighten and swell. The stranger was surrounded in a halo of light. I shut my eyes tight; the light was blinding. When I opened them, the light was gone and the dark eyes were replaced with the most beau-tiful, green eyes I had ever seen. They looked like emeralds, and yet, I could-n't see the face that held these priceless jewels. I wanted this being to wrap me in its arms and protect me. I reached out to touch this inviting figure but my fingers grasped only air. It was gone and I felt empty. I felt sad. I felt lonely. I awoke.

I ran my hand through my damp hair. I could feel a warm tear burning on my cheek and wiped it away with the palm of my hand. My throat ached, not just when I swallowed, it was a constant burning accompanied by a dull throbbing. My alarm clock read 5:30. I rubbed both eyes and drug my tired body from my full-sized wrought iron bed. Despite the darkness of the dream, I felt unusually cheerful that morning, unlike every other day since Alex left.

When I stepped out of the door that morning, I immediately noticed a thick blanket of snow lay across the ground and how the air smelled fresh and crisp. There wasn't enough snow to make a snowman, just enough to be pretty. The roads had already been plowed, but some of the slush had refrozen, leaving spots that were dangerously slick.

Cautiously, I pulled onto the highway that led into town. I hadn't gone far before I noticed a snow covered car pulling off the gravel shoulder and onto the road, now directly behind me. I slowed to a near crawl, motioning with my hand for the car to go around. They slowed, but held steady a measura-ble distance from my bumper. I motioned again to the driver, this time more visibly, waving my hand outside the cracked window in the icy morning air. The car stayed close behind. The driver had no intention of passing.

My heart was beginning to race. I took a couple of deep breaths, the air was still cold inside the car and I could see my breath. I shivered, my gloved hands tightening around the wheel as I focused on the road ahead.

I looked into my side mirror. Two headlights beamed dimly behind me in the hazy, morning light, and I wondered if perhaps I was being followed. I pushed harder on the gas and the snow-covered car behind me sped up but did not pass.

I pressed harder. I could hear my tires spinning beneath me, grasping, searching for even the slightest amount of traction to keep them on the road. The car that was tailing me was closer now. I glanced in my rearview mirror, hoping to catch a glimpse of the driver, but the warmth of my breath in the cold car had left the mirror foggy. With my gloved hand, I wiped away the tiny droplets of water and squinted my eyes. The tint on the car behind me was illegally dark, not a chance of seeing in. The car was approaching closer and closer and then, without warning, I felt myself being pushed from behind; the slightest tap on the bumper launching me forward, my tires spinning wildly, my hands holding steady on the wheel, my foot pumping gently on the brakes.

I couldn't believe they were trying to run me off the road. I felt incredibly helpless. I eyed my bag that was resting in the seat beside me, then reached my hand blindly inside to feel for my phone. Just as I grabbed it, I felt my car being slung forward, catapulting across the ice, but this time, the tires were not able to regain their grip on the road. My body flung back in my seat. The rear of my car swung to the left and the front end followed like a dog chasing its tail. My car was spinning fast, but my world was now in slow motion.

It was a solid sheet of white outside my window as I spun, as if a swirly white blizzard had spontaneously formed. I counted the spins: one time around-I wondered if I would hit the telephone pole up ahead, two spins around- I shut my eyes tight and prayed that I would land in the ditch instead, three spins around- I wondered if it would hurt. My life was flashing before my closed lids, images advancing through my mind like the pictures on the View-Master toy I played with as a child: my new house, my parents, the scar on my mother's arm, Cocoa, the sea, beautiful mountains, sandy beaches, fairy tale castles, Alex at the lake behind my house, Alex kissing me, Alex standing on the bridge in my dream, and then, on the fourth spin, it stopped . . . there was nothing. My car had come to a standstill on the edge of the road. My hands were still clinched tightly around the wheel and I opened my eyes slowly, preparing for the worst. My head was spinning and my heart was beating heavy beneath my puffy, black ski jacket when I saw the car in question moving slowly past me. And then, like a switch had been turned on, I felt strong and invincible. My breathing slowed as I gripped the cold handle of my Honda and opened the door, finding the bravery to stare my assailant in the face.

What my intentions were, I'm not exactly sure of, but within seconds of climbing out of the door, my body froze. I was unable to move. It wasn't that I was standing ankle deep in a drift of snow. I was frozen solid because of what I saw at this new angle, what I couldn't see from inside my car, what I couldn't see when my pursuer was behind me. It wasn't a car that was tailing me, it was an SUV, a thin layer of snow covering it; spots of shiny silver peeked out and sparkled in the now emerging sun. As the SUV continued slowly past me, I caught a glimpse of the license plate. Snow had melted away from plate, clearly revealing the letters F-O-R-C-E, and my chest cramped. The silver SUV that sparkled beneath the snow revealed the same personalized plate that I had seen on the first day of school. It had been at least four or five months since I had last seen this shiny, silver Range Rover and now it appeared out of nowhere, driver still unknown.

I was late getting to school and soaking wet from sloshing around in the snow. My hands were still trembling as I opened my locker.

"What happened to you?" I was shocked by the monotone voice that came from beside me; it had been a while since Claire and I had spoken, more like months.

"It's been a long morning," I answered, struggling to control my anxiety.

"You're all wet. Did you get in a snowball fight before school?" she scoffed.

"No, someone tried to kill me, that's all," I answered dryly.

"Well, I can see why you're so upset. It all makes sense now."

"You think I'm kidding?" My anxiety was changing quickly into anger. I looked at myself in the mirror hanging inside my locker and stared into my own big, blue eyes. A film of fluid had collected over them almost instantaneously, weighing heavily on my lower lids, about to spill over at any moment. I shut my eyes tightly and counted to ten before opening them to stare at the face that everyone seemed to hate. I had never been popular, this much I knew, but so far no one had ever tried to kill me.

"Oh," she said in a hushed voice, her eyes beginning to sparkle with interest. "What happened?"

I explained to Claire the events of the morning, and she seemed captivated with every detail; that is until I described the SUV that ran me off the road and the personalized license plate that read F-O-R-C-E. She looked taken aback; the curiosity that was previously on Claire's face twisted into a something that resembled disbelief.

"The car you're describing . . . that's Chloe's car. Chloe moved in November . . . that was four months ago, Rae."

I was silent. My mind was cranking round and round, trying to sort through this new information. What Claire said seemed logical; Chloe had moved and I remembered the exact day that she did, the day that I saw her in the office, the day I found out that Alex was gone. It had been four months since I had seen Chloe or Alex or the silver Range Rover. All of my suppressed emotions were beginning to surface, and without another word, I grabbed my math book, shut my locker, and walked quickly to class.

All morning my head was spinning. What started out as a single theory quickly snowballed, linking previously separate pains and circumstances into one enormous and messy clump. I scrawled out my thoughts with a purple gel pen onto a piece of ruled paper in hopes of gaining a bit of clarity.

Chloe HATES me

Alex's shoulders stiffened when he saw Chloe in the hall. Do they know each other?

Chloe transferred schools just days after Alex

Chloe's silver Range Rover ran me off the road

Chloe is still in town

Is Alex still here too?

I studied the list. With my thoughts scribbled out in front of me, I could now see them in a different light, consider things I had never considered. Of course, I was still bent on finding out why Chloe ran me off the road, but in the process of searching for this answer there was something more that I hoped to find. Had it been a coincidence that Chloe and Alex had transferred schools just days apart? It was an idea I had toyed with on occasion, and even though I felt silly and a bit paranoid for considering such a thing, it was a theory I would no longer discredit. Was there some sort of link between the two? I wasn't sure, but for the first time since Alex's departure, I felt purpose. It was a purpose with two parts: one of which was to find out what Chloe's interest was in me and secondly, but most importantly, I hoped that where I found Chloe, I might also find Alex. I knew it was far-fetched and unreasonable, but it was the only thing that was keeping my heart beating at the moment.

I swung by my locker after third period and found Claire shuffling through a stack of papers. When I approached, her eyes moved from the stack she was holding in her hands and focused on me. I exhaled audibly, not bothering to turn in her direction.

"Looks like you've dried off a bit," she smirked as she glanced around the side of her locker door, looking me up and down.

I shrugged my shoulders without saying a word. My indifference seemed to spark a bit of interest because she continued to study me. She had a different look about her. She was shining with curiosity and excitement. I couldn't relate. My chest was still throbbing. I was sure that I had an indentation of the letter "H" in the middle of my sternum from the emblem on the steering wheel of my Honda Accord, and my feet were finally thawing, leaving my boots damp and soggy. I was in no mood to dance around the topic at hand. I needed answers and at this point I didn't mind asking.

"You said that Chloe moved . . . do you know where?"

"No," she said. Her eyes moved back to the stack of papers in her hands and she began to shuffle through them once again.

"You were friends with her, right?"

"Um, not so much." She had an uncomfortable look about her.

"Look. I'm sorry if I caused some sort of rift between the two of you. If I did, I didn't mean to."

"It wasn't entirely you fault," she said with a smirk.

"I know that Chloe didn't like me, I mean, that wasn't hard to get."

"Don't take it personally. Chloe doesn't like anyone."

" I just never thought that she hated me enough to want me dead."

"Well, you could have passed for Chloe's twin, you know. But you're prettier than she is. Maybe she's jealous."

"Jealous enough to commit murder? That seems a bit extreme."

"I suppose. Oh, I know! I don't know why I didn't think of this before." Claire looked up from the stack of paper. "Maybe she wanted Alex for herself. She stared at him all of the time. I mean, she couldn't keep her eyes off of him. Couldn't keep her eyes off the two of you together. That would explain why she left just days after he did."

"Okay, you are not helping."

"Sorry," she apologized, but she didn't sound like she meant it. "So what are you going to do?" Her eyes were flickering, sparkling, and I could tell that she trying her hardest to come up with a plan.

"I don't know. I'm sure that you have a suggestion."

"I do, actually. You could drive by her old house and see if she's still there," she offered. "I mean, if you knew where she used to lived."

This was something I hadn't considered and where it would take me, I wasn't sure, but it was a starting point, and the only inkling of hope that I had.

"And if by chance you know someone that is an office aid, myself perhaps, then maybe that someone could see if Chloe's files are still stashed away somewhere."

"You would do that . . . for me?"

"Let's just say that Chloe and I never really saw eye to eye. Besides, she tried to kill you; that's the least I can do. I'll see what I can find and then I'll meet you at the Book Nook after school. You know where the Book Nook is, right?"

I nodded without saying a word and watched Claire bounce quickly away.

Claire no longer seemed cold and distant. She had warmed. Something changed in Claire's dark, brown eyes that morning. It was something I hadn't seen before, something I hadn't counted on. That something was intrigue. She found hope in my story, a glimmer of excitement in this small, prairie town. And whether or not she knew it, we both now shared the same determination. The darkness was reeling us in; begging us to play its game. A game that was probably dangerous, but the challenge made it all the more appealing.

I arrived at the Book Nook after school; there was no sign of Claire. The store was filled with the aroma of crisp paper and brewing coffee. I could get lost for hours in the aisles of books and that's just what I needed right now to distract me from the waiting game I was forced into playing. I quickly found the mystery aisle and glanced at all of the new releases. I opened each one and read the jacket before I decided on one that fit my mood, which was sneaky and invincible, a very deceiving and dangerous combination. I walked over to the café, paid for my book, and ordered my usual latte with three Splendas, non-fat milk, and my new added detail of light foam. I couldn't stand when they handed me a cup half filled with foam instead of the warm, mocha colored liquid that I craved.

I opened my book, hoping to read a chapter before she walked through the doors. After only finishing the prologue, I looked up and saw Claire's jet-black hair breeze past the top of the science fiction aisle. I waved her in my direction and she scampered toward me, her hands already searching inside her backpack.

Her eyes were dancing with excitement as she pulled a piece of paper from her bag.

"Well?" I asked with a bit of impatience.

"Chloe's files weren't exactly transferred to another high school when she left Bartlesville," she said, pushing toward me a piece of paper that revealed a long list of dates. She pointed to the last date on the paper, it was November, the first week in November. It was a week that brought back painful memories. It was the week that Alex left me.

"Are you saying that she dropped out?"

"It looks that way." Claire paused. "The part I don't understand is how she got into the Bartlesville School System to begin with. Look at the address at the top of the page. She's from Tulsa. She's been attending Hollbrook Academy since kindergarten."

"What's Hollbrook Academy?"

"It's just the most expensive private school in Tulsa."

"Maybe she got into some trouble and her parents wanted her in a different district, who knows."

I picked up the paper and took a closer look. I glanced at the address and I was shocked and a little confused, but not as confused as I was when my eyes drifted up several lines to the date that was typed neatly at the top of the page.

"Forget the address. Look at the date above it."

Claire pulled the paper closer so that she could see.

"She was born in '88? She's two years older than we are? She flunked?" Claire had a confused look about her.

"I don't know." I turned to the second page of Chloe's transcript and carefully counted each year and the perfect grades that followed.

"Did you not read this all of the way through?" My expression was no longer able to hide my surprise.

"I skimmed it."

"Well, you missed the best part. Chloe was the valedictorian of her graduating class. She hardly flunked." Right now I was thinking about how it would be better for me if she had. At least there would be a reasonable explanation for her presence. Chloe couldn't keep up with the academic pressures of Hollbrook Academy. Private schools were tough. I knew from experience. But even on paper Chloe was perfect which left only one explanation: Chloe was in Bartlesville because of me.

"So she couldn't get enough of high school, or what? I mean . . . I can't wait to get out of this place."

"You and me both."

"Shouldn't she be at Harvard or something? It looks like she has both the grades and the money. Just one of her shoes cost more than my entire wardrobe. I don't know why she would want to be hanging out here."

"How did she get in? That's a better question. It's not typical to be readmitted to high school. Especially after graduating with honors."

"You'd be surprised the things that money can buy," Claire snorted. "So, for reasons that we are unsure of, Chloe Pierce drove two hours out of her way just to repeat her senior year. That doesn't make any sense. And now she wants you dead. This is crazy."

"Pierce?" I paused, swirling the thin, wooden stick around in my coffee.

"What?"

"Her last name is Pierce?" Somehow I already felt like I knew her better. She was no longer just the dark and mysterious girl who didn't like me; she was no longer the dangerous girl who was following me in the snow. She had a last name, and that made her seem more human, and that made me feel even more invincible.

"You didn't have to do this, you know."

"Well, I have a favor to ask. I was kind of hoping that I could come with you if you decide to go by her house. Would you mind?"

"Of course not. I'm ready to go now, if you want," I said eagerly.

"I can't tonight. Let's go tomorrow after school. Besides, there's just one more thing I need to show you." I could hardly imagine anything better than this.

"Just let me know if I'm crossing the line here. I thought that, while I was at it, I would check into Alex's files. I hope you don't mind. I was in the office that day when you came in asking about him. I also know that he and Chloe seemed to come and go around the same time," she said with hesitation, as if she had most certainly crossed the invisible line and was now standing directly on top of my toes. I didn't mind. My heart was pounding now and all traces of invincibility had vanished. I felt weak, helpless, and sick to my stomach.

She pulled another sheet of paper out of her bag and pushed it in my direction. I struggled to read the words in front of me. I was reading, but without comprehension.

"What does this mean?" I asked after studying the paper for a moment. It was basically blank. Only his name, address, and three months worth of records from Bartlesville High School were printed on the single sheet of paper.

"I don't know," she said helplessly

"There has to be more than this. His files should indicate where he transferred from; they should say where he went." I could feel tears burning behind my eyes and I tried to hold them back. Claire squirmed uncomfortably in her seat. I took a deep breath, still fighting the urge to sob. I had hoped that seeing this paper would make me feel better, that it would put everything to rest, and that it would allow me to move on. Now, every single emotion I had felt was magnified.

I lay on my bed trying to sleep. Thoughts of Chloe were now put on the back burner as I focused on how the love of my life had vanished into thin air. The tears that I had tried to hold back this evening were released and I buried my head in the pillow and let the wetness fall from my eyes without control, without caring.

## CHAPTER SIXTEEN

*T*he phone rang, waking me, leaving me startled and confused. It was still dark outside. I looked at my clock and it read 3:45. There was something about the phone ringing in the middle of the night that sent fear running through me. Immediately, I took myself back to a night last May when my father was on assignment. A young girl had been found in a rundown building in De Wallen, a red-light district in Amsterdam, and needed immediate medical attention. My parents hadn't told me much, just that she was really sick and scared and Dad was going to help to make her safe. I remember how I thought that it sounded like an explanation for a two-year-old. When the phone rang late that night, my mother was informed that my father had been taken to the nearest hospital. There had been an explosion in the building my father had been called to. He had been in the alley behind the building when the bomb went off and even though he hadn't been hurt, I can remember feeling angry. Not angry at him, but at his job. I couldn't imagine why one girl's life was more important than my father's. I knew that it was selfish, but he was my dad.

The phone rang once more before it stopped. I waited, wondering if one of my parents had gotten it. My parents' bedroom was downstairs but I could still hear them, their voices carried up over the balcony and into my room. I slid out of bed and sat in the carpeted hallway that looked down over the living room. I nervously ran my fingers up and down the spindles of the balcony, straining to hear their conversation. I rubbed my swollen eyes and put a hand on my pounding head. It took me a second to remember why my eyes were so puffy to begin with, and then, the sickness swept across me as if I were entering into the pain again for the first time. I could hear my father's voice, the click of the phone setting back onto the cradle, the sound of two voices softly whispering and finally, crying; the soft muffled cry of my mother. I eased down the stairs and knocked timidly on their already opened door, announcing my presence.

"Who was that?" My voice was laced with concern. I felt sick. I wasn't sure that I wanted to know the answer.

"That was Papa. Irene had a stroke and she's in the ICU." He spoke quietly. I could hear my mother, still crying a muffled cry beside him.

Ever since I could remember, my father called my nana Irene. Of course, I always called her Nana, but I had to admit that I loved hearing him say her name. Irene. Irene. Irene. I could say her name a thousand times and never get tired of hearing it.

Irene . . . Serene . . . Pristine.

Her name was something immaculate and safe, a place to hide when you were scared, a fluffy, white cloud that formed into a pleasing shape, and a shelter to escape the coming storm. I could see her lying in the hospital bed with needles and bags of saline and machines with loud, beeping noises.

Irene . . . Machine . . . Saline.

Her name no longer sounded immaculate. I no longer felt safe . . . I felt scared.

My mother was choking back sobs. Of course, I knew she was grateful that this didn't occur while we were living overseas, but I think she figured there that would be more time until something like this happened. We hadn't even been back a year.

"Is she going to be all right?" I asked hopefully.

"She's stable; we're going to drive up tomorrow morning to be with her and Papa."

I knew he was hesitating, fearful of upsetting my mother.

"You'll be missing some school, Rae. Why don't you go on back to bed and let me take care of Mom," he suggested.

"Okay," I hesitated before walking over and kissing the top of her head.

The last time I saw Nana was in July, just after we made the move to Oklahoma. It was the first time that I felt emptiness inside the walls of her pink and white kitchen. Nana was still there, her body anyway, but her mind was somewhere far away, somewhere nobody else could go. On the night before we left, I was lying in bed when Nana walked into the room, the far-away expression had disappeared and for a few moments I had my Nana back. She slipped into bed next to me and I ran my hand down her silky, grey hair.

"Do you want to hear a story, Sunshine?"

"Yes."

"It's a sad story, but it has a happy ending. Do you still want to hear it?"

"Yes."

"Okay, then. Once upon a time there was a little girl by the name of Irving. She lived in a tiny town with her daddy. Not a single brother or sister and her mother had died while giving birth. So, you see, it was just the little girl and her daddy. But her daddy was a mean man, and he did mean things to the little girl. At night, she would pray to God for an angel to come and take her away from her daddy, but an angel never came. As she grew older, her daddy grew more violent and her prayers began to change. She prayed for a bolt of lightening to come down out of the sky and strike her daddy on the head, because she was a scared little girl and she didn't know any better than to pray a prayer like that. After years of unanswered prayers, the little girl's heart grew as hard as a rock and she could no longer feel the pain. She stayed like that for quite sometime. As years went by, the little girl turned into a woman and, without meaning to, fell in love for the first time. But there was one problem that she didn't know how to fix. She found it very hard to love when she had grown so hard. When she tried to open her heart once again, all of the pain from her childhood came rushing back.

"One night, after her father had drunk himself to sleep, Irving packed her bag, snuck out of her bedroom window, and hopped into her boyfriend's truck. She thought that the further she got away from that tiny town, the faster her heart would mend. She thought that she could leave the pain behind, but she couldn't. It didn't take long before that young man asked

Irving to marry him and of course, Irving told him 'yes' because she loved him very much. 'Surely,' Irving thought, 'marriage will cure my broken heart once and for all.' Irving married that young man and he loved her with every last bit of his heart, but Irving's heart had yet to change. She just knew that love would save her, and it was true, there was indeed a portion of her life that her husband had saved. But no matter how good his intentions, he could never fix her heart. Less than a year later, the couple discovered they would be expecting a baby, and while the young man was filled with joy, young Irving was terrified to raise a child when her heart was still as a stone inside her chest. One very cold morning late in November, before the baby came, Irving wrapped an old, yellow blanket around her shoulders and went outside to watch the sun rise. It was on that morning that Irving's heart was healed. As the sun rose in the sky, her heart opened up and no longer hurt. She felt a peaceful, wavelike ripple through her body, and it was at that moment she knew God was there for her. At that moment, her heart was healed. And although she didn't understand her past or why it had happened, it was the first time in her life that she felt stronger because of it. She felt a newfound strength in her heart and that strength spread from the tips of her fingers to the ends of her toes. You see, the man in her life could only save part of her, and when she was finally ready, God was able to save the rest."

The far away look had returned to Nana's eyes, but for a moment, while she was speaking, she had come back and I knew with all of my heart that she had come back just so that she could tell me that story.

I couldn't fall back asleep. I had never really considered sickness and death to this degree. I never realized how much it would hurt. Maybe it was because no one close to me had ever been sick in a life threatening way. Of course, our family had experienced tragedy, but I had never lost someone that I loved. My parents had lost Laney, but I had never experienced that type of loss, not really . . . I never knew her. Life was something that I had always taken for granted. Some warm tears squeezed their way through my already swollen eyes and rolled down my cheeks. I began making a mental list of all the things that I needed to tell . . . to ask Nana.

I was scared to see her now, so frail and sick in a hospital room. I was also scared to see Papa. I knew the hurt he felt would show in his eyes. I didn't know what I would say to him, what would be the right thing to comfort him. I had always expected them to be there, in their little house doing the things they always did. The tears were falling harder now, and I quietly sobbed into my damp pillow.

The next morning, I awoke to the smell of breakfast cooking. I ventured downstairs, unsure of the mood I might find. My eyes felt swollen and foggy from the tears the night before, and I rubbed them trying to clear my vision. My mom was cooking, which wasn't a good sign.

"How are you?" I asked.

"I'm good, considering everything," she said while flipping the pancakes and turning the bacon. The kitchen was a mess. Flour covered the countertops, measuring cups were stacked beside the electric mixer, and eggs dripped down the side of a metal bowl.

She set down the spatula, grabbed a wooden spoon, and began to stir the eggs around in the nonstick skillet.

"They're not scrambling," she panicked, shaking the pan on top of the stove.

"Helps if you have the gas turned on," I said, noticing the knob was in the off position. I walked over and twisted the knob, hearing a click click click before the flame ignited and began to heat the pan.

"Let me do this," I told her as I fought to get the wooden spoon out of her clinched hand.

"Fine." She surrendered, loosening her hand and sliding onto one of the bar stools facing me.

"Have you heard from Papa yet?" I wondered.

"He called this morning. Nana's doing better. She isn't talking, but she is able to move her right hand a little. The doctors are hopeful, but they're just not sure how long it will take for a full recovery, or if a full recovery is even possible."

"What time are we leaving?" I was trying to determine how much time I had to gather my things, make arrangements for someone to pick up my assignments, and call Claire to tell her our plans for tonight were off. The plans that seemed so insignificant now.

"In a few hours. Dad tried to call the school this morning, but they didn't answer. Remind me to try them a little later."

"Where is Dad?"

"He went to the neighbors to see if they could watch Cocoa while we're gone."

"Oh," I said as I handed her a plate of food and then grabbed two pancakes for myself, skipping on the bacon and eggs, and headed up to my room to pack and call Claire.

The car ride was quiet, so I stared out the window, admiring the trees and the early spring flowers. Only a trace of snow was left from the day before.

Today, the weather was warm, a mild sixty-three degrees. Once again, I was reminded of all things hot and cold. The pure beauty of it brought a bit of order to my chaos. The many different shades of green that lined the road had replaced the barren trees of winter. I was learning about different types of trees in AP biology. There are trees that winter cannot change called conifers. They hold strong through the dark, cold spells. Their growth is slow and steady. Then there are deciduous trees that cannot tolerate the cold. They lose everything during the winter, everything that makes them beautiful. But spring always brings them back, stronger and more deeply rooted. It is like they are being given a second chance. Nature is so simple and perfect. I thought about how humans are much like trees; some stay strong through pain while others break. If Papa was a tree, I wonder what kind he would be. Would he stand strong through Nana's sickness, or would he lose himself during this dark time? I knew my papa; he would stand strong.

Nana was still in the ICU. Papa met us in the lobby. The atmosphere was cold and unwelcoming, and the smell of sickness made me feel lightheaded and my knees began to buckle. I felt nauseated and jittery. Cold beads of sweat were forming on my forehead. I took the nearest seat in the lobby. All of a sudden, I didn't want to go back to her room. I was scared of what I might find. I was scared of finding someone I didn't know lying in the bed, someone who had changed beyond recognition. I was scared of seeing the Nana I did remember, sick beyond repair. I felt helpless . . . HOPELESS. I held my head between my hands and breathed deeply . . . in and out, in and out. I listened to doctors talking to nurses, nurses talking to families, families crying, families pleading, families mourning. I stuck my fingers inside my ears. I didn't want to hear. If I didn't hear, if I couldn't see, then perhaps this would all go away. The hospital would go away and I would be lying on my bed, waking up from this nightmare. I didn't want to feel. Peeking between my fingers, I watched Papa and Mom walk back to Nana's room. All was not clear. All was not well. I wished that I could tuck myself back inside my hard and comfortable shell . . . but it was gone.

Slowly, my dad walked over to me, his head was low and he sat down sluggishly in the chair beside me. He was quiet for an uncomfortable moment before he spoke.

"Nana's not doing so well, Rae." His head was down, still not making eye contact. It surprised me that he had called her Nana.

"But, I thought that she was doing better this morning." My voice crackled and pleaded.

"After Papa called this morning, she had another small stroke, they have increased her Coumadin, but she isn't responsive. They've asked us to say our goodbyes."

"How long do they think she has?"

"They're not sure. Nana and Papa had both decided that if anything like this were to happen, they didn't want tubes and machines keeping them alive."

"But I'm sure there's something they could do to help her, to make her okay." I was pleading again.

"Rae, Nana's lived a long and happy life. Papa has accepted it. He said that Nana knew it was her time. All week she had been talking to him like she had only hours left to live."

"Do you believe that? You know, in that sort of thing? That someone can tell when they are about to die." I had never actually considered it, maybe because I had never lost anyone before. To me death just seemed like the loss of a person, you know, the body. But when I listened to my father's words, Nana's death seemed more like the passing of a soul, a soul that was going on to live for eternity, a soul whose body was too weak to hold it anymore and the thought sent warmness and unexplainable peace throughout my body. I felt a warmness that wasn't present when Carly spoke of the dead. When Carly spoke of the dead, it seemed cold and uncertain, like a spirit in limbo with no real place to rest. With Nana, it truly seemed as though her spirit would go some place final, some place better. It felt like hours that my mom was at Nana's bedside before she came out. She looked shaken, but I could see acceptance in her saddened eyes. She came and hugged me tightly, laying her head on my shoulder.

"She's gone, Rae. I just wish I would have had more time with her. I wish I would have had a warning that this was going to happen." Her voice held regret for all of the years she was away from Nana and Papa. How long had they been so frail, how long had they needed her help? "I guess time just has a way of slipping by. You should go back and see her. She looks peaceful. I don't think she felt a bit of pain," Mom swallowed hard, her eyes were wet with tears.

"Did she know you were there with her?"

"I think so. Why don't you go back with Dad," she suggested.

Nana's room was quiet. All of the machines had been unplugged and the IV had been removed. She did look peaceful, just like Nana always did. It was something that I had tried to prepare myself for, but looking at her lying in that bed brought out all of my emotions at once. I felt so much at the same time. I felt sadness and grief. I had unanswered questions. I was feeling things that I had never felt before and considering things that I had yet to consider. I could feel the cold, winter wind blowing in my direction. The light was fading. The days were becoming shorter and darkness was settling in. Would I ever be the same after experiencing this loss? Would my mother ever be the same? Would her face light up again after all of this sadness? I needed her face to light up again for me. It felt like I had weights strapped around my ankles as I walked over to my nana's bed. Each step taking more work than it should have. I touched her hand. Her skin felt thin like tissue and it was already cold to the touch. I ran my hand down her silky, grey hair and then I kissed the top of her head. "Nana," I whispered into her ear. "Life hurts, Nana. Where do I put the pain?"

Mom and Papa stayed at the hospital to take care of the necessary paperwork and to begin making arrangements for the funeral, while Dad and I went back to Papa's house to take care of anything we could there.

I sat down on their olive green, velveteen sofa, the only sofa I could remember them having, and I began to turn through the pages of an old scrapbook. So many pictures of my mother; she was so young. I loved my nana's scrapbooks. She lined the pages with pictures, scribbles of dates, places, thoughts, and old letters were haphazardly tucked into envelopes and stuck to the pages. Her scrapbooks told a story. Each page was filled with emotions, laughter, and tears. It brought me back to that time as if I had lived it right along side her. I continued to flip through the pages, now approaching my mom's high school years. I studied a picture of my mom and her older sister Eva leaving with their dates for the senior prom. My mom was wearing a lacy, baby blue gown. Her sister was wearing a much tighter fitting, purple dress that looked beautiful with her wavy, charcoal colored hair. Eva's eyes were bright blue like my mother's . . . like mine. I didn't know much about my Aunt Eva, other than that she had died years ago. My mother didn't talk about her sister much. Once, when my family was visiting my grandparents and I was sitting on the sofa looking at the exact same picture, I asked my mother what my Aunt Eva was like. "She was the black sheep of the family."

That's what my mother told me, and I remember my nana getting mad. "She may have chosen the wrong path, but at least she found the right one before it was too late," Nana corrected my mother. They didn't look much alike, except that they shared the same blue eyes. I had never understood until this moment why I looked so completely different from my mother and father. I had even questioned whether or not I belonged in the Colbert family. But as I studied the photo of Eva, I realized that I more closely resembled my aunt than either one of my parents. I had her almond shaped eyes, her wavy, black hair, and her nose. And there was something about the expression on her face that I found in mine when I studied myself in the mirror. It is a strange thing how genetics work. I continued to flip the pages through my parents' wedding, laughing at their attire and their hair. I turned to the next page and let it sit open, unsure what I was looking at. It was Mom, Dad, and Laney, of this I was certain. I had seen a picture similar to it before. They were wearing the same clothes, and Laney was around the same age, but this was taken in a different spot. In this photo, they were standing in front of a glistening lake, surrounded by tall trees. It was a place that I had never been and a place that I had never heard them speak of. I read the notes that Nana had scribbled.

Sue, Will and Laney. September 13th, 1990 — Alexandria, Minnesota.

Alexandria, Minnesota. Alexandria, Minnesota. I repeated the words silently, over and over again in my mind. Those two words, they sounded so familiar to me, yet I was sure I had never been there. The rest of the book was filled with pictures of me ranging from the age of one to the age of seven. I flipped to the last page, which held a picture of Mom, Dad, and I waiting outside a hotel with a mountain of luggage. Under the picture, Nana had scribbled out a few words.

Sue, Will, and Rae leaving for London.

Sadness swept over me. I knew the present and the future stopped for Nana when we moved overseas, but I had never felt it like this before; I had never stopped to consider her loss. It was as if her memories had ended with the final page of the scrapbook.

I set the book aside and went back into the kitchen to help my dad fix dinner. He wasn't fixing anything fancy tonight: chicken and dumplings with some veggies, the perfect comfort food.

"Dad, what were you and Mom doing in Minnesota?" I asked, hoping he would be able to fill in all of the blanks.

His face turned white as a sheet, not the reaction that I was expecting or hoping for.

"I was just looking at Nana's old scrapbooks," I offered, hoping that my reasoning might bring a little bit of color back to his cheeks.

"Oh." My father turned his still pasty face back toward the pot on the stove. Without saying another word, he returned to stirring the pot of dumplings with a long, wooden spoon. But I couldn't let it go.

"Did you go there a lot?" I asked, still trying to determine why that town seemed so familiar to me.

"No, just the once." He was still stirring the pot gently, making sure the dumplings didn't stick to the bottom.

"Humph." I wasn't even partially satisfied.

Later that night, Mom, Dad, Papa, and I were sitting in the small living room reminiscing, remembering Nana in all of her glory. I sat next to my mom on the green, velveteen sofa. I couldn't help but think of the last time I had spilled my heart to Nana, about a year before her memory started to go. I remember what she was wearing that day: a pair of tan Bermuda shorts that showed off her long and slender legs. Her skin was taut for her age, but her arms sagged underneath and jiggled a little when she walked or when she was stirring a pot on the stove. She was wearing a solid white tank top, and I could see the softness of my nana's arm wiggle as she whisked some of the hot, chocolate pudding into the eggs that she had cracked into a bowl beside the burner, tempering them before she returned the mixture to the saucepan on the stove. It was the July before I turned sixteen, and Nana was making me a chocolate pie for my birthday. My grandparents always celebrated my birthday in the summer, because they never actually saw me in September, when my birthday actually fell. On that particular day, it was smoldering outside, too hot to go to the pond and fish with Papa but just right to play a game of solitaire at the table and watch Nana cook. The window unit in the kitchen was turned on full blast, blending the smell of Nana's Shalimar, the freshly cut roses on the counter, and the chocolate pie filling on the stove into one delicious and intoxicating fragrance. As usual, I had something on my mind and under normal circumstances, that something would have never escaped my lips. But I was in my nana's kitchen, and there was something about that kitchen that coaxed me into speaking. Once a year, I would fall apart on her kitchen floor and with a few simple words, she could always put me back together.

"I think my parents hate me," I told her. "They love their jobs more than they love me. All we do is move around. I have no friends and they don't even care. I think they've sold their souls to A-Omega."

I could no longer hear the sound of the whisk beating against the saucepan, but I felt Nana's eyes hot on me even though she didn't say a word. I was staring at the hand of cards I had dealt myself. All of my aces were on the table. I picked up the two of hearts that sat face up on one of the stacks and placed it on top of the corresponding red ace in front of me. The card under the two was still face down so I flipped it over. It was an eight and I couldn't play it, so I started to shuffle through the cards in my hand by threes. I was stuck and I knew it, but I didn't dare look into Nana's eyes and so I continued to flip through the cards without purpose.

"You know nothing about selling your soul. You should never throw around words like that." The tone of Nana's voice was foreign to me. The soothing voice I was so accustomed to was now stern and almost angry.

"There is a time in life when you must protect and a time in life when you must fight. Someday you will understand that your parents are doing both. It may be a year from now or it may be ten, but one morning, you will wake up and realize that you are called to do something and it will most certainly be something difficult. If you watch and learn from you parents, Rae, they will teach you everything you need to know."

And with that, Nana turned back to the stove and began to stir.

I wish that I had asked her what she meant. I wished that I hadn't made her mad. The angry Nana was not the Nana I wanted to remember. I wanted to remember her golden skin and how it smelled like baby oil and perfume. I wanted to remember her silky, grey hair that she kept in a short bob. But most of all, I didn't ever want to forget her voice, how it was so soothing and her words so filled with wisdom.

"Remember the time Mom wanted you to pull out those ratty, old bushes in the front yard? She had asked you for months and you said you'd get to it. Remember you came home one evening from work and she had a chain on the back of the truck with the other end tied around those awful, old bushes."

"She always was a determined woman. She always said if you want it done right, you've just got to do it yourself," Papa chimed in.

"She pulled them out, too. Sometimes I think her spirit was too big for her tiny frame."

They burst into laughter and quietly, I got up off of the sofa and slid my bare feet across the shaggy rug to the back door. Just as my hand grasped the door handle, my mother began to recall another hysterical Nana moment. I stood still with the door cracked only an inch and listened. I needed to hear one last story of the Nana that I remembered, something that I could bottle up and save forever.

I stepped out of the door into the cool, night air. We hadn't set our clocks forward yet, so darkness was still coming early. Quietly, I shut the door behind me and was alone, just me and the stars. I looked at the blinking objects as they hovered over me. They were so tiny, and yet I was the one who felt incredibly small and insignificant. It was the first time I had been alone under the stars since Alex had taken me to the water tower. I felt close to him for the first time since he left, and I wondered if he, too, were lying under the stars somewhere tonight.

"Are you here, Alex?" I whispered quietly, knowing how foolish I sounded. And of course, there was no response.

"Are you here?" I whispered again, this time with desperation in my voice. I heard nothing but the rustle of new spring leaves being blown by the Missouri wind. Out of the corner of my eye, I saw something shiny like a jewel shoot across the sky and then another and another. They continued to fall until I swore I had seen at least eleven or twelve. I lay in awe, remembering Alex tracing the perfect arch in the sky, a map for the star that burned through the atmosphere. I remembered the wish I had made that night and wondered if it had fallen through the crack in my broken heart. I had wished that Alex and I would be together forever, that nothing would keep us apart.

Although the first eighteen years of my life were far from perfect, I had never wondered why. I had never asked my parents how Laney died or how my mother had received the large scar on her arm. I had never questioned their careers nor had I ever asked them exactly what it was they did. Maybe I was afraid that they wouldn't tell me. Maybe I was afraid that they would. Regardless, I had dealt with life in my own way and it was working well . . . until Alex came along. With just one look, he softened me. With one kiss, he melted me down and formed me into someone new, someone I no longer recognized. Life no longer looked the same. My eyes and my heart were open and for the first time in my life, I was now questioning everything . . . eighteen years worth of questions that I needed immediate answers to. I lay in bed, tossing and turning. I wasn't exactly tired, but in a quiet, dark house without a TV, what is one to do? Something was bothering me, and I couldn't leave it alone. The words "Alexandria" and "Minnesota" were ringing over and over again in my mind. The pallor on my father's face when I asked him about the tiny town did little to curb my interest. I got out of bed quietly, walked into the living room, and crept over to the sofa where I had returned the scrapbook several days ago, being careful not to wake anyone in the process. I carried it back to my room and turned on the lamp beside my bed. I let it fall open to the page of my parents and my sister standing amongst the beautiful trees and the lake of crystal. Alexandria, Minnesota. I studied the photos for a moment before noticing a small envelope stuck to the top of the page. I hesitated before opening the envelope and unfolding the tattered letter that was stuffed inside. I took a deep breath and began to read, hoping to find an answer to the question that was eating me alive: What was it about this place that seemed so familiar?

*September 10th*

*Mom,*

*Sometimes I wonder how you and Daddy did it for so long. I love what I do and I owe that to you and Daddy, but I have never been one to patiently wait. One step at a time has never suited me and yet, I have a career that requires me to do just that. For the past five months, Will, Laney, and I have had the luxury of a much-needed sabbatical. As you know, we were in the process of preparing for our upcoming assignment in January. But that is what I have written to tell you. We have received correspondence from A-Omega that the date for the assignment has been moved up. We will be leaving tomorrow. I am scared. All of this is just coming so fast. I wish that I could have your faith right now because I cannot see how any of this will work out. I have never had such a bad feeling in my entire life. I am sorry to say that, even though you and Daddy are still actively involved in A-Omega, I cannot disclose the location of our assignment. You have every right to know and I am very sorry. You have been waiting for this moment just as long as I have. I do not know how long we*

*will be gone and I'm afraid that our only correspondence will be by mail.
I will write often and keep you as informed as I possibly can, but A-Omega
has made it clear that the details of this assignment are confidential. The
mission depends on it. I love you. Tell Daddy I love him, too.*

*Sue*

I glanced down at the picture once again, this time taking note of the
details, and I immediately felt coldness spread through my body. I had seen
a picture like this before in the scrapbook at my parents' house. Little Laney
was wearing the same short-sleeved heart top and blue jeans, and she had the
same curly, blond pigtails. It was the same Laney that Carly had described.

Just days ago, when I had been flipping through my nana's scrapbook, it
was the name of the town below the picture that seized me. But now, after
reading the letter, it was the picture that captured my attention more than
anything else. The picture looked different to me. Dangerous. I couldn't help
but wonder why Nana had tucked the letter from my mom into an envelope
on this particular page. Was the letter in some way linked to the picture? I
studied it, re-reading it. Nothing was adding up. My parent's career. A-Omega.
Secrets in which my mother could not divulge, not even to Nana. This letter
did nothing to appease me; instead, it only left me wanting more. My parents
had secrets that I knew nothing about. I folded the letter carefully and, as I
was sliding it back into the envelope, found another piece of paper. I pulled
it out to find that it was another tattered and worn looking note. Once again,
I carefully unfolded the piece of paper and began to read.

*Dear Charlie and Irene Roth,*

*It is with our deepest sympathy and regret that we write to inform you of the tragic events that occurred on the night of September the 13th.*

*As you were previously informed, your daughter Sue, her husband Will, and your granddaughter, Laney, were on assignment with A-Omega. We are certain that you were informed of the complications that could potentially arise, as the date of the mission was moved forward by four months. Late last night, the Colbert family was involved in a fatal car crash while on assignment. Your granddaughter, Laney Colbert, was killed by the impact of the collision. Your daughter, Sue Colbert, is being held in the ICU and treated for internal bleeding and lacerations to her right arm. Will is doing well and following orders to keep this assignment confidential. There were ten individuals involved in the accident on the night of September 13th, but only three survived. The package entrusted to Sue and Will was beyond repair, but the contents of the package were saved and, despite the gravest of circumstances, the objective of the mission was carried out. Sue and Will are under strict orders to remain silent about the assignment and their present location; however, we at A-Omega will keep you well informed.*

*We thank you for your patronage and your faith. You will be greatly rewarded.*

*Arm yourself well,*
*A-Omega*
*Ephesians 6:10-18*

I now knew why my parents had always been so secretive about the scar on my mother's arm. I knew the accident that had left the scar on her arm was from the same accident that killed my sister Laney. What I didn't know was that my mom felt responsible. What I didn't know was that she not only felt remorse for the death of my sister, but for six other people who died that night. It wasn't just a scar; it was the memories the scar brought back. I remember tracing it with my finger when I was little and she would grimace as if it hurt. I now realized that it wasn't a physical pain. I closed my eyes and let images flash through my mind. My mother's scar. The picture of Laney. The sickened look on my father's face when I mentioned Alexandria, Minnesota. And then, the number thirteen. All at once, my eyes popped open. I was considering something that, just moments ago, I hadn't considered. It was not a coincidence that my nana had placed the letters on this particular page. The picture and the letters were connected. They were connected by dates. Countless times I had looked through Nana's scrapbook. Why had I never noticed this before? But there was still something eating away at me. Something didn't add up. Hastily, I dug through my bag and pulled out my notebook and purple gel pen. What I did know was that there were four events that occurred on September 13th, 1990 and, without wasting any time, I began to scribble down the facts in shiny, purple ink.

- The picture was taken in Alexandria on September the 13th
- The car crash on September 13th happened while my parents were on assignment with A-Omega

- September 13th was the day that my sister died.
- September 13th was the day that I was born

I stared at the list, unable to finish the puzzle. Very important pieces were missing and without them, I would never learn the answer to my original question. Why did the town of Alexandria seem so familiar? What I concluded was this: based on the dates in Nana's scrapbook, Alexandria, Minnesota, was the destination for the assignment. A chill fell over me, little pins and needles creeping over every inch of my skin. In the letter, my mother had told Nana that she was scared. That she had a bad feeling. She had been right. My sister died in Alexandria. That explained the pallor on my father's face. But there was still one bit of the puzzle that I could not place. If Alexandria, Minnesota, was the destination, if the letter from A-Omega was correct, and if the mission had ended in tragedy on the night of September 13th, then that put my mother in Minnesota on the night that I was born. My chest felt tight. I couldn't breath. I was born on the night of the accident. I was born in Alexandria. There was no way that I could have been born in Missouri. My head was now throbbing. My parent's had lied to me. But why? Who were they trying to protect? Themselves? Me? A-Omega? I had not been looking to answer any of these questions. I had simply been looking for the answer to one and only one question and still, nothing could explain why the name of the town sounded so familiar. My parents hadn't mentioned it. In fact, it seemed quite the opposite. For the past eighteen years, they had done a very good job of keeping not only the town, but also the events of September 13th buried beneath a stack of lies. But still, my mind echoed the name Alexandria. I closed my eyes and tried to sleep, but the wheels continued to crank round and round. It was as if someone was whispering it in my ear, pushing me to think harder, and encouraging me to move forward.

Alexandria . . . Alexandria . . . Alexandria . . . and then it stopped, and then I knew. Alex's mother . . . she had died in a car accident there. Every bone in my body was telling me that this was no coincidence. I needed to find out more. I wished that I could just pick up the phone and call him, that would solve so many of my problems right now. Instead, I pulled my laptop out of my bag and tried to pick up a signal. Of course, my papa didn't have wireless; he didn't even own a computer. I picked up a couple of signals from the neighbors, but they all needed passwords. I contemplated sneaking out and taking my parents' car to the nearest all night coffee shop and wondered if my papa had set the alarm, the alarm that my parents had installed for them. It was the only modern thing in the house. I bet he didn't even use it. I remember them fighting over the box on the wall after it was installed. He had said that they hadn't needed one for seventy years, so why would they need one now. But in the end, it made my parents feel better, so the argument was dropped. I slid out of bed and headed for the front door. The red light on the box was on. I sunk down to the floor and wondered how I would wait until tomorrow to find the answers I was looking for.

# CHAPTER SEVENTEEN

$M$y footsteps were inaudible. I was weightless. I was inside a small cottage. The walls were made of crystal. Sparkly, translucent walls that revealed the beauty of the outdoors. The walls that surrounded me were unfamiliar, but certain objects inside brought me to a familiar place: the floral ottomans tucked neatly under the sofa table, the books and the way they were stacked on the shelf, and the crack in the upper right pain of the large glass door. It was the little details that seemed familiar, but foggy. I had been here before. My chest tightened, and I could hardly breathe when I saw a radiant silhouette moving toward me. It was Alex, and all of his ruggedness was gone. His face was glowing. Gone was the scar near his eye that I traced with my finger. Gone was the freckle on his lower lip and the pinwheel eyes that hypnotized me. In their place was something more brilliant, something that words could not describe. I could see through him and yet, as I reached out to touch him, I could feel his skin with the tips of my fingers. I felt my own skin; it seemed real enough, but it too was opaque and shimmering. There was music in the background. I couldn't hear it, but I could feel it waving gently through my body, pulsing harder and harder. I felt his arm, gentle around my waist as he led me to a large window overlooking a lake. The world outside was a collection of tall, green spruces and pines, and the horizon, an endless, translucent blue. He slowly turned toward me, putting his hand on my cheek and parting his lips to speak. He hadn't uttered a single word before he began to fade. My fingers reached out into thin air, grasping for any piece of him that I could hang on to. But he was gone and the house that was surrounding us was fading as well. I looked down at my arms; they too were beginning to disappear and the fading continued until there was nothing left but darkness. It was as black as night.

I woke up in a state of panic, drenched in sweat and forgetting almost immediately what caused me to wake in the first place. It didn't take a second for me to remember my mission for the day. And thus, the details of my fascinating dream faded as my worldly concerns took over. I felt guilty that my mind was preoccupied with things other than my nana's death and her funeral. I knew that Papa and my parents still had many arrangements to make before the funeral later this afternoon, and if I was lucky, I might be able to sneak out for a couple of hours this morning.

I headed to the kitchen; everyone was up and had already eaten. They were sitting around the table looking through pictures of Nana. They had pulled one out of the box that I had never seen before. It was of Nana, probably from about twenty years ago, I guessed. Tiny children that looked malnourished and filthy but full of love, surrounded her and Papa.

"Where was that picture taken?" I inched my way closer to the small, wooden kitchen table. I picked up the worn picture for a closer look. Nana looked tired in a way that could only come from lots of work and sleepless nights, but I could see a love in my nana's eyes so bright that it overpowered the dark circles that lay beneath them.

"India," Papa replied.

"What were you doing in India?" I asked with surprise in my voice.

"We were on an assignment for A-Omega."

I looked at my papa, shocked. I'm not sure why I was taken aback. I knew that Nana and Papa had been the reason my mother and father had taken an interest in A-Omega to begin with. But Papa had always been a quiet man, and he never talked about their lives outside the walls of their Missouri home.

"Are you hungry, Rae?" my dad asked as he sipped his coffee. He was trying to change the subject and I knew it. "We saved you some French toast."

"No, I was actually thinking of going to get something. Is there a coffee shop close?"

"Oh, I don't know why you can't just eat here," he protested.

I gave him a look that let him know I needed a little time to myself, and he dropped the argument. There were certain topics that my dad didn't enjoy discussing, and I guessed by the look on his face that he thought this might be one of those occasions. My mom was preoccupied with Papa, and I felt an overwhelming wave of guilt rush over me.

"Are you sure you don't mind if I go for an hour or so?" I asked half-heartedly.

"No, go on. We won't be leaving here until after lunch," my dad reassured me, tossing me the keys to the car. I gave my mom and Papa a hug, then forced myself to walk, instead of run, to the door despite my anxiousness.

I drove around for at least fifteen minutes before seeing a sign for free wifi in the window of a small coffee shop. My stomach was growling, and I parked the car hastily and headed to the door. The coffeehouse was small but quaint and occupied the bottom floor of an old but completely remodeled home. The inside was decorated with an old fashioned bar and beside the bar was a glass case lined with pastries. Bright, vintage, floral prints made loose hanging curtains that fell to the floor. The floors were a light, maple colored wood, and the room was filled with espresso colored tables and chairs. I ordered a triple shot latte with skim, four Splenda, and light foam and then sat down and turned on my computer. Perfect, I had internet access. I wondered how Papa got by without it. I didn't know where I would start and then I wondered if I would find anything from eighteen years ago. The thought had never crossed my mind until now. I may not find anything at all.

I typed in the words "Loving" and "Alexandria." Nothing about Minnesota turned up, so I narrowed my search to "Loving, Alexandria, Minnesota" and hit return. To my surprise pages and pages bounced back. I began opening each search result, scanning them, searching for the word "Loving" or anything to do with a fatal car crash. One did capture my attention, and I clicked on it. I read to about the middle of the article, which described the lack of land for sale around Lake L'homme Dieu. The article went on to say that rich oilmen in the midwest originally purchased most of the land during the Great Depression and the land had never left the families' hands. There was apparently controversy over tearing down the original cottages to build new, mansion style homes. It showed a few pictures of the cottages, and I wondered why someone would want to destroy the history that their family had shared for nearly a century. I didn't see the key word "Loving" anywhere in the article, so I went back to the search results, and began clicking once again, now realizing this could take all day.

I narrowed my search even further to Loving, Alexandria, Minnesota, Car Crash and hit enter. I looked at the search results; only two bounced back with any information at all. One of them looked promising, so I clicked on it and began to read. The article appeared to be a scan from the original dated September 14th, 1990. My eyes began to read faster, my mind unable to keep up. I read and re-read the article

*Tragedy stuck the small, fishing town of Alexandria, Minnesota, late last night. Paul Loving 29, Sarah Loving 29, along with their two-year-old*

*son were killed when a driver, whose truck spun out of control, struck their vehicle. The Loving family died at the scene. The Lovings have been vacationing in Alexandria for generations.*

*The driver of the other vehicle, Will Colbert 27, was released with minor injuries. Sue Colbert, 26, is still being held in the ICU. Laney Colbert, 2, daughter of Will and Sue, died in the crash. Slick road conditions from heavy rains seem to be the cause of the accident. No charges are being filed.*

*Laney Colbert and the Loving family will be greatly missed. Funeral services will be held on Friday for the Loving family in their hometown of Bartlesville, Oklahoma.*

A tiny black and white picture of a man and woman was below the article. The woman had long straight hair that framed her thin face. Below the picture it read: Paul and Sarah Loving 1961-1990. I sat frozen, my eyes glued to the picture of the woman in the article and my mind racing back to the picture of the woman in Alex's room. It was her, his mother. I went over the facts again and again, my mind not able to catch up with what my heart already knew. I glanced back at the article. I highlighted the text and then cut and pasted it into word, so that I could pull it up at Papa's house.

I slipped my computer into my purse, zipped it up, and walked out of the café door to my car. I felt very close to robotic on the drive back to the house. My body seemed to do only what it needed in order to get me back to Papa's, but my thoughts, my spirit was elsewhere, somewhere far away. I pulled into the drive and slid out of the car without purpose. My mind, which had previously felt overworked and tired, now felt numb and achy. My parents could tell I was shaken, but they didn't question me. I'm sure that they were thinking I was a typical teenager, dealing with the loss of a loved one in my own way. I wished it were that simple. Although hard, I could handle the things that were supposed to happen in this life. I was having far more trouble dealing with something that appeared to be supernatural. I was also troubled with the idea that I could very well be crazy.

A large crowd gathered after the burial and brought mountains of food. They stayed until they could tell that my Papa was tired and then began to excuse themselves one by one. As if there wasn't already enough food, Mom, Dad, and I spent the next couple of days making small portion dinners that we wrapped in foil and placed into the freezer for Papa. We went through all of Nana's belongings, sorting them into piles. There was a pile for things to be donated and another pile for the things that we held dear. I was busy sorting and picking through her closet when Papa snuck quietly into the room. We had tried to keep him busy while we were rummaging through Nana's things. It seemed almost cold and inhuman to be going through a dead loved one's belongings so shortly after their passing. But we would have to go back to Oklahoma soon, and Mom thought we should take care of it so Papa wouldn't have to. Carefully, Papa sat down on the edge of the bed without saying a word. He was holding a large and bulky box in his arms. I turned to face him, sensing that he was here for an important reason.

"I saw you up the other night looking at this," his voice cracked as he opened up the box to reveal the large scrapbook filled with memories.

I could see sadness consuming him, and I wondered if the funeral this afternoon had made Nana's death final.

"Your mother has no interest in it," he said. "Brings back something painful, I reckon. And I have all of my memories stored up here." He pointed a crooked finger to his hairless head.

"I don't know what to say, Papa." I reached out and grabbed the large book as he pushed it across the bed in my direction. Carefully, I ran my fingers across the cover of the book. "Irene spent hours on this book. It tells a story, you know. If you look hard enough at all those pictures in there, they'll tell you something that words cannot."

I knew he was right. Sometimes words could be deceiving; one seemingly simple sentence could be taken many different ways. True meaning was found in expressions and body language. In photos, true meaning was sitting right in front of you. There truly was so much more to see in a picture.

"Thank you, Papa, I'll take good care of it," I assured him.

He put his hand on the corner of the four-poster bed and pushed himself up slowly. I think that he had aged several years in the few short days that we had been here. He walked to the door silently and started to pull it shut behind him.

"Papa!" I shouted. I caught us both off guard. Papa turned his wrinkled face toward me.

"Yes, Rae."

"Um . . . I just wanted to ask you something. Um . . . ."

"What is it, Sunshine?" he asked, still standing by the door.

"I was just wondering, I mean, you never talk about it much, and Mom and Dad won't tell me, but I was wondering why you and Nana decided to work for A-Omega?"

Papa now moved slowly back toward the bed where I was still sitting, bending his knees slowly, lowering himself to the mattress. He paused, not speaking a single word, and so I spoke again.

"I know you don't talk about it much, and it's fine if you don't want to tell me . . . but I always meant to ask Nana, I just never got the chance."

"It's not that I don't like to talk about it, Rae; it's just that your parents have never thought that you needed to know. Irene and I have always been open about what we do. Certain events have changed our lives in ways that we could never have imagined possible. We never wanted to keep it from you but your parents, well, they've never wanted you to grow up, either. I suppose they just wanted to protect you from the evils of the world. But hiding and protecting have never been the same in my book. I think you've grown into a fine young woman and, if I dare say so myself, I think you are ready to hear the truth.

"It was really your nana who decided to dedicate her life to A-Omega. There was a time in her life that was very, very dark. When I met Irene Irving, I knew that I had to take her away with me. I thought we could leave her pain behind when we left that little town and I think that, in a way, she thought so, too. I thought I was the hero, I thought I could be the one to help her, to pull her out of that darkness. But I learned that some pain is too great, and it leaves a scar on the heart too deep for man to heal. But I've always loved Irene. From the moment I saw her, I loved her, and I knew that she belonged with me. I asked Irene to marry me, but it wasn't until she was pregnant with your mother that something inside of her changed. She says it was God. Maybe it was God. God does work in strange ways. But it was most certainly the life growing inside of your nana that gave life back to her.

"One night, she came from work late and had pain written all over her face. She had seen something that night on the way home from work that she couldn't repeat. For a solid month I couldn't get her out of bed, and I feared she had climbed right back into her shell. But then one morning she got up with a determined look on her face. She had decided to help young girls like her. She wanted to make a difference in their lives, she wanted to change the world. I asked her why. I couldn't understand why she would want to submerge herself in darkness when we had worked so hard to pull her out. I wanted to keep her safe. I wanted her all for myself. It was on that day she said something to me that I will never forget.

"She said, 'Charlie, to open your heart to someone means exposing the scars of the past.'"

"You see, Sunshine, your nana's heart was open when she helped girls like her escape. Every time she reached out her hand to help one of those young girls, another piece of her heart was healed. Really, they helped each other in a way. For so long, she had tried to protect herself and then one day, she knew that it was time to fight. Your nana was a fighter, Rae. And that is why we worked for A-Omega."

I was left to myself again, my mind now preoccupied with the book he had so graciously given me. I flipped it open to the page of my parents and Laney and studied it once again. They seemed so happy, truly in love, and Laney so tiny and innocent. A thought crossed my mind. It was something I hadn't considered until just now. I had pictures of Alex on my camera. Up until this point, I had been relying on my painting in art class to remind me that he did indeed exist. I remembered I had packed my camera and searched frantically through my messy bag until I found it. My heart was racing. How I had longed to see him just once more. I couldn't believe that I had forgotten. The pictures would still be on the memory stick.

I began scrolling through the pictures, one by one. I hadn't looked at them since they had been taken. I had snapped a few of him at the park and he had taken a few of me. The background of each picture had turned out perfectly; the tall trees behind him boasting their bright fall leaves. But strangely, a rippling effect occurred in the middle of the image, in the exact spot where he should have been. It was a perfect circle, a rippling, wave of darkness, a black hole with nothing in it, and pain began to shoot through my body. It ached, and it started to twist my stomach into knots that I couldn't begin to unwind. Tears were swelling in my eyes and then rolling quickly down my cheeks. I wanted him back. I needed him to wrap his gentle arms around my calloused soul. I needed my safe spot, my security blanket, and my comfort.

I slid the camera back into my bag, now realizing that bringing it out in the first place was a bad idea. I had more important things to do besides sit here and wallow in all of my grief. I had to make a game plan. I needed to get to the bottom of this. I had to know where he was, why he had left, and where he had come from.

"I need to find out where he is . . . I need to find out where he is." When I repeated these words out loud, they seemed to strike me in a new way. I frantically pulled my computer from my bag and turned it on, impatiently waiting for the ancient laptop to wake. The computer lit up, and I clicked on the Word icon at the bottom of the screen. I opened up the "Alex" file began to re-read the document, carefully scanning the article until I found what I was looking for.

*Funeral services will be held on Friday for the Loving family in their hometown of Bartlesville, Oklahoma.*

I had been so focused on the fact that my parents had killed Alex's entire family that I hadn't even noticed the part about his hometown. Alex was from Bartlesville.

Why did he say that he was from Minnesota?

I was sure of nothing anymore, but I did know that I would investigate this until I found the answers that I needed, even if it took a lifetime. This new adventure gave me hope, quite possibly a false hope, but any kind of hope was better than being miserable. This newfound discovery made me feel close to him in a way that I hadn't felt since our last night together at the water tower. I now had purpose and drive and the first place I would begin my search would be at the Bartlesville cemetery.

# CHAPTER EIGHTEEN

*I*t was a cool, spring day with a slight chill in the air. A veil of mist was falling from the sky and the smell of the blossoming Bradford Pears was overpowering and pungent. But I still had my window rolled halfway down, allowing the coolness of the air to awaken my senses. I couldn't believe what I was doing. It seemed crazy and irrational. I had come up with a thousand explanations for the newspaper article, but none of them made any sense at all. The most reasonable explanation was that I was going insane.

The cemetery was easy to find; Bartlesville only had one, but of course, it had never caught my attention, as death was not something that crossed my mind until my nana died. The hard part would be finding the gravestones, if they even existed.

As I stepped out of my car and walked toward the arched entrance of the cemetery, a chill stole over me that had nothing to do with cool, spring air. It reminded me, once again, of what I might find.

Without any plan in mind, I headed to the far end of the cemetery and began glancing at the names on the stones, but there was nothing. I must have looked at over a hundred stones when I realized that they were in order of date. I was now in the early 1900's, so I made my way to the middle of the graveyard, skipping over what seemed like thousands of stones. The thought of what they symbolized was unsettling. They represented humans that lived once just like me, who once had lives, families, loves, hurts, sadness, and excitement.

I stopped at a beautiful headstone carved from granite. The name engraved was Walter Urby, 1901–1975, Beloved husband, father, and grandfather. I felt peace knowing that he had lived a long life, and I wondered if it had been a happy one. I wondered how he had died. I wondered where he was now, not his body, of course, but his spirit; that I would never know was disturbing.

On occasion, I had considered life outside the human body, but until this moment it had never seemed so real. I had thought of angels and demons and spirits, but more in a cartoon character sort of way, just as Alex had suggested. I wondered if spirits were hovering around me, watching me weave between the graves. I rather hoped they weren't. I didn't like the idea of being watched.

I moved to the next stone, which was much like the last, made of granite. I was beginning to get sidetracked from my original purpose when a voice from behind me made me jump.

"C'help yeah ma'am?" An older, peculiar looking man who was dressed in a pair of jeans and a blue, button up shirt was standing directly behind me. His facial lines were sharp and his face thin, accentuating all of his features. His voice had a thick, southern drawl that was a little out of place for Bartlesville.

"I don't think so." I had unintentionally held my breath since he startled me. I responded, sucking in a chestfull of air when I spoke so that my answer sounded more like a gasp. Aware that he had frightened me, his features now softened.

"I take care uda grounds round here."

I'm sure that he was trying to reassure me that he had a purpose for being here and that he wasn't some sort of scary man that hung out in cemeteries.

"You lookn' fer sumpin' particular, I jus' thought I might help ya."

"Um, yes. The Lovings," I replied, still unsure of my safety.

"Well, ya know what year they passed?" he asked.

"1990."

"Gettin close," he said as he began walking forward at a rather quick pace. I wondered if he knew the precise location of all of the stones. I quickly dismissed the thought; it did nothing to ease my anxiety. He continued to weave in and out of the large pieces of stone that landscaped the huge mass of land.

"An here we are." He ushered me to the stone and then lingered for a moment as if he had something more to say. "I'll leave ya'lone now," he said, putting to rest anything further he might have wanted to add.

"Um, thank you."

Finally, the groundskeeper turned around. I watched as he walked away at a much slower rate than he previously moved. I waited until he neared the middle of the yard before I dared to turn my back on him, still spooked and slightly on edge by my whereabouts. I was now facing the stone, and I read the inscription.


Sarah Anne Loving

1961–1990

Beloved wife and mother


Her tombstone had been carved from white marble. Some withered flowers lay on the ground in front of the stone, which left it looking neglected rather than beautiful. I wondered why the groundskeeper hadn't cared for Sarah's stone, but then again, I wouldn't want to be the one to remove dead flowers from someone's grave, at least not without replacing them with fresh ones. I ran my hand along the cold stone and then stepped back to look at it from a distance when I noticed that it did not stand alone. Slowly, I took five steps to my left and knelt down in front of an identical, white marble marker. I ran my fingers across the engraved words as I read them.

Paul Michael Loving

1961-1990

Beloved husband and father

The questions I had been suppressing since I had left my papa's all jumped at me at once, and I could in no way sort through all of my emotions. I felt angry because of the lie Alex had told me. I couldn't imagine why he would tell me his father was alive. Was he embarrassed? Was he an orphan? The thought made me sad. Was he uncared for, so much so that he had to teach himself everything, take care of things that I had always depended on someone else for? That explained his maturity. This new reality invaded me with a sorrow that I had never experienced before. I didn't know what to do with this new dimension of myself that thought about others. I wasn't sure if I liked it and the way it made me feel. It was much easier to just be self-centered.

I stepped back once again to look at both graves. I glanced to the right and saw a miniature version of the two tall, white, tombstones. When I saw the tiny gravestone, my mind jogged back to the article I had read. A baby had died in the crash. My stomach twisted into a large and tangled knot and nausea crept its way through my body, but still my comprehension had not caught up with my senses. I inched my way over to the small, stone. I knelt down and ran my hand over the cool and smooth piece of stone. I held my eyes closed trying to prolong reading the inscription on the tomb. Still, my body felt what my mind was not ready to accept. I glanced down and read the engraved letters.

Alex Michael Loving

1988-1990

Beloved only child of Sarah and Paul

Only child. The words rang in my ears. This couldn't be possible. My mind was racing when I heard a sound so startling that I must have jumped ten feet in the air.

"Hey there, Sunshine."

I flipped around. The voice that came from behind me was familiar. It was the same voice that could make me melt over and over again, and yet, there I stood, frozen in a capsule of ice, unable to move. I could feel my lungs begin to tighten. Each breath I took became labored and I began gasping for air in little gulps. Death was surely at my doorstep.

"I'm sorry about your nana." His warm voice chilled me to the bone. I couldn't respond. Each breath took more work than I could muster. Everything seemed to be spinning and then it went black.

I will never forget that moment, when his touch brought me back: electric warmth replacing numbness, heating me from the inside out. The mist from earlier had dissipated and when I opened my eyes, the sunlight shown so bright that I shut them once again. I focused instead on every other sensation: the tingling that was spreading through my body, the intoxicatingly familiar scent that surrounded me, the familiar gentleness wrapped around my body, and the warmth of his skin on mine. I felt safe like I hadn't in so long. I shielded my eyes with my left hand and looked up into his with disbelief.

"It's okay. I understand if you wonder what I'm doing here." His voice was smooth like honey.

"I . . . I . . . " I couldn't spit out a complete sentence. I wasn't sure I could even form a complete thought. I reached up and wrapped myself around his neck, holding him tight, not intending on letting go. It was Alex. All of my anger, my sadness, and my questions had just slipped away. Months' worth of feelings had just vanished into nothingness. One moment in his presence made everything okay.

"I didn't want you to find out this way," he whispered in my ear.

I leaned back, just enough so that I could look him in the eyes. "How did you know I called her Nana?" I asked, pulling from my pre-blackout memory.

He ignored my question and stared back at me painfully, as if the time away from me had been just as treacherous for him.

"Where have you been? Why did you come back? What . . . what are you?"

A normal reaction would be to slink away, but this in no way felt like a normal situation. The questions were now free flowing from my lips and uncertainty and longing was filling a place in my body where fear should have been. I turned my head to look at the tiny gravestone and then I looked back at him with a blank and helpless expression on my whitened face.

"Which question do you want me to answer first?" His voice still smooth and his face flawless in a way that was not possible on this earth. No one could be that perfect, that beautiful. I lay in his arms, spellbound.

"How about we find a better place to discuss this. Someplace other than the cemetery." He was making a suggestion, and I began to wonder who was running this show. For months now, I had envisioned what I would say to him if our paths were to cross. I imagined that I would be the one in control. He had hurt me. He should be begging for my forgiveness, giving in to every one of my requests.

"No. No way." I pushed myself out of his arms. "I'm not leaving until you answer some questions." The creepy feeling that I had associated with this deathly place was now the only proof I had that I was not crazy. It was the only way I could convince him to tell me the truth. I had his gravestone behind me. For all I knew, all three stones would miraculously disappear as soon as we left, and I would be left blaming my imagination once again.

"How do you explain this?" I pointed to his father's stone.

"That was my father . . . Paul," he said with surprise.

"Why did you lie to me about living with your father?" I asked, my voice now reflecting the anger that had been building up inside of me for months.

"I never told you that I lived with my father. It was something that you assumed."

I thought about it for a moment before I decided that he was right.

"I can't believe that you are asking me about my father when there's a gravestone marked with my name right behind you," he said with surprise.

"I was getting to that. It's just . . . I'm not quite sure how to ask that question yet." I paused. "So, is that your stone? Are you really here with me or are you buried down there somewhere? Better yet, am I going crazy?"

"Yes, it's my stone. And yes, I am here . . . with you. And no, you're not going crazy."

"How can you be here with me if you're dead?"

"I can't imagine what you must be thinking."

"If you're dead, then what does that make you?"

Alex parted his lips as though he was about to speak, but I was not yet ready for him to answer. "You're an angel, right?" I spat, hoping he was an angel rather than a demon, but really wishing he was just a normal, teenage boy and this was some huge misunderstanding.

"Not an angel." The expression on his face told me that he was holding something back.

"A ghost?" A hard wrinkle began to form in my forehead like it did when I was anticipating something painful.

223

"More of a spirit trapped in a human body for the moment." He appeared amused as I desperately attempted to make sense of this situation, the corners of his mouth twisted into a smile.

"Well, isn't that what I am, just a spirit trapped in a human body?" I tried to sound convincing. Alex only shook his head in disagreement, a smile still on his face as he studied me. I could tell that he was enjoying himself, watching me try to solve his riddle.

"The accident? Do you remember what happened?"

"Yes."

"I'm sorry. I'm *so* sorry. How can you not hate me . . . my parents?"

"It wasn't your parent's fault, Rae, and it definitely wasn't yours."

"Of all people, why me? Why did you fall in love with me? You could have loved anyone."

"Wasn't there anything that was familiar when you saw me for the first time?" he asked hopefully. The amusement had left him, and I could now see desperation in his eyes.

"I guess. There were things about you that did seem familiar but it was more what I felt than what I saw. Does that make sense?"

"Yes." He looked down, and I thought that he seemed only partially satisfied. "We've known each other for a long time, Rae. Longer than you think."

"For how long?" I gasped.

"Since the beginning. Minus the eighteen years of your life that you've been on this earth."

"I don't understand."

"We're soul mates."

"And?"

"And then we were born . . . to this earth, but my life here was ended almost before it even began."

"Why are you different from other spirits? Why do you have a body? How come I can feel you? Why are you here?"

"Most spirits don't want to come back; they aren't looking for a way to come back. Generally people's lives are complete when they die. It's like a book that's been read from cover to cover. Everyone has a purpose, and they either figure it out or they don't; regardless, they are given the time. I wasn't given that time and that makes me different."

"So, were you in Heaven before I met you here on Earth?" I quickly remembered how he so vaguely replied "up north" when I asked him where he had moved from. Only now did I see the humor.

"Not exactly."

"Were you in Hell?"

"I wasn't in Hell, Rae."

"Purgatory, then?"

"No, but it felt like Purgatory some of the time."

"Then where were you?"

"A place that I call the Halfway."

"Why the Halfway?"

"Because I was halfway between Heaven and Earth."

"I didn't know that such a place existed. I mean, before this moment I wasn't even sure if Heaven existed . . . and now . . . "

"The Halfway is a holding place of sorts, a place for those whose bodies were separated from their spirits prematurely . . . before their appointed time."

"What was it like?"

"It was lonely; numbing at times. When a human body dies and returns to Heaven, the soul has no recollection of earth. I suppose that is because earth is a place of sadness and there is no sadness in Heaven. Likewise, when you're born to Earth, you have no recollection of the Heaven you were in before you became human. All memories of Heaven are completely erased. I don't think humans would last a day on earth if they could remember the happiness they experienced before they were pulled from eternity. This is how it's supposed to be . . . ideally . . . if things were perfect. It's the natural order of existence. But for me, because I was halfway between, I could see and remember the Heaven where I began and the earth that was an enormous sea below me, swallowing whole every living thing that was born unto it. The earth truly is a tragic place to be."

"Finally, something we agree on," I said. "So were there others there with you?"

"There were some, but not many."

"Did it hurt to die?"

"No." He was silent for a moment, his lower lip tucked behind his top lip, his eyes serious the way they always were when he was deep in thought. "Dying is no different than a bird hatching from an egg. When the bird is ready for life, the shell cracks and the bird continues on, leaving the shell and all memories of the shell behind. Our spirit is what defines us, Rae. Our body is just a shell that houses our spirit while we're here on earth. When our spirit is ready, we leave our shell behind. We move on."

"Why now, why didn't you come back sooner?"

"It was a matter of timing. I had no choice."

"Did you come back for me . . . just for me? Are you going to take me back with you? I'd be fine with that, you know."

"Yes . . . I did come for you, but not to take you away. I'm not planning to remove you from this earth, if that's what you're asking me. You're really sick, you know. Morbid in fact . . . no offense."

"None taken," I huffed. "You know, it would have been fine with me if you would have come sooner." I immediately began to imagine what my life would have been like with Alex around.

"Believe me, I wanted to. It's been just short of torture for me being able to see you and not being able to touch you."

"You could see me?" I screeched.

"Did I leave that out?"

"For how long?" I was appalled.

"I've pretty much seen the last eighteen years of your life."

"That could be a little embarrassing, depending on how much you remember," I said. "Sooo . . . exactly how much do you remember?"

"Pretty much everything."

"And you still love me?"

"How could I not? I find your awkwardness endearing."

My face had turned ten different shades of red at the thoughts my feeble, human mind could remember of my imperfect existence.

"Could you see everyone or just me?"

"I could see anyone or anything that my human body encountered during my two years of life on earth. But mostly, I saw you."

"Could you see my parents?"

"Yes."

"So you knew my parents before you even met them. No wonder you were so relaxed. You knew exactly what to expect."

"I guess that's one advantage I did have," he said with a smile.

"That doesn't seem quite fair. That must have been perfect for you, having this unfair advantage over me. You played on my weaknesses."

"The halfway wasn't my choice, Rae. It was hell for me most days. There were so many times I wanted to touch you, protect you, hold you when you were sad, even if it were only for one moment. I would have traded anything for that chance."

"You should have."

"I wanted to, I wanted you. But my wanting wasn't enough to make that happen."

"And yet . . . you left me again." Alex didn't say a word. I was being a

227

bit harsh, and I knew it. "So, where have you been for the past couple of months?"

"At my family's cabin in Minnesota."

"Why would you want to go back there of all places? That place holds such bad memories for the both of us. For our families."

"Alexandria is where I took my last breath as a human. I needed to reconnect."

"But you've been gone for months."

"It's complicated. It's torture when I'm away from you. I've spent seventeen years in the Halfway living with that torture, and it is something that has never gotten easier. But when I'm with you, it tortures me that I can't give you what you need. It's painful to see you and know that I have only hurt you worse by coming to you in the first place. I was selfish for letting you fall in love with me. It pains me to touch, you because I know that it is my touch that will break your heart one day, the day when that touch is no longer there."

"Are you trying to tell me that you're going to be sucked up to Heaven sometime soon?" I asked, my mood now somber.

"I hope I'm not sucked up to Heaven. That sounds rather painful. But, I also don't know if I'll be able to stay forever."

"You know I won't let you leave me again. There are things I can do to prevent that from happening. I'm not scared."

"You're not ready to come back with me yet, Rae."

"I would die for you . . . so that I could be with you. I can leave this world behind," I said between labored breaths.

"Well, if you're dying for me then you are dying for the wrong reasons."

"I don't know what reasons are right. I do know that I can handle the idea of my heart beating its final beat . . . I only fear the torture that each beat brings when you're away."

His expression was somewhere between pity and remorse.

"Look," I sighed. "You're here now, and I just need to know. Can you still see me? I mean, if you're not with me then can you still see what I'm doing, like through a crystal ball or something?"

"It doesn't work that way."

"Then how does it work? How did you know my nana died?

"I still keep tabs on you. It's just harder now. I needed to know that you were okay. I saw you at your papa's house with the scrapbook and at the coffee shop digging into things about our past." My mouth was hanging wide open in astonishment. I could hardly believe what he was telling me. He had been there with me, so close and I hadn't even known.

"And then, I saw you at the funeral."

"You're like my own personal stalker . . . not that I mind."

"You make it sound like it's some sort of joke." He rolled his eyes. "I just couldn't do it all over again. For much of your life, I looked at you in your sadness and I could do nothing to help you, nothing to make your life better. It was like there was this invisible wall separating us from one another. I could see you and hear you and love you, but only from a distance. The part that hurt the worst was that you didn't even know I existed. It was when you were lying on the back porch at your papa's, and I heard you whisper my name that I knew it was time. You're smart, I knew you would figure it out and I wanted to let you. But I also wanted to be there when you did."

"And so you were."

"And so I was."

"Come on, let's get out of here." He wrapped his arm around my waist, just the way he always had, the way that made me feel safe.

"I always knew you were too perfect, too perfect for this world. Now I don't have such a complex with you being an angel and all."

"I told you, I'm no angel."

"If you say so."

We walked in silence for a moment and he pulled me closer.

"So, do you have like superhuman strengths too? Can you fly?" My voice was unable to hide the excitement.

"I'm sorry to disappoint you, but while on earth, I have a human body just like you."

"Oh." I shrugged, trying not to let the disappointment show. "Can you do anything superhuman at all?"

"Well . . . I do have a few tricks up my sleeve."

I remember him saying that once before, the night at the water tower. The night he had traced an arc in the sky and let the star fall from the Heavens. If these were the type of tricks he was talking about, I would say he indeed had superhuman abilities.

"I'm not leaving this instant, I can't give away everything in the first day."

I was becoming more and more dissatisfied with the privileges that his holy deadness provided.

"I didn't think soul mates were supposed to keep secrets." I nudged him.

"It's not a secret if I intend on telling you, it's more of a surprise."

"You know how I feel about surprises."

"You never have been very patient, have you, *Sunshine*?" His face broke into a thin smile.

"Do not call me that. I hate that name."

"Okay, *Sunshine*," he said with an impish smile. "Us being together . . . it's not going to be easy. You know that, right?" There was a degree of seriousness in Alex's voice.

"It feels easy to me. It feels easy right now."

"Let's just hope it stays that way."

"So, where do we go from here?" I asked him.

"I guess you probably need to go home."

"And after that?" I now felt like a four-year-old asking my parents, "Are we there yet?"

"Patience, Rae, Patience."

# CHAPTER NINETEEN

$S$chool had become worse than a chore. Alex had decided against enrolling to spare confusion and too many questions. School was just short of torture for me. I kept track of each tick the clock made, counting down the minutes until I could see him again. I longed for our time by the bridge in the afternoon.

I hadn't told my parents about his return; I didn't enjoy lying. I wasn't good at it, either. I knew they would ask me where he had been, and I was pretty sure they wouldn't take me seriously when I told them he was somewhere near Heaven. I was also certain that I would become one of my mother's patients on the psych ward if I tried to explain to her that Alex was really dead. Besides, I didn't know how long we would have before he left again. My parents seemed more than pleased by my improved mood, and in order to keep them that way, I decided to leave them in the dark about all events concerning Alex Loving.

I had about thirteen missed calls from Claire when I got back from Missouri, half of them frantic and eager. I avoided my locker by bringing a fully loaded backpack to every class, and thus, I also successfully avoided Claire. I was now between a rock and a hard spot. I had asked Claire for help, but now that Alex was back, I had to be careful of what I told her. Besides, my attention was diverted away from the Chloe conspiracy theory that I created out of pure boredom as I focused on Alex now more than ever. I wondered what I was thinking, making Chloe into something dark and dangerous. I also wondered if I had imagined some of the details of that snowy day in March: the license plate, the make of the car. I knew that Claire would want to continue the conversation where we had left it, so I did my best to avoid her.

The weather was now warm and all the trees had their bright, green leaves. They looked full of life and so happy, almost as if they were capable of possessing emotions. I could feel them smiling down on us as we lay looking up at the sky, captivated by each other's voice and infatuated by one another's presence.

"Tell me how we first met."

"I was assigned to you," he said, very matter of fact, like it was just yesterday that all of this happened. Alex was lying on his side atop the bright, green blades of grass, his elbow perfectly planted into the ground and his head resting upon his hand. He was wearing a hat today, covering up his mop of chocolate waves. He looked irresistible. I fought the urge to reach out and pull him close to me. It took every ounce of my willpower not to kiss him impulsively.

"How romantic," I said sarcastically. "Were we married?"

"Being married is more of a human ritual and, as you know, marriage doesn't necessarily work out the way it was intended."

"So, we weren't married?"

"We were much more than that. We had something so much stronger than any physical bond here on earth."

"Did we have a house?"

"Yes, we had a house."

"What was it like?"

"You don't want anything to be a surprise, do you?"

"You know I can't stand surprises; besides, it gives me something to look forward to."

"Most people don't look forward to their death, that's sort of morbid, Rae."

"Most people don't know what they're missing," I retorted. "So tell me about our house."

"It's perfect. It's a small house on a lake. Glass windows make up the walls so that we have a beautiful view of the forest and the water."

My heart stopped beating for a moment. His description brought back memories of the dream I had at Papa's. The small, crystal cottage, the floral ottomans tucked under the bookshelves, and him, so beautiful and perfect standing in front of me, so real just before he disappeared.

"What's wrong?" he asked

"Nothing, it's just you're being so vague. What was the inside like?" I was beginning to wonder if it was decorated with my current taste. I wondered if it were cluttered and messy. Had I been predisposed to sloppiness since the beginning of time?

"Some things are just beyond words. There's really nothing to compare it to here on earth."

"Did we have a bedroom? Did we sleep together?"

"We didn't sleep, so no, we didn't have a bedroom."

"Never, not even a little nap?" I immediately thought of all the things I would be able to do without sleep. Sleep was really just a waste of time. Even though I wished I could do without it, I was rather cranky if I didn't get enough.

"What did we do if we didn't sleep?"

"We found plenty of things to do."

"Were we in Heaven?"

"Yes."

"Tell me more about Heaven."

He paused for a moment not saying a word.

"Think of the best day that you've ever had, your most perfect moment, and then imagine that moment never ending. That's what Heaven is. Your own idea of perfection . . . for an eternity."

"Did you love it there?"

"Yes."

"Do you love it here, on earth?"

"I love you. And you're here."

"Is our love different here on earth, different than it was up there?"

"I'm still learning about loving you here on earth. It's not like before. I'm not sure if you're aware of how grueling it can be inside the body of a teenage boy."

"And what do you mean by that, Alex Loving?" I asked, batting my eyes in his direction.

"Listen. I want you to know this. I don't want you to ever think that I didn't warn you. I cannot give you the things in life that you want or that you may one day want. Marriage. Kids . . . "

"I just want you . . . that's all."

"But you see, Rae, I can't even give you that. My time here is not guaranteed. I can't promise you anything."

"You and me . . . we really aren't that different. My time on earth is no more guaranteed than yours. My existence is just as fragile. But I will promise to love you forever, as long as forever is on this earth."

"You're right," he sighed.

"What about marriage? Do you think we could ever get married?" Alex shook his head with regret, like he was wishing that he had never mentioned the word marriage. "I wouldn't care if we had only a year. I want to marry you. Is that possible?"

Alex stopped shaking his head and his lips spread into a smile. "Are you proposing to me, Rae Colbert?"

"I guess so. The way I see it, I either marry you or I become an old maid. You wouldn't want that now would you."

"If we did decide to get married, do you really think I would let you propose to me? I guess I'm a bit traditional and even though my two years on this earth as a human didn't provide me with a plethora of worldly knowledge, I do know a little bit about being a gentleman."

"Are you saying that you might want to be my husband?"

"It's tempting. I have considered it. I just don't see how it would work."

"You know, you've only been back a couple of weeks and already it's hard . . . all of this sneaking around. I want to be with you, but I don't see how we can be together here."

"I've considered that, too. I think it would be easier to just tell your parents about us . . . about me."

"Are you crazy? My parents are shrinks. They're head doctors. Stories like ours are a dime a dozen. They would lock us up and throw away the key."

"I doubt it. They have already met me, and I seem to recall that they liked me . . . at least your father seemed to. You didn't mind introducing me to them, did you?" he asked, poking my arm playfully.

"No, I didn't mind, but that was before I knew that my parents killed you and your entire family. That was before I knew you were dead. I'm sure you can see the difference."

"They'll never put two and two together. They won't figure out who I am . . . I mean who I used to be. I think we should tell them."

"We can't. You underestimate my parents. You underestimate my mother. Did you not see the look on her face when I introduced you? If my mother didn't have a practical side, I think she would have already figured it out. I mean really, if you didn't want them to know, don't you think you could have a least changed your name. I mean, that seems like such a small detail compared to all of the other hurdles . . . like for instance coming back from the dead."

"Well . . . I kind of like my name." He laughed. I didn't feel so light-hearted at the moment.

"We're not telling them," I said with finality.

"Well, what's your bright idea, then?"

"We could run away . . . so that we could be together. I'll do whatever it takes to be with you."

"Where would we go?"

"What if I said I would let you pick?"

"You know this world better than I do. You used to live in Europe, how about that?"

"I was thinking somewhere a little closer."

"How about Minnesota?"

"Talk about morbid." I couldn't imagine what he was thinking, wanting to move back to a place that was attached to such negative circumstances.

"Like I said already, Europe would be pretty cool."

"I'm not moving back to Europe, okay. Europe doesn't hold the best memories for me."

"How about you choose, then. I can't seem to get any answer right today."

"I'm sorry. I'm just a little nervous, that's all." I stopped short, watching Alex carefully pull a scrap of paper from his pocket. "What are you doing?"

"Do you have a pen?"

I rummaged through my bag, finally pulling out a marred and stubby pencil with no eraser. "Here." I handed it to him. "Why do you need it?"

"Just a little game." He ripped the paper in half and handed me a piece. "Now, write down five places that you would like to live. I'll do the same and then we'll draw. That makes it easy."

"Okay." I hesitated. It seemed fair enough. Quickly, he wrote down his five choices and then handed the pencil over to me. I took a little longer to choose. Honestly, the idea of moving again made me sick to my stomach. I wished we could just stay here, but I knew it wasn't possible, not now.

"Done." I told him, and then slid the pencil back into my messy bag. He took the slip of paper from me and tore it into five pieces, folding each piece in half and adding them to the others that were resting inside the hat he had taken off his head.

"So, who gets to pick?" I asked.

"You can, if you want." He gave his hat a little shake.

I reached my hand inside the hat, touching all of the slips of paper. I felt nervous that our fate literally rested in my hands. Finally, my fingers fell on a slip of paper, crisp between my fingers and perfectly folded, and so I lifted my hand out of the hat and held the slip in front of Alex.

"I drew, now you get to read it."

"Wow, I feel privileged." He slowly unfolded the scrap of paper and immediately a smile formed on his beautiful face, but he didn't speak. He just sat there smiling.

"What!" I shrieked.

"It must be fate."

"What!" I shrieked again. "This isn't fair. Give me the piece of paper," I demanded. He handed it to me, still smiling. I opened it quickly, a look of disappointment immediately consuming me.

"Minnesota?" I sighed.

"It's just a game, Rae."

Frowning, I took all of the scraps of paper out of the hat and shoved them into my bag.

"What are you doing?" His expression was a perfect combination of baffled and amused.

239

"Just making sure that all of our bases are covered."

"Did you ever stop to think that maybe this is all just going to work out? You've always tried to control everything, ever since I've known you, and I'm not only talking about your eighteen years on earth. You've been doing this for an eternity."

"Hmmm, I guess some things never change," I responded obnoxiously.

"All I'm trying to say is that maybe you should just wait and see what happens. Everything doesn't always have to be so planned out."

I responded with silence.

"So, what are your plans after you graduate?"

"I already told you. My only plan is to be with you."

"Besides that. You have to have some sort of thoughts about your future, right?"

This was a discussion I had been trying to avoid. Maybe because I knew what I was expected to do, but what my parents wanted for me and what I wanted for myself were two totally different things.

"My parents want me to go to college. They want me to be a doctor, like them. I am good in science, I guess," I said without any enthusiasm.

"But what do you want?" he encouraged me.

"I love to paint. I would like to go to art school," I told him nervously. My nervousness stemmed from the fact that I had never told anyone that before. I was always too afraid someone would say that it was not practical, or that I didn't have the potential.

"I say you're more of a Picasso than a Florence Nightingale."

"Actually, Florence Nightingale was a nurse, not a doctor."

"Freud, then. I see you as more of a Picasso than a Sigmund Freud."

"We'll see."

"Your future is important. You should really be thinking about what you want to do with it."

"Now you sound like my parents."

"Well, maybe they're right." Alex sucked in a deep breath before he continued. "Look, I wanted to come back sooner, you know that. But I didn't have that choice. You know I love you, but that's not the only reason I'm here. And I hope you know that you're here for more of a purpose than to just love me. Your future, and what you decide to do with it, is important, Rae." Alex laid down on the soft, lime green blades beneath us and began nervously pulling bits of grass from the ground.

"I'm glad that you have some sort of purpose in life, but unlike you, I wasn't let in on all the secrets. I was just dumped here on this earth with all of my awkwardness. I have been shuffled around from country to country. I barely get enough time to learn about my surroundings, much less myself." My face was now hot with frustration. I was frustrated that I was eighteen and didn't have the slightest idea who I was. And to make matters worse, I was being chastised because of it. "All I know is that when I'm with you, that's when I'm the happiest. I don't want anything to change that."

"I'm sorry. I guess I forget that it's not so easy for you. I mean, it's not so easy to see the big picture when you're standing so close to it."

"As opposed to watching my life from Heaven? Is that what you're trying to say?" Sarcasm was still heavy in my voice.

His face lightened, a hint of understanding was beginning to develop and the left side of his mouth started to curl in a tiny smile.

"You said you went to a lot of art museums in Paris, right."

I wondered what the drastic change in subject was all about, but instead of questioning him, I shrugged and gave him a simple one-word answer.

"Yes."

"Okay, and you went to the Musee de l'Orangerie, right?"

"One of my favorites." My vocabulary was increasing against my will. He had a way of calming me, bringing me back down to a simmer.

"And you saw a Monet while you were there?"

"You should know, haven't you been watching me for all of my eighteen, uneventful years of existence?"

"I guess I could rephrase that. Do you remember seeing a Monet at the museum?" he asked. He was beginning to sound annoyed, and I was still unsure of what point he was trying to make. I didn't quite understand how my purpose on this earth correlated with an art museum in France.

"Yes," I said, my mind jogging back to the large painting of water lilies, the single painting that circled the entire room.

"Do you remember how, when you're standing up close, the painting looks like lots of large splotches on an extraordinary canvas, the splotches not making sense and in no way seeming to fit together?"

"But when you step back, then you see the true beauty of the painting."

"Exactly." His eyes were fixed on me like he was trying to determine if I had made any sense of his analogy.

"So, you're saying that instead of a Picasso, you could see me more as a Monet?" I asked.

"No, what I'm saying is that in many ways your life is like a Monet. When you try to look at it up close, in the present, it can look confusing. But when you step back and look at your life in retrospect, you gain clarity. You can see the whole picture. I guess you could say each experience is one splotch of paint in your great masterpiece of life."

"Oh." That was all I could say after his deep and meaningful analogy. I was still trying to take it all in. "You make it sound so. . . easy."

"Thank you by the way," he murmured.

"For what?" I asked, feeling totally clueless once again.

"For letting me live vicariously through you. I would never have had the chance to see some of the earthly beauties and wonders of the world if it hadn't been for you and your parents who drug you there."

"I'm sure it's nothing compared to the place where you were." I was truly surprised by his interest in my mundane world.

"No, it isn't. But still, it's fascinating to see what humans are capable of. They are capable of such beauty when they put their minds to it."

"Do you think we would have found each other if, um, it weren't for the crash? I mean, if you were still living in the human sense of the word."

"Of course, we just might not have figured everything out right away."

"I bet we would have. I knew that you were something special the first time I saw you. There was something familiar about you."

I lay looking up at the sky. This moment was perfect. I couldn't remember being this happy.

"This would be it."

"This would be what?" he asked

"My moment. This would be my moment. You said if I could remember my happiest moment it would be Heaven. This is my moment. I have never been so happy."

"Me neither."

"I could think of one thing that would make me just a little bit happier."

"And what would that be?" he said with reluctance, as if I were going to ask him for the world.

"Just a little kiss. That's not too much to ask, is it?" I inched my way closer to him until he was warming my entire body.

"You're doing it again, Rae."

"What?" I asked, trying to play innocent.

"Tempting me."

"I don't think one little kiss is going to hurt anything," I begged. His willpower was driving me crazy. I had dreamt about his kiss from the moment he left. It would have been better if he had never touched my lips with his at all. Then I wouldn't know what I was missing. It was like he was depriving me of a drug that I needed to keep my pathetic body alive.

"Not going to hurt anything, huh? Patience may not be one of your stronger traits but persuasiveness definitely is," he whispered as his body came closer to mine. He pulled me to him without hesitating and wrapped his arms around me, bringing me to the place that I felt safest. The strength in his gentleness never failed to surprise me.

"Marriage, that's what you want?" he said, smiling as he brushed the loose hair back from my face.

"I just want you, forever. I want you to promise that you will never leave me again."

"Rae . . . I just don't know that . . . "

"Just kiss me," I interrupted. My heart was pounding.

"Okay," he hesitated before he pressed his lips to mine. He held them there for what seemed like an eternity. I couldn't think of a better way to spend my eternity than this. He pulled back gently, his beautiful face now holding me captive.

"I could get used to this."

"You see what I mean, Rae Colbert. I have no control of myself when I'm around you."

"Control is overrated," I told him, as I leaned in for another bit of Heaven.

# CHAPTER TWENTY

*I* had an idea for today," he said, trying to hold back all of his excitement. I was becoming quite good at reading his emotional status through his eyes. They say the eyes are the window to the soul, and I couldn't disagree.

"What's your idea?" I asked, trying to sound equally enthusiastic. It didn't take much for me to be content. My idea of fun these days consisted of sitting at the park talking to Alex, hoping that he might touch me, because it was the warmth of his skin that reminded me that he was real, that I wasn't crazy. Besides, I can't deny that even the slightest touch of his fingers across the top of my hand was invigorating. I was well aware of how pathetic that sounded.

"I was going to take you somewhere," he answered, being careful not to give too much away.

"Like a date?" I asked, the enthusiasm in my voice becoming genuine. Alex and I hadn't been on a real date since before he left. We had been careful to be discreet about our meetings since his return. I had tried to convince him that flaunting our relationship could in no way benefit our situation. I had yet to ask him what would happen if my parents found out about us. I guess my hesitation was because I didn't actually want to hear the answer. I didn't want our fun to end.

"Yes, like a date," he confirmed.

"Well, where are you taking me?" I already knew his answer before I even asked. He had no intention of telling me.

"It's a surprise!" He smiled, once again, satisfied with himself for keeping me in the dark.

"How did I know you were going to say that?" I scowled.

"Don't worry, it will be fun."

"What if someone sees us?"

"I don't think we need to worry about that." He sounded confident, so I dismissed the idea of getting caught; however, there was something appealing to being so secretive. I felt like I was breaking the law. I felt like I was tasting the forbidden fruit and that made my attraction to him all the more intense.

"Okay." I dropped the subject and tried to relax and enjoy the fact that I didn't have to be at school all day. The prospect of Saturday and Sunday was what got me through the week. The weekends, for the most part, gave me uninterrupted Alex time. That is if the parents didn't ask too many questions.

I stared at the old bridge that stretched out in front of us, our secret spot in the middle of the park. It was secluded and beautiful. I never had to worry about us here. This neglected area of the park had been forgotten when the new section was added. We seemed to be the only ones who appreciated the dilapidated bridge and its rundown surroundings.

The irises were blooming now, a little earlier than normal. I always admired the beauty of nature, thanks to my dad. He was the one who taught me most of what I knew about plants and trees. We used to take walks when I was younger, and he would educate me on every species of plant and tree that we saw. He was a walking encyclopedia of horticulture. My dad grew up on a farm and as a boy, his entertainment came from taking nature walks and exploring the riverbeds of his Missouri farm. I found it fascinating. I loved that about him.

"My mom thinks I went for a run," I said as I pulled myself up off the ground. He followed my movements with precision. "What time are we leaving on our hot date?" Excitement returned to my voice.

"Around five or so," he replied. "You might want to spend some time with your parents before we go. I mean . . . you don't want them to start asking questions about where you're spending all of your time, do you?"

"You're probably right," I reluctantly agreed. "I think I'm going to at least attempt a run. If I come home smelling like roses instead of sweat, they may begin to wonder where I've been all morning. Do you want to come with?"

"No, thank you." His tactful choice of words did not seem to fit with the look on his face. Alex could not stand the idea of exercise. I guess he would really have no use for something so unremarkable. "I don't understand why you enjoy it so much," he continued.

"Well, Alex, exercise is what we earthlings do to stay healthy." I turned, pulling him near to me and giving him a quick peck on the lips. "I'll see you tonight."

"Tonight," he said, repeating my words.

"Where should we meet?" I asked, jogging in place.

"Just meet me here. I'll be waiting."

He watched me as I ran off toward the newer section of the park, heading for the trails. I didn't usually jog the path unless I was in the company of others, but there was much more to look at on the path, plus I was already here. I continued to jog as I pulled my dark, black curls into a ponytail. I started out slow, then began to build speed. I could hear each step that my feet made on the path. It was so quiet out this morning, as if every soul in town was still at home enjoying their Saturday morning. Silence was usually something that I cherished. I was a fairly quiet person, but today, the silence of the path made me feel both insecure and vulnerable. I pushed play on my iPod, listening to the mix I had created this morning. The music took away my anxieties. I took the path that was familiar to me, the one that I ran during practice. It stayed close to the main road and had very few areas of complete seclusion. I continued on, my mind beginning to wonder about Alex's plan for the evening. I was excited. I had to admit, I rather enjoyed all this sneaking around. I couldn't stand the thought of him leaving again. I had barely survived his last departure; I knew my heart would be too weak to bear the loss of him again.

The whistling of the wind interrupted my thoughts. I looked down at my left arm where my iPod was secured and saw that the play list was complete. When I looked back up, I found that, while I was deep in my thoughts, I had jogged all the way to mile marker four. I was now just yards away from the tree that looked like twisted taffy; however, unlike before, I drew nearer to it without caution. Exactly as it had happened in my dream, I felt the path beckoning me closer. The dream had been disturbing, but even more unsettling than the dream, was the fact that just days after it occurred, I found myself standing in front of the twisted tree that was the hallmark of my nightmare. I will never forget how I felt at that moment. I felt something almost supernatural stirring inside of me as I considered how my dream had come to pass. It was surreal. It seemed preposterous and the mere craziness of the idea allowed me to erase the notion from my mind. But things were different now. My boyfriend had come back from the dead and the shadow of doubt that used to follow close behind my every move was gone. Nothing was impossible. Alex was proof of that. But could nightmares really come true? I knew the answer lay ahead of me, and it was half curiosity and half determination to prove my nightmare wrong that pushed me forward onto the hard, dirt trail. Once I was fairly deep inside the cover of trees, I realized this trail was nothing like the one in my dreams and a wave of relief washed over me. The path in my dreams was dark, but today, bright streams of light shone down on the ground below and the leaves above were sparse but green. The forest was busy with animals and the surrounding noise only further convinced me that my dream was, in fact, just a dream. I paused, remembering the invisible force field from my nightmare and how it stood in my way when I attempted to retreat. "Crazy," I scoffed. But then, with a bit of hesitation, I turned my body in the direction of the twisted tree and began to walk toward it. I expected to feel resistance, but I felt none. My dream was a dream and I was not crazy, I silently told myself. And I was just beginning to believe it when I neared the end of the forest and saw what lay ahead. Instead of light at the end of the tunnel of trees, as in my nightmare, there was only darkness. I glanced over my shoulder, contemplating whether or not to run the half-mile back to the tree or to continue into the darkness. Without considering the consequences, the darkness reeled me in.

I was now on a narrow, asphalt path that ran like a vein through a field of waist-high native grass. The path I was on was as flat as a board and I could see for miles; I could see nothing for miles. The tall native grass did little to block the strong gusts of wind and it seemed as though every step I took forward, I was blown two steps in the opposite direction.

It was still mid-morning, but the sky had turned a deep, charcoal grey; only hints of light filtered through the clouds, shining like diamonds onto the black asphalt. I looked around and found that I was still the only runner out this morning and all of my forgotten anxiousness flooded through my body once again. In reality, the path was unfamiliar, but I had seen it in my dreams. I had just decided to turn back when I saw a man coming toward me. He appeared out of nowhere, not walking on the path, but through the grass instead. The sky was growing darker; ominous clouds began rotating above us. My intrigue prevented me from moving. I felt like a deer staring into a set of headlights. His features became clearer as he neared. His features provoked in me an unexplainable fear and yet, I stood still, motionless. I felt myself slipping into a dream like state, but I knew this was no dream.

As he neared, the sky grew even darker. All of the little diamonds on the pavement began to disappear one at a time and the sky turned a yellowish-green. The man stepped onto the path, standing several yards away; still, I was unable to move. He stood in the center of the path, unlike a friendly jogger who might move to the side to let others pass. There was nothing about his positioning that suggested he was going to let me by. His eyes were fixed on me and panic began to tear through my body as I recalled the familiarity of the situation. I was surrounded by circumstances that I had seen in my dreams, but standing on a path that my feet had never crossed until this morning. I looked at the man in front of me and realized it wasn't his appearance that made me cringe in fear. His appearance wouldn't attract any unusual attention. He was attractive, hypnotically so. He was tall and muscular with an angular face and dark hair. His wispy bangs fell just above his eyes. His eyes held a certain familiarity. They brought about so many feelings at the same time: panic, sadness, despair. My legs felt heavy and my feet felt as if they were sticking to the pavement. We were alone and he was moving closer. He stopped; only a few feet now separated his body from mine.

"I don't believe your mother would approve . . . your being out here alone like this. You always have been a pathetic, little girl," he said, curling his lip in disgust. "I don't understand it, really . . . but I suppose it's not for me to understand."

I continued to stare at him. I was speechless. I could not find my voice. His voice was sticky and thick, but not the honey-like smoothness I found in Alex's. His expression changed to one of amusement, as if he were looking forward to what he would do next.

"I've come here to take care of something that I should have done a long time ago. I'll try to make this as painless as possible." He stiffened, a smug smile emerged and then, while my legs were still cemented to the ground, he lunged at me with surprising strength, pinning me down.

My head hit the hard concrete beneath me, sending an immediate and excruciating pain through my entire body. I felt something snap and pain rushed to my arm and I screamed in anguish. His hands were gripping my throat leaving my arms free to move in defense, but it pained me too much to do so. I choked, my legs kicking in the air desperately. I could feel my oxygen supply running low. The air seemed thicker and my lungs felt heavy, as if there were a heaping pile of rocks stacked upon my chest. It hurt. I couldn't believe that just weeks ago I was begging Alex to let me die, to go back with him and leave this awful world. My life was flashing before my eyes and fear consumed me. I wondered if I would make it to Heaven. I had always considered myself a decent enough person. I had never intentionally done anything to hurt another human being. I'm not sure I would go so far as to say I was a good person. I had always wondered what it would be like to be a good person, a truly saint-like person. I knew the kind; the kind that always does the right thing at the right time, without even thinking about it, without a hint of selfishness or greed. It was like it just came naturally. If I had been that type of person, I may not have feared the fate that lay ahead of me. My body was in constant battle with my soul. It was no longer the idea of God and goodness that perplexed me. To be good seemed a hard task, yet simple enough to understand. Still, I wondered if everyone struggled as I did. Despite my struggles with holiness, it was the idea of evil that I couldn't grasp. Evil was something I had yet to experience. It wasn't until this moment that I found pure evil, that I stared it in the face. I stared back into the deep, dark eyes of death, trying to replace them with the gentle, green eyes that I so longed to see.

The scant light that was surrounding us began to fade, each second growing darker. I knew that it wasn't the sky that was dimming; it was my life that was quickly fading away. I would soon be nothing more than a memory. And then, without warning, as I was preparing to take my final breath of air, my assailant was violently jerked away from me with one forceful swoop. My eyes were not prepared for what I saw when I opened them. I was certain that I had died and was now in the Heavenly realms. Was there a battle being fought over my soul? At that exact moment, the clouds began to part and a magnificent ray of sunlight forced its way onto the path, surrounding a human-like form while leaving my assailant in the dark. Who was this person that had rescued me? The light and its source filled me with a new kind of fear, a fear that I had never experienced before. I wanted to run from the light and the person inside; but at the same time, I wanted that light to surround me, envelop me, and take me away. I no longer feared for my body; I feared for my soul. I was sure that I had taken my final breath, but still, I slinked back to the edge of the path, pulling myself into the tall, yellow grass behind me. The light grew brighter by the second until it was blinding, unbearable, and so, once again, I quickly shut my eyes and held them tight. But even in this position, it felt as though the light was searing through my eyeballs, simultaneously shooting pain and heat up the optic nerve into my brain, the intensity of the heat now awakening my sense of sound and smell. My nostrils were filled with the scent of rising smoke and looming rain. A noise like an out-of-control freight train now accompanied the mayhem, a deep, haunting, ripping noise that tore through body and soul. It seemed like hours before I felt the intensity of the light wane and the searing pain subdue. When it did, I lifted my lids with hesitance, but nothing could have prepared me for what I saw. A fight had ensued. One like I had never seen before, not even in the movies. Elements of nature pulled toward the two figures like magnets, creating a funnel of dirt, debris, and limbs. Native grass was uprooting from the soil. The tall, yellow, stinging blades whipped across my face, my arms, my legs. I seemed to be the only thing sticking to the ground, as though I was being held in place on purpose, forced into watching the fight that was unfolding before my very eyes. As the funnel grew larger with matter, the light became less and less, allowing me a better look. I shielded my eyes from the dust and looked at the monstrous tornado head-on. Flashes of flesh were peeking out of the debris—an elbow, a shoulder, a foot—protruding from this force of nature and then pulling back inside. The ghostly rumbling continued. My senses were now so overwhelmed that I wasn't sure whether to shield my ears or my eyes. The cloud of dirt and other earthly matter had shielded me from the brilliant light that, just moments ago, I could hardly tolerate, but as the battle drew on, debris began to settle and, once again, the light began to shine. I continued to stare until it became too bright for me to bear, so I closed my eyes in fear and discomfort. The smell of smoke had vanished and all at once, it seemed the earth was still. The next thing that I felt was warmth. It surrounded me and then a familiar voice filled my ears. I sat with my knees tucked to my chest, trembling, with fear still griping me so tightly that I couldn't force my eyes to open.

"You're shaking, Rae," the voice said softly. "You're hurt." I could feel my arm being lifted.

"Ouch," I cried. My eyes opened to examine the source of my pain, but they were detoured as I glimpsed a pair of familiar hazel eyes.

"Alex?" I whispered. His eyes were familiar, but iridescence had replaced his pallor, and all of the rugged features that belonged to the Alex I knew had been replaced with softer, more beautiful lines, chiseled cheekbones, and bright ruby lips. I could almost see directly through him. My eyes narrowed, the light still blinding, and so I shut them tightly once again.

I didn't fear him, as I should have. I felt safe and warm and desperately confused.

"Does it hurt?" he asked.

"Yes," I admitted, realizing now that my adrenaline was waning and the pain was swooshing over me in throbbing waves. He placed his hand over my mangled limb. I closed my eyes tight. I felt him touch my arm. It felt invigorating, and then the pain was gone.

"Better?" he asked in a smooth, honey-like voice that caused me to open my eyes at once.

"Alex?" I asked again, but this time there was no question, it was him. The light haloing over my boyfriend's body had disappeared, a cloud now covered the sun, and the sky returned to darkness. I had my Alex back. He wrapped me in his arms, my safe spot, my blanket of security.

"Is he gone?" I gasped.

"Yes, he's gone." He tried to calm me. He stroked my hair as I lay in his lap. I raised slightly to look around. He was gone. Had he just disappeared into thin air?

"I don't understand." My mind was so full of questions that I didn't know where to begin.

"What is there to understand?" he asked calmly.

My heart continued to pound and my knees were shaking uncontrollably.

"Am I dead?" I asked, not really caring one way or the other now that he was with me.

"No, you're not dead," he laughed.

"So, maybe I just had one of those near death experiences, because I know what I saw."

"And what is it that you claim to have seen?"

"I saw a boy turn into a demon. And then, I saw a bright and blinding light," I spurted out. I realized how foolish I sounded. The average person might think I was crazy or something like it. I was in love with the non-living, I was being attacked by demons, and I was seeing bright lights surrounding angelic figures. My imagination was out of control. I was beginning to think myself crazy.

"I thought you said you weren't an angel," I said accusingly.

"I'm not an angel," he replied, pulling from our earlier conversation.

"If you're not an angel then what was that light?" I asked, confusion still consuming me.

"I believe they call it the sun."

"But you looked, you looked so . . . ."

"You know what I think?"

"What." I knew my voice sounded desperate. I was desperate, desperate for him to give me any sort of explanation that would ease my mind.

"I think you think too much."

I scowled and hung my head.

"Are you trying to tell me that what just happened wasn't a big deal?"

"No, not at all. What I'm telling you is exactly what I told you before. There is nothing easy about us being together."

"Was he a demon?"

Alex began to laugh, obviously amused by something I had said. "You speak of demons like storybook characters," he chuckled, trying to straighten his smile into seriousness. "I can just picture the thoughts that are flying around in your head right now."

"Well, excuse me for using the wrong terminology. What would you rather me call him? He looked like a demon if I have ever seen one."

"And maybe he was just a man; in the same sort of way that I'm a man," he suggested.

"Did you kill him?"

"No, I didn't kill him."

He sounded annoyed.

"Well, where did he go then?" I turned my head, scanning the surroundings for his presence. I was lying in Alex's arms, several yards away from the apex of the storm which was a gigantic pile of debris. The square mile surrounding us was now completely barren. Not a single blade of grass remained. It looked as though a seismic wave had pulled portions of the path away from the ground and now the asphalt resembled a crumpled ribbon rather than something to run on.

"Let's just say he was a little scared of this," Alex said, patting patting his muscular bicep.

"Whatever." I rolled my eyes and then all at once, I remembered something that my attacker had said, something that struck in a new way. "I think he knew me," I gasped. "He said that my mother wouldn't approve of me being out on the path by myself. He said he was here to take care of something that should have been done a long time ago. I think he wanted me dead!"

Alex ignored me, his face turning serious once again as he scanned my body for scrapes, bruises, or blood.

"Are you sure you're alright?" Uncertainty rang in his voice.

My eyes were closed and my mind was still somewhere far away. I could not erase from my mind the eyes of my attacker. There was something about those eyes that made me feel desperate, a kind of desperate that I could not yet place but that I knew I had felt before. Was it a coincidence that someone had wanted me dead, not once, but twice in less than two months? I wanted to believe that my life with Alex would be perfect now that he was back, but every bone in my body told me that something much, much darker lay ahead of us both.

"Rae," Alex spoke again. "Are you okay?"

"Yeah. Yeah. I'm okay." I opened my eyes and all at once the darkness left me. "Looks like I just have a small scrape on my elbow. I think I will live. All thanks to you."

"Come on, let's get you out of here, it's getting ready to storm." He swooped me up in his arms and then gently set me down on my two feet, brushing all of the grass from my clothes.

"So, do you want to fly me home?" I suggested. "You know, it would be much faster."

"Let's not get too carried away with this superhuman thing, Rae," he said as he wrapped his arm around my waist, holding me in a more protective way than usual. "I wouldn't want you to be disappointed."

"Fine, but you know that at some point you will have to cave in; you said it yourself, I am impatient and persuasive. You didn't really think I was going to forget all about this, did you?"

"We'll just see about that. I'm guessing that patience is one area where you need a bit of work."

## CHAPTER TWENTY-ONE

*I* pulled into my drive and found my parents gardening in the front yard. The sky had cleared, not a cloud in the Heavens, and the sun was shining brightly. I guess Mother Nature couldn't decide what she wanted to do today.

For as long as I can remember, my parents had been deprived of gardening because we never actually had a yard; besides, even if we would have had a yard, we were never in one place long enough to watch anything grow. I guess they were making up for lost time, because it looked as though they had bought out every nursery in Bartlesville. Huge assortments of flowers were strung out across our yard.

"Doing a little planting, I see." I circled around the yard, admiring the purple salvia, the day lilies, the assortment of rose bushes that I had never cared for, some geraniums that my mom had set near several hanging baskets, flocks, creeping jenny, and a few small trees I couldn't identify.

"Do you want to help?" they asked hopefully, as I walked closer to them, taking a real interest in their purchase. I flashed them an "are you crazy" look.

"Did you take out a second mortgage on the house to buy all of this stuff, or what?"

"Oh my goodness, Rae! What happened to your arm?" My mom's voice was close to hysterical. You would have thought that, with her being a doctor, she would be in a little better control of her emotions. I knew that she was a shrink and wasn't accustomed to seeing blood, but I could only hope that she didn't act this way with her patients. She had explained to me that being in a medical setting was much different than being at home and that at home, she was a mom first and a doctor second.

"Oh, it's no big deal. I just fell while I was out for a run." It truly was nothing compared to the more severe injury that Alex had miraculously healed with one gentle swoop of his angelic hand. At that moment, something occurred to me. My mind flashed back to the night I fell down the stairs at school. Not a bruise on my body. Two others had been there that night. Could he have been there? Was he the one that called 911? Had he healed me?

"It looks like road rash to me. I've seen it over and over again. I'm sure it will leave a scar," she said.

"Great, way to be optimistic, Mother."

"We should go inside and get that cleaned up." Concern was still heavy in her voice.

"I can do it, Mom. And if you don't mind, I think I will help. With the gardening, I mean." I needed to be around someone. I couldn't stand the idea of being alone, even if it was in the safety of my own home. I didn't know much about demons, or whatever it was on the path today, but I was sure that they were not limited by boundaries.

"That would be perfect." She looked taken aback, but regardless, I seemed to have made her day.

I washed my arm off in the kitchen sink. I now realized why her voice was so hysterical. The blow that I had received as the boy crushed me down on the path had scraped all of the skin away from my forearm. It looked oozy so I washed it, grimacing as I pulled small bits of gravel out of my unprotected flesh. I found a bit of gauze and antibiotic ointment and wrapped it loosely around my arm. I returned to my mother, who was completely camouflaged in a hibiscus plant. I donned a pair of gardening gloves and grabbed a small shovel, waiting for step by step instructions on how to keep each plant alive as long as possible.

"How far did you run?" my mom asked with a hint of skepticism in her voice.

"Oh, I don't know. About four miles or so," I lied.

"You were gone an awfully long time," she continued to grill me.

"I ran into some friends," I lied again . . . sort of.

"Well, that's nice. Who?"

"What is this, the Spanish Inquisition?" I asked, becoming slightly defensive.

"I'm sorry, I know I should feel much safer here in Oklahoma, but I still don't like the idea of you just running around without any kind of supervision. Our family doesn't seem to have the best of luck, you know."

This was the first time in my life that my mother had ever verbally acknowledge the misfortunes of my family and for a moment neither one of us spoke. I noticed that my father had looked up from the hole he was digging in the front yard waiting, I suppose, to see if my mother would say anything more.

"I just feel like I am losing you, Rae. You're never home anymore. And I really don't like the idea of you running on that path all by yourself. There are weirdos out there, no matter where you live. You have to be careful." She paused, her eyes shifting nervously to the flowers. She picked up one of the black, plastic containers that, five minutes ago, had been the home of a pansy and began to twist it between her fingers. Finally, after cracking one of the thin, plastic sides, she threw it in the large recycle bin on the front porch.

261

"You do seem very happy now. Much happier than before . . . " She stopped herself in mid-sentence. She didn't like to use the word "Alex" around me for fear it would cast me back into the pits of depression like a spell.

Despite my mother's nervous behavior, I felt closer to her, closer than I ever had before. There was no shell separating my heart from hers. The pain was out there and we were dealing with it, in our own ways, but at least we were no longer ignoring the pain that was so real. I wasn't sure when Alex and I would be leaving, but I knew I would miss this when I was gone. I would miss her. I would miss them both. It's hard when you can't have what you want, but it's worse when you have the two things in life that you most want and you have to choose between them. I had always heard that you can't have your cake and eat it, too. I had never understood that seemingly silly figure of speech, but now I get it. You can't have it both ways. You can't have two totally incompatible things. I could not live with an angel and expect to fit in here on earth, too. I felt so selfish; I hadn't even stopped to consider what my parents would go through. I was their only child. They were losing their identity as parents. They had already lost one daughter. I was so selfish to make them go through it once again. Telling myself that I would visit often was the only thing that gave me comfort. But it just wasn't the same. Yes, I knew I would see them again, but it was the secrets that I couldn't stand. I mindlessly began plugging plants into the holes that my mother had dug to the recommended depth and then finished by scooping dirt around the flowers to fill in the empty spots.

"Dad and I are going to a movie tonight, and I think we're grabbing a bite to eat before it starts. I hadn't planned anything for dinner," she said apologetically.

"Mom, no offense, but that's nothing new. I am capable of cooking, you know. I will be on my own here in a couple of months, and you won't be there to take care of me anymore." I was testing the waters, trying to determine if she had considered my independence as regularly as I had.

"I know." Sadness rang in her voice, and I wished that I hadn't brought it up at all.

"Well, I'm done." I stood back to admire our work. "I think I'll go and get showered," I said, looking at my watch, amazed that it was already 3:30. The weekends had a way of flying by much too quickly. The water from the shower felt like fire running over my arm. I examined it while it was unwrapped, looking for anything that might indicate what sort of wound Alex had supernaturally healed. There was nothing. Other than the oozing open scrape, there was not a trace of anything more severe.

A fairly risky idea had been playing through my mind from the moment my mother said I would have the house to myself tonight. I didn't want to be alone, but I also didn't feel like going anywhere either, and the option of having Alex over to keep me company was becoming more and more appealing by the second. Convincing him of this wouldn't be hard, considering he was of the opinion that my parents should know about us, as well as our plans for the future.

Just as I thought, he agreed without hesitation. I slipped on my sweats and a tank top, so that my attire wouldn't arouse my parents' suspicions and waited for him to arrive.

I lay on the blanket looking up at the stars, Alex by my side. The warm night air was blowing over us. Crickets were chirping in the background, and we could hear the occasional howling of a coyote somewhere in the distance. It was perfect.

"This would be it."

"This would be what?"

"My most perfect moment. My Heaven moment."

"Mine too." We lay side by side without saying a word, observing the sky, his hand lightly touching mine.

"Alex."

"Yes," he answered. His voice seemed distant; he seemed a thousand miles away.

"When do you want to leave?"

"I just got here."

"No, this town . . . with me?"

"Oh." He paused for a moment to think it over. "Well, I think that's entirely up to you. You're the one who has to be ready. I mean, you're the one who is leaving everything behind."

"You're right, but I am ready. I'm tired of hiding."

"We'll see how you feel after graduation; besides, there's a little something that I need to take care of before we can leave."

"What's that?"

"You'll know soon enough."

"Why does everything have to be a surprise with you?" I asked, biting my lower lip in frustration. "We're talking about spending the rest of our lives together. We can't be keeping secrets like this." I now rolled over on my side to face him so that he could see the seriousness of my expression.

"Look, I'll make you a deal. I have one last secret and that will be it. I promise."

"That sounds reasonable."

"When will I find out this secret?"

"How about the night of graduation. That's just a couple of days away. That will give me some time to work a few things out. You can wait that long, right?"

"I think I can manage." We were both silent, but just for a moment, and then I disrupted the peace with my long list of questions.

"Can we talk about what happened today on the path?"

"What do you want to know?" he asked in a way that made me almost believe that there was nothing left to tell.

"So, how did you know where to find me? I didn't even know where I was."

"I followed you," he responded vaguely.

"You ran?" I could hardly believe it. "You must love me."

"I never said I couldn't run, I just said I didn't like to."

"What about the light?" I asked, not wasting any time. "What was that light surrounding you?"

"I already answered that."

"I don't think it was the sun. It was a miracle," I disagreed.

"Do you believe in miracles?" he asked.

"Until you came back, there wasn't a lot that I believed in, but now, I guess I believe that anything is possible."

"And you think today at the park would fit into that category?"

"Well, it's a miracle that you saved my life and healed my arm."

"Then what are you asking?"

"Not that I'm disappointed, because I'm not. I guess I just thought that a miracle would be more obvious, you know, like someone being raised from the dead or making a single loaf of bread feed thousands."

"You know a miracle doesn't have to be a blinding light show to be a miracle. They happen everyday; humans are just too blind to notice."

"I guess I just expected to see God, or at least the devil himself . . . but preferably God."

"Sometimes I think you live in a storybook, Rae." Once again he looked amused.

"And, Rae, just for future reference, in case you see another miracle anytime soon, it does help if you have your eyes open," he said, referring to the fetal position I had assumed on the path this morning; my eyes clinched tightly.

Now I rolled my eyes at his obnoxiousness. "Can we ever have a conversations about something serious without you turning it into a joke or avoiding the topic all together?"

"Well, I was seriously thinking that we should tell your parents about us. I am over at your house and everything. I thought that maybe you had a change of heart." He looked at me wishfully, puppy dog eyes and all.

"Not possible."

"They'll find out eventually."

"We don't even know how long you're going to stay. Right now, the most important thing is for us to be together."

As soon as the words left my lips, I was reminded of the painful truth. He would have to go. At some point he was going to leave me again. I watched as Alex rolled onto his back and stared up at the stars. By the look on his face you would have thought that I had shattered his dreams. In a way, I understood why he wanted so badly to tell my parents. I couldn't blame him for wanting a family; he had never had one, not really. The family that he wanted was the same family that I had always taken for granted.

"How long will you stay?" I could hear pain in my voice as I spoke.

"The longer I am here on earth, the weaker I become, the more human I become. Even though I'm not exactly human, I'm not just a spirit anymore either."

"What do you mean weaker? Weaker how?"

"Weaker physically, weaker mentally. Each day that passes, my memory of before becomes less and less."

"Will you have to go back soon?" I gulped.

"Would you still love me if I was merely human?"

"Are you leaving me again, tonight?" I asked with finality.

"Do you promise you'll love me when I can't save you from evil demons or even from yourself?"

"I promise. I promise anything to keep you here," I gasped.

"You promise then to love me when I get old and have grey hair and bad breath?" He questioned me further. I scrunched up my nose and pretended that I was reconsidering.

"Yes, of course I do. I just want you here with me, forever."

"Okay, then I guess I have no other choice but to stay with you, forever," he said thoughtfully. "For as long as forever is on this earth. What I'm trying to say is that I will do my best to not get sucked up to Heaven any time soon."

This was something I hadn't counted on. I knew we had time together, but I had also been preparing myself for his departure ever since he arrived. I was too overwhelmed to speak.

"Look, I think after all that's happened today, I'm going to hang around here tonight."

"My parents will be home in like thirty minutes!" I shrieked.

"I'm just saying that if you see a car on your gravel road tonight, don't worry, it's just me."

I had no problem with that. I was an easy target and I felt much more at ease knowing that he was close. I no longer felt safe unless I was wrapped in his arms. I wanted him to hold me all night. I wanted to leave now, to leave this town behind, and to begin the new life we had talked about.

"Thank you," I whispered. "For taking care of me . . . for coming back . . . for loving me."

"Shh," he whispered, and he touched his finger to my lips.

I pushed his finger away. "There's one last thing that's bothering me."

"Let's hear it," he said in an unusually drawn out voice.

"I've told you about my dreams. That day you found me in the park . . . you know, before you left me." He rolled his eyes as if he were dreading the direction the conversation was going. He hated when I brought up the several months that we spent apart; it made him feel guilty, and it was something he avoided discussing at all costs. "That wasn't the only time I had a dream like that. What happened in the park today, with the exception of a few little things, is exactly how I dreamt it. Every last detail."

He was silent, still staring up at the sky, still very far away.

"What do you think that means?"

"I don't really think it's all that strange. It's called having a sixth sense. Maybe your dreams were just a warning."

I considered this for a moment before assuming that he was correct. I had heard of this sort of thing before, people canceling flights because they dreamt their plane would crash and then finding out that their dream had been correct, that their dream had told the future.

"Do you think that makes me weird?" I asked

"Yeah, a little maybe. But you ain't got nothing on me."

"You're right; I'm not even sure we're in the same league," I laughed.

"Do you think that means our future is planned? Do you think that means we have no choice what happens to us?" I continued.

"Well, if that were so, then we would just be pawns in one great big game of chess," he answered.

I paused for a moment before considering something else. "Do you think we're messing up some sort of universal plan, you being here, you and me being together? If we were pawns, do you think we would be cheating?"

"Maybe, but I wouldn't have it any other way." He rolled over on his side so that he was now looking at me. He put my face in his hands and moved me so that I was looking directly into his eyes.

"You know what I think?

"What?" I whispered.

"I think you think too much."

"Maybe."

I climbed the stairs to my room and looked out the window. His car was there, barely visible to the unsuspecting eye, shining under all of the beautiful stars. He was there to protect me.

I lay in bed replaying the events of the day in my mind. Alex hovering over my assailant, defeating him without even lifting a finger, without even laying a hand on him. His bright eyes and his iridescent, angelic face were so different than the features of his human body. The Wonder Woman I so wanted to be for Halloween when I was just five-years-old was quickly descending from the pedestal I had put her on. She would be no match for Alex the angel. I now realized that the human mind is easily satisfied with its own creations, not even realizing the wonders that are right in front of us if we only opened our eyes and looked. Miracles did happen and they were happening to me. I had secretly wished for a supernatural experience and it had been delivered; not in the way I had imagined it would happen, but He delivered none-the-less. Nothing had been spared. I had never understood God before this moment. In fact, I wasn't even sure He existed. But now, after everything that had happened in the past few months, I was beginning to understand. God didn't always use miracles to accomplish things here on earth. Sometimes He used the things here on earth to accomplish His miracles.

## CHAPTER TWENTY-TWO

*O*ne last secret. One last secret. These three words rang over and over in my mind while I was out for my morning run. They were bothering me, infuriating me, consuming me, and I didn't know why. And then, as if a bolt of lightening struck me, I knew. I was still bothered by the fact that I had never been able to keep anything from Alex. He knew everything about me. He had a whole stack of secrets that he dangled over my head. He taunted me with them and I had to admit, I was a bit envious. He had this advantage over me for the last seventeen years. It now dawned on me that he no longer had the same advantage, at least not to the extent he did before, when he was in the halfway. He was on my turf now, and I couldn't help but be tempted by the idea of having one final secret of my own.

I had four days left until our pact was final; four days left until the secret that would end all secrets. It wasn't as if I had to create something elaborate; there was a little something already brewing. In fact, it was a puzzle that was begging to be put together, a mystery that needed to be solved. It was a nagging that wouldn't seem to leave me alone and this something was Chloe Pierce.

Since Alex's return the Chloe conspiracy had been put on the back burner; however, it didn't mean that all of the questions I had before weren't just as troubling. And now, after being assaulted for the second time in just under two months, I knew that I had two options: fight or flight. I had no intention of sitting around and waiting for the next attack. Alex suggested that I might have a sixth sense. If he were right and my dreams were a warning, then I could not ignore the fact that, in my most recent nightmare, there had been both a man and a woman searching for me. Last fall, I saw Chloe slip off onto the path that was marked by the twisted tree. What did this mean? Was it a coincidence that I almost met my demise on the path that she liked to frequent? Had she been trying to lure me onto the path behind her? The blurred face of the woman in my dream could have been Chloe, I suppose. And the man in my dream could have been the same man who had attacked me on the path yesterday morning. But who was he? How did he know me? What was it about his eyes that looked so familiar? Why did he want me dead? And if he was with Chloe, then how were they connected? These were the answers that I needed to find.

I had saved all of Claire's voicemails and in the last week, had played them over and over again out of curiosity. The first couple of messages sounded normal. It was the last of the messages that had captured my attention. Claire's voice was frantic. The voice that was so robotic and predictable was gone; it was now laced with emotion and concern. The change intrigued me almost as much as her purpose for calling, which I assumed was Chloe. I filled my head with different scenarios that would cause her to be so out of sorts. Had she gone to find Chloe on her own? Did she find her? Had she gotten hurt? Had she learned something new, something that I hadn't considered previously? The truth was . . . I wanted to know. This wasn't something that I could leave unfinished. Besides, I would have to face Claire at some point, and I would also have to come up with an excuse for my apparent rudeness.

It took the rest of my run home to come up with something believable, something worthy of dismissing my recluse behavior, and something convincing enough to have her help me once again. I thought of everything from mountainous stacks of homework to creating some medical condition that had caused me to semi-permanently lose my voice. I decided on a partial truth. I would tell her that I was distraught over my nana's death, and it was all I could do to pull myself out of bed every morning. It was an exaggeration, but not a complete fabrication.

I ran up my gravel drive and, once again, I found my parents in the yard gardening. I pulled my cell phone out of my pocket and scanned through the numbers in my directory before clicking on Claire's. I took several deep breaths before I touched the number and waited for it to ring. It rang three times before she picked up. Her voice sounded less frantic, but still not the monotonic voice that I usually associated with Claire.

"Hello."

"Claire?" I asked. I did want to be certain I was speaking with the right person before I began spilling my guts about my plans for the next four days.

"Hey." She sounded upset with me, and with good reason.

"I did get your messages . . . and I'm sorry it's taken so long to call you back." I didn't realize how guilty I should actually feel until the words escaped my lips. She had done me this gigantic favor, and I had blown her off. I was a terrible person. I was a terrible friend. I knew she would totally understand my reasoning for doing so if I told her the truth: that I had found Alex, but she was going to have to settle for the prefabricated excuse that I had so carefully come up with just moments ago. I told her about my nana and the rough time my family was having with it. I told her that things were better now, and I was ready to finish what we started.

"Rae."

"Yeah."

"I have to confess."

"What?" I could handle anything now. I had a boyfriend that had come to me from the dead. There was nothing on this earth that could shake me.

"I tried calling you like five or six times but. . . ."

"Try more like thirteen times, Claire. It must have been something important."

"Well, at first I called like five or six times. I was concerned about your nana. By the way, I had no idea that she died, and I'm so sorry. But anyway, I called to see how your nana was and to see when you thought you would be back . . . I waited over two weeks and I didn't hear anything, so, I um . . . " She didn't appear to want to finish the sentence. Was she afraid I would be mad? "I couldn't wait any longer, Rae."

"Any longer for what?"

"I went to her house, to Chloe's address, the one that was on her transcript."

"And." She now had every last bit of my attention.

"You were right, Rae. She's still here."

"You saw her?" I gasped. I took several deep but silent breaths trying desperately to regain my composure. If what Claire was saying was true, then I was right. Chloe could have been following me that cold spring morning, but why?

"No, I didn't see her." My hopes sank quickly and just as quickly I realized how truly self-destructive I had become. I knew that it would be better for me if Chloe hadn't returned, if Chloe hadn't followed me, if it wasn't Chloe's car that I saw. Was I really that desperate for an adventure that I was willing to possibly endanger myself in the process? I decided the answer was yes; after the terrifying events at the park yesterday, I felt a little on the invincible side.

"I did see her car parked in the drive."

"I'm not crazy, then. She was following me. What else. Did you look around? Did you look in any windows?"

"No. That's why I called you. I thought by going to her house I had already crossed the line. I mean, this is your thing, not mine. By the way, it's a great house, Chloe's, I mean. It's huge, one of those older homes around Utica Square."

"Do you want to go back? With me?" I was rather hoping she would say yes; even though I felt unusually invincible after yesterday, it would be nice to have someone by my side, someone to share in this secret that I was keeping from Alex.

"Are you kidding? I'm in. I thought you'd never ask. Actually, I kind of thought that you had been avoiding me . . . but I'm glad you called."

"When do you want to go?"

"What about in the next couple of days?"

"Um, I don't know. What about tonight?"

"I just have this huge final project in debate that I'm trying to get finished. What's the rush?"

"I have to find out before graduation. It's a long story, but I think I'm leaving again and I need to find out before I go."

"Well, I guess we *could* go tonight, if I spend most of the day at the library."

"What time?"

"It needs to be dark, and it will take us a good forty-five minutes to get there."

"Eight o'clock?"

"Eight it is," she agreed. I shut the phone and headed up to my room without saying a word to my parents. I could feel their eyes following me to the door, and I knew their curiosity was getting the better of them. I had been a bit odd lately; my overly enthusiastic demeanor was so dramatically different from my state of depression during the months after Alex left. Out of the corner of my eye, I saw my mother shrug her shoulders, look at my dad, and then return to her gardening. At least I was a teenager, because pretty much everything could be blamed on erratic teenage hormones.

The clock by my bed read 3:30. I didn't know what I was going to do with myself from now until eight. I fell back onto my unmade bed and looked around my room. I wondered how much I would be able to take with me when I ran away with Alex. I wasn't someone who liked to have things just to have them; I never had much growing up, but there were definitely things in my room that held sentimental value and the newest addition to the collection was the scrapbook my papa had given to me. I decided to pull it out of the box that it had been lying in since I returned home from Missouri. I wondered if I might see the pictures differently now that I knew the story. It would allow me to look at other details that perhaps I hadn't focused on before.

I sat on the edge of the bed and quickly thumbed through the pages until I found the one that I was looking for: the last completed page of the book. I had flipped through the scrapbook dozens of times but, because they were blank, I had never bothered to look at the pages in the back. Yet today, I felt prompted to do so. The emptiness of the pages was no longer unsettling. They reminded me of a blank canvas: pure and white with the potential for color. A new beginning. A fresh start. Maybe Nana's story didn't end with the last page of pictures. Maybe she was leaving the book for someone else to finish. Without thinking, I jumped off my bed, walked over to the bulletin board on the wall, and pulled off a couple of pictures of my family. My nana's story would not end. I would make sure of that. Carefully, I taped a photo onto the first blank page and, with a feeling of satisfaction, turned to the next. At first I didn't notice the white slip of paper that was pressed flat into the middle of the book. It blended into the page. Unlike the other letters that I had found, this one was unaccompanied: no pictures, no envelope, and there was a complete absence of Nana's scratchy handwriting. It was a crisply folded slip of paper that was wedged into the binding and held in place by age. Without thinking, without considering the repercussions, I pulled the letter away from the binding and began to read.

Dear Mr. and Mrs. Colbert,

On the twenty-third day of June, A-Omega received intelligence that a certain package thought to be safe is now in jeopardy. For the past couple of months, we have been attempting to eliminate any problems that might hinder the delivery of said package into your hands. Under optimal circumstances, this package would have been delivered for your safe keeping at a later date, just as we had previously discussed. We can no longer wait. The risks are much too high as we have already learned. We feel that the package would be safer in a more remote location and have confidence that you will do everything in your power to protect it.

We at A-Omega cannot emphasis how important it is that we get this package to safety. As physicians, you are well aware that there will be some care involved. The package will be in grave condition when it arrives, but not beyond repair. However, we must inform you that the requirements for this mission may exceed your level of expertise.

The arrangements for delivery will be simple. Your family will be arriving into the Minneapolis/St. Paul International airport at 6:15 PM on the evening of September 12th. As we at Omega have already informed you, this should be a very simple operation, but in the case that complications should arise, we will have arranged for a contact to meet you at the airport. Your contacts will be Paul and Sarah Loving. They will be equipped in areas that you are not. Transportation will be prearranged and a vehicle will be ready for pick up at the transit center in terminal 1-Lindbergh between concourse C and G. You are to follow your contact to the designated place of safety and wait for further instruction. Your family's patronage has not gone unnoticed.

Arm yourself well,

A-Omega

Ephesians 6: 10-18

I shivered, coldness swept through my body and electric warmth resided in my calves and toes. I could not breathe. So many questions had entered my mind that I couldn't sort them out. The infamous date: September 13th. My birthday. My sister's day of death. And now, it was another important factor linking my family to Alex's. What had my parents been up to? And Alex's parents? They had not been two couples out on a catastrophic evening drive as I had previously thought. They had met. They had both worked for A-Omega. Who were my parents? My parents were shrinks. Head doctors. What business did they have with a package? And Alex's parents? The letter indicated that they would be able to take care of the things that my parents could not. What was this organization, A-Omega, and what did it have to do with me?

I placed the book back into the box and pushed myself up from my bed. It had just occurred to me that maybe Alex knew more than he let on. He wasn't telling me everything and in my book, that was the same as being dishonest. Five minutes ago, I was feeling guilty about having a secret of my own, but now, with all of this newfound information, I did not have a single reservation.

At just before eight, I pulled into the high school parking lot and found that Claire was already there, waving her hand out the window of an unfamiliar car. She convinced me into letting her drive because her mother's car was less conspicuous and because she already knew where she was going.

What's in the backpack?" Claire asked, taking her eyes off the road and focusing them on the green backpack in my lap.

"Stuff, you know. A camera. Some walkie-talkies, binoculars."

"You came prepared."

"Better safe than sorry." I shrugged my shoulders. The truth was, after the events of the last month or so, I couldn't be certain of what we might find, and if I did find something, my father's high dollar, Cannon, digital SLR would help me capture it. Claire continued in the direction of the city, the bright streetlights flashing though the dark, night sky. I could see the glowing of downtown Tulsa getting closer; it was 8:45 when she took an exit off the highway, and my stomach began to twist into knots. She made a series of turns through the dark streets before she came to a stop in an alleyway that ran behind several large estates.

"Is this it?"

"No, it's down about a block or so. You didn't want me to pull up in front of the house, did you?"

"No . . . of course not."

"Are you nervous?"

"Why, can you tell?"

"You just look as though you're about to get sick, that's all."

"So, do we have a game plan?" I asked.

"I'm just along for the ride. You tell me."

"I think the first thing we should do is see if there are any lights on and then see if her car is here. If everything looks okay, I'll take a couple of pictures of the house."

Claire rolled her eyes. "What do you need a picture for?"

"A picture's worth a thousand words."

She nodded in agreement and then made a sort of rolling motion with her hand that seemed to say "and then . . . ."

"Well, I don't know, maybe look in the windows. I brought flashlights," I offered as I pulled one out and handed it to her.

"Do you want to split up?" she asked.

"I guess so. Here," I said, reaching into my bag and pulling out a walkie-talkie, which she accepted. I gave her a quick overview on how to use the walkie-talkie and then decided it was now or never.

"Let's do this," I told her with as much confidence as I could pull together. We both opened our doors as quietly as possible, but every little movement seemed to echo in the still, night air. We walked in silence, neither of us saying a word, and I wondered if she was as terrified as I was. Where was the invincible feeling I had just several hours ago?

"Here we are," she whispered.

"You're right. This house is a monster." It wasn't really a house; it was an estate, a mansion. It came close to some of the castles I had seen overseas. The grey stone exterior rose up at least three stories and spread out across the multi-acre lot.

"The lights are out," Claire fervently pointed in the direction of the house. "I'm going to walk around and see if the Rover's here. Just stay where you are."

I held still, not wanting to disturb a single twig that lay on the ground. I was standing directly under a large, oval shaped window on the side of the estate. The streetlight was shining on it just enough for me to see that the different shapes and colors of the stained glass made a picture. Of what, I couldn't tell.

"The Rover's gone. Let's look around. You go around that side of the house, and I'll meet you back here."

"What if her parents are home?"

"I don't think anyone's home, Rae. The house is dark."

"What about a butler or something? You can't have a house like this without having a butler or some sort of help."

"Rae, do you want to do this or not?"

"Fine, but keep your walkie-talkie handy in case I need something. Oh, and only use it if it's an emergency."

The stained glass window fascinated me, so I snapped a picture of it in hopes that the flash would allow me to capture the image that lay within. My legs were shaking as I began to walk. I pulled the flashlight out of my bag and clipped the walkie-talkie to my belt loop. There seemed to be something covering the windows, so looking in was a futile effort. I made it around the house in no less than half an hour and with no more information than when I started. As I rounded the corner, I saw Claire's flashlight shining on something that appeared to be an opened cellar door.

"You want to?"

"No!" I quietly shrieked. "That's breaking and entering."

"This might be your only chance to find out whatever it is you want to know."

"What is wrong with you?" I now felt sick to my stomach and was ready to call it quits, or maybe just call Alex.

"What's wrong with *you*? You're the one who planned this whole thing and in my opinion it's been a big waste of time. We don't know anything new."

"All right, all right. I don't think now is the time or place to argue over it. What if someone comes while we're inside?"

"Oh, I'm not going inside. I'll be the guard dog. If anything changes, I'll beep you on your walkie-talkie."

I gave her a precarious look before I stepped cautiously into the cellar. My flashlight beamed into the darkness, revealing a room filled with unpacked boxes. I moved the flashlight around the room, finally, letting it rest on a set of stairs several yards in front of me. Without hesitation, I took small steps over to the staircase. I swallowed hard and then, carefully, I advanced toward the glowing hallway above.

I reached the top of the stairs and clicked my flashlight off. Tiny flickers of illumination were lighting my path. I looked out of the doorway and saw that the light was coming from iron candelabras that were attached to the walls and held five lit candles each. The walls were made of stone, like a castle, and the floors were worn and dark in color. The smell of melting wax filled my nostrils with something pleasant considering my surroundings. I stepped out of the basement and into a large, wide, hallway that led into a gigantic and open living room. The room had large, heavy, velvet drapes that hung from ceiling to floor; I now realized why the house had looked so dark from outside. The ceilings were high with thick beams running across them. I was no expert on period design, but the inside of the home looked like some sort of medieval castle with rustic furniture, candelabras, and heavy curtains, but it was the stone walls that gave the estate a castle-like feel. I was in awe of the artwork that hung on the walls. It was ancient, and I was sure that it was authentic and priceless. I pulled out my camera, and without thinking about damaging the priceless pieces, I began to snap pictures of each painting that hung on the wall. It was after the camera made its last snap that I realized I had gotten sidetracked. I wasn't here to admire ancient artwork that should be hanging in a museum somewhere; I was here to find out about Chloe Pierce.

I walked over to an antique wooden piece that looked like a desk and I ran my fingers across it while taking notice of a note pad that lay on top. The watermark of a lion was barely visible atop the cream colored paper. At the top of the notepad, PIERCE AND ASSOCIATES was printed in red. I snapped a picture of the pad of paper, then glanced at the bookshelf that took up the majority of the opposing wall. I ran my fingers across the books' ancient spines. Now this was a bookshelf that put not only mine to shame, but Alex's father's as well. There were some books on religion, but I noticed there wasn't a single copy of the Bible to be found. There were lots of books on ancient history dating back to before Christ. Books on Antiochus Epiphanies, Julius Caesar and the Roman Empire, Alexander the Great, Cyrus the Great, and other men whom I assumed were historically powerful figures but knew nothing about. There was no way I could possibly read every title, so I took a multitude of snapshots. The bulb flashed and at the same moment my walkie-talkie buzzed; Claire's frantic voice followed.

"Rae. Are you there? Pick up."

"I'm here."

"Get out. Now. They're home."

Words couldn't describe how fast my feet were moving across the old, wooden planks. I made it to the basement opening in record time and hustled down the stairs without taking my previously careful precautions to keep the creaking to a minimum. The stairs whined and squealed as if they were going to break at any moment, but I continued on faster and faster down the set of old, wooden stairs. It was when my flashlight shone on the last step that I felt my foot catch on something rough. I was now flying through the air. My flashlight flew from my hand, and I found myself lying face down on the hard, concrete floor. My chest hurt. I took in tiny gulps of air, each breath painful. I couldn't get up; I lay on the cold, concrete floor, barely moving, letting out short and labored breaths, while my eyes filled with tears of pain. I reached for the loop on my jeans where I had clipped my walkie-talkie, but it was gone.

"Claire," I grunted in a voice too shallow for anyone but myself to hear.

I felt hopeless. I was in Chloe Pierce's dungeon, soon to be her own personal prisoner. I was envisioning the torture chamber that would so appropriately fit into a setting like this. It was while I was envisioning the chains and cuffs on the walls that my eyes focused on the glowing beam from my flashlight.

The light was resting on the boxes I had seen on my way in and the halo of light made visible the letters "A.A.M.S." that were written on the front of the box closest to me. They would mean nothing to most people, but to me, it meant only one thing: Amsterdam American School, the school I attended in Holland. I knew I had to see what was inside. I used my arms and pushed myself up off the ground, grimacing from the pain that was tearing through my body. I held my side tight and inched closer to the box. Squatting down, I picked up my flashlight and opened the box and began to look inside. It was stacked with several yearbooks and what appeared to be a rather large scrapbook or photo album.

"Rae. Are you still in there? You've got to get out of there, now." I ignored the warning that came from the walkie-talkie, which was lying in the dark somewhere on the other side of the room, and shone my flashlight across the floor toward the stack of boxes. All of the boxes were labeled: Missouri, England, France, Holland, Croatia, Germany, Czech Republic, Italy, and last but not least, a small box labeled Oklahoma sat on top of the others. I pulled my camera from my backpack and began to snap a few pictures of the boxes and their contents. With the pain still blazing through my body, I blindly reached my hand into the box, pulled out a thick, brown, leather binder and stuffed it into my bag.

"Are you crazy?" What took you so long?" Claire shrieked as I approached the top of the cellar stairs.

"I fell."

"Are you all right?"

"Not really, I think I broke a couple of ribs."

"We've got to get out of here." Her voice was more frantic than ever.

I did a slow jog back to Claire's car, still tightly clutching my side. Slowly, I slid into the front seat letting out a long and painful moan. Every breath I took brought back the same pain I experienced during the initial fall. Claire slid into the driver's side, not saying a word; she just stared ahead out of the front windshield.

"I think that's the most fun I've ever had," she droned.

"I don't know if I can fully agree with you," I said with a painful look on my face. "Can we go now?"

Her car pulled out onto the main street, but it wasn't until she merged back onto the highway that my pulse began to slow and my body began to relax. As the adrenaline waned, my mind was becoming still enough to consider the meaning of the boxes in the basement. There was a box for each country I had lived in. Before I could fully grasp their meaning, Claire's voice broke the silence.

"So, what did you find?"

"Nothing," I said blankly.

"Come on. You were in there for over thirty minutes. You have to give me a little more than that." She was trying to rationalize with me and I knew this.

The way I saw it, she didn't need to know anything. I had taken all the risk, so I would give her as much or as little information as I saw fit. I explained to her the décor of the house in such detail that she seemed appeased. She began to tell me her version of the story; the story of how we barely escaped by the skin of our teeth. It sounded like a story she was planning on repeating over and over to just about anyone who would listen, so I reminded her that every last detail about tonight needed to stay between us. She looked disappointed and began to sulk in a very obvious way. I hardly cared.

"Claire."

"Yes," she said, still sulking.

"You said, 'They're home.'"

"I know."

"Who are 'they'?"

"Chloe and a boy who looked about our age."

"Did you see what he looked like?"

"I got a pretty good look. It was dark, but I was close. Plus, it helped that they were standing right under the lamppost by the garage. He was about the same height as Chloe and thinish."

"Did you see his face?" I felt my chest beginning to tighten.

"Just for a second. He had dark hair . . . high cheekbones, that's about all that I could tell." It was like I was frozen, I couldn't move, I couldn't respond. Of course, Claire's description could have described a handful of people, but something inside of me was confirming that the man that Claire saw with Chloe was the same man on the path yesterday morning. The pain in my ribs began to disappear as my senses, instead, began working together to link together the pieces of something much, much larger. "Oh! I almost forgot." Claire startled me, pulling me out of my reverie. "He had a tattoo on his arm. It was a lion, I think." She paused, and I swallowed the hard lump in my throat. All at once, my dreams began to blur with reality. I could see perfectly the tattoo on the forearm of the man in my dreams: a lion done in black and red ink. Before this moment, the tattoo had seemed so insignificant, but now, under a different set of circumstances, I realized that this tattoo was the link. The tattoo in my dreams was the same tattoo as the one on the arm of my attacker and on the arm of the boy with Chloe. Lions. They seemed to be everywhere, even printed onto a simple, white pad of paper in the Pierce estate. And then a chill swept across my body, little goose bumps formed on my skin as remembered the cold night in Prague when I stumbled across a storefront with the image of a lion on its large, plate glass window. I closed my eyes as I tried to remember the name of the business. The fuzzy black and red lettering was beginning to come into focus: International Relocation and Job Placement Services. But there was more. I pushed harder, trying to pull from my memory the name of the business and then, all at once, the name that I had been searching for came into view. Bold black and red letters flashed behind my tightly clenched lids. Pierce and Associates. I gasped, my ribcage throbbing as I sucked in a chest full of air. I began to remember how, on that night, someone had been following me. The boxes in the basement of Chloe's mansion suggested that the Pierces had been tracking me for years. My mind was swirling. There were things that didn't make sense, things that didn't add up. But this I did know: Chloe and the boy on the path were working together, and the Pierces . . . well . . . they wanted me dead. My dreams had become a reality. Alex was right; my dreams were a warning. But there was still one unanswered question: who was the boy on the path, the boy who lived in my dreams, and what relation did he have to Chloe Pierce?

"It wasn't Alex, if that's what your wondering."

I whipped my head around so that I was now facing her. "What?" I had almost forgotten. She thought this whole thing was about finding Alex. She had no idea how complex this had become. I changed my look of surprise to one of disappointment just as she turned toward me.

"I know you wanted to find him and I'm sorry, Rae. Sorry about your ribs, too."

She pulled into the school lot, and I thanked her over and over again while, at the same time, trying my hardest to make myself appear as distraught as possible over the fact that Alex was still MIA. At this moment, the only thing Claire Kirpowski knew was that this stakeout had been a complete flop, and I wanted to keep it that way.

It was completely dark when I pulled into my driveway, not a star in the sky. Nighttime in the city is so much different. In the country, you only have the stars to light the sky, and when they're gone, you can barely see your fingers at the end of your arm.

I walked in the house and flipped on the porch light. I made my rounds to check that all the doors were locked tight before setting the alarm and then I took two Tylenol PM for the pain that had returned to my ribs and the still lingering pain in my arm from yesterday morning. I wasn't sure how I would explain this most recent accident to my parents, or to Alex. I wondered if Alex *could* heal me. I wondered if he *would* heal me since I had lied to him. I knew that I would rather deal with the pain than tell him where I had been. Besides, I wasn't completely over the fact that Alex was trying to keep me in the dark. I couldn't understand why he would want me to be so uninformed. How could my ignorance benefit either one of us? It's not that he didn't tell me things. He had in fact enlightened me. But the light came only in tiny bursts, not allowing me to see very far ahead, and I wanted to see the whole picture. I wanted to know why he had come back and when he would be leaving. I needed to know that we would be okay.

I went to my window and peeked out of the blinds. The porch light beamed to the end of my gravel drive where it stopped and rested on Alex's cream and brown Wagoneer. He was there to protect me once again. He was hidden so well that I hadn't seen him when I was driving up the road, but I was sure that he had seen me. He was trying to keep me safe while I was out looking for trouble. It seemed as if we were moving in the opposite direction, and I couldn't imagine he would be pleased when he found out what I had been up to. I shut my eyes tightly and replayed the events of the night, but the more

I strained my mind, the less sense I could make of anything. What I did know was that Chloe, and quite possibly her whole family, had been tracking me for quite some time. What I didn't know was why.

# CHAPTER TWENTY-THREE

*I* awoke this morning to what sounded like a marching band in my living room. I was reminded of the pain in my chest as soon as I opened my eyes. I held my ribs tightly to prevent any unnecessary movement and begrudgingly drug myself out of bed. I descended the stairs and walked into the living room where I found my father holding his pointer finger in the air, waving it in time to the OU fight song that he must have just recently downloaded. Up until this point, I had successfully avoided the topic of graduation and my plans thereafter. This could only mean one thing: the pressure was on. Graduation was several days away, and I would have to be answering to someone about my plans for the future. My parents had no reason to believe I would be going anywhere other than OU. I hadn't protested. Not verbally, anyway. I'm sure my body language told them I wasn't exactly thrilled. I took one look at him and then, without a word, turned and made my way back up the stairs for my room.

My dad was set on The University of Oklahoma. He told me that it would be a good excuse for him to go to the football games. Although I knew that this was partially true, I told him it was just an excuse to keep me under his thumb. He agreed that there might be just a little truth in that. He was concerned that I had not put much thought into this huge milestone in my life; in reality, I had put more thought into it than he knew. I had applied to eleven schools including OU. It was my secret.

I sat down on my bed and reached into my nightstand, pulling out a handful of papers. Each paper was haphazardly stuffed into its original envelope. I thumbed through the pile of acceptance letters: The University of Boston, The University of Oklahoma, The University of Arizona State, The University of California-Berkley, The University of Florida in Gainesville, The Kansas City Art Institute, The San Francisco Art Institute and finally, the envelope in the middle of the pile, The University of Minnesota Twin Cities. After that day at the park, the day when Alex and I drew out of his hat to decide our final destination, I took all of the slips of paper home and applied to one college in each of the states. I sent off eleven applications, and I received eleven letters of acceptance. This did nothing to make my decision any easier; however, I couldn't help but wonder if fate would draw us back to Minnesota. I pulled the acceptance letter from the envelope and ran my fingers across the top of the paper, feeling the texture; it felt so smooth and perfect. The Twin Cities had been his idea. At first, I had objected. The idea of leaving my parents without saying goodbye was hard enough for me to swallow, but if they found out that I had fled to the exact place that had caused them such pain . . . well, it would be like rubbing salt in their wounds.

In the past few weeks, the idea of Minnesota was growing on me. I was fairly certain that Alex was leaning toward the land of 10,000 lakes, and I was becoming enchanted with the idea of it as well. I was born in Alexandria on the exact night that he died. I was entering this world just as he was leaving. It was far fetched, even fantasy perhaps, but I did wonder if our souls had passed each other by.

I stuffed the letters back into the drawer of my nightstand and gingerly leaned backward onto my bed, supporting my ribs as I did so. I was ready to leave everything behind so that I could be with him. I couldn't believe how I had changed. I had been so independent and stubborn less than a year ago, not even allowing him to open a car door for me, and now I was giving him my entire life. The obnoxious sound of drums and horns that had invaded the entire second floor was now gone, so I ventured down the stairs to give this morning and my father a second chance, but still hoping to evade the conversation of college that was so apparently on my father's mind.

I began to replay the events of the last few days: the park, Alex's secret, Claire, the stakeout, the boxes, and, of course, the tattoo. I couldn't help but feel slightly on edge as I considered how my recurring nightmare for the past year had become a reality yesterday morning. No portion of the dream was left out: the setting, the chase, the eyes, and the light. The details of the attack were still vivid in my mind, but it was the eyes that I couldn't erase. They were hollow and empty eyes; they were eyes that I had seen before. Who was he, this boy who wanted me dead?

"Well, good morning your Royal Highness." My father was sitting on a barstool with his legs crossed, sipping a cup of coffee, and reading the morning paper. It seemed as though his jets had cooled down a bit. What it is about football and fight songs that get men so riled up I will never understand.

"Good morning," I said with apprehension in my voice. "Looks like you're still reading that junk they call news." I looked at him from the corner of my eye to catch his reaction.

"No one ever said that all news was supposed to be good and no one ever said the world was a perfect place to live, either."

"Well, I'm glad to hear that someone else thinks the same way that I do."

"So, are you ready for graduation?" he asked as he focused on the paper. The unintentional long pause caused him to look up from the article and study me from above the wire rimmed, reading glasses that sat toward the end of his nose.

"Why don't you push those glasses up a little bit so you can actually see through them . . . ?" My voice faded as I noticed the irritated look forming on his face. "I just mean, you're always looking over the top of them, I really don't see how . . . " my voice faded again and I twisted my mouth in discomfort as I realized that I was in for a talkin' to.

"Any thoughts on college?"

"Not really," I said, walking over to the refrigerator and pulling out the milk for my cereal."

"You don't like OU, is that it?"

"It's not that, Dad. I like OU, it's just that . . . ."

"What?"

"I just haven't made up my mind, that's all."

"I think it's a little late to apply anywhere else, you don't have a whole lot of options." I remained silent as I poured the milk over the top of my cereal.

I shrugged my shoulders and took my cereal back up to my room, not looking back to see the expression of bewilderment on my father's face. I could only think about one thing and that was transferring all of the pictures from last night onto my computer, so I could see them more clearly. I plugged my memory stick into some sort of device that I didn't know the name for and then plugged that device into my computer and immediately the pictures began to transfer. I picked up my coffee, grimacing in pain as I did so, and I waited. I waited for nearly fifteen minutes while my ancient, dinosaur of a computer tried to keep up. I was thumping my finger on the side of my bed anxiously when I remembered that I hadn't replaced my father's binoculars. Reaching into my bag, I pulled out the binoculars, clutched my side once again, and headed down the stairs. I placed the binoculars back on the shelf. Still holding my side, I started out the office door just as my father was on his way in.

"What are you doing, Rae?"

"Nothing," I said through clenched teeth. The pain was blazing through my body. I tightened my chest in an attempt to prevent my ribcage from moving.

"What's wrong with your side?"

"Nothing," I responded immediately as I removed my hand from my ribs. "Nothing" seemed to be the only word willing to come out of my mouth at the moment and it did "nothing" to ease my father's suspicions.

"I should have a look at it, anyway."

"You're a shrink, Dad."

"And you would think that I would have a better understanding of whatever it is that you are going through. But at the moment, I think I would have better luck fixing your side."

"Whatever." I rolled my eyes, and my father turned around and went on about his business.

I took the stairs even more slowly and by the time I made it to my room, the pictures were up on my computer. The first picture of the stained glass window had turned out better that I had expected. The flash had captured perfectly the image of a lion with wings, surrounded by lots of pieces of brightly colored stained glass. Somehow I wasn't surprised. The next twenty pictures or so were of the artwork hanging on the stone walls of Chloe's mansion. I scanned the pictures until I found the one I was looking for: the notepad. The image on the pad of paper was just as I had remembered: the watermark of a lion with a full mane. Its mouth was opened wide as if it were about to devour its prey. Next, my eyes fell upon the images of the boxes in the basement. These were the ones I most hoped would turn out. The images that I had taken of the outside of the boxes were perfect, no glare, and I could make out the writing. The pictures I had taken of each box's contents could have been better. From what I could see, each box contained lots of photos and composition pads, as if someone had been taking meticulous notes. I flipped back to the photos of the boxes' exteriors. My eyes focused on something that I had missed the first time. Behind each box that I had taken a picture of were other boxes stacked up against the wall, stacked tall until they reached the ceiling. The flash had picked up something that my eyes could not in the darkness of Chloe's dungeon. I strained my eyes to read what was printed on every box that stood against the wall. The markings appeared to be dates; dates too out of focus to read. I was no pro at Photoshop, but I thought that with a little work, I would be able to read the numbers with ease.

The days leading up to graduation were a blur, full of the organized, group activities that I loathed: the class breakfast, the class pictures, the rehearsal, and the assembly. The upside was that it did indeed make the days fly by, bringing me closer to discovering Alex's last and most enticing secret. The downside was my full agenda, which left zero time for lunch at the bridge. He hadn't seemed too disappointed. In fact, he had been rather preoccupied in the details of his last big surprise. I could hardly wait. The suspense was killing me. Since I had met Alex, I had gone from being a rather controlled and even keeled person to an absolute ball of nerves with so many highs and lows and lots of inbetweens. But after much anticipation and preparation, the day had finally arrived.

I ran the black robe between my fingers before pulling it off the hanger and slipping it on over my jeans and tee shirt. It symbolized so many things. It symbolized all of my hard work. My 4.0 grade average had opened the door to many colleges, thus giving Alex and I more options for our future. The robe also symbolized my freedom. I would no longer be uprooted on a consistent basis. I planned to make only one more move and that was with Alex. Gone were all the bullies and cliques of high school; gone too was my shell. It felt nice. I felt free. But mostly, the robe signified a change in my life. I would no longer be with my parents. I would begin my new life with Alex, location still unknown.

My stomach had been nervous all day. I wasn't sure if it was due to the anticipation of walking across the stage in front of thousands of people or if it was the eagerness I felt for this specific day in general. Today was the day of the final surprise, the secret to end all secrets. I walked down the stairs in my black robe, the cap still in my hand because I was unsure of how to get it to stay put on my head.

"Well, look at you," my mom said. There was something about her appearance that was peculiar, but I couldn't put my finger on it. She looked a little pasty and tired.

"I'm so proud of you, Sunshine." Her eyes were dewy with tears. "You look beautiful . . . so grown up."

"I do? Do you think it's the eyeliner?" I asked, batting my eyes at her.

"No, I just think you look more mature...and happy. You look like a woman who knows what she wants." I considered for a moment that she had called me a woman instead of a girl and decided I liked that.

"That's because I am, and I do."

"Good, that's all I've ever wished for you, your happiness." Her face was now as white as a sheet, her eyes glossy.

"Mom, you're looking a little ghostly. Do you feel alright?"

"Oh, it's nothing. I've been nauseated all day. I always get that way when I take my vitamin on an empty stomach."

I twirled my hair around my finger as I studied her face.

"I'll be fine," she said, trying to sound convincing.

"You know, if you don't feel good, you don't have to come tonight. It's no big deal, really. I'll be on the stage for less than a second, and I'm sure Dad will take lots of pictures."

"I'll be fine," she repeated, again, in the most reassuring tone she could pull together. I couldn't help but notice she also seemed a little short of breath.

"I promise. Now come with me and let's figure out how we're going to get that cap to stay on your head."

She rummaged through several drawers in her bathroom until she pulled out two, black bobby pins.

"Now, I'm just going to slide these in on either side. They'll slide right out when you pull off your cap to toss it."

"Thanks, Mom."

"Look at you." Her voice echoed as she stood behind me in the mirror. I can't believe this day is already here. It seems like just yesterday that I was holding you in my arms and making your hair into pigtails. Her eyes began to well up with tears.

"Don't make me cry, because you're about to, and then all of this make up that I worked so hard on is going to start smearing across my face," I lovingly warned her.

"Point taken. Sorry."

We started to walk back out to the kitchen when I stopped her.

"Mom, you do know that what ever I decide to do, I mean after graduation, that I love you and Dad and that I will always love you."

"You make it sound as though you're saying good bye, Rae. We'll only be two hours away. It'll take some getting used to, of course, the empty house and all, but we'll manage."

"Just saying, Mom." The subject was cut short when my dad walked into the bathroom, shirtless and sweaty from doing yard work in 90-degree weather.

"Who's that pretty girl?" he asked.

"Beautiful woman." My mother corrected him as she looked at me with what seemed to be awe in her expression.

"You'd better get in the shower, Will, we have to leave here in thirty minutes."

"Don't you worry yourselves, little ladies. It won't take old Will more than ten minutes to shower and shave."

"I think I'll lie down for a minute while you're getting ready, Will."

I looked at my dad with concern and then we both looked at my mother. Mom seemed to interpret the concern on our faces. She continued to breathe heavily.

"I'm fine and I will be fine . . . . and I'm going."

So much noise filled the auditorium; laughter and chatter bounced off the walls giving me the beginnings of a migraine. I looked around the room, so many different faces, each with the exact smile, with the exception of mine. Yes, I, too, had been looking forward to this day, but not for the same reason. I hadn't picked out a school, or a job, or a place to live, but I knew what my future held and I couldn't wait to start it. I turned to look for my parents in the crowd. There had to be at least 2,000 people in the audience and that did nothing to calm my nerves. I had never enjoyed being the center of attention, not even for a few, short seconds. What if I tripped over a cord, or up the stairs, or what if Chloe had plans to sabotage me while on stage? I let out a deep breath and tried to remember Alex's words of wisdom from earlier this week. I did worry too much, and I needed to stop. I continued to scan the audience when I saw a shadowy figure standing at the top corner of the balcony at such a distance that his features were not distinguishable, but I sensed his presence. When our eyes met, he waved at me, and I couldn't help but smile. It was Alex, and everything was going to be just fine. I sat down in my assigned seat with all of the rest of the "C's", waiting for the commencement to begin, and before I knew it, the entire ceremony was over. I could barely remember walking across the stage; it was all a blur, but as I looked at the rolled up certificate in my hand, I knew it was over. I had done it. I was finally free.

My mother still had a pasty look about her when I met up with her and my father after the ceremony. I convinced my mother that she needed to go home and lie down; my father agreed. This left my evening free: no explanations and no excuses.

I wasn't thinking about the multitude of graduation parties that were going on around town; instead, I was thinking that I was truly happy and completely fulfilled. But as we lay in silence on the deck at Alex's house, staring up at the stars, each uneventful second that passed began playing on every one of my nerves, making me even more frazzled. Tonight was the night that he would share with me the secret to end all secrets. Of course, I knew that the surprise would be a good one, but his hesitation was causing me to imagine the worst. Just as I was beginning to run through all the possible negative scenarios, something shiny caught my eye. I glanced down at his hand; I was now staring at the brilliant reflector of light. He was holding a small, blue box with the lid flipped open. Inside sat a thin and delicate, diamond-encrusted band. He pulled it gently from the box and held it between his fingers.

"You didn't think I was going to let you call all the shots, did you?"

"You never do. I didn't imagine this would be any different."

Alex was still holding the ring between his fingers, his lips curled into a nervous smile.

"It's so shiny, it looks like little stars. I told you not to."

"Do you like it?"

"I do."

"Should we see if it fits?" he asked, waiting for me to nod before he slid the perfect, jewel-encrusted ring onto my finger. His hand shook and his voice quivered.

"I love you, Rae," he said, kneeling in front of me. "If I could offer you what we had before, before we were on this earth, then in a heartbeat I would. But if marriage is all that I can offer while we're on this earth, then I hope that one day I will . . . "

"Wait a minute," I interrupted. "What do you mean, you one day will?"

"Just let me finish." He cleared his throat before he began. "Rae, I promise to be with you forever, for as long as forever is on this earth. I promise to keep you safe and to love you and take care of you. But above everything else, I promise that when this life of ours is over, our love will have only just begun . . . I promise that I will love you for an eternity. I know that you wanted to get married but an engagement ring just seems so mundane and worldly. Our love is greater than that. I want you to know that my promise will last forever. This is a promise ring, Rae. A promise to love you . . . forever."

My chest felt heavy. I couldn't breath. I wanted to say something, anything, but nothing would come out.

"Oh, I almost forgot," he said, brushing my hair away from my neck and moving his fingers down my neck until he found the clasp to the chain which held my locket.

"I couldn't help thinking that you might not want your parents to see the ring, so I thought you could just wear it around your neck for now."

I looked down at the ring that sat so perfectly on my hand. It would most certainly not go unnoticed, and I decided that he was right. I pulled the jewel from my finger, slid it onto the chain around my neck, and let it dangle in front of me.

"Here, let me put it back on you," he offered, turning me in the opposite direction and once again, delicately sweeping my hair over the front of my shoulder. His fingers on my skin felt the same as the first time we touched: electric, stimulating, intoxicating. His touch still sent tingles through every inch of me and made my heart do summersaults in my chest. To be with Alex had been my greatest dream. For so long, it seemed out of reach, unattainable and now he had made me a promise. I should have a feeling of contentment, but I wanted more. Of course I wanted marriage, but when he spoke of our lives and our love here on earth, he made it sound so insignificant and a piece of me wished for that something more, the love we had before. A piece of me wished we could skip straight past this worldly love of ours and start our eternity together. He made it sound so appealing, and I hated that he could remember that part of us while I was left in the dark. I wanted what we had before, even if it was just a little taste.

## CHAPTER TWENTY-FOUR

The emergency room is such a dreary place; coughing, aching, bleeding, screaming, crying, and pain don't really fit into my idea of an ideal evening, but scared is what I mostly felt at this moment . . . and anxious. I felt anxious because I was waiting in the lobby, alone, for my dad to update me on Mother's condition. I had no details. I only knew that she had been delivered by the EMS themselves, which could hardly be good.

I sunk my head down into my hands and pressed my eyes hard until I saw nothing but darkness with the occasional flash of light that came each time I rubbed my lids. In the past couple of months, my life had become extremely complicated. It was obvious that I was being followed. My boyfriend had come back from the dead, and to top it all off, someone was trying to kill me. But now, my mom was the one lying in the hospital bed and somehow I felt to blame. I *felt* scared. I wished that Alex could be here to comfort me. I loved how he calmed me, how he soothed me, and convinced me that everything would be okay. I pulled my head from my hands just in time to see a nurse coming from behind the secured double doors. I tried to steal a glance inside, but the long, narrow nursing station that wrapped around the front part of the room blocked my view.

"Rae Colbert," the nurse said, her voice just above a whisper. Her eyes scanned the lobby, looking for anyone that would fit the description of an eighteen-year-old girl.

At that exact moment, I had a strong sense of déjá vu. Icy surges tore through my body as I looked at the slightly overweight nurse who was clad in a pair of navy blue scrubs and clogs. This moment felt surrealistic. My body was reacting to my surroundings, each sound and smell adding to this strange familiarity: the nurse's voice and how she called my name, the dim light, the hard uncomfortable chairs, the large fish tank that looked tiny in the enormous lobby, the baby crying somewhere behind me, and the overuse of sanitizer to kill the smell of sickness. It was when I stood up slowly that I felt weakness and doom come over me. It was this final emotion that sent everything over the top. I had desperately tried to erase this darkness from my memory, but when the nurse called my name, I was quickly reminded of the night last year when I was surrounded by very similar circumstances. It was the night that my father had been in the explosion in Amsterdam. That night my mother and I had nervously paced the lobby of the ER, waiting for an update. I had never before felt so helpless. There was a split second during that time when it felt as though something was working against me, something evil.

Every sensation I had during that moment in time became permanently linked with a feeling of impending doom; the same feeling of doom that I had at this moment.

I flashed back to that cold night in May; I was walking toward the nurse with my mother by my side. The nurse opened the heavy, double doors and walked us back to my father's room. I heard the sound of crying babies, my nose burned from the smell of antiseptic, I focused on the wrinkled scrubs that clung to the nurse's body, I heard the sound that her clogs made on the hard, cold floor, and Bernard Bodin. I gasped, sucking in a chestful of air when his name passed through my mind. Bernard had been there that night. I recall the look of satisfaction on his face as he surreptitiously rounded the corner in the ER. I remember being surprised by seeing him there. I also remember being surprised by the expression on his face. It was a face that was free of any sadness, but it was his eyes that I will never forget. They were unmistakable. They were so hollow and empty. I froze. I had made the connection, yet it seemed so unreasonable. The hollow, empty eyes of my attacker belonged to Ben, but the man on the path hardly resembled the gangly boy with wire rimmed glasses that I remembered.

"Rae Colbert," the nurse called again. A pleasant smile crossed her face when she saw me walking toward her. Immediately, my thoughts shifted to my mother.

"Is my mom okay?" I panicked.

She walked hastily in front of me while ignoring my plea. She stopped abruptly in front of a partitioned room, grasped the curtain with her free hand, and jerked it open. I saw my mother's little body lying in the bed, a single needle connecting her body to tubes and bags. She was covered with blankets. She was surrounded by monitors and the steady beep, beep, beep in the background let the nurses know that her vitals were within the normal limits. My dad was sitting with his head tucked into his hands. He startled when the curtain was pulled and his eyes went from glassy to warm when he saw me. He lifted from the faux leather recliner beside my mother's bed and joined me in the hall. His hair was sticking out in every direction. He looked tired and disheveled. The nurse began to fiddle with the tubes attached to my mother's arm. She pulled out a vile and hooked it up to the tubing, watching as a steady stream of blood flowed into the little glass container. She then pulled the vial away from the tubing and replaced it with another. She repeated this process around five or six times, scribbling with a sharpie onto the labels of the little, glass tubes before she exited without saying a single word, leaving the curtain open behind her. My dad pulled the curtain shut and looked at me with concern.

"Is mom okay? What happened?"

"She was having chest pains, she thought she was having a heart attack." He looked flushed. "There was nothing I could do. It's not like we have a supply of Nitroglycerin just lying around the house."

"Huh."

"I called an ambulance. I have never in my life felt so helpless. I am a physician and I could do nothing for her but call an ambulance. I should have seen the signs. I should have insisted that she come in to be checked after how badly she looked last night."

"Wait, Dad. Did she have a heart attack?" I felt sick. I remembered my mother standing in the kitchen this morning. She looked healthy and happy and fine. I couldn't help but remember how badly she was feeling the night before. Dad was right, we shouldn't have ignored the signs: her whiteness, her shortness of breath, and her nausea.

"The doctors around here think it might just be anxiety, you know, considering all that's been going on in the past couple of months with Nana and Papa and with you going off to college soon, but I don't think so. They took blood. We should get the results back in about an hour."

"What are they looking for?"

"Medications in her blood stream that might have caused something like this. They asked if she was on any medications and I told them just a daily vitamin. She's not taking anything else is she, Rae?"

"No . . . um, not that I know of."

"And of course, they'll be looking for the CK enzyme to determine if it was indeed a heart attack."

"What do we do?"

"Just wait. That's all we can do."

"Does she need anything?"

"No, she's sleeping right now."

"Is she going to stay the night here?"

"I don't know. Right now there's a lot I don't know, Rae."

"Can I go in?"

"Go on in. I'm going to step out into the lobby and grab a cup of coffee. You want some?"

"No, thank you."

I walked into the room, pulled the curtain closed behind me, and fell into the recliner beside her bed. I stared at her tiny body; her soft, brown hair was still perfectly coiffed, her nails were painted, and there was a hint of lipstick still lingering on her mouth. She looked perfect as usual, but this time so frail and helpless. I wanted to know what happened and I wanted to know now. I had never been too good at the waiting game. I reached out and touched her hand and it was icy despite the mound of blankets that lay on top of her. She should be the one with the stethoscope and the white lab jacket. She should be the one standing over the bed not the one lying in it. My dad entered with a steaming cup of cheap smelling coffee in his hand, muttering something about all the damn red tape in the hospital, and then he sat down on the hard chair opposite me. I could see his tired face sadden, and I wondered if seeing my mother lying in a hospital bed brought back memories of the crash, the night Laney died.

"Mr. Colbert." A stiff looking younger man appeared in my mother's room. I glanced at the nameplate that hung on his white lab jacket. Jeffery Connelly, MD. It was as if the letters, MD, were supposed to make me feel more confident in his level of expertise. I looked at my father, and I could tell that we were both thinking the same thing. He looked at us with warm eyes. He included me as he explained my mother's condition, so I decided that I liked him okay. My dad, on the other hand, still had a look of skepticism across his face.

"Will and Rae, right?"

"Dr. Colbert," my father corrected him. "And yes, this is my daughter, Rae."

"Okay, Dr. Colbert and Rae . . . I have a little bit of good news and a little bit of bad news," he said.

I couldn't help but think how cliché that sounded. Next he was going to say, "Which do you want first?"

"Which do you want first?" he asked in the exact way I imagined he would.

"The bad," my dad answered through clinched teeth.

"Sue did indeed have a small Myocardial Infarction."

"A what?" I spat.

"Heart attack." Both Jeffery Connelly, MD and Dr. Colbert responded in unison. "We found small amounts of the CK enzyme in her blood sample."

"Impossible," my father said incredulously.

Jeffery Connelly, MD, offered the lab results to my father. "It looks like there was a bit of muscle damage as a result of the MI, Dr. Colbert."

My father continued to scan the lab results shaking his head and muttering under his breath. Finally, he looked up into the Jeffery Connelly's eyes with a look of desperation. I thought that for the first time in my life, I saw defeat in my father's eyes, and it scared me.

"So, what's causing this? Sue's healthy. We're healthy. We're the textbook definition of heath, doctor. We shouldn't be here." My dad looked shaken.

"That leads me to my next point, which is somewhat better news. We also found higher than normal levels of potassium in her bloodstream. This is both good and bad. Good, because the high potassium level leads me to believe that

Sue isn't suffering from anything chronic. However . . . ". He paused, trying to think of the best way to ask the question that was on his mind. How could he be tactful about the fact that he thought my mother had over-medicated herself?

"Do you know how Sue might have gotten ahold of extremely large doses of potassium?"

"I thought potassium was healthy," I added my two cents.

"You can get potassium from your diet, and yes, in the right doses it is healthy, but . . . Dr. Colbert . . . as you are well aware, there is no way that Sue could have had potassium levels this high from diet alone. Levels this high generally come from taking potassium in higher than recommended doses over extended periods of time."

"What do you want me to do?" My dad's voice sounded weary.

"We'd like to keep her overnight, just to monitor her. With all likelihood, she'll be going home tomorrow afternoon."

He pulled a compact book from his lab coat and flipped it open rather quickly to a page that had been dog-eared. He then turned the book to such an angle that my father and I could see.

"If at all possible, I would like for you to familiarize yourself with this picture, Rae. This is a picture of a potassium pill. Now, I'm sure your father would like to be the one to stay the night with your mother . . . but if you could go home and have a look around the house . . . and if you come across anything that looks like the pill in this book, call up here and let us know."

"It looks like a vitamin," I told him, noticing its whitish color and oblong shape.

"Sue's a physician for Pete's sake. I think we can trust Sue to answer for herself," my father spoke through pursed lips. His normally cool and collected demeanor was quickly reaching its boiling point.

"I'm not suggesting anything, Will, um, Dr. Colbert. I'm just trying to cover all of the bases. However you choose to look at it, the potassium is in Sue's blood stream and right now, my objective, as your wife's physician, is to determine how it got there. If we don't . . . well . . . this could happen again."

"I understand." My father nodded. The doctor's answer seemed to extinguish the fire in my father's face.

"We'll be moving Sue up to a room shortly. Which one of you plans on staying the night?"

"I think I should be the one to stay . . . Rae . . . if you don't mind." His eyes were pleading with me.

"That's okay. I'll go home and see what I can find." My father looked relieved.

"That would be helpful," Doctor Connelly added. Your mother will be fine, Rae. Go home and get a good night's sleep." Dr. Connelly now turned toward my father. "We will certainly run a few more standard tests to make sure there's nothing more serious going on. I don't expect to find anything. All of her other labs appear normal."

"I gave my dad a hug and a quick kiss goodbye before I leaned over my mother and kissed her softly on the cheek.

It was 9:00 PM when I arrived home and the house looked quiet and dark. I pulled into the garage and shut the garage door quickly behind me before getting out of the car. I left the car door open to keep the garage lit while I made my way to the switch on the wall. The garage filled with a dim light. I then went back to shut the car and glanced over to the side entrance that led from the garage into our back yard. It was locked. I walked into the house and shut the door behind me. I glanced at the alarm on the wall that had not been set and rolled my eyes at my parents' good intentions.

I started my search in the laundry room where my mother kept the ibuprofen, cough syrup, Tums, Nyquil, and so on. I fumbled with the bottles, looking inside to check the contents. Tiny, round, brown pills; medium sized, chalky, round tablets in a variety of fruity colors; and purple colored syrup filling a very unsuspicious cough suppressant bottle. I found absolutely nothing.

I walked quickly towards my parents' room, flicking the switch in the hall to light the way. I fumbled through my mom's side of the dresser but found nothing resembling a bottle of medication. I moved on to their bathroom. I opened my mother's medicine cabinet and immediately saw a bottle of vitamins setting on the shelf in front of me. I pulled the bottle off the shelf and read the label: "Women's One A Day." I opened it and pulled out a white colored, oblong pill: "Exhibit A." It appeared to be a vitamin; it also looked like the pill in Dr. Connelly's book. I turned the pill over and noticed the inscription M 15 etched lightly into its surface. I laid the pill on the counter and then began to rummage through my father's personal hygiene products. The same sized bottle was sitting on his middle shelf. Turning the bottle around so that the label was facing me, I read "One A Day," and then pulled a similar, white, oblong pill from the bottle, "Exhibit B." It was similar with one exception; this pill had "One A Day" imprinted on its surface. I held the two pills side-by-side. Other than the inscription and an almost unnoticeable variance in color, they were identical. In that instant, I knew what I had to do. My heart was racing and my feet moved so effortlessly beneath me that I felt as though I had flown to the garage. I got in my car and locked it before opening the garage door.

At 10:05, I pulled into Walgreen's. I walked in like a girl with purpose, not even taking a moment to glance at the boy behind the counter who said, "Welcome to Walgreen's, can I help you find anything?" I promptly returned to the front of the store with a bottle of "Women's One A Day" vitamins and placed it on the counter. He gave me a strange look, and I wondered if it were part of the job requirement to analyze each and every customer's purchase.

I refused the plastic sack, grabbed my bottle of pills and receipt, and walked out into the parking lot. I glanced over my shoulder, slipped into my car, and locked the door behind me. Without hesitation, I pulled "Exhibit A" from my pocket: the oblong, white pill with M 15 inscribed on it, the sample that came from my mother's bottle of vitamins. Next, I opened the new jar of "Women's One a Day" and pulled out "Exhibit C" A medium-sized, white pill. I held the two side-by-side. They look remarkably similar. I flipped "Exhibit C" over and stared at the words that were etched into the pill, "Women's One A Day." My heart stopped. They were not the same. Someone had swapped the pills. Someone was trying to hurt my mom. And then, my body shuddered; someone had been in our house. I pulled out my cell and dialed Alex. I summed up the events of the night, ending with the clincher that someone was literally trying to give my mother a heart attack.

He was waiting for me on the front porch when my car pulled up the gravel drive, just as I had hoped. His Wagoneer was parked right in front of the house as if there was no longer anything to hide.

A few tears rolled down my cheek, and he wiped them away and told me it would all be okay. I believed him.

"There's something I need to check," I said, pulling away from his warm body. I unlocked the front door and walked into the house. I made my way over to the desk in the kitchen that housed my laptop.

"What are you doing?"

"I want to find out what kind of pill this is."

"Can I see it?"

"Sure," I said, pulling it from my pocket. I pushed my laptop on and waited for it to boot up.

"Where's the other one?" he asked.

I pulled "Exhibit A" from my pocket and handed it to him. He studied them side-by-side. Firefox was now up, and I Googled M 15 and the word "pill" and then clicked on the first search result. The word Oxycontin appeared at the top of the page and below it was a picture of a small, white, round tablet that looked nothing like the pill in Alex's hand.

"That's not it," I sighed.

"Try 'M 15' and 'potassium,'" he suggested. I clicked on the first result. An image popped up of an oblong, white pill that looked remarkably similar to the one in his hand.

"I think we've found a winner," he exclaimed.

"Yeah," I replied. But somehow I didn't feel as though I had won anything at all. It was final, someone had tried to kill my mother and I couldn't help but feel that I was somehow to blame.

"Are you tired?"

"I think I'm more scared than tired."

"Your mom's going to be fine. You know that, right?"

"I'm not so sure." My voice quivered. I shut my laptop and slid out of the chair, leading him into the living room where I collapsed onto the sofa. Alex sat down close beside me, his lips brushed across the top of my hair. I could hear him breathing, shallow and slow.

"Alex."

"Yes." The warmth of his words radiated down the back of my neck. I turned sideways so that I was facing him, studying the scar beneath his eye, studying his lips and the freckle that lay perfectly in the lower, left corner. I then lifted his hand, noticing again the tiny freckles that fell across the tops of his fingers. Gently, he moved his hand away from mine, brushing the side of my cheek, running his fingers across the top of my shoulders and down the back of my neck before stopping on the clasp of my necklace. I could feel the tips of his fingers, warm, moving across my cool skin and then they stopped when his fingers finally rested on my ring, which lay just below the nape of my neck. He began to slide the ring up and down the silvery chain that was holding it.

"Were you there that night? That night at the school when I fell down the stairs."

He didn't say anything for the longest time. He continued to move the ring on the chain; he appeared hypnotized by the smoothness in which it glided and then he stopped. He looked up at me as he spoke.

"Yes."

"There was someone else there with us, am I right?" I asked as I remembered each distinct sound in the hallway that night and the shadowy figure by the stairs.

"Yes," he said again.

"Who was it? Who was following me?"

He was quiet. Uncertainty crossed his face.

"Remember, no more secrets," I reminded him.

He exhaled deeply. "It was Chloe Pierce."

Now I was silent and I felt sick, but not at all surprised. It was the answer that I had expected.

"What did Chloe want, anyway?"

"I wish I knew. It would make everything so much easier."

"When I woke up that night in the hospital, I hurt everywhere, but there wasn't a single broken bone, not even a scratch. Pretty remarkable considering the spill I took, don't you think?"

"I guess so."

"It was you that healed me. Just like you fixed my arm that day on the path."

"Let's not get too carried away."

"You're not going to tell me, are you?"

Alex sat silent beside me, still moving my ring up and down the chain.

"Well, isn't that something. You fixing . . . I mean saving my body like that over and over again."

"That's the least I could do, considering."

"Considering what?" I asked.

"Considering that you're the one who's saving my soul." Judging by the immediate look of regret on Alex's face, it was clear that he thought he had said too much.

"How's that?"

"It's a long story."

"We have plenty of time."

"It's just . . . there are two parts to the story and to understand one part you'll have to hear it all."

"So, what's the problem?"

"I don't know," said Alex nervously, obviously torn between our oaths to tell each other everything and his lingering desire to keep me in the dark. "I feel like I would be breaking the rules if I told you."

"You're breaking all kinds of scientific rules just by being here. I don't see what it would hurt to break one more."

"I'm just not sure that it's my story to tell, that's all."

"No more secrets," I reminded him quickly.

Alex let out a sigh of defeat and fell back onto the arm of the sofa. We were now separated by a single cushion, but it felt like we were on opposite sides of the world. His eyes were fixed on the living room ceiling and when he spoke, there was a hint of despondency in his voice. "Eighteen years ago, your parents received a set of orders." He paused, still staring up at the ceiling. He had barely begun and already I was questioning where he was taking me. "Their sole responsibility was to keep you safe. And I am not talking about the way most parents keep children safe. There were procedures involved . . . orders that needed to be followed, orders that your parents didn't

315

necessarily agree with. And so, after your sister died, and shortly after you came into their lives, they left A-Omega and tried to protect you on their own. They tried to do it their way and then, when you were about seven years old, they came very close to failing. They had no choice after that. They needed help. Why do you think they moved around so much? Despite what you may have thought, it wasn't to torture you, I can guarantee you that."

"They moved because of their jobs . . . because of A-Omega."

"That's partially true. But who exactly do you think A-Omega is? It was A-Omega who gave your parents the orders to begin with."

"I still don't see how you and I fit into any of this."

"I'm getting to that. Several months before your eighteenth birthday, your parents began to panic. You would be graduating in less than a year and going off to college. They wanted this for you. They have always wanted you to have a normal life. But they knew you weren't ready to be on your own and they would no longer be there to protect you. They voiced their concerns to A-Omega, and A-Omega agreed. They were given orders to move to Oklahoma and stay put. They were told only to have faith and trust that it would all work out for the best. And that brings me to the point in the story where I answer your question. I didn't explain this to you before, but I have a purpose for being here. I have loved you since the very beginning. I've already told you this, and I know that you don't doubt it. But I was not supposed to let you fall in love with me, I was sent here for one reason: to protect you. That's it. By letting you fall in love with me, I have only complicated things. You see, there is a time to protect and a time to fight. It is my responsibility to protect you until you are ready to fight. And when you are, my job here will be done. I will move on to where I belong. So you see, by letting me save your body, you are in turn saving my soul."

"My nana used to say that: that there's a time to protect and a time to fight. She told me that one day, I would understand that my parents were

316

doing both. She said that one day, I would wake up and find that I was called to do something. She said it would be something difficult."

"She was right, you know."

"Well, I just never thought I would be responsible for saving someone's soul. That's not difficult. That's impossible."

"Nothing's impossible."

"I don't want to be the one who's responsible for your soul. You don't need to protect me. And I don't want you to move on without me. You told me you would stay."

"I told you I would try. I'm not sure I have much of a choice in the matter. Like you said before, neither one of our lives are guaranteed."

I wasn't sure what to say. I was sure that Alex was waiting for me to say something in return, but when I looked at him, his mood had changed. The determined crease between his eyebrows was gone and little lines began to form around his eyes. It took me a moment to realize that Alex was laughing.

"What? What's so funny?"

"Oh, I don't know. I was just thinking about how, between the two of us, I was given the hardest task . . . you're keeping me busy, you know. You're not the easiest person to keep safe."

"That's not very nice." I stopped to consider what he had told me and immediately I felt burdened. "What if I do something wrong?"

"You're doing everything right just by being here . . . and by staying out of trouble."

I was quiet for the longest time. Originally, I hadn't intended on telling Alex about the stakeout, about creeping around the Pierce estate, but now, after everything I had discovered, I didn't see how I could possibly keep it from him any longer. It was just that I wasn't quite sure how to go about it. I knew he would be mad, but I couldn't think of any better time to tell him than now. Besides, if I didn't tell him now, it would be just the same as lying. We weren't supposed to keep things from each other, not anymore.

"There's something that you need to know," I told him as I bit my lower lip and swallowed hard. He looked at me with a blank stare, but he lacked the surprise that I had anticipated.

"I snuck into Chloe's house the other night," I said bluntly. He looked furious.

"Are you mad?" I asked.

"Mad would not be the right word to describe how I feel right now." He looked back up at the ceiling, fuming.

"Rae, I'm trying my hardest to keep you safe, and then you go and start playing with fire. You go and hop right into the den with all of the lions. No part of me can understand why you would do that." He paused. I didn't say anything. His attempt to make me feel bad had backfired. Anger was building up inside of me. If he had told me the things that I needed to know in the first place, I wouldn't have had to take matters into my own hands.

"Before I came here, I could see you and so many times I wanted to save you. I'm here now and I can save you, but I can't see your every move like I could before. If I can't see you, if I don't know where you are, then I can't protect you."

"Maybe you don't need to protect me from everything."

"I've already told you that I do."

"Well, you don't need to protect me from the truth. The truth I can handle. What I can't handle is the fact that, for the past eighteen years of my life, my parents have been lying to me. I don't need lies from you as well."

"I have never lied to you."

"Your lies are ones of omission."

"I have always told you the truth . . . whenever you ask. What else do you need to know?"

"I need to know everything. Now. I need to know who attacked me on the path, and I need to know why."

"Well, I don't know why . . . "

"But you do know who," I interrupted.

Alex shifted positions again, inching closer so that we were no longer at opposite ends of the sofa. He cleared his throat and nervously smoothed his hair. "His name is Bernard Bodin." His voice quivered, and I felt my body go cold and numb. "You've met him before, but I have known him much longer than you have."

I wasn't sure why mouth was hanging open in astonishment. I had suspected Ben, and Alex was only confirming my assumptions. That Alex knew Ben shook me to the core and left me baffled, but it was the undertone of nervousness in Alex's voice that made me so uneasy. I had wanted to know every last detail and now I had a sinking feeling in the pit of my stomach that I was about to get more than I bargained for.

"I've know Ben for almost eighteen years. I met Ben in the halfway." He exhaled deeply and his eyes darkened. "There was a third car in the accident that killed Laney and my family . . . the Bodin's car. Ben and his parents died that night."

"But the newspaper said there were only two cars." My mind flashed back to my nana's scrapbook and the letter that I found stuffed inside the envelope, the one that A-Omega had written to my grandparents. The letter indicated that ten passengers were involved in the accident, seven of which died in the crash. But only two vehicles were mentioned, I thought. Quickly, I tallied up the casualties: Lovings 3, plus the Bodins 3, plus Laney. It added up. There were three who survived the accident: my mother, my father, and, because that was the night that I was born, I supposed that I was passenger number ten and survivor number three.

"Everything about the scene of the accident indicated there were three cars involved, but the third car, the Bodin's car, was never found," he continued. Police assumed that it landed in the lake not far from the road. They even sent in a diving team, but nothing turned up."

"So, Ben was there with you in the halfway?"

"He and I arrived in the halfway just moments apart and because of that, we became instant friends. He was a couple of years older than I was at the time of the accident, so he looked after me like a big brother might. He was nice and very charismatic, if you can believe that. We each had our own visions of earth, and we shared with each other everything we saw. It was our form of entertainment. I shared you with him, and he shared his family with me. We told each other stories about our lives. Of course, I had only vague memories, but Ben told me stories of his family and of the Pierces. He told me about his home and what his life was like. He loved to look at you through my eyes when I would let him. He loved to see what you were doing. It was very innocent at first. I thought nothing of it. But as we got older and my passion for you grew stronger, Ben grew dark. He, too, developed a passion for you . . . an obsession of a different kind. He was waiting in the halfway for his moment. He was planning to destroy your life and there wasn't a thing I could do about it."

"How do the Pierces fit into this?"

"Carl and Eva Pierce were close friends of the Bodin's. They were Ben's godparents, his very rich godparents."

"So, that's the link between you and Ben; you were in the halfway together. Carly was right. He was different, just like you're different," I said, referring to the aura-less boy with no thermal reading. "But what about Chloe. I can understand why Ben might want revenge. He wants to take from my parents what my parents took from him: family. But why does Chloe want me dead?"

"Chloe is to Ben like you are to me, Rae. Chloe is his other half; his evil other half, but they're soul mates none-the-less."

"Is Chloe dead, too?"

"No. Chloe is very much alive."

"Why didn't you tell me sooner?"

"I was hoping the problem might go away."

"Not talking about the problem doesn't make it go away. This is not something that you can just brush under the carpet."

Alex let out another deep and frustrated sigh. "Obviously."

"Is Chloe an only child?"

"Yes," he said without hesitation.

I didn't say a word. I could only think of one thing: I survived the crash, and that I merely existed was reason enough for Ben and Chloe to want me dead. Ben had lost everything that night: his mother, his father, and even himself. He knew that my parents had lost a daughter in the accident, but he was playing tit for tat; he would not rest until they had lost two. It was because of me that my parents could never have a normal life, and it was because of their need to protect me that our family had never settled down. The implications were far greater now; it was no longer just my life that was in jeopardy; now people I loved were getting hurt. I was dangerous to anyone who came near me, I always had been. I never had the choice. I was the threat. No one could possibly be safe when I was around.

"Alex, I am the cause of my parents' pain. We can't wait any longer. We have to leave. I know that I wanted to run away with you so that we could be together. And I know that I am not a patient person, but I could have been patient if it meant waiting for you. But, by trying to protect me, my parents have put themselves in the line of fire. I can no longer be patient. We have to leave now. I can't let anyone else get hurt."

"What will you tell them?"

"I don't know yet . . . as little as possible."

"When do you want to leave?" He slid his arm around me. I leaned closer, resting my head on his shoulder. For a split second, he rested his lips upon my ear and then just as quickly, he moved away, as if he were intending on telling me a secret but then quickly changed his mind.

"I have to make sure my mom's okay first, but then I'm ready."

"Have we decided where were going?"

"I was thinking we should go to Alexandria . . . Minnesota."

"Are you sure?" He looked surprised. I now had his full attention.

"I want to. I want to see the place where your family stayed. I want to be in the place where our souls first crossed on this earth. Alexandria is where it all started, all of this pain. I think if we go back to the place where it all began, we might find some answers."

"You'll love it there."

"What do you need me to bring?"

"Just yourself. That's all that I have ever needed."

"But what about all of my . . . ."

"Shhh," he whispered. "You think too much."

## CHAPTER TWENTY-FIVE

$M$y mom came home from the hospital late the next afternoon. Her color was back and apparently so was her health. Everything had checked out fine at the hospital; unfortunately, things had not gone so well here at the house. I was about 99.9% sure that I was not going to tell them about the potassium pills I found, but there was still the .1% of me that thought they should know it was no accident and of course, that it was in no way my mother's fault. I wanted to tell them that it was my fault and because of it, I would be leaving. If I could say it that simply and be certain that I would get no protests then I would have no trouble telling them the truth. I knew it wouldn't be that simple, and I knew that I could explain none of it without telling them about Alex and Ben. It would be hard enough telling my parents that Alex had come from the halfway, but if I had to tell them there was not only one dead boy floating around but two, my parents might just put me in a straight jacket and assign me to a padded room.

Today was the day. I had just twelve hours before Alex would be here, and I had a mountain of things to do in the meantime.

I began to rummage through the wooden box that sat on top of my bookshelf; it housed a few miscellaneous items of importance, including a checkbook for my savings account. I had exactly six thousand dollars in this account. It was money that I had been saving my entire life, but it wouldn't make a dent in the amount that I needed. I dropped the checkbook into my bag and started down the stairs for my car.

I pulled into Quicktrip about ten minutes later and when the lady at the counter asked to whom I would like the money order to be made, I told her The University of Minnesota, office of admissions, in the amount of one thousand-five-hundred dollars. This would be my deposit, and it would secure me a spot. I was perfectly fine tagging along with Alex wherever he went, staring at him, touching him, hearing his voice, feeling his warmth. But Alex was insistent that I study art, and since he couldn't convince me into going to Paris to do it, he settled for a school in Minnesota, instead. The clerk handed me the money order and I placed it into the pre-addressed envelope along with the acceptance letter I had signed and a form which I had filled out in advance. I licked the envelope, placed a stamp on it, dropped it in the mailbox right outside the door, and last, but not least, checked it off my list of things to do. The certified check was an afterthought, but I was glad that I had considered it. My parents had access to my savings account, and a check written to The University of Minnesota would totally blow my cover.

The next stop was the bank and this was the errand on my list that made me the most uncomfortable. I had not been the one to set up my account when we moved to Bartlesville, and although the account was in my name, I was pretty sure that my father's name was on it as well. I tried to pull myself together. I had to appear calm and confident so that the teller would have no reason to question why I was pulling out all but five hundred dollars from my savings. One phone call to my father from the bank manager, and my plans with Alex would come to a screeching halt. I walked into the empty bank, filled out a withdrawal slip, handed the teller the slip along with my ID, and just like that, she gave me cash, no questions asked. I thanked her and walked quickly out the door before she changed her mind. I pulled my watch out of my bag. It read 5:15, and I headed back home to spend some time with my parents and pack.

Things seemed back to normal when I walked through the door. All memories of the hospital had vanished into thin air. I wasn't sure what was going on with my parents. They should be fleeing, running away or something. But instead, they were in the kitchen, and my father was cooking dinner while my mother was watching him from a stool behind the bar. They seemed happy and for the next few hours, I tried to erase from my memory what I was about to do. I tried not to think about the fact that I would soon be turning my parents' lives upside down.

It was now 2:30 AM and the house was quiet. I started to scratch out the first feelings that came to my mind on a simple piece of white copier paper, my penmanship sloppy. The words that seemed to make sense in my head appeared bizarre when they were finally laid in front of me. The words had also provoked several large tears that I was completely oblivious to until they splat onto the letter of farewell that I was writing. The wetness puddling on the ink until it absorbed, leaving the letters smudged, blurry, and barely legible. I took the sheet of paper in my hand and crumpled it into a hard ball before tossing it into the trash. I glanced over to my packed bag lying on the floor by my closet. He would be here soon. Soon, I would be leaving my parents behind, the only part of my life that had ever been constant and trustworthy in my eighteen years of existence. They had been my rock and I felt like I was tossing them to the wind and it broke my heart. If only I was able to tell them the truth. If only I was able to make them understand why it was that I needed to leave. It was for the better, for all of us really. I was the one who was dangerous. It was me that they were after.

Frustrated, I walked to my bookshelf and grabbed a packet of stationary. My parents deserved better than chicken scratch on a piece of copier paper. I held the package of papers that were embellished with a glittery "R" for Rae, but I set it back down. This was a no frills type of farewell, and I decided that a plain piece of copier paper would suffice.

I walked into the bathroom, and studied myself in the mirror. I swallowed hard, taking notice of the movement my Adam's apple made behind my thin neck as I did so. My face looked tired and gaunt. I walked back into my room and flopped onto my bed, starring at yet another blank sheet of paper. Its blankness made me feel sick; it reminded me of the task at hand. My stomach was a huge knot as I considered what I was about to do. This was not a letter about feelings, but it was most certainly a letter about love. I loved them, so I had to protect them, and I would have to lie in order to do so. I would have to lie to keep them away from me at all cost. I was not a good liar, but it had to be perfect. I had to make everything as normal as it could possibly be considering that I was leaving the house in the middle of the night with Cocoa and very few of my personal possessions. It had to be perfect, and it had to protect them. If there was one thing that I learned in the past couple of days, it was that I was dangerous. I had ignored it for too long. I had responsibilities and with that, I let all emotions escape me as I picked up my pen and began to scribble out a few hardened words of endearment.

When I finished, I picked up another piece of paper and addressed it to my father. I then scratched out a few words in black ink on the plain, white sheet of paper, ending with the words "I hope this makes sense" and "I hope you understand." I then folded the letter, put it into a priority envelope that I had already addressed to the clinic where he worked, and dropped "Exhibit A" and "Exhibit C" into the envelope.

It was time. I looked at the clock; it was 4:30 AM. I gingerly folded in half the letter addressed to both of my parents and printed Mom and Dad on the front. I set my pen down and slid off my bed. I had never really known myself before this moment. I had never really known what I was capable of until now. As I looked around my room, I realized that all of the things inside this room told a story about me. I had picked these things. The cross over my bed reminded me of the faith that I had as a child and the faith that I had forgotten as I grew. The books on the shelf told me that I had been interested in romance long before I realized. The yellow bird that hung from the chain in the center of my room no longer reminded me of a tiny creature in constant flight. The bird now represented freedom. Perhaps I was still flying, or fleeing, but this time, I was finally free to choose. I cautiously untied the string that kept the bird suspended in the center of my room and placed it gently inside my bag. I was free.

I glanced one last time around my bedroom of almost a year and then I laid the letter to my parents carefully on the top of my neatly made bed. I grabbed my luggage from beside the closet door and slid the priority envelope discretely inside.

"Come on, girl," I cooed as I patted Cocoa on the head and turned off the light to my room.

I climbed into the old Wagoneer, and for a fraction of a second, I got a glimpse into the life of my nana. Just like her, I was running away with the man that I loved, the man who was trying his hardest to protect me. I often wondered how she felt when she left her father behind. Maybe she felt relief. Maybe she felt free. At that moment, I realized that my nana and I were just as much alike as we were different. We were both in love with men who were determined to save us and we were both on the run. But she was running away from abuse, and I was running away from two wonderful people who were trying to protect me from it. I no longer needed to hear her story about the day she left her father behind. As I looked into Alex's eyes I knew how she must have felt. It wasn't that she felt relief or freedom. She felt that she had no other choice. I could only be reminded that my nana's life turned out pretty okay. I doubt that she ever regretted her decision, and I knew that I would never regret mine. This thought immediately sent tears streaming down my cheeks once again. It's strange to feel sadness during the happiest moment of your life. It doesn't seem fair to be so upset when something you wished for has finally come true. I felt his gentle hand on my cheek as he wiped the warm drops from my face. Without saying a word, he pulled quietly away from my gravel drive. I turned my head away from the window, not wanting to look at what I was leaving behind; instead, I turned to Alex and focused on what lay in front of me.

"You tired?" he asked

"Not really," I replied, as I stared into the darkness. "I think I've gotten my second wind."

The car was silent once again. The windows were down, letting in the warm, night air, and I could hear the faint chirping of crickets as we rolled slowly down the country road.

"Are they safe, now?" My voice quivered.

"They're safe."

"How can you be sure?"

"Because it's you they're after." Alex was absolutely right. The further I could get from this little town the safer my parents would be. An uneasy peace spread through my body, relaxing me, and despite my best efforts to stay awake, my eyes succumbed to the blackness around me, letting me forget all of my happiness and all of my misfortunes.

I woke some six hours later to blinding sunlight streaming into the car and the pungent smell of manure. I rubbed my eyes to clear my vision and immediately began to knead my neck in order to smooth out the large knot that had formed just where my shoulder began.

"Good morning, *Sunshine*." His laughter filled the car. I imagined that he was laughing at all of the new ways he could incorporate my least favorite nickname into a sentence. I rolled my eyes. If I hadn't been so groggy, I would have protested.

"Where are we?"

"Missouri."

"Missouri," I repeated. "How ironic." I sighed as I stretched my neck to the left and continued to press on the large, gumball sized knot in my muscle.

"How do you mean?"

"Missouri is where my nana and papa ran off to, much the same as I am doing now with you. Papa still lives here . . . remember."

"Do you want to swing by? I know where he lives."

"I hardly think that's appropriate, considering." I twisted my neck to have a look at what Cocoa was doing. Her lean body was stretched out long in the back seat and she was sound asleep.

"You're right, but if you want we could still stop by and say hello."

"No, we can't leave a trace."

"I'm sorry, Rae. I am sorry that it turned out this way. It's not fair for you to have to make a choice."

"It isn't a choice. You're what I want. I know I can't have both . . . not right now," I answered as I slid closer to him.

"You know, you can take that ring off the chain now and wear it on your finger, if you want." A smile spread across my face.

It was something about the words that he said and the way that he said them that made this moment so real. I reached behind my neck and carefully unlatched the clasp before sliding it off the chain. It was beautiful. I slid it onto my finger and held my hand out so that we both could see. It symbolized our life together. It symbolized a promise. And maybe it would not be a perfect life but it would be a life with no secrets.

# CHAPTER TWENTY-SIX

*H*ours later, we pulled into town. The sun was setting quickly, and I traced my finger down the passenger side window as I looked at the beauty that lay outside: the tall pines, the flowers in a multitude of colors, the quaint, family owned stores, the park across the street with children playing, and the old couple that was out for a stroll. This town was full of life. This town would be my new home and for the first time ever, I felt as though I were truly living. I closed my eyes as he drove out of the city limits to the lake on the other side of town. Lake L'homme Dieu, French for "Man of God." Maybe this move would be different after all. I could feel the winding of the road. It was a place that I had never been and yet it felt so familiar; I could almost sense each curve the road made. It seemed to be an infinitely perfect ride, and I didn't want this moment to end. The window was barely open and the cool breeze coming off the lake was sending goose bumps up my arms and legs. I opened my eyes and could see the lights of the town fading gradually as we crossed the bridge; they were replaced with the light of the stars. The noise of the car on the bridge made a softer sound, almost as if we were floating though the air, suspended between Heaven and Earth; I thought what a peaceful place that is to be. The car came to a stop and Alex shifted into park.

"Come on," he said, "I want to show you our new home."

It was dark. Dark enough to accentuate every star in the sky. The perfect contrast of light and dark was stunning. There were three cottages in all, but I could only see a faint outline of them as their white paint shone under the moon. A larger cottage stood near the lake and two smaller cottages were closer to the edge of the road. Alex was leading me around the side of the larger cottage, his arm wrapped around my waist, pulling me close to his body. Cocoa was one step in front of us and then, without warning, she howled and took off toward the water's edge. I could see her silhouette in darkness.

"I think she's going to be happy here."

"I told you she would love it. I think I remember saying that you would love it, too."

"It's beautiful, even at night." I could hear the soft crashing of the waves in front of me, and I watched for a moment as the moon danced on the water. The air was chilly, so different than the summer nights in Oklahoma. We walked through the back door into the living room. He swung open the door without even testing the lock.

"Seriously! Did you not lock up when you left?"

"No. I never lock the doors, you know that."

"Well, it's not like you left to just run an errand; you've been gone for a couple of months now." Cocoa brushed past my leg and scampered into the house. I could hear her sniffing around the room and her tail beating excitedly against anything that stood in its way. Alex's arm moved behind my back as he reached his hand to the left of the door and flicked on the light. All at once, the house became illuminated. It looked as if it had been decorated in the early 1960's and no one had touched it since. It was charming and enchanting, and I was sure that these walls held a bit of history and possibly an interesting story as well. Paned windows lined the walls and were boxed in with a worn, cherry finished wood. Cherry colored doors and hardwoods stood out brightly against the plain, white walls. An old, brick fireplace that had been painted milky white took up the front part of the room and I could only imagine how a smoldering fire would give the cottage a warm glow. The mantel was stacked with random tchotchkes including an old, Celestial clock that had the words "Time to plant your flowers" painted at the bottom. Three giant fish hung above the fireplace, and I thought that they gave the room a masculine feel amongst the yellow and green, plaid sofa and the floral chairs. The bookshelves were filled with a huge assortment of books, mostly classics with the occasional book on war snuck in between. There was a modest pine table with white chairs sitting to one side of the living room, a small desk with an old time telephone, thick, pleated curtains hanging over the windows, and large French doors that opened onto the deck.

I glanced around the room and saw the doorway to what appeared to be the only bedroom in the cottage. Alex seemed to be reading my mind.

"Um, I'll be staying in the back cottage. This one's all yours." A look of disappointment flashed across my face. "I'll bring your bags in and then I'm going to go unpack."

I watched him walk back out the door we had come through and disappear into the night. I walked the length of the room, running my fingers across the old pictures and books, then fell back onto the green and yellow, plaid sofa. I closed my eyes and tried to imagine myself eating here, sleeping here, painting here, kissing Alex, right here on this sofa, and possibly, one day, getting married here. I was getting further into my thoughts when the back door slammed shut and Alex emerged with all three of my suitcases, two in his hands and one tucked under his arm.

"This is everything. It doesn't seem like much."

"I've never really had all that much anyway."

"Well, I guess I'll leave you to unpack. I'll be back in a bit to check on you." Alex paused for a moment. His hand was resting on the doorknob, and he was twisting it back and forth nervously. "You okay?"

"I'm fine. I'm perfect," I whispered.

"You promise."

"I promise."

"I'll be right back," he assured me, then I watched him walk back out into the darkness.

I glanced at my three pieces of worn out luggage that lay on the floor by the back door and forced a smile. I couldn't seem to escape them. I had been so excited to rid myself of them when we had moved to Oklahoma and now, less than a year later, my life fit so neatly back inside. But it was different now. I was different. I couldn't help but think about the past few months and how I had changed. I had been sheltered for too long. My mom and dad had tried to keep me safe by running away. They had guarded my mind by lying to me. For most of my life, I had blamed them for my unhappiness, but I could no longer hold them responsible. They were only doing the best that they could. I knew that I was to blame for what I had become. I had taken matters into my own hands. They may have guarded my mind, but I had guarded my heart and, in doing so, I had chosen the strongest materials I could think of: steel and rivets, locks and chains. Nothing got in or out of my heart, and I was satisfied with that . . . until Alex came along. Without my knowing or wanting, Alex had set me free and the funny thing was, without the shell around my heart, I felt stronger now than I had ever felt before. I could now feel both pain and pleasure; they mixed together to transform me into something indestructible. Alex had given me so much. He had shown me how to love and how to feel. He protected me. He healed my wounds both inside and out. I was no longer a girl who moved without direction. I now had purpose, but at the moment, it was my purpose that was tearing me apart. I knew that I could not save Alex's soul without losing him in the process. I wanted to do the right thing. I wanted him to be where he was happy and where he belonged. But even more than that, I wanted him here with me.

The back door of the cottage opened, and I watched Alex walk in from the darkness.

"Whatcha doing?"

"Nothing . . . just thinking."

"About something good, I hope."

"Something bittersweet, I suppose."

"Look, I have something for you. I meant to give it to you earlier."

"Oh, like a house warming present?"

"Not exactly." Alex reached into his pocket and his hand returned with a white envelope.

"What is it?"

"Just open it."

I slid my finger through the top of the envelope, breaking the seal, and then carefully slid my hand inside.

"It's like Christmas," I said as I pulled out two tiny, oval shaped pieces of paper. My chest felt tight. I couldn't breath. I grasped for the locket that lay just below the hollow of my neck.

"Is this it? Is this Laney's locket? How did you get this?" My eyes welled up with tears as I stared at the tiny, oval shaped picture of my sister Laney, the picture that belonged on one side of the locket. I then stared at the picture of my two-year-old self that belonged on the other side. The locket was a family heirloom. It had been my nana's, and then my mother's, and then my mother had given it to my sister Laney, and after the accident she had entrusted it to me. I had, in some strange way, felt connected to Laney when I wore it and when it was stolen, I felt an overwhelming sense of guilt. It was all I had of Laney and when it was gone, that connection, that closeness went with it.

"You're not the only one who's been sneaking around the Pierce estate," he confessed.

"How did you know it would be there?"

"I told you, from the halfway I could see everything and everyone that crossed my path while on this earth. My path did cross with Ben's before I died; even if it was just for a second, our paths still crossed. Of course, we were both together in the halfway for a good fourteen years and being able to see Ben on earth was something that I had never considered; that is, until he left. Fortunately for me, it was something Ben failed to consider as well. I could see his every move and he had no idea. Even though I couldn't protect you from him, I studied him at work. I learned a bit more about him, all so that I can protect you from him now.

"And the locket, he took it? He's the one who stole it?"

"You guessed it."

"What does he want with the locket of all things?"

"I don't know, but I do have to say that the Pierce estate is a little creepy. You can understand why I was so upset with you before. You had no business going over there."

Tears were flowing down my cheeks, although I wasn't sure why. Perhaps they were tears of happiness. I was happy that I had him with me, that I had my locket and the picture of Laney back in my possession. But I was scared. For the first time, I was scared of what lay ahead of us.

"I told you it wouldn't be easy, Rae."

"I know," I whispered

"Don't cry. Please don't cry," he begged me. "I thought the pictures would make you happy."

"They do." I kissed him softly. "Thank you." I wiped the tears from my eyes and cleared my throat. "I have something for you, too."

"Ooh, it *is* like Christmas."

I walked over to my luggage and began to unzip one of the three suitcases. "It's in here somewhere," I said as I rummaged through my bag. Not finding what I was looking for, I zipped it back up and tried another. "Ahh, here it is." I pulled out a medium-sized, rectangular package, walked back over to the couch, and patted the cushion beside me. Cocoa jumped up next to me and began to paw at my arm, begging to have her ears scratched.

"Not you, Cocoa."

"It's okay, I can just . . . sit on the other side." His mouth twisted into a smile.

He took the package, set it in his lap, and began to feel the edges, as though he were going to try to guess what was inside.

"You'll never guess it."

"I told you that I had a few tricks up my sleeve and guessing what's inside of presents is one of them."

"Oh . . . seriously," I scoffed. "Are you going to unwrap it or not?"

"Of course," he said as he ripped into the paper. An enormous smile spread across his face. "So, this is what you've been hiding in Mr. Bradley's closet, a giant painting of my head," he laughed.

"You don't like it, do you?"

"I love it; it's just that you paint me to look more handsome than I actually am."

"You underestimate yourself."

"No, I think it is you who underestimates yourself. You're talented, you know."

"Thank you." I blushed.

He set the painting down on the coffee table, and he pulled me into his arms. He looked into my eyes for a moment without saying a word and then brushed my hair behind my shoulder and began to whisper a song.

*A year was like a breath to me*
*A long, a labored sigh*
*To see you was the death of me*
*To see you pass me by*

*The sea was dark*
*The sky was gray*
*I whispered to you anyway*
*I close my eyes*
*Pretend you see*
*Wishing you were here with me*

*Oh please don't tell me different*
*I can try or just pretend*
*Oh please don't tell me different*
*Just please don't tell me different*

*There I was transparent*
*A shape, a light, a sound*
*Here a shallow breath*
*A beating heart is what I've found*

*I love you*

*I thought you should know*

*That I'll never let you go*

*You're beautiful*

*If only you could see*

*But of course, you've always been to me*


*Oh please don't tell me different*

*I can try or just pretend*

*Oh please don't tell me different*

*I don't want for this to end*


*I watch atop the tallest hill*

*The earth below me standing still*

*A raging sea with you so near*

*I wish you knew that I was here*


*I reach out*

*I touch the air*

*Your skin, your smile, your raven hair*

*My world changed that night*

*From black to blue*

*I dreamt you dreamt about me too.*


"This would be it. This would definitely be my Heaven moment," I whispered.

"Mine too," he whispered back.

After all that I had been through, I still don't have all of the answers. But what I do know is this: behind every human life there is a purpose and for every hardened heart there is a key. My heart was open and now, I was ready for anything that came my way. I knew that there was something greater out there for Alex and me, more mysteries to be uncovered. But for now, we both knew what we were put on this earth to do, the reason for our existence. Our souls had crossed, our earthly bodies had touched, and our lives had become intertwined. He was meant to save my body, and I was meant to save his soul.

## END OF VOLUME I

CPSIA information can be obtained at www.ICGtesting.com
Printed in the USA
LVOW041932131112

307203LV00004B/1/P